The Woman Who
Lived in a Prologue

Nina Schneider

HOUGHTON MIFFLIN COMPANY BOSTON

1980

Library of Congress Cataloging in Publication Data

Schneider, Nina, date
  The woman who lived in a prologue.

  I. Title.
PZ3.S35952Wo   [PS3537.C5413]   813'.5'4   79–18595
ISBN 0–395–28211–X

Printed in the United States of America

V 10 9 8 7 6 5 4 3 2 1

Above all, to
WILLIAM MAXWELL

Everything is very simple . . . astonishingly simple. A woman is born, grows up, marries, goes shopping, has a son, deceives her husband, apparently takes care of her home, loses a son, does works of charity, gets bored, and dies.

Everything is so simple . . . everything turns out so simply in the end that at times I think that only murderers deserve to benefit from the immense peace which usually settles in their look, in that happy look which didn't believe in the simplicity of things, in the dull simplicity of adultery, in the daily simplicity of usury, in the diaphanous simplicity of bestiality.

— CAMILO JOSÉ CELA

Contents

Characters

Ariadne:	The Woman (1900–1973)
Daughter of:	Abidah Azzair (1868–1933)
	Hera Azzair (1872–1954)
Wife of:	Adam Arkady (1892–1961)
Mother of:	Absalom (1919–?)
	Ariel (1921–)
	Aaron (1923–1944)
	Benjamin (1926–)
Grandmother of:	Dinah (1945–)
	Daniel (1947–)
Friend and mistress of:	Jeremy Starobin, M.D.
	(1881–1954)
Lover of:	Paul Matthew Donant (1901–?)
Sister of:	Reuben and Ezra
Niece of:	Giselle and Joshua Schleifer
	Cassie and Heinrich Volkmann
Cousin of:	Jessica Schleifer
Mother-in-law of:	Jethro Meyers
	Ricardo Cordovero
Others:	Grandparents, a lifeguard, several *Talmudim,* cousins and *cousinas,* schoolmates, nurses, an unnamed infant

Prologue

MORE THAN 5730 years from Genesis, the planet ticking like a bomb under camouflage, and here I sit poised over a throbbing eclectic typewriter, an old woman in a room that smells of wood ashes and drying immortelles (all I could rescue of my helichrysums), staring out at my garden where frost has blackened the asters and silenced the bees.

Only an optimist practiced in taking long views could see this as a setting for a prologue: hoarfrost hanging from the shrubbery like shrouded mirrors; a few wintry birds mincing on the glassy lawn. And I'm no spring chicken either. Actuarily speaking (and my late husband often did), my time is up. Yet I wake every morning to the sensation that my real life is waiting, immanent, like an embryo whose atoms are about to be assembled.

My mother, the Pragmatist, would have snorted at the sight of me ankle deep in false starts. "So, it wasn't perfect in golden America. So, slowpoke, set the table already and let's eat what there is."

My father, the Exegete, would have scanned the cross-indexed palimpsests of his mind in my defense. "Keep trying,

I

Ariadne. God confides in us that He Himself was dissatisfied with His beginnings, or why one version of the Creation in Genesis, chapter one, and a second version in Genesis, chapter two?"

"You want an answer?" My mother would have chimed in her big bell contralto. "The first Genesis was boring. Day one, day two, seven days in a row, creating and lecturing. The Adam and Eve one was a botch, too. What He did to women, that Father in Heaven."

I can see her, with her fine flair for the specific, sever an overmellow pear with one chomp of her square white teeth, then plunk down amiably to allow my father the pleasure of a few pieties. (She had no patience with anyone else's.)

"You miss my point, my love." He gives his well-trimmed mustache a prefatory tweak. "By beginning the Creation again God sets his children an example to strive for perfection. As in resurrection, reincarnation, transmigration, the soul continuously reborn continuously improves. Zohar-Kabalists await the day when all incarnated souls will be perfected into purity, thus heralding the Messianic . . ." and so on and on.

Having borne four children I know how tedious it can be in labor not to proceed uninterruptedly from first dilation to delivery. Get the water boiling. Get the midwife. Get the doctor. Get the forceps if you must, but get through it. Head first if you can. If not, feet first, breech presentation, Caesarean section . . .

"The only thing you must not do," Jeremy, my dear physician, would have advised, "is give birth piecemeal. Thanks to Ambroise Paré, who developed the procedures for podalic version, there is a way to rescue the entangled infant and deliver it whole instead of breaking it up to extract, as they had to in the Dark Ages."

Jewish mother, father *and* doctor to invoke, yet I keep rummaging backward for my beginning as if my womanly aspects

2

were so many costumed parts I had played. I qualify, I qualify as an identity. There is no reason why my rib cage should feel like an emptied aviary. If I have a CIA dossier (and it's a rare concerned citizen who doesn't), the fixed points of my life can be retrieved and replayed on the taped memory of a computer: daughter of; wife of; mother of; mother-in-law of; mother-in-lieu of; mother-in-loss of; grandmother of; widow of . . . and if the fingermen aren't all thumbs, also mistress of; lover of. In the realm of data I am all precision.

If only I were able to slip into one role that fitted me well, or at least as well as expected, I could locate myself and chart my existence from there. I could stop muttering "Where do *I* begin?" But to whom at my age can I refer the question? Do I imagine, if I keep riffling, an answer will come to me, crawling with quotations like aphids fat with honey sucked from Time's perennial hosts? Let me make clear: I do not mean *"How* do I begin?" (The dust settled on that question when we were teenagers — T. S. Eliot, the century and I.) I mean, where do *I* begin, I whose teeth have become more omnipresent than a baby's; white skin/amber hair reversed to amber skin/white hair, undone, I am done with, done with the womb, done with the morning faces of children, the amorous cries of men, re-signed, I have resigned even my garden.

It is my season to be serene. I can afford to go bask among the widows. My husband, Adam, left me well provided for, and Benjamin, our youngest, has expanded the family computer business. But I am not ready for a semitropical exit. Dwindling though I am I have not absolved myself from responsibility to a life. Mine.

Now that I can no longer be ordered about by the urgencies of brooder mash; having settled down, a fowl in season no more, out of the range of the cock-crow lords (only an Oedipal cockerel tries for the old brood wing), there is nothing to keep me from flying off in search of my personal drama. My problem is,

3

I've been pottering about with my egg basket for so many years that I have a suspicion I have become the actions I've scratched out. Chicken! And what does an old hen, one that's done laying, have to talk about except eggs lost in cabbage patches, chicks, mash, and the pecking order? And who but a fox has the heart to praise a chicken's voice?

The fact is, I'm frightened. Here I stand, retired servant of the species, my freedom and my evening-college diploma in hand, ready to take off. The wind is ruffling my draggled feathers. My scrawny legs are unsteady. But I'm taking off. I'm eager to discover my own life, whatever that is. I have survived the unrelenting authority of family needs, the petulant tyranny of domesticity, the sensual abnegation of matrimony, the prodigal cruelty of offspring, the aberrant gratifications of adultery, the whimsical expectations of those tombstone angels, my grandchildren; the entire womanly life for which I was promised I would pass into the land of the self-possessed adult. And I tell you, I have been lied to.

Under the guise of privilege I have been robbed of a life I could call my own. My training is useless, my education out of date. I am irrelevant, expendable, obsolete, yet I'm burdened with a hungry something . . . I don't know what. I have carried this tenuous *I* through decades of indenture to the Big Barnyard. As my deliverer knoweth (Jeremy, that is), an ectopic pregnancy tends to be fatal to the bearer unless the foetal cluster shrivels and aborts of itself. But this *I* has fed and slept and stirred in me, remaining active in my hopes and restless in my fears. It is long overdue. Like each of my four children it resists being born. It too must be induced to leave its little paradise of sloth even if it survives as the laziest bed-hugger of them all.

Unfortunately, just as I've gotten into "doing my own thing," as my grandchildren inexplicitly put it, I am told I'm too late; that there is no point in retiring to my dacha to produce a novel about a woman who feels, with Shakespeare, that "what's past

4

is Prologue." Now that my real life is waiting, now that the embryo has grown teeth, developed desires, would emerge and utter in its own person, now *they* tell me: the novel is dead.

Dead or alive, I've been expectant for so many years, begun dilating, been forced to contract, that I have no choice but to push ahead. On the way to the labor room it is as irrelevant to scream "Wait, wait, I've changed my mind" as to consider what figure your issue will cut one Sunday in a *Times* to come. On the delivery table *birth* is the cogent miracle. It alone can separate bearer from borne. Unless it's a false pregnancy.

Tumescence, merciful heavens, nothing but tumescence?

No. It can't be. I know precisely when and where conception took place.

5

BOOK I

Mosaics

The wide plains of my memory and its innumerable caverns and hollows are full beyond compute. I can glide from one to the other. I can probe deep into them and never find the end . . . The power of memory is great . . . Yet it is my mind; it is my self. What then, am I, my God? What is my nature?

— ST. AUGUSTINE

Daughter of:

The beauty lies in the discovery . . .

— GEORGE HERBERT

CONCEPTION took place at a stove, a common black kitchen stove. It took place on the opening day of the fishing season the year my first-born was nine and I was twenty-nine.

My recollection of the event is sharp; sharper than of the tooth of that child (and Absalom teethed early and sucked late) and keen, though perhaps not quite as keen as the pain that recurs like a corrupt dream too slowly understood each time I am reminded of a certain slap in the face when . . . No.

If I accept what bubbles up in the potluck of memory (in memory everything that happens, happens now) what signs will I set to divide the years from the years?

Why not a simple sequence of numbers?

I have my reasons, the most cogent being that I have always found it extremely difficult to defy my father's prohibitions. And in my father's house there was no numbering.

* * *

"Arnie, set the table."
"For how many, Mama?"

9

"There could be . . ."

"I can count. Let me count."

"No, no. With the rabbi here it's not allowed."

"Not allowed to count?"

"Come, I'll show you how to count and not to count. So. You say *not: not* one, *not* two, *not* three. Don't make cat's eyes at me. I didn't think up that foolishness. Go ask the gentlemen why it's *verboten*. It will keep them busy while we finish up in the kitchen."

Both my father and the rabbi rise to the question. I remain between them; the fine prickly emanation of Turkish tobacco, European cologne and clean linen surrounding me, my father's index finger resting on my shoulder, making its physical claim.

"A good question," the rabbi lilts. His beard is a gold cloud drifting over my head, his voice rocks out of it. "It is written, 'Satan rose up against Israel and moved David to number Israel.' "

My father picks up the theme and enlarges it delicately. "The anger of the Lord was kindled against Israel. He moved David against them to say, 'Go, . . . number Israel and Judah. Go . . . from Dan even to Beer-sheba!' " His finger presses the point into the hollow between my neck and shoulder. "Second Samuel, twenty-four."

The first voice lifts courteously to the challenge and intones, "Why doth my lord the king delight in this thing?"

"A military gloss."

"Gloss? Your source!"

Quotation and erudition have collected the dispersed guests, who submit as water under oil.

Says my father modestly, as if to me, "Who is to say who stands first?"

Say I, "Put the smallest first, Daddy."

"You have your reasons, my little Topaz?" My father bites the dexter side of his mustache to hide a half-smile.

The two principals draw closer. (Oh these insidious debates: body approaching body, the veiled contest taking on symbolic force.) I am ringed about by these aerial players. To the music of a drone chant, bright words whir like birds in and out of leafery. "Heretical." "Incompatible." "Pythagoras." (Ring-a-rounda-rosie, pocka-fulla-pozee)

At my eye level one button of the rabbi's gabardine is sewn with lighter thread than those above it. This puzzles me. My father places his palm tenderly on my head, then rapt in discussion he allows a caress to pass down to my hair. Not once. Not twice. (I am *not* counting.)

"Duad proceeding from Monad from whence their Trinity."

"Clearly denies First Cause." (Caress.)

"In order to avoid receding into Infinity, First Cause is necessary."

"Kabalistic." (Caress . . . caress.)

My mother calls impatiently, "Where is that daughter of mine?" (Ashes, ashes, all fall down.)

Slowly I withdraw from under my father's hand.

"Hurry, slowpoke, set for twelve," she scolds.

* * *

Kitchen or Kabala? Kabala or Kitchen?

What's wrong with opening in the kitchen? Heraclitus of Ephesus said to the people who found him warming himself at the kitchen stove, "Enter, for the gods are here also." Not in *my* mother's kitchen. No philosopher could have generalized from it. My mother's kitchen could have been submitted as a sample of modern history or avant-garde art: random and disorganized; full of found objects; fortuitous as paint hurled at a canvas.

Most afternoons, when my cousin Jessica and I came home

from grade school, the breakfast dishes were still undone. My sociable mother would have spent happy hours at an auction, or seeking out bargains at a street market where she was a favorite with all the pushcart folk. She would have stopped for a gossip or an exchange of letters from the old country and a glass of herb tea with her sister Cassie, who lived in the apartment below us. If her hunger for society was still unsatisfied she might go a flight higher and visit with her other sister, though Giselle's immaculate presence was in itself a rebuke, and the best that could be expected from her was a lecture on the virtues of straight hems, an ordered schedule, or vegetarianism. My mother's peregrinations would bring her back to our kitchen approximately when all the chores of evening converged.

"Mama, why can't we do like Aunt Cassie and Aunt Giselle, finish breakfast things at breakfast time, then begin preparing supper the right way?"

"What's the difference how we begin so long as we eat?" She waved her hand. Soap suds dripped over tomatoes waiting on the sinkboard. "You are your father's daughter to the dot. Always with the Beginnings. Did God begin the world this way or that way? We should begin the day that way, not this way. The meal should begin with soup even if I like nuts first. Should the chess begin with this opening or that one? Does some family begin with Rabbi Nachaum or with Rabbi Eliezar?"

"How did I begin, Mama?"

"*Oy vay!* Not that again. I told you, the stork brought you."

"But before that you said . . ."

"I forgot to buy sugar. Go borrow a cup from Aunt Cassie."

My mother had a point. My father's daughter had absorbed a sense of the finality of openings from watching my father play chess, not with my mother, but with my uncle Joshua. Like Masters, the two men would exchange a few opening moves, scan the board, and in recognition of all that *should* logically follow, nod decisively . . . one in defeat, one in victory. They did not argue to take back moves, falsely crying, *"J'adoube, j'adoube,"* or persist in the hope that if they fuddled along, an opponent would weary and fall into perpetual check by oversight, the way my mother did when my father was winning. My mother could inject chaos even into that tight world of sixty-four squares. Head to one side, tongue tight between her teeth, eyes too bright with shrewdness and anger, the flimflam of her amateurism was so apparent I wandered away as I never did when the contest passed to my father and uncle.

*   *   *

The hush of the half-holiday Saturday descends. The viridian plush drapes shut out America. Two tapestry armchairs that my mother rescued from a storage auction are occupied by two Eastern potentates: Uncle Joshua, a stock of Sumer by way of Astrakhan; and my father, Abidah, an offshoot of a Goth on a pliant Circassian. (What recourse did she have when her owner said, "Come thou, visitor, enter into my handmaiden." These scratches have been seen on a harem wall: "My heart bleeds. I am defenseless.")

"Ariadne," my father calls, "set up the *Schach*."

I know my privileges. On the chessboard, carved and inlaid by my father, I set each combatant on its center of fruitwood: the queen on her own color . . . then *König, Laufer,* crenellated *Turm* . . .

Both men rest before the engagement. My uncle's head is thrust back, tipping upward the black triangle of his beard. I try to picture him as a smooth-faced four-year-old dropped from a Cossack booty cavalcade, tears sticky on his black fur lashes, freshly orphaned, as I have heard he was found.

As my mother comes out of the bedroom my father glances up. Ignorant though I am of facts, I apprehend the expression of gratified desire. I move away from his side to lean against my uncle's thigh. He responds with gentle pressure. En passant, his lonely arm circles my waist.

I complete my service. The obsequious regiments are drawn up in ranks. Uncle Joshua draws white; his advantage. He becomes first mover. Under the hand with black hairs and diamond ring lie infinite possibilities. He determines an opening gambit. A little white pawn trips forward — P-K4.

My father faces the immensely contracted field. (The state of the universe at any instant, as John Stuart Mill remarked, is a consequence of its state at the previous instant.) There is a quick exchange accompanied by a click as of triggers. A white and black pawn are declared expendable. I put them in the box, they are dead, poor *Bauern*. Uncle Joshua completes the maneuver for which he calculated the sacrifice. Done!

He leans back into the gros point flanks of the caparisoned horse. Banners frame his head. My father, bending forward from the tattered tapestry arras with its silenced motto, reviews his troops. He lifts his hand over the battlements. His king's bishop makes a bold flight and settles. B-B4. My uncle covers a smile.

My father scans the board. He sees that his move is, logically, fatal. The battle is over in a skirmish. "It will be *Schach, Abidah.*"

"*Schachmatt!*" my father concedes. "Charousek and Tchigorin."

"Budapest 1889."

I go quickly to the kitchen. I do not wish my father to see that I willed him to lose.

The afternoon is not complete until I bring the tray with the exiled silver tea holders and my grandmother's teaspoons; the men stir cherry preserves through their golden tea, and my father holds toward me a spoonful of tea-soaked fruit. A speck of preserve clings to his russet mustache. The spoon is warm and sweet.

"Play a slower game." I put my arm around his shoulder.

"For my Topaz, a study game," my father says.

My uncle nods his slow consent, absently.

This is a different game, a positional one. I am permitted three questions. I may also suggest one play, which they will expound move by move, as it relates to the tradition of chess praxis. I make a fortuitous suggestion: Queen's gambit declined.

"A Daniel!" says my uncle, "a sweet little Daniel."

"My daughter could become a Master. If only she were a boy."

Perpetual check!

My father troubles his lower lip with a scorched forefinger. My agitated brother will never have a head steady enough for the cogitations of chess. My uncle sighs. He understands only too well that simple and faithless as a long visit to her mother, his elegant wife, Giselle, has again abandoned him. She has taken their child, my playmate Jessica, with her.

"Oh my daughter." His boyish lashes are wet.

"Oh my son."

So they sit and grieve.

*   *   *

My father's daughter? My mother's daughter? I put it in that order because my father was the one people noticed first. He made a precise impression, like an etching in which nothing without spiritual significance remains. My mother took on solidity more slowly, after first enduring a "how did she ever get him?" stare. She was massive in her pragmatism and, like the heroes of modern Russian fiction, Darwinian in her capacity to survive. My father had the heroism to resist death of the spirit; my mother, of the flesh. Together, my parents might have made one hero.

Still in the night my father calls, "My daughter, set up

15

the *Schach.*" And still my mother determines otherwise. "My daughter will finish up in the kitchen."

What of me was formed by an alliance with my father? What, as a retort to my mother?

Last night I was awakened by a volley of explosions. Before I connected them to steam banging in the old radiator pipes a dream assailant struck me a blow across the face. My father materialized. "What are you doing with that beachbum . . . that baseballnik?"

A bronzed lifeguard disappeared into sleep mist, sneering like a disdainful otter. My inelastic blood vessels pounded in my ears. I took breaths, counting slowly . . . one . . . two . . . three . . . four . . .

Again my father appeared and delivered his divine pedagogical disapproval. "Is that my daughter counting? Recant!"

I sat up, and stuck my feet over the side of the bed.

"I'm not counting, Daddy; I agree with you. Lies, damned lies, their numbers seriatim, their axioms of causality. There's no First Cause. I'm older than you were when you died and I've learned about addition that subtracts; about men at arms who lie still to be counted; about love when arithmetic of experience contracts the *he* who was infinite into the finite *they?*"

Unexorcised, the figure who had sleepwalked out of my destiny emerged again. Behind that blow. Since I alone could have summoned this ghost, I should take him up tenderly as if he were one of the children who had broken into my sleep. For if I orphan him, who can house him?

* * *

Scenes arrange themselves. Behind a scrim of fog, lustered figurines rotate in carnival tableaux. The music over the water is

16

Let me call you sweetheart
I'm in love with you . . .

Sea girls in white ruffles, summer-sweet boys in blue blazers, billow and dip, whirl away from each other and twirl back.

"It's like a carousel, it makes me dizzy," I say as I return to his arms. He hums a turn with the band.

"A carousel!" Dip . . . two . . . three . . . "You're a funny kid." He spins me from him and draws me back. "Scared of the roller coaster? With me holding you!"

My love (I knew neither modifying number nor nickname then) — my love was a lifeguard with a chipped front tooth to prove he had forcibly rescued a drowning man. He was one of the "others," the bronzed, the natives who leap and do not stumble. (How they shine in the light of envy!) All summer I had watched as *they,* like adolescent seals, dived off his catamaran in the open sea, or sported around the lifeguard stand in a herd into which, only ten days earlier, he had drawn me, smile by crooked smile.

"Here, catch it! Yeah, you, the strawberry blonde."

The ball lands in my quiet lap. "Hey! Bookworm! Get on that base!"

"Get your nose out of that book, peach-cake. Tide's pulling out, come talk to me while I keep an eye on the small fry. Some mothers think the ocean is a bathtub."

"Carry your books home, kiddo?"

"Come down early in the morning. We'll comb the beach."

"Storm last night churned up shells and glass. Sit down, I'll buckle your sandals. Hey! Pretty feet."

"Meet you on the boardwalk after supper. Sure you can. It's still light. Go out the back door."

"How about being my girl at the Labor Day dance?"

*

There is a scene with my parents.

"A lifeguard!" my father cries as if stabbed. "Maybe he plays baseball, too," he adds, in broken tones.

"He's a senior in high school. He's working to pay for college." My shrewdness sprouts with my love. I do not add that his eyes, his Irish eyes, are irreverent and unsad, that his black patent leather hair hangs straight across his brow like the prince on the cover of the *Crimson Fairy Tales,* the one that shows him parting the shrubbery behind which the Sleeping Beauty (altogether passive) is about to be kissed awake. (Oh, no villain can be more selectively secret than a child!)

"Fourteen years old and your daughter wants to go dancing with boys." My father bites the sinister side of his mustache and rocks his head, keening.

"The other girls will be dancing and I'll be the only one at the social who has to sit with my parents and the babies. Everyone will see we're greenhorns." (Leave it to children, they know just where to slip in the knife.)

My mother speaks up. "It's true. In America . . . young girls . . . different customs . . ."

"Amerikaaa!" My father cracks the word against his tongue. Gall floods his taste buds. "Amerikaa has customs? You saw the Sunday papers? The Vanderbilts after dinner in the library. A room full of books, but, no, they don't read out loud after supper like common people. The butler stands with a tray of fine Copenhagen and dolled up in egret feathers and diamonds they throw china it should break against the marble fireplace. That's in Amerikaa, custom!"

In the end, my tears and my mother's willingness to let me go prevailed. My love was permitted to escort me to the end-of-season social.

He could dance and he could whistle too.

Oh let me call you sweetheart
I'm in love with youuuuuuuu.

and la la la and twirl away from the family chaperonage of supper to the privacy of the dance floor.

Oh let me hear your answer,
Say you love me tooo

He glittered at me, all electric. I scattered hectic flutters at him like a courted peahen.

He spiraled me outward from the crowded center to the thin edge, to the deserted dock, away along the breakwater, out to the last rocks of the jetty. Under the heaped clouds all the little ships flashed colored lanterns and glowed welcome from cabins rocking in the cradle of deep sleep.

It was a soft September night. One of those tropical masses that creep up Long Island ahead of hurricane season had thickened out of the sea; a white sea with no height to it, only that it sloped upward into mist that lolled down on it, oppressive as wet hair. Between ocean and sky the line was dim; dimmer than my consciousness of forces gathering outside my girlish pictures of love, in which my self was poised with myself in varnished views more vivid to my senses than its vigorous presence beside me.

Our drift was toward the dark. He leaped from the high wall to a low-tide beach and with love's light wings I flew after. Carrying our shoes we walked along the hard margin, stopping to kiss now and again or only to fall back and gaze at each other's faces that were vague as clouded moons; two moths swaying toward each other, vibrating before our lips touched.

"Love," I whispered (speaking for myself).

"Honey-baby," he sighed.

19

At our beach we sat down at the base of the lifeguard stand. "How about a swim, honey-bunny?" he said. "I'm burning."

"At night? It's not allowed."

"Listen, Miss Goody Two-Shoes," he recited as if reading the sign above us: SWIMMING PERMITTED ONLY WHEN LIFE-GUARD IS PRESENT.

We laughed so hard we fell into each other's arms. He smelled of hot sand and seaweed charring under a driftwood fire.

"Is there a lifeguard present? I ask you and I answer, yes indeedy sweetie, there is a lifeguard present and he permits us to go swimming."

He took off his jacket and made a pillow for us. We lay looking up at nothing, saying nothing for a time.

"Come on. It's so hot. Let's go. I'm going." He jumped up and landed with his legs astride my outstretched legs.

(So he stood and stands engraved on my sensual memory: manly hand glimmering against white shirt; thumb and fore-finger on pearly buttons; that sapient gesture, a directional pointer along my bewildered amorous trail, retained in after years, the power to direct my blood from my heart's caves to the cage of my pelvis.)

He unbuckled his belt. In carnal delicacy I closed my eyes as his white flannel trousers slid downward. I felt the sting of upflung sand as he jogged away.

He was, after all, not naked. Far off, a patch of white under-shorts was suspended among mists that coiled into being in the turbulence between air and water. His trunks tapered up into the darkness and his legs down into invisibility. It seemed as if the sea could suck him down with one sigh, or the mist lift him into itself like white arms and he would be lost. Only his voice would be heard crying with the gulls on the salt air.

"Coomme ooon innn . . ." Already he was only a voice.

Behind me were the dim lights of the road, before me

the darkness into which he had gone. Gone. Gone.

I let the weight of starched ruffles pull my dress down me, and stood shivering in the voluptuous dark. I considered my petticoat and dropped that. A whiff of talcum powder and lemony body arose from it. In cotton bloomers and brassiere, hands pressed against the hard fullness of my breasts, I ran toward him.

"Commmmme onnnn . . ."

Surf frilled around my ankles. It barely broke into wavelets, and even where the land shelved downward and dropped into the channel, the water rocked around the buoys and swelled without breaking under the windless air.

"Smells like lightning," he said.

"How does lightning smell?"

He plunged away. "Like gunpowder." His words floated back to me.

"How does gunpowder smell?" I called.

"Like Fourth of July." He dived under a shallow roller and emerged sleek-haired, bobbing on the viscous calm. "Come with me, I'll take you out deeper."

"My hair will get wet — they'll see."

"Tie your braids tight on top with your ribbon. I'll swim backstroke and keep your head above my chest."

He slid under me and drew me out after him. My teeth chattered.

"What's the matter? The water's warm," he laughed.

"I can't see the shore!" I gripped his shoulders.

"Hold on tight, sweetheart, you're safe with the lifeguard."

He was a strong swimmer and I flowed easily above him, my limbs touching and being touched by his, delicately, through a film of water. We exchanged gentle kisses, lips cool, tasting of salt. We swam and floated so until sheet lightning, which had been rattling like silver foil in the distance, crackled closer.

"We have to get out," he whispered and languidly pulled for

shore, towing me along until I could feel grit and shells where the receding tide had dropped them.

He lifted me. Oh Mother! Oh Father! Like flying. Like dying. At each step brushing my nose with his lips.

"My honey-baby has a cold nose and a warm heart!"

He carried me up the beach steps, past the boathouse and a faintly lit row of bungalows that seemed already to be receding into autumn.

"Folks not home yet," he said.

No doubt they thought me somewhere in that swarm of young on the dance floor.

In the bathroom, I removed my wet underclothes and hid them in a towel. What to put on? Not my brother's hand-me-down stringy robe. This was the occasion for my father's gift, the watered-silk robe I had kept rolled up in its tissue paper.

On our porch swing I nestled in his arms. Rocking, swaddled in darkness I accepted his kisses and murmurs. He ran his hand over the extravagant fabric and left a wake of sensations on my flesh beneath. For me, a well-developed nymph a molt or two away from maturity, these were wilderness enough.

"Mmmm," I murmured and rubbed my face against the bristle of his cheek.

"You don't have anything on under that, do you?" he whispered. His kisses became more lingering. But I still kissed from the book. Partly I needed to have my feelings affirmed as significant; partly I was still too unformed and uninformed to be certain of what they signified. At each kiss, as my sensations fulfilled and surpassed my imaginings, a joyous confidence suffused me. Joy took the shape of my body and filled it.

Hesitantly, or experimentally, he parted my robe. At the touch of his fingers a tremor of timidity shook me, but was soothed under a new languor. Encountering no defenses, he extended his caresses. Like a log slipping into water, I wavered, sank, rose and floated on my own current. Intact.

Supine on the swing, his murmurs deepened into moans. He groaned. Did I draw him to me?

(It would be an absurdity to attempt to conceal my adolescence from my age, but I feel a twinge of suspicion that some ideal may be defending itself, even now at my dirt brink, from the real.)

I drew him to me.

"Yes?" he breathed against my neck.

"Yes," I whispered happily.

"Yes, honey, yes, sweetie, yes I'm in love with you." Hoarse and urgent. "Yes. Sure thing I love you. La la."

Suddenly it became one of those Happenings in which the performers act without cues, without reference to each other. For him the scene had become a prior activity, a prologue mounting toward a climax. For me this prologue was ample play.

With a moan he thrust himself at me. Our weights shifted. Instead of being beside him I was under him. My breath was slammed out of my mouth and nose. His ankles trapped my ankles, his chin pinioned my shoulder, his fingers pressed separate points into my back.

For a dazed moment I lay still, succumbing to a passivity that waited for physical assault, a submission to clouded intuitions of underness. Then I began to struggle. I tried to pull away, to push him off me. His grip tightened. I twisted. He twisted with me. "Hey! Hey. That's not nice. Let me go!"

"Let me baby, let me, damn you, let me!"

In my ignorance, I might well have. But the violence in his body, the ferocity in his voice, alarmed the childhood still in me. Raging down on me was this Halloween mask: sightless skull, white eyeballs, broken tooth fang, and from the twisted jagged hole of mouth dribbled, "Let me, let me, let me, let me."

"Stop, stop, stop . . ."

Body roiled, spurred, teeth at my neck, at my mouth, chipped tooth-edge cutting into my lip, fly-trap kisses. I fought against his grip; wriggled one shoulder free. His mouth came down on my bared breast . . . "Aaahhh" he snarled.

"Uggghhhhh!" My mouth filled with phlegm. My nipple under his lips felt long and whiskery as if a soiled pen-wiper had stiffened up from my breast. My nose ran tears. Snicker and rumor took suffocating shape. A man on top of me! A man on top of me! And against my bare belly the snake — the Snake that defied God Himself.

Panic gave me strength. I arched my back. With all my might I pushed and half disloged him. The swing lurched and creaked under us and suddenly he slid and was sitting on the floor, blowing wet coarse whiffles through his mouth and nostrils. Only a moment, then he lunged back, repeating, "Let me, honey, let me." I clawed. He clawed back.

He flung his arms around me in a lifeguard's stranglehold. Against my flailing resistance he forced me backward. His arm muscle was pressed against my mouth and bulged in like a gag. Collecting all my fear I bit down as hard as I could and hung on for blood. He recoiled. But before I could slide away he grasped my loosened braid, noosed it round my throat, and yanked. Pain scalded my scalp. Tears were forced out of my eyes. I gasped and gulped for air.

"Bitch . . . you stupid bitch! Bitch! Bitch!" He rattled my head; banged it against the iron of the swing; a seagull breaking a clam. My blood beat in my ears as if it would erupt in a final roar. An unimaginable cry ascended in me on waves of terror and nausea.

So he held me, by the hair, the way a breaker mounts, crests, and rears for seconds before it hurls itself down into its undertow, drowning surf, sand, foam and flotsam with it. Protests chattered through his teeth. He snarled, whimpered. Still grasping my hair, he freed one hand, reared back and whacked me right across my face. Whack!

That blow. With it everything collapsed.

A spasm shook him. He threw me from him to the floor. Breath hissed out of me as from a clam dropped by a gull. A strand of hair shuddered in and out of my mouth but I hadn't the strength to raise my hand to brush it away. I saw I was naked. My robe lay on the floor by his feet. Dully, I drew it to me with my toes.

Drops of sweat beaded his chest and throat and rolled down like strands of tears. He was breathing uneven sobbing breaths. He glared at me. Oh, if looks could kill!

"That's it. That's Daddy's good girl. Cover yourself. Cover yourself you damned hot . . . bitch."

Far down the street the sound of hurried footsteps.

He pulled himself up from the floor. Shook both fists under my nose, a chimp menacing his tormentor. Dropping both hands over his groin, he doubled the Latin street gesture of swearing by the genitals. Moving from side to side like a mechanical man; uttering hoarse gutturals at my atrocious and thrilling virginity, my first love hobbled down the porch steps and out of my life.

I stumbled into the bathroom, locked the door and turned on the taps. I cried. I cried like a beaten child.

*   *   *

Ripeness is all. So it is well written. But where wrought? Not in flesh. Perhaps, in the artless realm of nature, the spring bud does not ache into flower as it fits its consent to the bee. Perhaps two ephemeridae slit their final membranes and emerge, correct in the calendar of moonlight. Their parts collect. Their mechanisms lock. But in the human realm every course of events is the sport of chance. Error is heaped on probable error, though art and memory shift the scenes to contrive life in accord with models. Oh my daughter, as the egg is pricked, do we not bleed? Oh my sons, as the prick is egged, also?

25

Give or take half a century, what should I have said? "My Irish cupid, you have tampered with the life of a myth." But he was the illiterate future, and he — I have since rehearsed the scene and delivered numerous ripostes to empty stairwells — he would have said, skipping a stone expertly through seven wavelets, "Tell that to your old man, bookworm, that stuff is Greek to me." Or how about a Shakespearean thrust? "You don't have to be the Queen of the Night to waken to an ass's head" (I have since fingered the fur on its ears).

Ah love, in a fading western literary light! If Juliet cues, "What satisfaction canst thou have tonight?," no fumbling prompter should set Mercutio onstage with his "O, that she were an open et cetera, thou a poperin pear."

But the prompter does muddle. And we? . . . We concoct. We concoct ideal simplifications and as these fall apart we reshape them out of our diminishing residues of hope. Unless suckled by wolves we architects of bric-a-brac spend ourselves trying to bring our sentiments of how things should be into being. Not once, not twice, but until desire fails; as if pressure of wishing and thinking could force our romances into existence; a willing of unicorns, a lifelong effort at reification.

My grandson Daniel, being a philosophe-activist, put it more vehemently. "We must loosen Plato's death grip! There must be an end to sacrificing life to forms."

"You say it will be better without forms. What a time to tell me!"

"Never too late to learn, old lady." He lit two cigarettes and passed one to me.

"Thank you, Humphrey Bogart." (That boy. Everything is a drama with him.) "When your revolution takes over, will the nonforms you impose be instruments of liberation?"

"So I believe."

"Power will not change your purposes? You seriously believe yours will not become one more system of brutalization; you will not use violence in the name of your moral necessity, or as a means to your ethical perfection?"

"No violence." (His early-Lenin air and the way intensity mutes the green of his eyes to gray, like leaves scudded underside in a storm, remind me of my son Absalom.) "We are violently opposed to the war in Vietnam but we'd rather not resort to violence."

"What about bombings?"

"Only symbolic targets, if we have to."

"Symbolic targets have no hands and feet, Danny?

"Our only alternative to military enslavement by the criminal powers that tried to destroy Cuba, that assassinated the Kennedys, Martin Luther King, Malcolm X, Fred Hampton . . . may be to blow up the centers of military power."

"If you talk like that on campus can't they take away your draft deferral?"

"They can do anything they damn please and get away with it. This whole Vietnam War is a Pentagon plot to destroy our country. It is a worse plot than their most paranoiac, zenophobic, anti-Communist fears could have created. It is draining our country morally, economically, physically and spiritually. It is setting the world against us and our people against each other."

"O.K. O.K., Danny. I'm with you but answer my question."

"They can take away my deferral, yes. With an A average and entering my senior year I should be O.K. One thing you can bet on, I will not go to Vietnam."

"Of course you won't. Let's not cross that bridge. Maybe this insane war will end soon. In the meanwhile must you shout defiance from the housetops and the law library steps? 'Bombing centers of power!' 'Symbolic targets!' My father, your great-grandfather, would have said you are feeding from ideas ex-

27

pressed by Bakunin and Nietzsche in their most obstreperous moments: invaluable fellows on the first day of a revolution, disastrous on the second."

"My ole man don't talk that kinna' fancy, man." He thinned his lips into a straight line, flared his nostrils, and achieved a parodic resemblance to his father, my son-in-law Ricardo. "You're damn tootin' he'd give me what for. The bastard would button up his officer's coat, like, snap on his Jesuitical look and wham, turn me over to the inquisition, or the military police, *for my own good.*"

"Come on, Danny, you're exaggerating. Anyway, you can hide out with me. We'll fit up the chimney room in the attic where the runaway slaves were hidden on the escape route to Canada, or so the real-estate agent said when I bought the place."

"Then I'm all set for a healthy mind in a healthy body. You'll hoist up picnics — a bird and a bottle — and what was it the guard gave the prisoner in solitary in *Grand Illusion?* — a flute. And we'll have an ongoing chess match. Your move comes up in the basket, my move goes down."

It wasn't enough of a joke. We were both silent while he prepared us drinks. Neatly he stirred my sherry flip with his finger, the way his uncle Benjamin does. "No sweat. You will be rewarded for your services to my revolution. When I am chairman you will be commissar of . . . what do you want, name it."

"Window boxes."

"You have it. From sea to shining sea the country will be a blaze of geraniums and petunias."

"Is that how much you've learned from gardening with me all these years? How about north-facing windows? Will you provide begonias and ivy or will the sun shine for your revolution on both sides of the street?"

"Just so *you* are on my side, Granmaw."

"Just so *you* promise to hold my hand when we face the firing squad in the first counter-reform. You'll have to be brave for us both. I'm too old to run and I'm a proven coward."

"If we have to make a getaway I'll carry you pickaback. I swear it. Now may I eat the rest of the biscuits?"

He crammed a warm cheese biscuit into his mouth and smiled chipmunk-cheeked.

(In the reversibility of time he was four years old and we were planting bulbs on a windy autumn morning; he, crouched in the protective hollow of my body, repeating after me, "An early tulip [pat down hard], a late tulip [pat down hard] early . . . late . . ." Crisp and neat, like his grandfather, Adam, and his mother, Arie, he endowed any act with immaculateness retaining a look of clean fingernails and white linen even when shoveling manure.)

He stared out the window. "Speaking of gardens, don't try to dig up the bulb bed, old lady. Leave it for me. How would you like Dinah and me for company next weekend? I could pick her up at the office after my last class on Friday and we could make it in time for dinner."

"Suits me perfectly. Anything special your sophisticated palates crave?"

(The blessed thing about grandparenthood is you don't have to defend yourself from doting. It is also your last chance to imagine you can create happiness for children.)

Gloomily, Danny troubled his lower lip — the same gesture as my father's.

"Danny, have you tried to talk to your father? I know he has an infuriating authoritarian manner, but he *has* worried himself into an ulcer about your getting into deep trouble with the army."

"My father has an ulcer from his temper, not from worrying about anyone else. He is from the ice age. He has all the petty vices of a Spanish grandee who lorded it in the colonies. He's

29

a redneck! A Nixon admirer! A Johnson supporter! You should hear him pick on Mom. His offspring don't leap to attention when he enters a room because she brought us up according to that Communist, Dr. Spock. Her mother — that's you, Grandma — is a misguided bleeding-heart liberal who encourages fine young men like me to be draft evaders, instead of urging us to do our duty and napalm the Vietnamese."

"Me? I don't give legal advice at the peace center. I serve coffee and cake.

"My father and I have had our last quarrel. We have absolutely nothing more to say to each other, ever."

"Maybe you should have said . . ."

By the puckering of my mouth with salt *I* should have said, *they* should have said. But oh, the silence between generations. I have learned them all, already, learned them all. Children. Their circular fashion of forsaking. I too have wept and prayed, more passionately than to any unconsenting adult, "Oh speak to me, my life's sweetness, my darling, enlighten me. Don't you care, my heart, humble as a button, fallen on the shrouded plain? Come out, come out, wherever you are. Come back, hard hearts. Is there any cause in nature that makes these hard hearts?"

They answered me with silence. Longer and longer silence.

Who would be a parent? We, who wake clinging to a wet pillow crying the name of a child, departed, left no addresses, consider Romeo and Juliet.

*   *   *

"Everything in the dark," my father said, "dark as ignorance and as violent. No one saw those two. They barely saw each other. Masks, moonlight, a secret chapel. They even took poison from each other's lips in the dark."

The book lay between us; American high-school student

bringing Shakespeare-in-English home to the foreigner, her father.

"Is that daughter of yours crying again?" My mother's voice belled from their bedroom. "That girl. At every paper tragedy she boohoos as if she invented tears."

"I'll be in soon," my father answered. He handed me his cologne-scented handkerchief. "It *is* very sad; two rich, pampered, only children who didn't believe they could die, die. Imagine those parents."

He riffled the pages for a text to moralize the action. "Willful children; bumbling between friar and nurse. (Miserable marriage counselors were you both.) Old fools. Safe drugs!"

"They were trying to help."

"What might we have been spared if those children had walked in by the front door instead of flitting up and down rope ladders playing forbidden games. In-and-out-the-window, Statues, even playing dead. Juliet should have come in out of the night garden and said, 'Father, I would like to marry Romeo. Can you arrange that?' "

"Her father had just arranged her marriage to Paris."

"And an excellent match, too; better than the one she arranged for herself between one step of a dance and another."

"I don't believe in arranged marriages," I said, fresh from pursuit-of-happiness novels.

"Why not? You think ignorance and inexperience are diplomas for life?" The umber flecks darkened in his green eyes. (Even when distressed he had that appropriate beauty found in old photographs of serious gentlemen who believed they owed the world getting on in; whose index of excellence was sterling character combined with honed intellect.)

"They fell in love at first sight."

"In the dark? By smell? Like two animals. Paris was too refined for her. Those Capulets had bad blood; parents, child, nephew, even their servants were infected. Wooden-headed

31

Hauskerls following *Lumpen* nobility; the idle rich itching for a fight, breaking their boredom with bloodshed *Pogromniks*."

"Romeo tried to avoid fighting," I said, "after he was secretly married."

"That's what comes from secrets. If Juliet and Romeo were crazy to have each other, their parents would have had to come around. The duke would have arranged it gladly. Reconciliation of two warring factions would have brought peace to Verona. Shakespeare's audience worried more about bloody feuds than about love. Only in America they don't understand civil war in the streets. When the prince says all are punished, he means all extremists are punished. Shakespeare understood that. The audience did too. In politics, in religion, in love, should be a measure. Read Hegel. Understand synthesis.

"Look at the text," he said. "You've left out something Shakespeare didn't. 'Can you love the gentleman?' her parents ask. On Sunday the girl says yes, on Thursday she kills herself. Romeo, the same craziness. Before the dance he's fainting for Rosaline. One minute later he can't live without Juliet. Temperament! Temperament!"

He struck a match so hard it split, then brandished his glowing cigarette. "Don't you see, child, old Capulet was doing what every father should. He chose a man of good character from their milieu and arranged a secure dowry." My father sighed for his expropriated possibilities.

"I wouldn't accept a dowry if you had one to give, so don't feel bad."

"Before you throw out an old custom, Ariadne, find one that makes life more human."

"What about happiness, Daddy?"

"*Amerikanischer* Santa Claus. Can you believe those two spoiled children would have escaped unhappiness? Unhappiness is also life. But an orderly family life, making a decent living, a peaceful city, freedom to study, the right to discuss, to play a game of chess, time to think about how to make a better world — ah, my daughter, those are blessings to call happiness."

"What about individual rights?"

"Spoiled rotten. A world in which we and civilization are sacrificed to one another's whims." (He could envision society slowly climbing to more rational levels up Hegelian triads of thesis, antithesis, synthesis. But neither his education [Torah to Talmud — Mishnah and both the Palestinian and the more dialectical Babylonian Gemaras — thence to Kant, to Hegel] nor his buffeted history, inclined him to the logistics of romantic individualism.)

"I would not permit you to have a date — Phew, what a word; why not a fig? — with a rowdy like Romeo. No matter how rich and handsome. What a milieu! Now take a man like the guest the rabbi brought last Sunday. Adam Arkady. He is a suitor a father would choose, if he could afford the dowry: from a noble Sephardic family, educated, makes a good living, has a refined character. He plays a strong chess, too."

"He doesn't look as if he had trouble with temperament," I said.

"Temperament is for Caruso, in *Pagliacci,* not for family life. By us it is written, 'Bind not your daughter to a man of moods.' "

*   *   *

Had I known my future, I might have said, "You succeeded, Father. The man you bound me to has no moods."

And he would have said, "Your husband is a good steady man from a good family. The apple does not fall far from the tree."

And I: "No one could accuse Adam of an excess of temperament."

And he: "You are a malcontent."

33

And I: "That is probably true, but all the same you were a tyrant."

Suddenly we find ourselves on dangerous ground. Two enemies who desire nothing more than to break out of the trenches and embrace. But even on this posthumous field I do not know what terms could establish peace.

Dear God! Dear children and grandchildren. Must life always be lived as a retort? Will no one correct a hypothesis? Where, O where, is the synthesis?

Some day our genetic helixes will be pinned down and numbered as part of our dossiers. Master synthesizers will act as marriage brokers. Mates will be drawn to one another by the magnetism of tape and not by the dubious attraction of opposites, which is compounded of curiosity and a hankering for what is not ours. As Jeremy used to say, "The marriage of opposites may be good for the species, giving the widest range of genes, but a lifetime of having nothing in common is hell on couples." What a marital and even parental millennium we can expect when computers take over!

What can't a computer do these days? Dating, mating, tracing, bugging. It can be taught to play chess. Not brilliantly, but adequately. (It never occurred to me to ask my beloved Paul if he played chess. Perhaps it is not a preoccupation one expects of a man who can dance barefoot in a cabin by a brook; a man whistling there to a lovely and delicate tune; imitative it is true of Bach's *Erbarme Dich,* but reminiscent of liturgy and hauntingly wild all the same.) As a matter of fact my husband, Adam, a computer expert as well as a chess Master, designed one of the first chess programs. As he explained it to me, "The capture-tree depicts all the possible partial capture-moves for a given piece after you code in the first move." (Always the critical first move!)

The mention of matchmaking computers brings my granddaughter, Dinah, to mind. She telephoned me this morning, and, as usual when she calls from the office, we peppered our conversation with computer jargon.

"This is your long-distance analog flashing, Gran. Input: do you want to get married again?"

"Throughput *and* output: positively no, thank you. Have you gone into matchmaking?"

"No, I'm programming the software for a computer-dater. Uncle Benjamin doesn't want to refuse the slot-machine company outright. He's letting me see what I can make of it."

"Do you put your trust in the computer-dater?"

"Date-for-a-Mate? Absolutely. I swear I do, my very own gran." (She picked up that expression registering voters in the South.) "If there is one noble heart profiled into its storage bank the mechanism will retrieve him for me quick as a printed circuit."

"What are you feeding in?"

"The works. Alpha rays, biorhythms, astral awareness, horoscopes. When I get through, the gismo will tell us under what conjunction of signs to be married. We'll live happy as chickadees in your bird feeder."

"Given up, Fate-Mate?" I asked.

"Look around. What kind of fool do you think I am? Chance on him random? Probability near zero. The computer works as the brain should. So trust it. I have this hot prospect for you, lovey, 'Retired English professor: well-educated, dominant, extroverted male seeks compatible female. Special interests' Get this, Gran! 'Shakespeare and gardening!' "

"My treasure, that is an offer I can hardly refuse. Wait. What's his sign?"

"Taurus."

35

"Too bad. Our ecliptics would overlap and cancel each other out. But it is sweet of you to think of marrying me off, Dinah. Did you have anything else in mind?"

"Old shrewdie. What do our horoscopes say about you, me and Danny for the weekend?"

"Danny has already spoken to me. All the signs agree, come ahead love. I'll be going up to the dacha on Thursday. Will Vincent join you?"

There was a pause and a sigh. "Not unless our conjunction improves before then."

"Play nice, kiddies, play nice." I said.

*   *   *

In the fictional world, incidents are supposed to add up to a right course, a revelation. But these tableaux I see behind me — an event here, an event there — float apart as I study them. Scenes invade and impinge on scenes, impervious to order. It's very modern, it shouldn't upset me, but it does. Given five random dots, I try to connect them. Ten inkblots become a Rohrschach in which I am driven to trace my biography. In aftertouching memory I try to formulate patterns; I want every gesture, every incident to fall into place as part of a becoming.

Once in Athens (I had gone there hoping to meet my son Absalom) a sudden skirmish sprang up and caught me in an agora at a distance from my hotel.

Under a faultless blue sky, from between scenic white walls, military tanks converged, turrets revolving ominously, like bully boys indolently closing in on a victim they will brutalize. Ping. Zing. Dust spangled down onto the hewn hair of caryatids and onto birds nesting there. The flock rose in a cinder cloud (how the heart rises to their perturbation!), their ashen shadows reeling on the glistening façades.

36

Instantly the market was hurried away. Neat unyouthful farmers, privation scratched into their dry, thoroughbred faces, fled down streets and alleys behind black-veiled matrons. Mourning cries flowed back.

Shutters and doors were banging shut. Bolts clanged and screeched as they were jammed into place. House gates and shop grates slammed ringingly down. The square was emptied of life so speedily I found myself standing alone. Then I, too, ran.

I shoved against impervious doors, and rattled locked gates. When a church door yielded to my push. I lunged in, crossed a vestibule and dashed through another door. It slammed behind me. The latch-tongue clattered, a tumbler rattled and clicked.

When I stopped panting I tried to turn the knob. It was locked in place. (What better sanctuary than a church, even if I was alone in it? The sexton would be along in time with a key.)

Considering the modest entrance, the interior was unexpectedly grand. Though it smelled of disintegrating plaster and decline, from the lavish mosaics that glowed from domes, apses, naves, along all the walls and from the narthex as well, it had known splendor.

Riot sirens continued to sound. Militant chanting surged and died, swelled and died again. Gunfire rattled farther and farther off. But no one unlocked the door. Wandering about, hoping to find a side exit, I felt like an intruder. Cherubim with corroded lamps defended the access to the sanctuary. I could have used prayer but Christ Pantocrator was scowling down from a gold-tiled dome. The tablets of gratitude were in Cyrillic characters, which I couldn't read. There were mosaics all over the place but they too proved hard to decipher, they were so deteriorated.

In niches between vaults and arches, memorial candles guttered beneath the upward gaze of martyrs, more mortified by time than they had been wracked for their faith. Arms, legs, haloes, attendant birds and beasts had fallen away from moldering walls. Whole scenes were undecipherable though separate details remained that were very affecting; two noble-headed disciples, their embrace intact, had had their lower limbs and draperies reduced to granulated stains on the wall. A curve of iridescent blues and jeweled greens might have been part of a peacock's spread tail. The disembodied muzzle of a lamb seemed to be nibbling a garland.

The more closely I studied each mosaic the more it floated apart into fragments and patches and then into isolated tesserae — cobalt, indigo, amethyst, violet, gold — each bit unrelated to other bits. I could no more hold together an entire mosaic than I can my floating recollections.

Hours passed. The shafts of stained-glass colors that had been banding the chalky marble floor grayed as the light behind the windows faded. Restive and tired, I sat down in the center of the church where I could be seen by the sexton if he came to unlock the door for services.

I glanced back at the mosaics. Suddenly, it was as if a curtain had been drawn aside. What I had failed to see from up close was perfectly evident from the distance. Each mosaic was part of a story. The church itself was part of it. Arches, vaults, niches, pendentives, columns were intrinsic elements in a unified whole. A golden dome was also a dome within the mosaic temple in which a little girl in cobalt blue was being presented; Mary, small as she was, going forth "into her fate" as Rilke says. A circle of rosy light from a window fell on the Annunciation. Between two rough columns Joseph lifted his thick cap slowly off his head. The journey to Bethlehem curved across an arched span, Mary riding forward on a high-stepping white steed, Joseph walking bowed behind, the variegated green hills receding on an actual recess; the entire procession suffused with the unquenched glow from hundreds of thousands of gold tiles. Delicate patterns were repeated, unifying the whole, like amens or lyrical refrains. Tile by tile, slowly, like strength from suffering, the story had been put together, exalting the life of Mary, her suffering and her Son's.

It would have made historic sense for Greek mothers to have found sanctuary here, rather than for me, a Jewish American, a bystander, while the Passion was being re-enacted on the streets; the ruby-red blood of their sons being shed.

Compline and evening song went uncelebrated. The smell of scorch cut into the scent of cold incense. I fell asleep. When I woke in the early damp, a different slant of light revealed a chancel door within the carved railing. I found my way out via a spiral stone staircase, a subterranean crypt and a narrow door that gave out on an alley of cypresses and sunken gravestones. It was the hour of no color. I crept along the unpeopled streets, past empty tourist buses, overturned vans — sucking in my guts, crouching low to the wall, tense as a cat, yet aware of a curious tingling of lust. The blue light of an ambulance ascended, revolving toward the Acropolis. From the hill came scattered volleys, but my own death did not occur to me.

*   *   *

Why, after having been lodged in some cave of my memory for decades, do those hours of accidental sequestration return, hauntingly ambiguous now?

I think I know what the old men and women are doing; their far-sighted eyes focusing on nothing, their self-absorption reassuring at the last. They are tracing the repeat in their pattern. Under the impact of the oncoming fog the depriving light disintegrates the scenes. The past is a shifting mosaic. Blues melt into greens. The foreground dissolves. Old land routes and waterways are mazed with detours. Air lanes are dangerous with invisible peaks. Yet in clear bursts of brightness, by reflection and indirection, markers are discovered in the time-drowned sea. Explicit revelations of the main design lead back, lead back . . .

39

How I Became an American

Never become a refugee. Kiss the rod. Eat bark. Stay where you are.

— ROBERT GRAVES

FOR AN OPENER I had expected that an event or an unevent would present itself: like Moses in the bulrushes, a situation with a promising future in spite of its dubious past; or like my American brother, Ezra, a fully diapered neonate, who, the aunts assured six-year-old Jessica and me, had been found that very morning in a cabbage patch.

Birth? There's nothing distinctive about being born unless you can repeat it, like Christ or any other resurrection god. To me, my birth was no event. To my parents it was a catastrophe. En route to embarkation for America my mother slipped on a slick of ice in a railway station. I arrived prematurely with bronchial complications and no travel papers. My father had to go ahead without us, while my mother made her way back to her parents with two mewling and puking children. A minor war broke out. We were sucked into a "vacuum of power," and became another dossier in the Jewish Refugee Problem. (To speak of the Jewish Problem is to postulate that it is the Jews who are the problem.)

There is logic as well as tradition for opening on Arrival. ("Oh, my America, my Newfoundland" and all that.) For one, it is an opportunity to give my mother her due, belatedly (and what daughter does betimes?). She clearly demonstrated that any future we might have depended on making our way past customs. For another, on the steamship coming here she introduced me to the very American idea that a new life could be had, not through reincarnation or transmigration, but simply by transportation.

"Don't cry for Grandpa, Arnie. You'll meet your father soon. We'll begin a new life in America." (Like so many falsehoods parents tell to children, this one raised more anxieties than it allayed. What would happen to the life to which I had grown so attached?

*   *   *

Ellis Island. A health official inspects and stamps. Deified but not ennobled by authority, distancing himself with two sticks, he pokes as at caged chickens. Who among us is for wringing? Clutching his not-quite-perfect papers, an adolescent boy, pimply, skinny, orthodox side-curls, is pointed aside. A closed family breaks open. The shawled mother tries to pull the cluster back together. The moving pointer menaces. The youth waves the others on and floats backward, a blown petal on the wind of maternal lamentation. Number now, and see who is gone from among us.

My mother of the survivor's farsight tunes up her German lieder Voice, throws her fur-lined cape over her magnificent lumber-girl shoulders and sings out, *"Guten Tag, Herr Doktor."* I try to curl myself into the fur but she shakes me out of this foetal posture into my full stance. I am breathing in lifelong drafts of cowardice.

(From then till now, I suffer a foreigner's melancholy at change of place, and qualms of seasickness ride up from my

42

deepest gut if I so much as put my hand to the doorknob of a room that is unfamiliar.)

The dog-faced official checks off the cape ("Such a cape, my child, you can imagine! Your father, god bless his hands, designed it for me when I carried you"); her own hair coiffed high, no ghetto wig, no shawl, a blue velvet hat — she is George Washington crossing the Delaware. My blond brother stares ahead with unblinking shocked eyes. The officer meatily fingers one of my Saxon-invader curls, nods approval at our clean fair skins and exonerates us of orthodoxy and poverty.

"*Schönes Mädchen,*" he says into my mother's black lustrous eyes. She lifts me to his level. "*Sag' danke,*" she says, making it obvious she is superior to compliments from him. Something in him clicks its heels. He ushers us forward. "*Guten Tag, gnädige Frau.*" Another gate opens before us.

My mother and I are shelling peas and rehearsing our entrance into the New World.

"Clean! Your faces were certainly clean!"

As usual, my stomach turns queasy at her next words. "If the Herr Doktor had known I had to wash your faces with spit!" (Whose spit? The question rose automatically each time she spat out those words.)

"Your body," my mother rattles a quick handful of peas into the colander, "I should say 'your body, what there was of it,' was covered with sores and scabs, bones like spiders' legs. If the doctor had ordered me to undress you, we would have been locked into quarantine to be eaten by lice, or gotten pox, or been sent back to wherever they thought they could get rid of us. But your face was pure cream. Not a mark. God heard me. While I was carrying you I prayed every day if a girl, don't let her inherit my complexion."

She places a hand against her cheek to cover the fine warp

43

of scars left by acne. Cinderella of the slashed adolescence, she grabs a pea pod and splits it open, triumphantly. Winner take all. It was on her broad feet the prince had slipped the magic slipper, and not on her beautiful sisters'.

"Your faces were clean. That's what he could see. Heidelberg Herr! But your brother's swollen heart, his rickets, his broken nerves . . ."

For my damaged brother, a moment of silence.

We take up our next scene, which is acted at the Last Barrier.

"So. We have our Red Cross papers. We have our own names. I never liked the Greek names my father gave us but from Hera why Hannah? From Ariadne it's better Anna? Reuben is harder to spell than Robert? Who is this Robert in the middle of the family? From Genesis . . . at least the Bible they teach here?"

(A sneer for American education.)

"Out in front of that gate is supposed to be waiting the relative who answers for you and takes you out of Immigration. You think wives didn't wait for husbands that never claimed them? You're wrong. They sat. They and their children. Unclaimed parcels — with numbers.

"So. Each time the gate opens, there is a honking and fluttering like geese at food pails. Relatives throw themselves into each other's arms. Wives, children last seen as babies . . . Look . . . Look . . . God in Heaven, it's Rachel . . . it's Abraham . . . Here . . . Here . . . The screaming! The crying!"

Crying is my cue. My mother and my next line are waiting. Simply, "Daddy wasn't there!" But I let it hang between us, unspoken. I continue toying with the curled stem of a pea pod. She picks up the colander and heads for the sink. "What's the matter, you don't remember?"

I have rehearsed this impertinence since our last performance. "It's only, if there was such a big crowd, Mama, how could you know in *one* glance that Daddy wasn't there?"

"Getting smart! How could your mother know her husband wasn't there?" She looks down her formidable nose at me with that edge of contempt the strong have for the frail. "I looked! I had eyes like a hawk in those days. You know your father and you can ask? So handsome, so tall. Where else in the world have you seen such a color hair?" She glares out of thin-lidded eyes too acute for me to endure.

I might have answered "On my head." But granting we had the reciprocal antagonism of rivals, I was not the one in power.

She sloshes water through the peas, slopping some onto her shoes and the floor. "How could I be sure? Go give the barley a stir, and don't burn yourself, peanut." (And let those who play your clowns speak no more than is set down for them.)

I surrender unconditionally. "Tell me, Mama, why wasn't Daddy there?"

She is free to launch into her best part.

"Why wasn't he there? Red Cross. Red Tape. Their notification to your father I *myself* opened *a week later.*"

She takes two walnuts and cracks them together. They open neatly. (That year Aunt Giselle, returning to Uncle Joshua from one of her absences abroad, had turned her menacingly brilliant attention on vegetarianism. It was a foregone conclusion that our carnivorous family would be converted to her new faith.) "The Big Ones! They have their stamps. They have their rules. They have their uniforms. But for hearts, frozen onions. You know who cries from onions? Not the onions. If the Big Ones had hearts would the world be such a blood bath? Would a child cry for milk? When they cleaned us out of food, the pogromniks, I tried. I picked wild mushrooms, stole from gardens, ground acorns, cooked weeds. Children too weak to cry! That's a man's world. Would women allow it? I ask you!"

45

No more improvising for me. My next line is "When you saw he wasn't there, what did you do, Mama?"

"Do? You're here, aren't you?" She cuts down on the loaf of whole-grained bread. Her eyes are clear as eyes in the animal kingdom. Present-tense eyes.

Oh for the authority of her pauses; her innate sense of what Valéry called (and my lover, Paul, quoted) the "incomprehensible rule of the hiatus." Indomitable Duse. The bread knife rests in her hand. Once again the fur-lined cape is flung back, the defiant face raised to the indecencies that rain down on women from a patriarchal sky.

Now I see her beauty; in hindsight: a bust on a Viking ship's prow, a head on an Aztec ritual jug, a pitted marble caryatid. But then, little conservative with the mimsy esthetic of a little conservative, her mass embarrassed me. She loomed so. I wanted her to be demure, wistful, an exiled cameo out of an earlier age; if not the Gish sisters — beauty drifting toward us like the ghosts of earlier desires — at least my mother's sisters, whose charms were acknowledged to be authentic in love's romantic court.

"What did we do, child?" My heart takes flight with the flight of her royal pronoun.

What did *I* do, helpless child in the grip of realpolitik? *I* held on to her and shivered.

"I'll tell you what we did." The knife is mirrored in her eyes. "We walked right through the gate."

"Didn't the policeman grab you and arrest you?"

"Police!" (She hisses the word the way my grandson Daniel and his hirsute Bakuninites say "Fuzz.")

"I spoke to them in German and marched with my head held up." She makes a confidential aside: "If they ever teach you that the Germans lost a war, don't believe them. So. I look past the dog as if he were a heap of sawdust in my father's lumberyard, and I yodel out into the crowd — you know how I can make

46

an enormous sound without looking as if I'm trying — Youuu-uuuuu . . . Houuu . . ." (I put my hands over my ears.) "People turn around the way they do at my voice. I snatch my papers, saying *'Danke, danke, mein Herr,'* lift both of you in my arms — ach! such skin-and-bones children, and speaking in Polish I order you to wave and keep calling *'Vater. Vater.'*

"People are shoving from behind. You can't imagine the crowd, hundreds of people pushing, shouting, waving. The guard has just opened the barrier for a big family, which at once gets covered with relatives like a honey pot with bees. With all my strength, I push forward, and right away we are mixed in with them. The space fills in behind us, I bend down low to the ground." Her powerful body crouches over the peaceful kitchen linoleum. "I move like a big fish through water, without showing any motion above us or behind us. In front of us people separate like the Red Sea and, thank God!, we get on the ferry."

This is as far as we rehearse the event together. As she drifts to her reveries she whispers, more to herself than to me, "For a moment I thought you had forgotten the part about the gate."

Archaeologists and troubadours deliver us! How much of my mother's story was apocryphal? We need to verify those fragments of tales which float about us like pages torn from faded and ancient volumes . . . pages each of us feels condemned to piece together under penalty of mystical damnation; again and again to corroborate the testimony of those who have escaped to tell us. If we forget, there is always another wave of those Ishmaels, those Hagars of mankind to bring us the detail that substantiates Sojourn, Exodus, Auto-da-Fé, Destruction of the Temple, Diaspora, Holocaust.

During the Hitler period, by some linkage of interpolated data, my name and number were cast on the bloody flood and

I was given the option of swearing a false oath of cousinship for a Polish Jewess.

I took the matter up with my father's ghost.

"Should I sign the affidavit even if she is not related by blood?"

I can see that half-smile so precisely his, in which experience had not rendered tenderness obsolete. "Who is not related by shed blood?"

When the clerk at the refugee arrival center called her name and number, my imposter cousin stepped forward like a cloaked figure detaching herself from a Byzantine mosaic. She was the very one I would have chosen for kin from among those beind the barricade.

"Valegia, Pannje?" I retrieved the Polish words.

She answered in English. "This only valise."

"Is that one all you were allowed to take out?"

She looked at me; the famous dark eyes of song, but cool as a gunner's. "No, I am extravagant." Like dew on stone a smile condensed, then a giggle bubbled up.

"You learned extravagance in Berlin, in a factory?"

"I saved each day one part of my ration bread. I grew rich in stale bread. One day this rich woman came from factory to find barracks in flames." Again her smile, dew on marble. "My life's savings lost, I spend now everything."

The impossible fact is that laughter swept through both of us. While she laughed she rubbed her arm, the one with the indelible numbers.

How could I forget that gate? People can and do cast out of consciousness, or neutralize in myth, their painful passage out of the womb, as they put aside the intensity of loss of the nipple, the scented diaperings, those little instructions into masturbatory pleasure. But not a second Exodus. Within each our own

48

hearsay country, where broken images lie heaped like dishonored funeral stones, we pick over our pieces of rubble and try to reassemble them. Then one day, in an alien place, in a flash of déjà vu, an uninventable detail drops into place.

Whose spit washed my face? For some reason, truth hung on this. I coughed asthmas of rage over it, tried to surprise it under closed lids. Then once in the Caribbean: already a grandmother, I was lying on my deluxe hotel terrace, in sight of a shack within a clump of ragged palms. Idly, I set to thinking about it as a rearranged Winslow Homer that my daughter, Arie, might like to abstract for a painting if I photographed it: bleached orange planks, sienna soil, a woman's eggplant shape on long stick legs, conical head bent over a brown swollen-bellied baby. Suddenly a liverish tongue flopped out, slopped back and forth over the infant's eyes. I felt its roughness, felt the viscous spittle slip and slide against my stuck-together lids. Her spit!

What a relief when an unlikely detail emerges, not as distortion in a nightmare, but as corroborated reality.

The white ferry throbs, churns up a wake and pushes Ellis Island backward. A man in rabbinical kaftan breathes in gulps of fresh salt air. His black beard and expression remind me of Grandfather, whom I mourn as a lost father. Jowled farmer folk, heavy-headed as cattle, eyes clouded with mistrust, watch the river slide past, the city glide toward us. Sturdy women, in black skirts and white waists, stand determinedly upright. From between a clutter of roped bundles and straw hampers a single orange rolls toward us. A white-gloved hand withdraws. It leads to a brimmed hat ravishing with red and pink roses. My brother picks up the orange, wipes it on his sleeve, and without hesitation offers it to me. Gloved hands applaud.

We flow out with the crowd. A stupendous clatter showers down out of an elevated structure. Sunrays and dust spin through iron geometrics. My mother studies the scene, then leads us to a row of horse-drawn cabs in each of which sits a devil in frock coat and top hat, black whip in hand. All look equally ominous but among the hackmen a Polish ex-peasant reveals himself to her scrutiny.

She glances once behind her. In dreams I meet that glance, and moans strangle in my throat. She shows the driver an envelope. He nods, she steps up into the cab and disposes a child on either side of her. On the hackman's guttural we move forward. Jog. Jog. She tilts back her head, closes her eyes and smiles, a village Mona Lisa smile. A tear runs down the scarred ivory cheek. Her tongue whips out and licks it in.

My brother and I hold hands across her lap. The richness of privacy encloses us. Our spacious passage is slow. We rock in unison as the wheels revolve and sing over the cobbles. At a crossing pause we are level with a charcoal stove on a wheeled cart. The vendor cuts a long potato in half. It is gold. I tug at my mother's arm. She shrugs. "In America even the potatoes are golden." We are delayed beside a wagon on whose turning stage, also meshed in gold, children ride jeweled beasts. My mother sounds the syllables: "Car — ou — sel." A marvelous boy (one gold earring, black curls, audacious eyes) lifts boys and girls onto the backs of these magical mounts and straps them securely. Traffic carries us away. The music trails after. I am swept up in a wave of love and longing.

The streets ring with calls and sales songs: pots and pans, kraut and pickles, cabbages and potatoes. The carriage goes between pushcarts tended by women in black, shawls tied over wigs, by men in pious hats and shiny coats, in derbies and American suits. At the coachman's "Whoa, whoa!" the attention of the crowded street flows toward us. A woman at a second-floor window, arms and bosom at rest on a pillow, exchanges remarks with a woman sitting on the steps below. Boys stand up from their marbles. A knife grinder stops grinding. A junk dealer halts his "I cash clothes." At the back of the street a grocer in a white apron steps out of his shop, and tips his straw boater toward two men in bowler hats and dandy coats who are talking, lounging against two gleaming milk cans.

The cab door is opened. Both men lift their gaze to a woman and two children falling from the sky on a summer afternoon.

"Abidah!" my mother calls in her big country-bell voice.

A man flames up from his seat, rises in the air on one cry and slides to the ground. The crowd turns ecstatic. It surges forward, is waved back. It spreads the news — wife, children.

How often is it granted the happiness of participating in an event that concurs with the ideal? Ah, he died of joy! Bite your tongue, he fainted! In several languages he is pronounced unconscious but alive. We dismount.

So I first came to know my father — lying on a sunny sidewalk, his hat rolling merrily toward the gutter, two milk cans glittering like opera candles at his head.

We had come into the future. Now it was time for our history to have a happy ending. Now it was time for the children to play paradise in the sunlight. Where was the music we longed to hear? In whose hands were the cunning toys that dance and sing?

"Greenhorn" the girls sang grandly as they swept by me, affirming inness by shutting me out. "Boom. Boom. Here comes Boom." The boys taunted and chased Reuben and me back into the building. The shawled women stepped aside when my mother went bareheaded and unbowed to market. They sneered at my father. "Fresh starched shirt every day to the shop? On linen they eat? Flowers he buys? Showoffs."

Behind the windowpane my brother and I see a fresh-cheeked blond boy fill a used red satin candy box with steaming horse manure. He ties the ribbon bow and bides his time. Bess, the grocer's daughter, the buxom, dark-eyed daughter, traipses upstairs with soup for Mrs. Shalovitz, who is doing poorly. Back she prances, smoothes her apron. He comes forward, box in hand. Touches his cap. If he has a change of heart at her glance, at once saucy and shy, her trusting defiance of the shawled and wigged old women watching, he cannot retreat from his rape of the Jewess, because his compatriots, the little Cossacks, are whistling and whispering five feet away.

"No. No. Don't take it." But she cannot hear two children beating fists on the window and crying, "No. No. No."

She wants to be free of those immigrants on the stoop, those orthodox women in shawls and wigs, whose small hopes have already shriveled in the drought of poverty. She wants to be an American. Blushing, she takes the box.

As she unties, he retreats. Have you seen a sensitive mimosa contract in one spasm?

We stayed indoors, my brother and I, watching how every-one dodged with the jerky speed of characters on the penny-show. Men and women dodged horses, pushcarts, each other. Boys with skullcaps dodged boys with cloth caps; Italians dodged Irish, Jews dodged everyone.

Reuben's head shook more negatively, like palsy. Propped on pillows I coughed and rode wakeful isolation, listening to the adenoidal breathing of my always-ailing brother, my parents' sighs and whispers, the scuffling in the outside hallway, quarrels over the shared toilet, the cry of a baby with an endless earache. The higher mysteries waited for morning: the immigration officer tearing someone away for deportation; a dispossessed family on the street standing shamefaced among its possessions, a cup for pennies resting hopeless on top of a rickety chair.

*

"The children are fading away," my mother said.

"We must move to better air," my father said.

We ventured uptown, to another beginning, distant from the few kin, the shared Friday nights, the tenement life pouring over into the streets. Uptown, where the elevated train ended and there were private houses with shrubs and vegetable gardens tucked behind hedges and fences.

Uptown, where there were more Irish than Jews; more brogue than Yiddish, Polish, Russian or German, where tribal life was difficult to re-create; an isolation set in for which nothing had prepared us.

A green hill rose across the street from our apartment building. The day we moved in my mother and I picked daisies, then fell asleep in fragrant grass. I woke indoors, lying on a blanket behind a barricade of trunks and bundles. I was alone, my fear realized. I had been abandoned in steerage! Asthma coughs rattled in my throat. My mother scrambled through boxes, looking for the croup kettle. "What have I done to deserve two sickly children?" she said. "Don't cry, little lambs, you'll see, we are going to have a beautiful new life in America."

(Mother, with whom I never made my peace, our rivalries are ended, our secret fears and desires played out. Nothing disturbs the unfolding of our intention. I have you to myself. My head in your lap, I ride into sleep scented with daisies oxidizing into hay; the red and yellow trolley, high electrical singing of wire on wire, of wheel on steel, bell clanging, carrying the meadow away with us for always.)

*   *   *

Theologian and scientist, both have declared it. Any instant in time can begin Creation. According to Hoyle, there is void, then pouf there is matter. According to my father, the Talmud puts it another way. "It was the first night, but a number of

53

centuries had already preceded it. St. Augustine says, "There was no *then* before . . ."

But I should not parenthesize, if for no other reason than out of consideration for my cousin Jessica, who since our childhood has taken it amiss if she comes upon a parenthesis, be it delicate as two petals pressed between the paragraphs of a tale.

"For my sake, Arnie, go straight forward," she said to me not so long ago. "You know damn well if there is one thing that reminds me of my mother and sends me up the wall it's a story that spins around like a spider web. Our Greek-freak grandpa misread the chicken entrails or he would have named you Arachne." Jessica jumped up abruptly in the coltish nervous way she has retained.

"Calm down, Jessica. At over seventy, isn't it past time to stop griping about your mother?"

"She wasn't *your* mother; you can forgive her."

"Watch it, Jessica, any minute you are going to get bitchy."

"Bitchiness does not preclude affection," my old playmate flicked her tongue out at me, "as you should remember from your beloved Paul."

"Leave the room before I swat you. When you make biting remarks as if you were only joking it's time to put something soothing into your mouth. Go! Daniel and Dinah are due for the weekend, so the refrigerator is crammed."

"Yummy." She pranced on tiptoe, imitating herself as a child, rolling her eyes ecstatically, yet continuing to disparage me. "Do mother-feeders inevitably grow up to be grandmother-feeders, or do smart girls grow out of it? Good grief, Arnie, from nursing mother to catering grandmother nonstop. If I remember rightly, you carried casseroles to your assignations with Paul. If you die before I do, which omelet pan do you want to take to your reward?"

She skittered out of the room, a pained smile saying she couldn't help it. "Speaking of my mother makes me hungry." From the kitchen her voice floated, musical as *my* mother's.

I'm sorry dear soooo sorrrry dearrr
I'm sorrry I made you crrryyyy
Won't you forgive . . . won't you forget . . .
Don't let us saay goodbye . . .

* * *

Two little girls trot briskly on scene.

"Let's ask your mother to tell us a story." I presented the idea to my cousin Jessica.

"Aw no. My mother's stories are no good. Let's ask your mother."

"*Your* mother," I insisted.

"*Your* mother," she pleaded.

On the landing between both apartments Jessica hung back and I pushed forward.

"Maybe your mother will tell the one about the fish and the wishes. You know the one where she sings like the ocean. Don't you love it when she dances with a mop? That's a million times better than my mother's."

She cast enthusiasms before me until we were in the great white presence.

"Aunt Giselle, tell us a story."

"If you please!" She continued the scarlet paint stroke on the white porcelain cup.

"If you please," we repeated after her.

"Have you been good girls?" She appraised the finished poppy before she appraised us. (All the other ladies painted violets or pink apple blossoms.) "Your face is soiled as usual, my daughter."

We heard the voice of the critic and knew our pinafores were smudged, our stockings baggy at the knees.

"How is it that Ariadne's face remains clean? Go and wash, Jessica."

I reached out to comfort my unclean cousin. She shrugged me off and slumped out of the kitchen.

"Posture, Jessica! Posture! Young ladies who don't keep their backs straight develop hunchbacks."

Ah that quick talent milady had for imperiling any moment with guilt. Why had I exposed us again? I suppose that in love, children are no cleverer than adults. They also assume that those to whom they have given power over them will not use it to wound.

We were of an age. Why didn't Jessica simply push open the door that led to *my* mother, whose stories she preferred? Because love has its indomitable organization. I was enthralled by her mother but Jessica had submitted herself to me, and I chose the door behind which the tiger-lady was poised.

"Ariadne, my child, I am sure you were good. Was it a red-star or a gold-star day with you?"

(Whose child was I, did she say?)

Through her stock of bads and goods (she had no other means) I sensed praise, but in loyalty to Jessica I put it confusedly by, stiffening under the touch of her hand on my hair. Like a knife slipped back into its sheath, she withdrew.

"I will make things tidy first."

Rebekah at the well saying, "Drink, I will draw water for thy camels also" did not find more favor in the eyes of God's messenger than Aunt Giselle did in mine as she laid hands on the small disarray. Translucent cup set on wire stand, sable brush dipped into tincture releasing scarlet drops that sank, then dispersed upward in a pink current; palette of white tile sealed under a domed saucer, the whole private indulgence secreted behind an embroidered castle ruin framed in a silver oval and set as an ornament beside a flowering plant.

She unstopped a crystal bottle chased with silver vines. A rose unfolded, its essence caressed into Shalimar hands, clouding her jet wedding band.

"Why black, Aunt Giselle?"

"Oh Ariadne, daughter of Pasiphaë (I quote), I am in mourning for my life." (She quoted.)

A cool finger blessed my forehead with a touch of scent. Hashish! Sherbet! Assassin in a harem! I thrilled to the style with which she had wrested order out of our immigrant discontinuity.

Jessica returned, pink-and-white cheeks scrubbed to a blotched red, damp combed hair already springing up in black curls turbulent as her father's.

We were permitted into the Ur boudoir, a mere angle that had eluded the builder's greed. Aunt Giselle had curtained it off from the kitchen to form an alcove. No one would have dared her ever-ready outrage by drawing aside the drape. An eagle could not have established a more respected territorial imperative.

White shawl around her shoulders, milady composing herself for a Boldoni portrait could not more consciously have composed herself than Aunt Giselle in a chaise, a makeshift she had upholstered in the ash-color moiré of a surrendered mantua.

She must have made the decision on one of her pacing days.

The silk cape lifted out of black tissue paper, its border of steel beads spilling, with the fabric to the floor, she after it, on her knees, shears opening and closing with the click of locusts descending. It would have been like her to act it out in the cramped living room under her portrait of Giselle at the clavichord painted by an admirer in the halcyon season she had studied music in Vienna, the dishonored fabric like swan wings beating backward from her nineteenth-century shoulders to a toss of her arpeggio hands. Vienna, where she had taken the

57

name of Giselle as more appropriate on the concert programs she envisioned for herself than her given name, Iphigenia.

We drew up footstools, two boxes covered in black velvet and fringe that had entered America as an evening skirt, in the trunk with her stilled metronome and a rose-wood practice keyboard.

She began by wringing her hands. I never grew tired of imputing mystery to her desperate rituals. I leaned toward her. She leaned toward me. (Could it be she was my real mother?)

"On a dark and stormy night . . ."

At once I was held by the glitter of her totemic eyes.

". . . a band of robbers was seated around a campfire and the leader said, 'Jack, tell us a story.' "

I rose and fell with the currents of apprehension in her voice.

"And Jack began:
" 'On a dark and stormy night a band of robbers was seated around a campfire and the leader said, "Jack, tell us a story."
" 'And Jack began . . .' "

Jessica shifted. Aunt Giselle faltered as at a hiss.

" 'On . . . a . . . dark . . . and stormy . . .' "

That was it. No more. No less. The story that was always capturing the tingling apprehension of beginning without risking the melancholy of ending. For me it opened infinite possibilities.

Lightning above, firelight below, the leader, corsair ringolets blown back, rainwater multiplying mirrors as on an equestrian bronze rearing under the park lights, rainwater glittering on mustachios black as Uncle Joshua's, fingers of a raggle-taggle Gypsy on the top button of a rain-soaked silk shirt striped royal blue like my father's. And the leader said, looking into my eyes with promises he had fulfilled many times elsewhere, "Ariadne, my fair captive, you alone understand. You only have I spared of my prisoners to tell what will happen next."

For Jessica the story had no art, a round-and-round tale that went nowhere. But for me, even now, trying to tell my story as truthfully as I can discover it and finding myself as in a maze of mirrors that reflect a multiplicity of views, it suggests a possible model. I can suppose each character, saying in turn as my children sometimes did in the anxious middle of the night, "Tell me a story about me," to orient themselves in reality. It would be a dark and stormy night and we would sit by my fireplace and I would begin, "On the day you and I met . . ." Then I'd take up that single thread and together we would trace the path we had taken. And with each one I would go back to the beginning of the maze and say, "On the day you and I met . . ."

Well, suppose Jessica had pushed open the door to my mother's full-scale drama?

My sociable mother would be in the kitchen, ever-ready to put by what she was doing, most likely breakfast dishes sticky with scorched oatmeal.

My gorge rose at the smell of stale dishwater. At our entrance, her hands emerged from the sink, dripping. She wiped them on the apron improvised from a huck towel.

"Hello, rabbits. Hungry? Who would like warm compote? I just cooked a potful of bruised fruits. Peaches and plums."

"Yummy, yummy, yes, yes, please, please." Jessica, ecstatic, on tiptoe.

I felt I had already forced down the imperfect fruit, stones included. "I'm not hungry," I grumbled.

"That's why you're skinny and cough so much. See how well Jessica eats. That's why she's the family beauty. Such an appetite. A pleasure for a mother." Undaunted, full of gusto. "Hey. How about a piece of honey cake with walnuts in it. I got such a bargain; the end piece. With the compote it could be a party."

"Reuben," her voice rang out like a Swiss bell. My always-ailing brother stirred. "Get up, lamb, a party. Arnie, run down-stairs, bring Hillel and Becky. Jessica love, stay with me and serve out the compote." (A broad wink.)

"Not Hillel and Becky," I moaned. "I'll have to wash their faces and neaten them up."

"You're a big schoolgirl now and big girls have to help take care of younger sisters and brothers. I did the same."

"I'm the smallest in my class."

"That's because you got skipped. Read less and eat more."

"You aren't Hillel and Becky's mother. Why do I have to take care of them? Jessica's mother never makes her."

"What difference does it make who is the mother?" (What difference indeed!) "It's in the family. You have something better to do? Hide in your closet and read? Soon they'll call you cockeyes. Move! Move!"

It was Jessica's turn to comfort me as I slumped out of the kitchen.

At our cradling there had been no witches to perform an exchange, though had Aunt Cassie received the message, she would have obliged her sister Giselle, in this, as in anything else in her power, if not her proper province.

Jessica and I owed existence to one survivor parent each. My mother, with Jessica's father, could have led a migration across the desert, badgering the Lord for manna; while Jessica's mother and my father would have wandered at the end of the train pursuing arguments of brainy severity, and in a fit of theorizing, fed each other toadstools.

Aunt Giselle. Favorite. Potentate. The one who had seized

the right to cause others to suffer. In my mother's wedding picture she is in the foreground. Dressed in white as she always was except for her own wedding, for which she draped herself in Byron-black, she is filling the scene that should have been her plainer sister's. Through a strand of pearls her damning forefinger rests at the hollow of her throat, perhaps already tainted with the growth that stifled her too late to keep her from bewildering her daughter Jessica, and bedazzling me with her abracadabra in which I became her true offspring, a changeling who, by spiritual displacement, had been borne by her squat sister, Hera, while she had been forced to carry Jessica, her crude husband's seed.

My mother, Aunt Giselle and, dark as a raven clouded in forebodings, the third of the female triumvirate that ruled us, Aunt Cassandra. Runt of the litter, she clings to the edge of the photo as is fitting for one for whom there was never room at the breast. By the ungrace of place, family nurse and baby-tender; by the rasp of deprival, ascetic; by the rigors of displacement, philosopher. If there were clinical thermometers then, she had one tucked in her reticule or marking her place in a book on German health regimes or philosophy. Immediately after the picture was taken she probably cornered a wedding guest. As I saw her last at her husband's funeral:

Health regimes or determination, she had outlived her sisters, and, in her late eighties, bent and waxen as an old taper, she clomped across the chapel as if her shoes were weighted. She was waving legal papers at the rabbi, but swerved when she saw me. "Why here's Ariadne, how nice you could come!"

"Why are you running about doing these things? Here, let me," I said.

"So long as I can, I do!" False teeth clacking, she patted my arm as if I were the new widow. "We are all grass."

Her daughter and son, Becky and Hillel, one fat, one bald, shook their heads at my effort.

Aunt Cassie scrutinized me. "You will be cold at the cemetery. You always suffered poor circulation from your father's family. Do you exercise enough? Drink fluids? Here take my . . ." She began unbuttoning her sweater.

I grasped her hand, not kindly. "And you always tried to tell me what to do." At once childhood fury rose in me like gas in an old cistern. "You aren't my mother — don't take care of my health."

"What's the difference? I was like your mother; you were like my daughter." She clacked her ill-fitting teeth and hopped like a pleased skeleton. "Darling Arnie. What spirit! That's a healthy sign."

God knows what indecency I might have committed had a mourner not grasped Cassie's hand feelingly and murmured, "Peace on Heinrich's soul."

"Amen," she answered, then smitten by a thought she clutched my arm. "Maybe we should never be at peace?"

That moved her at once to the next thought and she brought out of her pocket a leather-bound volume. For a moment I thought it was a Bible. "I've been rereading Epictetus . . ."

"I think the rabbi wants us." Her son, the psychiatrist, with the practiced, ironic air of a Jewish cart horse, led the parade of her children and her children's children.

Yet, torn from my album, on the flawed brown print, she, too, retains the exoticism of those who had power and are dead.

*   *   *

"You were lucky, Jessica. Born in your mother's bed in Grandpa's house," I said.

"Lucky that my mother couldn't bear me or my father? She

62

kept finding reasons for taking me away from him and sticking me into schools in clean Switzerland. At least you had your father, Arnie."

"Until I was four I thought Grandpa was my father. Remember how he sang that melancholy song about a wanderer who had no homeland and no love?"

"He did that to torment Grandma. He was tone-deaf. "Grandpa never cared for me and I never cared for Grandpa ..." Jessica picked a raisin out of the cookie she was munching. " . . . not because he was tone-deaf, but because I was on Grandma's side."

"Why did you have to take sides?"

"Because married couples live in a state of warfare, undeclared when they are *happily* married. I remember, on one of our extended visits — I must have been seven years old — Grandma had a tooled leather bag filled with paper money that wasn't valid anymore. We sat by the porcelain stove and she let me throw the bills into the fire one by one. We watched them catch, glow red, then crinkle into ash worms. Grandpa came in unexpectedly. He said, 'I'm glad you found a use for that money at last.' Grandma closed her baby-blue eyes and murmured a prayer."

Family legend had it that her five brothers waylaid and kidnapped her from an elopement with a married Christian grandee, and as she was, baggage and moneybag, brought her to the rabbi and married her off, hugger-mugger, hush-hush, to my grandfather, a promising Talmudist with smoldering Spanish eyes (his family was of that Exodus) who having seen her pass, smiling to herself, had spoken for her.

In the magnesium flare of my parents' wedding photograph, she is an askew little parcel, tucked in front of her daughters' draperies. It's hard to tell if her doll face wears the tranquillity of a saint or the vacancy of the stunned — an arrested face under a wig made from her golden hair so rudely cut and clapped dead on her head thirty years and a dozen babies before this photo.

From behind his patriarch beard, Grandfather seems to be studying her, the uneasy gift that broke his pride in holy study and drove him from the scholar's bench to become a timber dealer. He traveled much, for he suffered not sufferance gladly, badge of his tribe though it be. As for his biblical studies, an Oxford don might have approved his reverse declension from Hebrew to Greek to Latin.

What I have left of him is a leaf-spattered imprint of me clapping to his Greek chant, his beard flying, harsh desolate face hectic with love for Homer and me, epic meter timed to the turn of his woodsman's stride up and down the tiled court-yard (reconstructed from memory and hearsay). My mother, his daughter, is saying to her mother, "He could make a child crazy with that Greek."

"There's Greek in this granddaughter, I tell you. Go away, women, take Reuben and Jessica with you. Leave Ariadne with me."

Having finished the cookie, Jessica began on her fingernails. "Nothing to sing about in either of our childhoods," she said, "but Reuben got hit hardest."

My brother Reuben, the loser, undoted on by either parent. Each day he acted the family victim. Hunted by our evaluating eyes, whipped by more intelligent tongues. Forgive me, Reuben, I was a puppy that yapped with the pack. I would expiate my part, for I dream you still, poor boy, black stockinged skinny legs, white sailor suit too bold for your diffident form. I remember the carrots you stole for us out of a neighbor's backyard; carrots we nibbled behind a white fence, the soft, forgiving green leaves flowing over our hands. Come out. Come out. All our sharp edges are blunted now.

"Come home. Your brother has fallen very low," the message read.

A knot of neighbors lingered on the street. I read in their glances that my father's telegram had been monstrously literal; yet I said good evening to the doorman and repudiated the guilt of the living that puffed up in me; the necessary pang that goes to the heart and persuades, against clinical knowledge, that the right person, the right regime, could have brought him back to coherence.

"Arnie," Jessica called gently, "come back, all is forgiven."

"From your mouth to God's ear, as my mother used to say."

"You can't blame yourself, Arnie. Every life is not your responsibility. And you can't blame your poor mother, a young woman caught between wars, pogroms and edicts while the husband she loved was trying to make it in America."

"She never forgave me for being born prematurely."

"You always had rotten timing."

"Did you know that in the general confusion of my birth, it went unregistered, which makes me a woman without a birthdate."

"Must be sheer hell on your horoscope reader, sweetheart." Jessica mocked.

"It doesn't touch your jade heart that I'm also a woman without a country? Every time a new atlas is published I find I have become an unlisted native of another political convenience."

"So what's new? You want to pass for a WASP?"

"It galled poor Adam. With no accurate birthdate and no official birthplace he could never locate me on his actuarial tables. 'If your input deviates you can't get an accurate throughput,' he complained."

"Those were his exact words?"

65

"As I live and breathe."

"No comment." Jessica pressed her fingers to her lips like a mischievous sibyl.

"Not to speak ill of the dead, as my father used to say. You know Adam was ahead of his time. Computer language is one we all have to learn."

"Not I. Not even if I never figure out my bank statement."

"You'll be left behind, Jessica. A computer novel is inevitable. Not only that, a woman will write it."

"I won't read it, but tell me why a woman?"

"Women's form and content will be fused at last. We've been conditioned to eat, sleep, play, think and make love in bits. We've been in training since we were old enough to be told to stop whatever we were doing and rock a cradle or serve tea to the gentlemen."

"Amend your pronouns, my sweet, I never rocked a cradle or waited on gentlemen."

"Your female partners waited on you?"

"Meow, meow! Be that as it may, why can't you write a Jane Austen type novel with a beginning, a middle and an end and sell it to the movies?"

"Aside from all else, because I don't have a country parish for my childhood, and neither does anyone else anymore.

"Count me out, Arnie. Learning English as a fourth, or was it fifth, language was hard enough when I was a child."

*　　*　　*

"Your father's name is *Abidah?* Stop twisting your handkerchief," Miss O'Rourke, the principal, said to me on my first day in American school. Her kohl-black curls lay on her forehead like lampshade trim in aspic. Two rounds of rouge crackled under her poll parrot eyes. A large agonized crucifix rode her green sateen bosom.

"Your father must have been given an American name when

they let him in. Adolph, Alexander, Arthur . . ." She waved an index card in her claw.

"Abidah," I whispered. "I only know Abidah."

"Speak up!" She slammed down the index card. "Where do you greenhorns get those names?"

"From the Bible, ma'am." I thought she wanted an answer.

"Don't be impertinent. Out of the Old Testament, no doubt. What language do they speak at home?"

I was afraid I would be slapped if I answered that it depended on who was talking to whom. I myself was doing my best to cultivate the neighborhood Irish brogue and wipe all other languages from my mind.

"Christ, these peasants! Monitor, sit this dumb Ariadne in the hall. Wait there till you find your voice." (The anterooms we have known, we the people.)

What sallies, what ripostes I could now utter! "Madame, you can find Abidah, the Father of Knowledge, in any biblical concordance," or "Madame, do Shulamith, Manassah, Avrom and Isaiah seem less appropriate to you for us than those Johnny-come-latelies of British peerage, Shirley, Sheldon, Mortimer, Harvey, Sydney or, for that matter, those deviationists Matthew, Mark and Luke?"

As for my name? Thinking ahead to my marrying a veritable King Solomon, no doubt, my father proposed Shulamith. But my grandfather prevailed with Ariadne. Grandfather, was that a sage thing to do? Wasn't it putting beans up the nose of destiny to give a puny Jewish female, destined to be a housewife and mother, the name of a Greek princess who betrayed her father and ran off with a gentile lover?

What's in a name? Ask Juliet. Ask Brutus. I'd like to ask you, too, Grandfather. Unfortunately military whimsey deprived me of that legacy also.

67

What's that you say, Grandfather; fashions come round? True. The space agency didn't scan a biblical concordance for their namings; American astronauts flew to the moon in numbered Apollos. Not one, not two, not three . . . They set their sights toward Mars, Jupiter, Mercury, Venus. They chart by the Milky Way, the galactic radiance named for milk that trailed from Juno's breast to kindle nightlights for a breast-fed world.

My voice?

Well, Miss O'Rourke, it would oblige me more than it could have obliged you, to find my voice. What voice will I discover? The sexless tenor of parody that throbs and slides off into shameless self-pity? In the presence of our transfigured carjunk, within hearing of random electronic tape beeps, within film memory of heaps of trashed shoes and eyeglasses husbanded orderly in the chambers of Augean-Auschwitz, in this damned light, what voice can anyone discover, dear hearts, that will flood your dry membranes? After such history, what fiction? When the Hapsburg conquerors dismissed the Polish taskmasters, German verbs dangled from every gaslight and weighed down forever the ends of my parents' sentences, and after them, mine. When at last I uttered in my beloved stepmother tongue (I learned to read it before I dared to speak it), I stiffened because I was afraid my refugee phonetics would be revealed.

Speak memory! But in what language? When the child I was lay sleepless on a made-up cot in a windowless corner loaned by another Jew "spawned in some estaminet of Antwerp," driven like us to the slums that were our America, I floundered on passport-crossed waves of speech.

Polish? Aunt Rysia, who worked as a bookkeeper. Her husband disappeared on one of those hayrides. The bribed peasant was a double agent. "My heart told me. When the *goy* (a sprinkle of Yiddish) didn't cross himself taking the money I knew, I knew . . ." What can you do? Scratch a Pole and you'll find an anti-Semite.

Russian? Uncle Boris, with one of his inventions. His family didn't have the money to buy him out of the Russo-Jap conscription, so he went west, poor man.

"It makes change — gives nickles and dimes for quarters and half dollars."

"They'll steal this from you too," my mother says.

"It works," whispered Boris. "I tried it." (He sold tickets in an elevated train booth.)

"Wunderbar," my father says in German.

Uncle Boris' waxy face bends over the glittering mechanism and my father's praise opens points of light in those remote intelligent eyes. (They did steal it.)

Flemish? That was dear Uncle Joshua talking diamond business with Uncle Felix and Tante Thalia, diamond-dusted leaves, later swept to South Africa with the trade.

German? That could be Aunt Cassie and Uncle Heinrich. He lost most of his eyesight for the Iron Chancellor, and his shop in a counterconfiscation decree due to his birth in Danzig when it was called Gdansk, or was it Gdansk when it would have been lucky to be Danzig?

The question of what language we spoke at home intruded on Uncle Heinrich's funeral.

*   *   *

The mourners barely filled two pews: Cassie, her son, Hillel, his wife with their children — a boy angel with pongee hair and blue eyes and a girl piquant as her grandmother Cassie might have been. Jessica, at fifty, porcelain-surfaced, a woman who had mothered nothing more corrosive than a cat. There were, also, several elegantly costumed old *cousinas,* rather like great-eyed monkeys playing Chekhov, a few patriarchal exiles, a taggle of befriended neighbors, a trio of incredibly emaciated

Hitler refugees, and the chief mourner, his daughter, Becky, between her two husky sons.

The rabbi conducted the service in Hebrew. Only a few old fellows from uncle's synagogue swayed through to the Amen. The rhythm, old as the destruction of the temple, failed to enter our mourning. We sat suspended, the rabbi watching us, working his silver brows in puzzlement. Then he began again, delivering the sermon, this time in English. Becky sniveled. I could see her surreptitiously wiping her nose with her hand. She had forgotten her handkerchief again, and I not there to pin it to her blouse as I used to every morning before school. "And we are all grass, and amen."

The gleaming doors opened and hired pallbearers marched forward, white gloves swinging solemn time, there being a great shortage of able-bodied men among us. They were almost upon the coffin, the mourners concentrating on the last decorum, when the rabbi raised his hand and signaled a halt. The break in protocol almost brought the bearers to life.

With the help of his cane, the rabbi made his way from his carpeted eminence to the foot of the plain pine box draped in black cloth. He placed his gentlemanly old hand beside the few white roses, like a Victorian wax arrangement, and in deep sad tones he spoke in still a third language, German. In the language of their vigorous male youth he addressed himself to Uncle Heinrich, the dashing student, the officer of the photo album, the cheeky groom with the waxed handlebar mustachios and uncontaminated boy-blue eyes. Only then did I feel I was mourning in the correct, memorial relationship. There he was! Uncle Heinrich, singing his slightly daring Viennese songs, accompanying himself, or my mother, on a little fiddle, two-stepping with the young ones; my father smiling indulgently at his friend, the card-playing barracks rowdy. ("It was easier for me to teach *your* father pinochle, Arnie, than for him to teach me chess after Joshua went to South Africa.") *"Gott, der*

Seliger, Heinrich" our pleasant uncle, Cassie's loyal husband, firm and loving father to Hillel and Becky, brother-in-law and in-deed to my father . . . *"und noch wieder, amen."*

Shalom, shalom. Next year in Jerusalem. On the shores of Babylon they wept to hear English, the language of the interrogating immigration officer.

*   *   *

Every creature has a native habitat but man. Swallows return to Capistrano. The entire population of European eels migrates thousands of miles to its spawning ground in the abysmal deeps beyond Sargasso. Adult salmon return from their sea life to lay eggs and die in their sweet source-beds. Halibut, seal, whales, caribou, golden plovers, robin redbreasts, monarch butterflies, wild geese, storks, they all have their itineraries. But all our roads have become maps of longing.

We are waiting in traveler's aid stations for unseaworthy carriers that never arrive on time. Antwerp, Alexandria, Cadiz, Gaza, Tarabulus, Odessa, Vladivostok, Ellis Island: the children are sitting on odd-shaped bundles tied with rope spun by conscripted soldiers' widows; they are guarding baskets woven of willow withes and reeds collected around laundry pools on the banks of blue green Argava, Yellow Kura, Blue Danube and hundreds of beloved tributaries of the Yellow, Red and Black Seas.

Compulsively repeating our disasters, we sip martinis in foreign airports waiting for flights that have been canceled, the isolating opacities of foreign tongues provoking imagined specificities of native happiness, while we finger our passports, memorize ticket numbers, fill in immigration and emigration forms. Hare Krishna, Algeria, Montreal, the Spanish Steps, Harvard Square, Haight Ashbury, Ibiza, Amsterdam, Millbrook. Count off, count up, count down, everywhere we are building homesickness colonies.

And Wife of:

"I'll look to like, if looking liking move:
But no more deep will I endart mine eye
Than your consent gives strength to make it fly."

— SHAKESPEARE

THERE'S TOO much gross talk about the weather. "Russian weather conquered Napoleon." "English weather destroyed the Spanish Armada." Do I, does anyone, feel less a human dilettante for having memorized that in school? Does anyone feel less a foreigner on earth for hearing Worldwide Weather Service report that the temperature differential between Albany, Casablanca, Lima, Paris, Sofia, Vienna and Zurich is a mere five degrees? Yet in my personal life that small differential has had consequences it would be hard to exaggerate. A small drop in temperature was enough to put a film of ice under my mother's feet, causing her to slip, and me to arrive prematurely. Had the mini-climate remained stable at 35 degrees I might have been born in America, under a more fortunate sign; my parents would not have been deprived of each other, and so on and on from then till now.

Kabalists, like my father, may maintain that everything is

correlated with the whole Creation, everything is mirrored in everything else. Scientific-minded types, like my dear friend and physician, Jeremy, may have envisioned an ecologically based worldwide morality, determined by scientific facts. "It's heaven or hell here and now," he said, "Darwin was a prophet. If a louse is dusted off in Madagascar, a walrus may indeed die of it in the Antarctic." But I respectfully submit that the weather, like so much else, should be returned to the local level.

My first hint of the enormous consequences that can ensue from slight shifts in mini-climate was given to me the summer day I fell in love with a lifeguard.

Sitting in my accustomed place on the sunny beach in full view of the open sea, salt wind saturated with seaweed odors running toward me with the tide, a sudden darkening gathered just offshore and rose like a misted goblet out of which poured a circle of fine hard rain. Within it, my bronzed lifeguard on his high catamaran raised exceedingly long oars in greeting. But I remained in sunlight. The glass emptied in a scatter of rainbows. Foam skimmed in and settled over stones and gravel. From somewhere, out there, not even sensed, sandpipers appeared. Out of the sheen between earth and sky, gulls soared and dived.

At that moment it was as if I had given myself to the laws of gravity. I who had never been to a dance had a sensation of concordance, of dancing together, nobody had to teach me how.

Had I been prescient I would have gotten the message that mini-climates would rule my life. But I wasn't. I had to learn the hard way that oracles are terse, they do not embellish.

Only a short time ago, on a fine autumn afternoon, en route to my country house, I drove out of fair weather through a screen of turbulent fog into lashing rain which glazed on the

74

windshield into sleet. From the opposite direction cars emerged in a slow cortege, headlights shrouded by snow. Two minutes later, slithering on a road that seemed to heave and slope maliciously, rubbery sleet pasting to the panes, I had to grip the steering wheel. My chest cramped, a current of high tension zipped through me. I felt as if I were being forced to lift something too heavy and had to go on holding it up. Considering that I have long ago topped the actuarial tables for women born at the turn of the century, I decided to stop at the nearest service center.

The counterman, steaming and panting as if he were a St. Bernard in service, made change for the telephone, plunked down coffee cups and elaborated on the weather. "Radio says a cold air mass met a warm air mass." (Cream and sugar . . . black . . .)

"I think it's those jet planes." (A woman in a plumed hat.)

"Drive you gaga enough to light up an orchid." (A long-legged girl with a small face like a rhesus monkey.)

"Never get my wife to believe I was stuck in a snowstorm." (A man drooped.)

*   *   *

I believe I would have been a spinster if a slight temperature differential had not dumped snow on the Jersey shore while rain fell heavily on New York City.

I say spinster because not butcher or baker or cloak-and-suit maker would have found approval in my father's eyes. It was sheerest chance that a prince came riding, a prince whose credentials my father respected: a pedigree dating back to the Diaspora. Exile having to do with protesting the Beylis trial for ritual murder (Kiev, 1913); European schooling, seminary prior to Swiss technical school. My father took the measure of level gray eyes, was at once at home with the courtly yet reticent manner, the overcast of homelessness, the medley of urbane accents, the rational priorities.

75

I should have suspected intention when my mother, straight-backed as ever, but neatened and restrained, was the one who carried in the tea tray while I was encouraged to show my modest accomplishments on the piano (I played "Für Elise" commendably; the "Moonlight Sonata" excessively) or to comment, maidenly, while my father and Adam played chess, or conversed — my father's references interspersed with Talmudic ironies, and inclining more to Kerensky and Trotsky, Adam's to the impending Balfour Declaration on Palestine. Stirring cherry preserves through Russian tea, they discussed the effect of America's entry at last into the war; Lenin's re-entry into Russia via the Finland Station — my father from the socialist viewpoint, Adam from the Zionist.

On taking leave, Adam bowed from the waist over my mother's dishpan hands and then over mine (odor of fresh cookies). Hand-kissing was not quite as intimate as I had imagined. His hand closed over mine in such a way that his lips lighted on his own fingertips. This gallantry of European schooling turned the boys I had known into mere boys. I twirled off to sleep in a dream of Vienna waltzes.

A perfect swain had fallen among us in godforsaken America. I was encouraged to unfold my parents' intention; stranger in a new land, so was he.

"May I, sir, escort your daughter?"

At last I, too, had dates. I was thrilled, particularly after the humiliation of being voted Senior Class Grind, and narrowly escaping Last Girl Likely to Marry by the votes of my fellow grinds on the newspaper staff. That year I had prayed hard to wake up boyish, breezy, bobbed, with a repertoire of camp songs and tennis scores. (I wince when I recall the questions I asked in class in the desperate need to have my presence marked.) I wanted to be flat-breasted and flapperish, or, second-best, pre-Raphaelite emaciated. I had a picture of Rossetti's phthisic model tacked next to my bookcase, and practiced composing my volatile, expectant expression in imitation of her languid, haughty mien.

"With her swollen neck stretched up, and her lazy eyelids, she looks like a goose being force-fed . . . and so do you, Arnie," commented my mother.

My mother's crudeness was a great cross for me to bear and, I felt, for my father as well. (That their marriage was full of life did not affect my judgment.)

"Did you fall in love with mother?" I asked.

"Your mother was the eldest of the sisters. Our marriage was arranged. In our day we didn't fall in love with a woman and then marry her. We loved the woman we married."

I had other plans. I would marry only for love.

I had envisioned my future down to the white gloves and wide-brimmed hat I would be wearing the day I met *him.* He would be tall, dark and handsome, wealthy, a professional with a touch of the poet. There would be a diminutive red rosebud in the lapel of his pin-striped suit. We would have instant profound intimate discussions about Nietzsche, Dostoievski and early death. We would read each other's poems aloud.

Adam did not match the description at all points. He was neither as tall, nor as wealthy — but he was a professional and good-looking. His silky black curls lay close as a helmet against his oval head. Like the Romans on the antique coins my father had made into earrings for me, his nose was thin and high-beaked, his lower lip full, his chin round and cleft. His eyes were a surprising light gray and rather far-sighted, which gave him the look of placing people at a distance.

"An aristocrat," my father announced, "a pure Sephardic type."

"His hands and feet are long and narrow, like your father's." My mother admired. "Such a gentleman."

He brought red roses and chocolates. "You look like the girl on the candy box, Ariadne."

I wasn't too pleased at his remarking my resemblance to the Sunbonnet Sue with pink bisque cheeks and rosebud mouth, but I tossed my head, heavy with its basketry of braids, and made "prunes and prisms" smiles to deepen my dimples.

On Sunday afternoons we drove to Central Park or up to Westchester. When we walked he held my arm, guiding me by the elbow around breaks in the path. He said little but I read much into his watching me feed bread crusts to the ducks.

He invited me to a friend's wedding. I wore a pale green tulle-and-lace shepherdess confection, with an hourglass waist and lowcut bosom. My father flicked the end of his auburn mustache, exchanged smiles with my mother and said, "We must have her picture taken." My kid brother, Ezra, clutched his heart and dropped to the floor in a mock faint. Already tuned to a sexual pitch, assured by the aura of approval from my keystone males, I blew a kiss to my rival, Rossetti's stately milliner.

When I went out with Adam no questions were asked as to when I would be brought home. It was assumed a perfect gentleman would return a lady before the pumpkin hour of midnight. There was none of that devastating acid evaluation to which any boy who might have escorted me home from school once, and once only, had been subjected. "Your father is a butcher, eh?" "You think the competition is too heavy for you to get into medical school? I see."

At home I found myself elevated. I was deferred to as a marriageable daughter. "I'll clear the table, Arnie dear, you finish your homework so you can be free on the weekend in case Adam asks you out." "Never mind taking the children to the library this Saturday afternoon, your brother can do it. You need time to wash your hair." "A study game of chess, daughter? Keep in practice; Adam plays a strong game."

My mother looked at me as if I had changed. "You're thin, but you're full on top, maybe you'll fill out the rest of you." I was the girl who would fulfill the parental daydreams; their princess, a prince. The plot presented itself with all the authority of a legend.

Adam had my father's approval (and as I've indicated, God spoke to me through my father), he had a Durant roadster, a proper job as an actuary in an insurance company and, for reasons to do with recent entry, a school sojourn in enemy Germany and a dreadfully overstamped passport, he was not drafted into the army. He was present. I was almost seventeen and frantically unoccupied in my own emotional behalf. Boxed in as I was, straining against my limited prospects, the least I could do was to develop a violent crush.

The opportunity to show off my domestic potential arrived in the form of a communiqué ominous with military stamps. Aunt Giselle, after several years in a Swiss sanatorium, was coming among us to die. Courtesy of military respect for death, she had been granted transport. She, with my cousin Jessica, would be arriving within three days. (Ship notices were kept to a minimum during war years.) She wished to be taken at once out of the city to the isolated farmhouse the sisters owned. It had been shuttered and boarded since the previous summer, and would have to be opened and made ready.

The socialist *cousinas* declared Aunt Giselle's action too self-indulgent in wartime. "I believe that for me life has ended and world history has begun," said their spokeswoman, who had heard Lenin address the Russian Socialist Democratic Labor Party in Cracow. The Zionist *cousinas* quoted Herzl, the Zionist leader, who noted that to establish a Jewish state, the list of requirements would include a coffin ship. "We also take with us our dead." But in spite of some theoretical disapproval they were all gathering to greet the Snow Queen.

There was a family conclave. When it ended, Adam's offer of help had been accepted. He and I would drive up very early Saturday morning. We would unshutter the house, ready it as best we could and return by ten o'clock that night. The others would hire cars for Sunday, drive up, settle Giselle and her sisters who would stay to nurse her. The husbands — Heinrich, Joshua and my father — would return Sunday night so they could go to work on Monday. (No one was heretical enough to think of taking time off from work.)

"We may be quite late in returning," said Adam.

"You will do as well as you can, I know." My father and Adam shook hands.

In addition to cooking and baking for the company that was bound to arrive to greet Giselle, I had prepared a hamper that would demonstrate what a potential mother-feeder I was. Then I spent hours deciding what to wear, settling at last on my newest: a burned-orange wool "costume" (designed by my father) executed in a cousin's shop; a peach-colored blouse that did not conceal the amplitude of my breasts, and a brown beaver hat with an artful brim. My mother decreed wool hose but I battled my way to ribbed lisle. At the last moment, I exchanged school ghillies for pumps with slightly raised heels. I slipped Tennyson's "Elaine the fair . . . Elaine the lily maid" among the cartons of soaps, scrub brushes and aprons — and sped down the stairs filled with the sensation that at last I was to play a vital part in an authentic adult drama.

My one regret was that every eye was not at every neighbor window to see us driving into the sunrise.

The air was so clear it seemed to have blown from the stars. Crossing the river on the ferry, we stood on the forward deck: the smell of brine was strong, the tide running in on a swell of steel rolling to a boil, gulls mewing above garbage-flecked foam, houseboats and barges taming the Hudson with domestic busyness.

He placed one hand over mine on the rail. "In Switzerland steep brooks and river banks are lined with stone. They straighten the banks and beds while they are about it. I can't imagine garbage dumped into their rivers." His fingers were long and tapered, his hands exceptionally well shaped — their length and slenderness sure signs of aristocracy, as my father had pointed out.

"I like the orange peel being churned up. It reminds me of coming over from Ellis Island," I said.

He pressed my hand slightly. "If I had the authority I would arrange for a preponderancy of orange peel." His words were wry but he looked amused: "In that costume you look quite Viennese."

"You look Tyrolean, but more worldly."

"What a learned opinion. Your sources?" He chuckled in his throat and pretended to cough.

"You are laughing at me," I said.

I had to admit my sources were a stereopticon slide and a postcard Jessica had sent me from Heidi land.

The rest of the crossing he was silent. But his hand remained over mine.

Beside me Adam seemed to grow intriguingly mysterious; as if there were many feelingful things he would say, as if it were propriety that prevented him from commenting on the emotions I felt swirling around us.

On the Jersey side the weather turned moody. Above Nyack there were still gray banks of snow. In protected crofts, buds were beginning to fatten and flush to celadon green. But between rocks, spring was held underground by heaped drifts. A brief sun flamed on an icicle cataract and went out. Fog blew in, yellow and cold.

Adam peered through the windshield. "Predictions were for fair and mild. I fear there has been a statistical error." Adam's speech retained the reconstituted effect of translation. As I suppose my family's also did.

The weather held until we arrived. He was admirably efficient and I a marvel of competence. A pair of demon workers, we approved each other through grime as I wiped windows inside and he removed shutters outside. A local farmer and his wife cooperated. For the sake of death they hauled in a cord of wood and primed the pump. Before we were finished, however, a warm air mass was overtaken by a colder air mass, there was a drop of a few degrees in the temperature. Snow began to fall.

"Better stop over," the farmer advised, "it will be a blizzard."

"Impossible," Adam answered.

"Impossible," I echoed.

"City slickers," he muttered as we took off.

Three hours later the road belonged to the storm. The roadster hunkered in snow over its mudguards, front wheels in a bank, windshield wiper paralyzed. Adam made a futile effort at backing out. The motor shuddered and died. He waited. Tried again. Dead.

"We can wait in the car until it's over," I said cozily.

"The car won't retain heat, nor will we, I'm afraid, if we are not moving. We passed a gas station not too far back."

He shoved the door open against haphazardly violent wind. A gust tore off his Tyrolean hat and tumbled it away. He stepped after it. His foot broke through new crust and sank knee-deep into a snow drift. His face blanched. Snow festooned his hair and eyelashes. I laughed. "You look like an iced cookie."

"Come along," he said.

I climbed out after him. Snow filled in over my shoes, rose up my legs, and seeped through my skirt. In no time my skin felt singed and scraped. A great beast of a spruce shook snow from its burdened paws. The car promptly disappeared from sight. Snow only slightly less dark than the sky whipped about like bolts of coarse sheeting flung out to entrap us. We were cloaked and encrusted in it.

"Can you see anything?" he asked.

There was only billowing darkness. After a time a vague bulk of darker shadow suggested shape. Slowly it took on volume, appearing and disappearing like a wreck rising and falling in a frothing sea.

"That may be a low hill ahead," I said, "or a building."

"It's a building but it shows no light." Wind cut into his words.

"Shall we chance it?" I asked.

"We can't stand here."

In three steps I had lost one shoe. In five, both of them. Blind and barefoot in the snow! Pellets of snow shot at my face, stung my eyes and bit my cheeks. Cold scaled my skirt, nettled my thigh, ran freeze tracks under my fur collar, cut into my neck and invaded my blood. I felt my circulation compress and squeeze upward like the ice cap of a milk bottle — yet I did not take in that we were snow-boxing in dead earnest with a Santa Claus who had turned maniacal. I went on trying to be an attractive young lady on a date, breathlessly tinkling on and off, wavering like a damaged music box.

"My little brother . . . once got hurt . . . playing in the snow. He cut . . ."

"Mouth closed. Breathe lightly," Adam commanded. "Hold on to me."

I clung. Slow breaths. Each a knife. Body heat steaming out on air. We pushed our way forward against the fleecy presence muffling us. I had become a tube of ice congealed inside a tube of freezing garments. I sank into a drift. It was a relief to rest out of windshot and snowblast.

"Must move." Adam bent over me. A cracked whistle separated each breath. "Up, up . . . must move."

Difficult, even impossible, to reach, the building appeared and disappeared. Ice crystals needled us. Wind bent us backward, held us in one spot. Breath breaking . . . egh . . . egh . . . foot forward . . . lift foot. Creak. Crack. Other foot . . . touched wood! A step. Another. Slow motion, we crawled up on all fours . . . slid down. Up. Stumbled onto a porch.

Snow lay against a door. Adam dragged himself forward, one hand, one knee; he drew himself up, leaned against the door, raised his hand, slowly, reached the knocker, breath wheezing in and out a tin whistle. Egh . . . egh . . . Knocked! Echo. Knocked again, louder. A blast of wind drove in. Ping. Ping. Ping.

The snow seemed already a recollection; I had only to let go and slide into insensibility. I lay still.

"Summer house . . . closed." He said it slowly, as if he too would be content to be immobilized, a large leaden wing disembodied, frozen in midair, distant from me in time and place.

He rattled the knob. Knock . . . Knock. The only sounds, our breath whistling and the ping ping of ice crystals against a rainspout. Neither of us moved. Surprised as if a wet glass had slipped from my fingers and splintered, it came to me how absurd it would be if we were to die in the service of Aunt Giselle's death. Knock . . . Knock.

From deep within the house a dog's yip surprised us. A second. Still another. A bark. The barks became queried, alert, aggressive, a dog awaking to its duty. Oh welcome, warm living beast. Right behind that door, barks, growls, scratches. A pale light flamed upward and traced frost webs through a window. The door slivered open. Wind blasted in from behind us and blew out the lamp. The door slammed shut.

"No. No. See I lost my shoes." I flapped my hands against the door. Adam knocked.

The door was reopened. A slumpy sack of a man in a long-sleeved woolen undershirt was buckling a suspender brace to his flopping trousers. An oil lamp glimmered deep in the room, where an immense woman was tying herself into a plaid robe. Sheets of newspaper were draped over furniture. The wind fluttered them.

"We're not opened for tourists yet. We're painting," the woman bellowed across to us. "Stop barking, Bonzo."

"No rooms." The man yawned and shook himself. A pair of tame bears befuddled out of hibernation, they peered out of their warm hollow.

"Merciful heavens, Henry, would you look at the snow that come up."

"Downright blizzard." Henry shook his hairy muzzle at the wonder of it.

"We've lost the road, sir."

"Better you come in and close that door. All outside's blowing in." Henry stepped aside.

"House tore up. Have only one room has a bed standing and that's off the kitchen in the borning room." The woman fixed us with a stare calculated to run through us like a truth serum. "You two married?"

Adam's hand actually moved back toward the doorknob! He was about to prefer my death to our dishonor.

(Nonsense, you say? But that's not what it was in 1917. Men *did* die and worms *did* eat them, if not for love, then certainly in defense of virginity. A female was classified according to the state of her hymen. On its intactness depended not only her earthly existence but her life hereafter.)

"We *are* married." I sobbed and collapsed among chairs and newspapers.

The woman shifted into maternal gear. "This child *is* froze, Henry. Get a bucket of snow. Say, the young feller looks mighty bad, give him a shot of booze. Get him out of those duds. Fire up the stove."

Unmindful of snow and water running off me onto the floor, she slapped snow onto me. Set my feet into and out of basins, cold to hot to cold again. Rubbed. Pummeled. When I lay back on the leather kitchen couch, shaken with fits of laughter and shivers, she forced me up. "On your feet. Walk. Must walk."

(Jeremy would have approved of her as a labor-room nurse.)

"Towels, Henry. Drink this ginger tea. Sure it's hot.

85

Swallow, walk. No, you must not sleep. Walk. Walk!"

The men were walking up and down, steaming glasses in hand, pungence of ginger and whiskey adding to stove wood smells. A bulky hand-knit sweater hung to Adam's knees like a child's hand-me-down. Pajama pants flapped about his slender legs, his reticent "yes-no" bobbing lightly on waves of Henry's roused garrulity.

"You two sure not dressed for snow. City folks give me a laugh. Better you stuff your shoes with newspaper, mister, if you want to get into them in the morning. A man needs oiled boots out here until June. Not much to a girl's duds." (He glanced covertly at my garments dripping on a line behind the wood stove.) "She'll be fine by morning, your missus . . . lost her shoes, eh! We'll find 'em come spring, heh, heh. April will fool you every time. Better keep walking, young feller. Drink up. Nothing like ginger tea and whiskey to scoot the blood . . . sprout grass in frozen armpits."

"Do you have a telephone by chance, sir?" Adam asked in a pause.

"Hear that, Mom?" He stamped his foot so hard the kettle on the stove rattled its lid.

"Doctor has a telephone. T'other side of the village. Closest one is in the general store, four miles if you want another dose of snow, heh, heh and he's shut till Monday."

In flannel nightgown and wrapper, decent and unfrivolous as my landlady's hands, I sat sipping ginger tea laced with whiskey. Currents of circulation burned, stabbed, itched, prickled as if I were trapped breast-high in a flourish of brambles. Stingers of hot and cold turned off and on through me. Alcohol, elation, confidence, giggly mischievousness buffeted with painful currents of returning circulation. I kept breaking into helpless spurts of laughter. Alive! I was alive. I was a treasure in a vault, my combination waiting to be sprung. But if Adam turned the mechanism in his mind, it didn't show.

86

His thin lips were compressed in worry or disapproval at my bursts of gaiety. His eyes were puffy like those of a child who has been crying; his skin blotched and puckered. His rules, like valued objects, were being buried under an avalanche of snow.

He cast a distracted look at me. That single glance penetrated me like a barb. Oddly enough, he too seemed to have been snagged on it. Clearly, my date, the world traveler, the older man in my life, the sophisticated foreigner, was frightened.

"We'll be all right," I said, as much to him as to Momma and Poppa Bear, who were hovering.

And so to bed.

Such a bed. A Mayerling bed. A Mother Goose feather bed. Carved, pillared, heaped with comforters, hot bricks tucked at the foot. The room was icy. But what a bed! It provoked senseless joy to nestle in it.

Adam lingered in the kitchen while I climbed in. "Oh good, aaahh." I stretched out. On the instant I rolled down to the soft center. I pulled myself back up to the far edge, stretched out once more, and again rolled back down. Once more. And yet once more I pulled myself to the edge, grabbed the edge of the mattress, and held on.

My back discreetly to the door, I heard Adam come in; heard him draw a chair to the bedside, take a blanket — fuss with it, settle into the chair. He put his feet under the quilts. A blast of cold tunneled through.

"Good night, Ariadne," he said.

That was it?

Flushed, flustered, yes, disappointed at my first experience with a man, alone, in a bedroom, I pretended to be asleep. I was still awake when his teeth began to chatter violently. He sneezed.

Maidenly modesty urged silence. But a lifetime of big sister, little mother, won out. "I think it would be better if you got under the covers. You could get pneumonia if you freeze all night. After all you've been through . . ."

He hesitated. He sneezed. He said, "Thank you."

"You're welcome," I answered.

Prudently, he entered. But as soon as his weight hit the edge he rolled down to the middle. Dislodged, I, too, rolled down. We bumped. Contact! We both gathered ourselves together and scrambled to the outer edges. Respectively.

"Pardon me," I said.

"My fault," he said.

I drowsed, rolled and sank into the depth. Rested and pulled myself up to my side again. Held on, drowsed, let go and rolled down. Each time we bumped, I said "Pardon." He said "My fault." We both said "That's all right," and climbed back again.

We each held on to our edge. He drowsed, he coughed, his breathing grew regular, his grip relaxed, and down he rolled. I held on, relaxed and rolled. We bumped, my soft against his hard. Out to the edge again, back in minutes, no word spoken, doggedly, each of us climbing back to our respective lines, fighting the malevolence of the mattress. Finally, too tired and frenzied to move, I dozed in the middle, leaving it to him to hold on. After a while he rolled down, bumped, and snoring lightly, lay in exhausted sleep against me.

Though I didn't know it then, a part of me rose, backed away in confusion, and left him. Something maternal filled its place. It is a moment to which I return, an old explorer stiff with cold, suffused with a feeling of despair that all which should have come into being never did — staring at the opening with jagged edges through which hope must have escaped.

Sunlight was jiggling rainbows on white walls and pillows. I was alone in bed. My dry clothes lay on the chair, a pair of someone's abandoned summer sandals beside them. When I yawned, the woman came in with a mug of coffee.

"How you, chick? Let's see your feet."

I stuck them out of the bedding. She examined them and ended with a slap and tickle.

"All there! That's what it means to have young blood. I'd 'a lost a toe, or been laid up stiff a month with my rheumatism."

"I don't believe you." I felt excited and snippy. She guffawed, woman to woman.

Sipping coffee, I looked out through a window framed in snow into a crystalline morning world: the sun casting clean elliptical shadows on the snow, from high up out of the current of clouds a shrill agitation of birds, sounds circling, spreading out and drawing in, piercingly fierce and exultant.

"It's spring up there this morning," the woman said, "red-tailed hawks mating. That sound goes on for days without let. Then you don't hear them again until next spring."

A white meadow stretched unbroken to the road, a distant brown line, along which a horse and snowplow were cutting toward the mound of car.

At the first telephone we stopped. "I told them we were all right and would explain," Adam said.

"I suppose they worried," I said. He gave me a pursed look but shook his head and said nothing.

The girl on a date still, I tried again. "Eskimos have a catalogue of words for what we call snow."

He concentrated on the wheel.

He drove the road home as to a funeral. I stared out of the window trying to match my spirit to his gravity and silence, but I was bubbly as a child enjoying the ride to the cemetery; and as unprepared for the enormity of the event.

The closer we got to New York, the fewer were the signs of snowfall. The city itself looked washed as it does after a heavy rain.

*

89

Who wants to be the victim of an Unevent: to walk into a Happening at random, a mere stagehand the floodlights catch dead center? It wasn't supposed to be *my* crucial event. It was Aunt Giselle's.

Trunks, trays, paraphernalia for rites of final passage crowded the foyer; the eccentric aunts and *cousinas* flocking to accompany Her Dying Majesty as if for emigration from an insulted Chekhovian dacha. When Adam and I entered, a quick retreat got under way. There was a heavy flapping as if crows with intelligent faces had flustered out of their swampy station, foreseeing a storm.

Aunt Cassie emerged from behind a steamer trunk, arms laden. At the sight of us, a ray of relief streaked across her memento mori face. She snuffled and wiped away true tears, twisting her head, a bird wiping its beak under a wing. "Oh Ariadne darling, she's dying. Her flesh is gone. Her bones are burning. She's drowning in pain."

She hurried away, whimpering, "My sister, my sister . . ." Attendants fluttered after. "Thin broth, maybe thin broth. She might be able to swallow."

Through the bead curtains I caught a glimpse of my long-lost playmate Jessica, her back straight against the far wall, one arm upraised, hand gripping her boyish-bobbed hair. She had grown tall, become finely drawn, like one of those elongated nineteenth-century models. She had emerged on the family sarcophagus, a cold figure of night. Only her splendid coloring divulged her begetting when (it was whispered) Uncle Joshua, after months of siege, had ambushed his Snow Queen wife-in-name-only and assaulted her.

I flung my arms out to her in a gesture of embrace, but she did not move. (I could not tell if she saw me from under downcast lids. Many years later, I caught that expression on a young hotel waiter, one of those beautiful Sicilian boys who pass in and out of bedroom suites bearing trays, their faces averted in chaste disapproval, demanding that they as well as the guest be accorded the fiction of invisibility.)

The parlor door opened. Alas, Aunt Giselle! The glory that was, become skull, horse's teeth, stranded keel of nose.

My father stepped out of the room, closed the door behind him, his face a cold mask. I thought he was iced over with grief for Giselle.

I was full of our adventure. I had wrestled with death, and won. I wanted to brag about it.

"Daddy, we were caught in a blizzard."

The last of the *cousinas* receded with rustles of gloom.

His gaze passed from my face, which glowed with windburn and exuberance, to Adam's where it remained fixed. I had seen my father's wild young brother, the successful businessman, the defiler, break into penitential sobs at the reprimand implicit in that visage.

Adam put up his hand as if to fend off accusation. I had an urge to protect him.

"Daddy, we were trapped in a blizzard," I repeated louder.

"An unpredicted snowstorm," Adam supplemented.

"What snowstorm?" My father's voice was somber. "We had no trouble getting from the pier with a dying woman. A burst of heavy rain."

"I assure you, sir . . ." Adam began.

"Daddy, it snowed where we were. The car got stuck. We nearly froze to death."

My father spoke as if I were not there. "You have become an American, Mr. Arkady."

"There was a blizzard, Daddy. We were lost . . . in deep snow. We almost died. We had to bang and bang on a door. See, I lost my shoes."

My father paid no attention to me. "I misjudged you," my father said.

Both men were in a perspiration of melancholy, both in remote, intent agreement about the catastrophic nature of a situation in which I was the central object.

"I assure you, sir, it was unavoidable. Your daughter is un ———"

(The daughter was me, standing there.)

"Who will believe you?" My father waved at the rooms behind him.

"I understand your position, sir." Adam bowed stiffly, as if a board were tied to the back of his neck.

"Who will believe you what?" I said from one to the other.

They regarded me with the abstracted air of two martyrs bent on suicide.

My mother emerged from the funereal parlor, her skin mottled under the white acne scars; face welted from weeping.

"Heartless girl! You had to choose today?"

"There was a snowstorm," I tried once more.

"So! You were too occupied to telephone until an hour ago?"

"There was no telephone where we were."

(My mother should have been a modern painter. To her, *surface* was *reality*. She had convictions that would have done credit to a French impressionist. She believed in and loved *appearance*. I *appeared* to have gone wrong, therefore I had gone wrong. But if my father was taken in by this appearance it was hopeless to expect any transcendent construction of the night from anyone, because to my father, more than to others, possibility was as pregnant as probability. Aunt Cassie, who might have been an ally, was immersed in the loss of the person she loved most. Her support would, in any case, have been discounted. She was a suffragette, an atheist and a socialist. Except for her attachment to Giselle, only the sorrows of the world were sorrow.)

"Disgrace!" my mother hissed and tiptoed back into the parlor.

The door was not quite shut. Whispers twittered and simpered. Words flew out in sudden coherence as when children play a game of passing a message from ear to neighbor ear, themselves startled at the end distortion.

The sentence reached us clearly. "What decent man will marry her now?"

"I will," I heard Adam reply to no one in particular.

He put out his hand. My father took it.

"This is not the moment for discussion, but you have my word," Adam added. At the door, both men shook hands again, formal, fastidious, grave as pallbearers.

Aunt Giselle died a week later in the country farmhouse and was buried in a cemetery as foreign to her as she was to it.

Adam and I did develop feverish colds. But our rise in temperature did nothing to cancel the events set into motion by the fall in temperature that had dropped a storm in our path.

"Arnie's getting married!" my brother Reuben taunted.

"Ugh, ugh! You're out of your milky mind!" my cousin Jessica said. "Disgusting idea."

My American brother Ezra made the only sensible statement of the period. "She can't get married. She's not a grownup."

I was surprised at the awe my match engendered.

The rabbi was so impressed that he called on me personally. "A distinguished family. Scholars and sages. Their line goes back to Kings. A great responsibility. I wish you many sons."

"Her family is weak in religion," the sexton remarked. But he had a pathetic daughter.

* * *

What, if anything, had happened? A trifling difference in temperature between one air mass and another, and we were engaged, our futures determined. Time and time again, I have been forced to concede the staying power of an Unevent. Here in my dacha, where nothing much happens anymore, where any glance might turn up an old journey recorded in ashtrays, bibelots, albums flaking with glue, or a framed photo of one of the children embracing a caryatid or, out of focus middle distance — was it Naples? — a rotunda with bronze portraits, their glazed eyes bent on a magnificent view, I focus on an Unevent:

In my journal I made no note of it. (I can be certain my beloved Paul didn't either.) We were hungry and we ate bread baked of a crude flour speckled with husks and flakes of unsifted chaff, the crust sprinkled with seeds that might have been poppy; they tasted of flint sweetened with oven-scorched ash. We were thirsty and we drank cider drawn from a cask in a farmers' market stall. We were silly by a brook; splashed and dispersed throngs of head-down reflected flowers; spat poppy seeds and crumbs back where their mother-field received them. We thwarted industrious ants. I munched a speckled pear. He licked the juice from my fingers. We delayed, as long as daylight allowed, the museum, the mansion, for which — with adjoining relics — I had allotted a dozen blank pages.

Yet that Unevent, that unrecorded hour from the middle of my life, reappears. Here in the west light my gauze curtains reflect that shallow pool. On the polished floor upside-down butterflies throb urgent antennae over red poppies whose black stamens glint among the barley not yet divested, not yet lying in sheaves.

*   *   *

The courtship became official.

The blemish of haste put on our engagement seemed visible only to me. To my parents Adam had been perfect before the snowstorm. After his impeccably appropriate response he was, if possible, more perfect.

94

April, May, June. Spring and all. We saw each other on Saturdays and Sundays. We went for drives and walks. Sometimes we went rowing. He spread his jacket on the seat to keep my skirt unstained. I trailed my fingers in the lake and admired his broad shoulders, muscular arms and slender waist. I filled his silence with my imaginings, and decided he was inscrutable and enigmatic as well as dark and handsome. He said "charming frock," or "enhancing jumper" or "becoming coiffure," which struck me as sophisticated. He endeared himself to my brothers and their friends by taking them to the park one balmy day and showing them how to dribble a soccer ball. I couldn't take my eyes off him, all in white, light-footed as a dancer.

At home the parlor was left to us. Door open. Gramophone records . . . he winding, I humming, my fingertips keeping solitary dance time, my whole body longing to follow. "Turkey-trot, bunny-hug, grizzly-bear? I'm sorry, Ariadne, I never learned American-style ballroom dances."

"Not even the tango?" (I thought every sophisticated Continental had spent afternoons at hotel thés dansants, but obviously I had been wrong.) I wished he would put his arms around me and try. But he sat smiling, smoking a cigarette, looking attractive. My parents sat on in the dining room, my father reading aloud to my mother, both of them glancing up shining with amiability at my passage to the kitchen to freshen the tea and get more cookies. (Certain appetites were admissible.)

Once, ages later, Adam and I, in a hill town, in the season of burned leaves, husks, tartaric diffusion of stemmed grapes, witnessed in dance a sacrament of fruition.

In the center of a circle, a middle-aged couple, field roughened, sturdy as banded wine casks, solemnly recapitulated forms handed down for generations. He revolved around her, alternating knee bend with leap and stamp. She circled, passing a veil before her face and withdrawing it. Enticement and flight. Formalized provocations and ritualized restraint. White kerchiefs appeared, one between each couple. Grape-stained fingers gripped the corners, no flesh touching in public. A broad-beamed couple opened a space, inviting Adam and me into the circle. Adam whipped a handkerchief from his breast pocket. How surprisingly native his click and bow appeared. He shook one corner deftly toward me. I caught it. "It is like a Chassidic kerchief," he said. "I believe, my dear, this is the kind of dance I can master."

Sunday dinners. Cooked by me. My brother Reuben seated to keep his shaking head out of Adam's view. My mischievous brother Ezra warned not to make sly remarks, glancing uneasy at big-sister, mother-inferior, playing favorites, heaping the interloper's plate with the best tidbits.

Adam took me to the theater. We saw *Maytime*. Everyone on stage sang and danced and was happy happy at the happy ending. Marriage. The sheen of happiness on the couple, even in its sham form on the stage, made me weepy.

"But you didn't ask me to marry you before we got stuck in the snow," I said.

"I planned to. I hoped my parents would meet you before I proposed."

"They live in Geneva, Adam, and there's a war. It could take forever for them to get here."

"A university has invited Father to a professorship here and arrangements are being made. I was waiting for news."

"Do you require their consent? You are twenty-seven years old."

"I was waiting out of respect. They have formal customs, somewhat more formal than American and . . ."

"Oh, I've been told. They are Sephardim; much classier than Ashkenazim."

"Tradition is important to them, as it is to your father." He answered seriously, his hands quiet in his lap. "Objectively, Ariadne, society is held together by small knots of convention of which marriage is one."

"I don't always agree with my father. He thinks a dowry is important and I think it's paying a man to take your daughter."

"Dowry is one of the conventions that have been found useful."

"I wouldn't accept a dowry. My Aunt Giselle went to her wedding dressed in black because Uncle Joshua's matchmaker brought up the subject. She wanted to break it off but he wouldn't give her up. They lived unhappily every after."

"Ariadne, it was you who mentioned dowry. I did not. Joshua and Giselle were probably not right for each other, or they would have overcome that misunderstanding."

"I guess you're right," I said, "but you do agree that people should marry only for love, don't you?"

"Then we have no problems. We love each other. My family will accept you when they learn what a splendid wife you will make."

"My family will accept me even if I don't marry you."

Each of us spoke with more hope than conviction.

I could feel tears coming on again. He put his arms around me and kissed my cheek. "You will be a model bride."

I read poetry aloud to him. One rainy Sunday afternoon I recited my new favorite: "The Love Song of J. Alfred Prufrock." " 'Oh, do not ask, "What is it?" 'Let us go . . .' " My voice soared to it.

My father appeared from the neighboring room. "What are you reading there about Michelangelo? I don't recognize it."

My father settled for a stay. He emptied a stub from his amber holder and lit a fresh cigarette. "How did you decide on mathematics as your field, Adam?"

"I always liked the subject. But when I was reading for my general philosophy requirements I realized I enjoyed Spinoza because the form of his arguments imitated the mathematical deductions of Euclid's geometry."

"I'm hopeless at math," I said.

"Arnie knows enough arithmetic for a girl," my father assured Adam. "She keeps the household accounts."

"One gift to my bride had better be a Chinese abacus. Factually, *abacus* comes from the Greek *abax,* meaning 'dust.' Perhaps calculations were made in it" — he leaned alertly forward — "with *calculi,* Latin for 'stones.' There are great opportunities ahead. One day mechanical computers will replace all tedious mathematical operations now done by humans. We've come far already."

"Go on, son." My father turned a respectful gaze on Adam, who inclined his head in acknowledgment of the newly bestowed title.

"Based on Napier's logarithms, Pascal in 1642 devised a counting machine using gears. Leibnitz" (a glance at me, "calculus, you know") "followed with one that could perform the four basic functions: addition, subtraction, multiplication and division."

"I don't altogether follow." My father's voice was warm with approval. "Perhaps you will explain one evening."

"It will be my pleasure, Father."

My father inclined *his* head.

Adam brushed his hair back briskly. "We must have more advanced computers. In the three years from 1915 to today we have Einstein's general theory of relativity, Cantor's theory of transfinite numbers, Eddington's calculations on the properties of stars, Lewis on valence theory, Max Planck's quantum theory. Imagine the mathematics Harlow Shapley required . . ."

"I can't imagine," I said, slightly jealous of the intensity Adam was giving to his subject.

"Arnie," my father said, "please fetch tea. As you were saying, Adam . . ."

On every side my victory was hailed, my good fortune envied. Word of my engagement traveled to school. Girls who had never included me in the category of "the girls" seethed. "How did he propose?"

"It's a secret," I had the wit to maintain.

"Who would have imagined you would be the first!" (So much for senior class predictions.)

"Never went to school dances, because she had a beau."

"A wedding this summer!"

The most popular girls in the class eyed me, the social zero, with perplexity and respect. They eyed themselves, measuring their more fashionable bobs and dimensions against my hour-glass curves and coronet of braids.

"Still waters run deep," said the tweedy English teacher who had loaned me her own copies of *Poetry: A Magazine of Verse*, patting my cheek approvingly when I said "Prufrock" was thrilling. "I had hoped you would go to college."

"Sly puss. Butter wouldn't melt in her mouth," the chinless librarian said drily and stamped my card, averting her face as if I had developed atrocious scales and a downy beak. She did her best, however, all the way to the altar; directing me to Hawthorne and Hardy, those champions of passionate women mangled through their ill-starred entanglements with men.

I became a favorite among my relatives. My parents reaped congratulations: their princess had hooked a prince. They were wreathed in verification. Day by day, the matrimonial machinery crunched forward, fife and drum corps of propriety and praise sounding their spirited commands. There was trousseau talk, guest lists, menus, linens, china, silver, furniture. My gown, my mother's, fittings, fabrics, swatches. My head was filled with dreams of domestic triumph, of a cottage small by a waterfall. Why, then, did I wake with a sigh?

It was a sullen wet spring and I would lie in the dark listening to the heavy rain, half dreaming. I was in a Gypsy's arms, he pressed me against his blue-striped silk shirt and lavished feverish kisses on my mouth and throat. I found to my surprise I was crying, and went on crying until I fell asleep, exhausted.

There was a craggy park in our neighborhood and one night in a thunderstorm I escaped the house and ran there, rain sliding over me, wet clothes slapping against my nakedness. No one saw a wild girl whirling, leaping, weeping for that fire which burned before decorum reigned. I scrambled up to the highest rocks and imagined leaping from them to my death. And wept for that. Then I ran recklessly down. I wanted to run until I fell down dead. I suspected myself of madness and criminal indecency. I remembered, once at the seashore:

I slipped from the crowded bungalow, escaped to the beach, ominously hot before a thunderstorm, lightning stabbing and crackling into fog, gun-metal surf soughing beyond the rock-pile jetties; took off my shoes and stockings, ran, welcomed the sharpness of pebbles and shells underfoot, galloped for impact, each shock shooting up my legs, trembling through hips and breasts aching like rocks grown sensate, my hair a mane blowing behind me.

At the far end a lone man entered the tunnel of fog, grew larger, advancing at a calisthenic trot; circular lift and roll of shoulders, muscular piston bare legs. Both of us steadily onward, two strangers tunneling toward each other. Neither swerved. At the last moment he curved away, too late. I thudded into him. Involuntarily his arms went out and around me, as one catches a child who runs full tilt crying, "Catch me. Here I come." He swung me round and round, laughing, "whee . . . whee . . . wheee . . ."

He stopped laughing, hesitated and put his lips to mine. Breathless, I panted against his mouth which slowly pressed down on mine. He drew me against him. We rocked mouth to mouth, body to body. Unknown sensations ascended and rippled out of me like water spurting in a fountain, my legs buckling under in a slow fall, mist and water rising round me, eyelids and mouth heavy with languor. My strength drained away. With a cry, my head fell back from him.

"Christ!" he muttered, kissed my throat, my cheeks, my mouth. My sight cleared. Whatever force had goaded me and shaken me apart in a stranger's arms was spent. Cool wavelets were breaking over my feet.

I pushed him lightly away, fingertips cold against his chest. Dazedly, he dropped his arms, stepped back and let me go. Very slowly, like horses moving in a dream, we separated. Slowly his arms and legs picked up their circular rhythm. My legs also rose and fell, he moving in his direction and I in mine. If either of us turned to look back, the fog erased our silhouettes.

There was no one to help me understand the furor that set me prancing. No contact probable to our flesh allayed the fever rising in my blood. I baked cookies with it. Stirred fudge. I polished, scrubbed, cleaned, helped my brothers and cousins with homework, picked up after my mother and every three days took from the library the maximum number of books — all hinting, none answering.

Books could no longer contain my ardor. I was exhausted by ambiguities on paper. I shed tears for Hardy's strong-willed heroines who defied convention, were ostracized and came to miserable ends. But "unhappiness is also life" and I longed to experience their urgency. King Arthur filled me with distaste. I much preferred Malory's Lancelot the Malfit who ran mad with love of Guinevere, who disobeyed the laws of knighthood and damned his soul to hell for passion's sake. No, nothing in literature prepared me for my discontent with my premarital condition. It was simply *fainter* than anything I had been led to expect. I should say, anything I had *imagined,* for, in fact, neither my father nor Adam could reasonably be expected to be so swayed as to run mad, eat grass, climb towers and swashbuckle against a cadre of outraged knights.

I preened with a white bathroom curtain draped to represent a wedding veil, endlessly brushed my hair, coiled and twisted it into a bun at the nape, burst into sudden rages and tears, blinked, gaped, sat with my mouth open, broke into sudden hops and runs.

There was Jessica, mocking me with "But you promised to marry *me* when we grew up" and "What makes you sure you'll love being married? My mother hated it and so would I."

I tried airing my doubts with my parents. "I don't know if I'm really in love."

"Love. Love. Love. That was your song before he asked you. Now it's settled. He wants to marry you; you don't know if you've changed your mind!" My father pressed his palms against his forehead. "Craziness. Temperament."

"I know I said yes." (I could not explain that I said yes the way Juliet said it about Paris. Before the idea was made flesh.)

My mother stitched into the monogram and jabbed her finger. She put aside the pillowcase and sucked the blood off her hand. "Bad luck to get blood on bride linens."

"I thought it was bad not to," I grumbled.

"What do you mean?"

(I don't know if other girls of my generation had a clear knowledge of the mechanics of sex, but I was hazy about what specifically our canaries negotiated under the flowered chintz cage-cover. I was the best-read girl in the class but I hadn't figured out how Tess of the D'Urbervilles *and* Hester Prynne got pregnant if they didn't want to. Or how, if they had wanted to.)

While I craved release from the smothering blandness of my life as daughter, big-sister and mother's helper, I felt rushed toward unspecific terrors. I was dying for experience, yet being marched blindfolded into the future. My bridal costume was exhilarating one moment and seemed to belong to some unknown grown-up woman the next. I was full of misgivings.

My father came in from his postprandial walk. It was only since my engagement that I had given up accompanying him.

"I met the rabbi. He told me *their* side had been offered a Rothschild," he said.

"Ah, millions! Such a girl must have millions." My mother said, "ah, millions" as if she had chanced on a half-acre stand of yellow chanterelles.

My parents talked to each other over my head, a mannerism they had developed since my engagement. It left me with the choice of eavesdropping or pretending I was deaf.

"She's from an orthodox house." My father looked accusingly at my mother, who, with her chaotic housekeeping, had long been mixing milk and meat dishes, though my father would have preferred to respect the ordinances, not out of piety but in deference to the culture.

"She's rich." My mother bit off the embroidery thread.

"Our Topaz got the best catch without millions," my father said.

"Without religion," she added, not to be outdone.

(I wish I had understood, when I was a child, that any topic can be ground down into ammunition in the conflict that smolders night and day between husband and wife — even between a pair of old-timers like my parents. I might have been cannier about allying myself totally with my father if I had realized that powder kegs were concealed behind their seemingly abstract debates.)

"If we're not rich enough to suit them, and not religious enough for his family, why should I marry him?" I asked sullenly.

"A refined boy from a refined family wants to marry her. Why should she marry him?" My father asked it of the air as if an idiot had spoken.

"My English teacher thinks I should wait and go to college."

"An old maid. She's jealous," my father said.

"Uncle Joshua is from a good family; he's my favorite uncle; Jessica loves him; he is your friend; Mama laughs and jokes with him; but Aunt Giselle hated marriage with him. Why?"

"Aunt Giselle was a sensitive woman," my father said.

My mother harrumphed. "My sister was too hoity-toity for anything but painting poppies on teacups. A husband she never wanted, children she never wanted."

"No need to speak ill of the dead," my father said. "Joshua is a good man but he was not refined enough for her."

My mother made a sour mouth. "You had a more suitable man in mind? Joshua is the one *I'm* sorry for. A healthy giant of a man who could have satisfied any woman."

"You say so?" It was my father's turn to sound affronted.

"I am sure." The venom in her voice frightened me. (In all the discussions of Genesis I never heard a word about the verse in which God curses Eve with desire toward her husband.) "Giselle was spoiled by my father. He gave her anything she wanted, made the rest of us give in to her, too. She had music lessons. And who was the musical one? Me. A father can spoil a girl for any man." She looked at him fiercely.

I couldn't believe they were quarreling in front of me, about me. My mind rebelled against the thought that they were not happy. If they were not, what chance did I have?

"Jessica swears she'll never marry," I said.

"Jessica? Another expert on domestic affairs!" My father lit a cigarette and made a visible effort to calm down.

"You have some objection to Jessica?" my mother asked. "A beautiful child who had a selfish mother."

"What about the *cousinas?*" I pushed ahead. "Most of them didn't marry. They went to school and worked. One is a dentist, one teaches German in high school."

"Since the war, that one has no job. What kind of life is it for a woman struggling without a husband?" My father scored his point with his lighted cigarette.

"They are beautiful girls," I said.

"Yes," my mother said, "clever, beautiful girls."

Again my father and mother exchanged hostile looks.

"When Ariadne was five years old, they were beautiful girls. Now they are old maids."

The *cousinas* old maids?

Too late for the marriage brokers, too soon for computerized matchmaking. From Moscow, Warsaw, Vienna, Berlin. A frieze of highfalutin working girls. Wouldn't marry any man on earth, not they! Socialists dreaming international fraternity; Zionists willing to settle for a Jewish homeland; organizers who mounted soapboxes in Union Square to denounce the greedy bosses responsible for the tragedy of the Triangle Shirt Waist fire. Among them were doctors, lawyers, dental assistants, bookkeepers, schoolteachers, shop stewards, pattern-cutters, women rumored to be more than they should have been; vaguely remembered women enshrined in fashions exalted by the taste of the time, their faces shaped to the desired expression; hair coiffed to the sensation, bodies held in the stance acknowledged to be that period's image of beauty. Everything conspires to enhance their desirability by concealing and revealing: wide-brimmed hats, the play of outdoor light sifting through leaves on real jewels, many-buttoned gloves, fragile silk shoes, sensual fabrics pin-tucked to underline the roundness of breasts, cunningly placed bustles to amplify the full haunches. Everything is shaped and draped, pinched and arched, everything reared to suggest forbidden caresses contradicting the downcast eyes, the cool profiles turned elegiacally toward snowcapped peaks of chastity — background mountains to be climbed.

A summer night, moths cindering in the lamplight:

Off with the petticoats, the camisoles, the corselettes. Heavy braids unlooped, two-pronged tortoiseshell hairpins tossed on my mother's dresser. Under lawn nightgowns, fertile hips, full breasts, white arms; everything lifts with each amber brush-stroke flashing through fiery hair, compelling as moonlight on snow.

In my ribboned bloomers, I leap from the carved headboard into the bounce of feather quilts among them, aromatic as wild mushrooms spread to dry, on the Brussels-lace field of their Aunt Hera's matrimonial bed.

They struggle with each other to catch and fondle me.

"Marry? No. Never!"

"Not even my daddy?"

"No, never . . ."

"No. No. Never. Never. Oh the slavery. The slavery . . ."

They sing, smothering me, their proxy child, with scented kisses, unmindful of a tear of maternity caught like a fossil grub in the primitive amber of an eye.

Old maids?

Did I want to become like them? Women visiting the patriarchal family on Sundays, hugging nieces and nephews. Women who went to political meetings, who picketed the White House in behalf of women's suffrage. (Four of their group had lately been sentenced to six months in jail for the offense.) Did I want to be like cousin Rysia, who supported herself as a bookkeeper? Or, since I had no exceptional talents, no training, become like the seamstresses in my uncle's clothing factory? What could I do — write verses like Amy Lowell, who dressed like a man and smoked cigars? She had Lowell money and was free to do what she liked. I was an ordinary girl and I aspired to normal things: children, a home, an enviable appearance. Also, if I didn't go through with the marriage to Adam, I might never be asked again, as my father implied. My honor had been impugned. I had spent a night alone with a man. Dozens of people knew about it. Gossip had flown like the feathers of a plucked chicken tossed on the wind. Perhaps I shared my father's fears that the outside world and I would prove untrustworthy. Or my mother's fears, that I was a puny specimen who would be left withering on the vine. Marriage offered the only way out of permanent daughterhood and spinsterhood.

I invented a cheerful grown-up married life, much like my mother's, but more orderly. My own housekeeping, my own children, my own market basket, my own spotless floor mop, my own husband to dote on, wait on, pamper and adore. And smile, smile, smile. I would be a more perfect helpmeet than my mother, a more devoted wife and mother, taking pleasure in giving pleasure to my family. I would no longer be a child. I would step out into my real life and act in my own behalf.

But what was the hurry?

"I don't want to be an old maid, Daddy. I just don't want to get married yet."

My mother, who hated embroidering, stitched doggedly on. "It's normal for a young girl to be frightened, Abidah. Be patient. She knows you want the best for her. She's shy."

"Who isn't shy! You were shy. I was shy," he declaimed.

"I'm not shy. I want to go to college. Be something."

"A wife is not something? Your mother is not something? A girl doesn't need college. She needs a husband to take care of her. In college you won't find a better man. Let Reuben go to college, so he can take care of a family."

"Reuben in college?! He can't even learn to play chess."

"You want to go to college, go! I'm not sending you."

"You're a smart girl. You can go to college after you're married, in the afternoon, before you have children. When you're a mother you can help your children with their schoolwork," my mother said.

"Enough nonsense," my father said, "I can't believe she is my daughter. All our lives we wish and plan and here comes a young man with all the virtues and this, this piece of foolishness doesn't know if she loves him."

"Listen to what your father is saying, dear. Would he wish you bad for your life?"

Were these the two people who had been my parents? Who had looked to me for advice about strange American customs like eating mayonnaise instead of horseradish with cold chicken; how it was an invitation, not a command, to visit school on parents' days; why it was not military conscription for my brother Ezra to join the Boy Scouts; which Washington was where; whether Gene Stratton Porter and/or Jack London would take their places in world literature. Where was the mother who had taught me how to walk barefoot in the woods without stepping on thorns? Was this the father who discussed Hegel and Shakespeare with me, who played chess with me as if I were an equal, a worthy opponent? Was this the person to whom the rational nature of man was not a subject of derision?

I turned from one to the other. "Why can't I wait?"

"You are waiting. Till the end of August." My mother sighed.

"Father, you always said, 'Study, build up a life of the mind. It's above riches.' "

He was pacing up and down, inhaling deep drafts of his cigarette, "Some other girl will be only too glad to take such a prize from you while your nose is in a book."

"He doesn't love me!" I cried.

"He asked you to marry him."

"Would he have asked me if you hadn't made a fuss? I'll never know. I'll tell you right out: his parents won't think *our* family is good enough. Can that come out well?"

My father waved away his doubts, but he paled. His cigarette glowed in midair. He recovered. "Your family is as good as anyone's. We've lost our money, but your mother traces her ancestry to Moses de Leon, the author of the Zohar. And I'm a workingman, a diamond-cutter, but my family is descended from Rabbi Akiva."

"I know, I know already, of whom the Talmud says that he left the paradise of mystical speculation as safe and sane as he had entered it. But Adam's family is high-class now, and we aren't."

I pressed forward. "Adam's in no hurry. I am in no hurry. You're the only one in a hurry, Daddy. Why are you pushing?"

My mother stopped sewing. "What are you hinting? Spit it out."

"I already did. He is in no hurry to get married."

My father went sallow. His mouth sagged. The bristles on his face stood out in separate spears. "Did he speak of not going ahead with the marriage."

(Ah, if only! If only I had had the wit to say "Adam said, out of respect for tradition, he would prefer to wait for his parents to come from Geneva before announcing the date." My father, out of respect for tradition, would have had to ask "Adam, would you prefer to wait for your parents before setting the date?" Adam would have said, "Yes, I think it would be proper

109

for the families to meet before." *His* parents would have said, "No, she isn't for you.")

For one moment there I almost had it. Then, as my grandchildren would say, I blew it. "He doesn't act like he's in a hurry. We've been going together for five months and when he kisses me good night he still kisses me on the cheek."

My father stared at me, then looked away as if he had come upon me dripping with taboo blood. His voice rang out. Was it with ice? Can it possibly be true, or am I with Freud's help reinventing a cliché? It had an overtone of triumph.

"God in Heaven! Where *should* he kiss you?"

He turned on my mother. "You heard what I heard? What kind of girl did you bring up? Emancipated ideas from your sister Cassie? Send her to college for more of them? I'll lock her up first. She can't be trusted. A man treats her as a father would wish. With perfect respect. For her. For her parents. That's not good enough for my lady. She wants to be treated like a . . . I won't name it . . . ."

My mother stepped between us. She grasped his arm. "Calm yourself, Abidah. She is a child. An innocent child."

He pushed her aside. I had never seen him in such flesh-and-blood fury. He had gone lemon ochre, his hands shaking, his eyes were red. "She wants a bum, a bum who knows everything, and wants everything. A lifeguard . . ." (How had he guessed?) "a bum who can't wait or won't wait, a filth in a hurry who doesn't care what happens to a girl. Marry her off quickly. If Adam finds out what she is, she'll end up on the streets."

Tears were rolling down his cheeks.

"Don't cry, Daddy. I'll marry. I'll marry."

I was crying too.

My mother signaled me to leave the room.

So Adam and I were married. And my father gave me away.

* * *

It's six A.M. I wish I could pick up the telephone and chat with Jeremy, as I used to at any hour, on any subject.

"Jeremy," I would say softly, "what shall we talk about?"

Alert on the instant, he might say, "Begin anywhere. What's the weather like?"

I had spoken aloud, and the hoarseness of my voice startled me.

In my garden, the earliest birds are remarking on the weather. To go outdoors I wrap myself in my mauve mohair cloak. Around my throat a wide velvet ribbon serves as a stake-tie to reduce the slight tremor of my head. These cameo costumes still, these affectations.

It's noisy. Birds are slandering each other. In autumn there is no love lost between creatures. The days of reproductive collaboration are over. Squirrels and chipmunks chivvy, each claiming the pod among leaves ablaze in their dying. Each creature feeds as if it were the last supper. As if it sensed that not all who are herded into the caves of winter will shake off the sleep of hibernation.

I peer down paths narrowed by tumbled walls of chrysanthemums. My hands are too arthritic for the pruning shears that might recover the alley of quince whose spring fires are being suffocated by thorned suckers. To whom shall I turn for help? (You know how help is nowadays.) The lily pool has leaked itself empty. It is too stained with leaves to mirror the stone cupidons. The children, my four burnished angels, are poised on tiptoe like shadow-fountain figures. I pass the picnic glade where Benjamin and I buried his dead bird; past the stone bench where Arie, my artistic daughter, a painter now, organized colored petals and made gnome salads that Aaron obligingly ate, displaying early the heroism that parachuted him from us; past the wildwood shrubbery where Absalom hunted God knows what.

III

I focus at the dead center of my formal garden where on summer nights we lay on blankets and studied the Milky Way. Here the children gave a performance of Hercules — played by Absalom — conquering the Nemean lion — played by Aaron; here in cheerful melancholy we sang our folk song repertoire of common heartbreaking things. Here Arie's wedding to Jethro took place. Where did it fall apart? If it was like most of our failures — merely a series of Unevents, forced, in memory, into causes and effects, tactical arrangements of hindsight. Black roses filled with early snow sway among ragged canes above the sundial.

No. This is not where I had hoped to go.

And Mother of:

The maternal instinct does not progress. It is born instantaneously
— complete, fully armed and bleeding. Whereas love has the gift of
tending towards its own perfection.

— COLETTE

DURING AN UNHURRIED convalescence in my childhood
the constellations were made animate for me in a book filled
with numbered dots. When lines were drawn in numerical sequence connecting dot to dot, stars, which till then had danced
indifferent asunder, were collected into shapes of augury. Had
I had my horoscope read at the time I don't doubt it would have
revealed that, like Tristram Shandy, "there had been the deuce
and all to do in some part of the ecliptic when I was conceived."

I was born under Aquarius, the servitor, the water-carrier.
And by some seemingly implacable astro-logic my life has,
indeed, been ruled by watery complications: birth precipitated
by a slick of ice, marriage by a snowstorm. And I have yet to
tell of the part a snowstorm played in my malformed love affair
as well as how the too early loss of amniotic waters required all
my children to be forcibly delivered.

I'm an Aquarian all the way: crossing waters, broken waters, frozen waters. (Frozen Aquarius? A bad sign for a gardener or a wife. Freeze and thaw will penetrate to the root and winter-kill. Freeze and thaw will break down rock.) Under my sign I have been dangled by my life line, have fallen in, and several times been saved from death by water.

Now after so many deaths, I who live and write this recall the oarsman, my father, guiding our boat through scattered light. Young and handsome as those who smile on us in dreams, he glints in the mirror discs, green, yellow, white, that dazzle the surface of a blue remembered pond. Gaily he paddles toward the applause of two shimmering figures on an arched bridge. Light flickers down through lace parasols sprigging summer gowns with random shadows; shimmers up from between lily rounds, doubling and dispelling a cow, knee-deep in shallows.

Oars dip and lift, whiteness falls in flakes of yellow, green, pink, flung into prisms in spray.

We float in *plein air.* (*Plein air?* Transparently filtered through Seurat, via Paul. I apologize for my lamentable tendency to borrow images from the referential males in my life. With a little help from time and art, my memory sifts and shifts the scenes, enclosing them in a continuum, like a child's numbered dots, or like an old woman tracing a repeat.)

Lift, dip, glide. Undisturbed, a whirligig beetle paddles its fringed legs among rainbows. A diving beetle slaps a bell of air under its scarab wing and sinks like a jeweled brooch beneath sunken stars of milfoil. A bubble pops in a fleck of scum. Underneath us spirogyra wave their lady tresses toward elodea. Wide as nets, cabomba's feathered reefs, unfathomably receptive, conceal silver minnows that streak continuously into its depths.

We should have floated in enduring sunlight; my cousin Jessica in unfading rose and I in gilded marigold, but a gesture tossed us back into time. It was by my hand. I reached down into the wake and lifted a festoon. Oh the gross reality behind that seductive appearance! Out of its element it was an ooze of slime that clumped snot-green to my fingers. I flung it from me. It flew toward Jessica and plopped, a cold glob on her warm knee. She jumped or fell against my father. An oar looped and flipped out of reach. My father grabbed for it. The boat tipped sharply upward.

Rising and then slowly descending weightless as flight in dreams, limbs disposing themselves, out of honey air I fell.

High maternal screams. "Look! Look! Catch her! Ariadne!"

Water closed over me. Water murky as dirty glass spread away from me in spirals. My dress ballooned. My hair flowed upward. I descended past goggle-eyed fish. A turtle paddled away exposing its pale belly. My father's length arced next to me, shot past. I saw the striped silk banner of his shirt and then his pale feet. Bubbles and nodules rose as I sank. His hand grasped my hair. What I next remember was the taste of slime in my mouth, my father rocking me in his arms, my mother wailing, "Dead, dead, dead!"

"No. No. No. I hear her heart."

"Her eyes are open . . . dead . . . dead . . ." The sharp cries of Aunt Giselle.

Dead? I was surprised that death had gone no further.

*　　*　　*

A summer night. Blankets. Fireflies and fireworks of stars scattering confetti through space. Stargazing with the children and Adam, I told how I had been rescued from drowning; like my father, drawing a moral from the story.

"So you see, Benjamin, it isn't safe to take the rowboat out by yourself even though, my darling, you are a splendid rower for a five-year-old. I would have drowned."

"You had to born us, so you couldn't drown," Benjamin answered, raising his head from my lap.

II5

"Since it was written in my stars, I suppose you four saved me."

"Mother, how can you fill their heads with superstitious piffle?" Arie, a silvered cat in the pale moonlight, stepped back from her telescope. "You are getting milky in the filberts. Honestly!" She sat down on the blanket and nestled against her father. "Dad, would you explain to Mother once again that the zodiac has been shifting in precession for centuries? Which means all astrological readings are nonsense."

Adam let his hand slip down her cheek and come to rest on her shoulder. "Our lovely astronomer is correct. Since planets and constellations are not in the sky positions they occupied when the astrological theories were first formulated, their use as predictive instruments is invalid."

Aaron, second son, assistant stargazer, aligned himself at once. "Mother seems to think stars attend births like fairy godmothers bringing gifts."

Absalom, who had been lying face upward, sighting through a celestial chart, sat up in my defense. "What about myrrh and frankincense and that newborn star?"

"Shifted in precession or not," I said, "I like to think I am threaded by stellar magnetism to my very own sign — that I'm part of a planetary procession."

"Make a wish! Falling star! Everybody make a wish," Benjie sang out. "I saw it first."

Adam smiled across at me, both of us awed by the fourfold miracle that had come out of our marriage.

*   *   *

I was charmed with married life. For an entire month I thanked my lucky stars. Early to bed. A festive air of pajama party without pajamas and with a man. Waking, surprised not to find myself alone in bed. A lifetime's isolation merrily undone by the cool silky body next to mine. It was so much more *interesting* than lying alone *imagining* what making love was about, my blood seething.

Untwine from each other at the first twittering of birds. Prepare the hot breakfast, he muttering "Oh my, oh my" between mouthfuls. Easily ply my craft, breeze through my chores. No mother's, brothers', cousins' litter to stumble over; no stale tea things to clear. Nothing to do but tidy up, dress, bathe, go to market. Time to read, write verses, talk on the telephone to Jessica, or my mother, or a girlfriend before preparing dinner. I flashed my wedding ring and said "My husband" as often as occasion allowed. "I think my husband would prefer potato-parsley dumplings with his chicken stew tonight." "My husband likes soft-starch in his shirts." "A copy of the *New York Times* for my husband, please." Content, yet keyed up, alert; a new awareness brought the world close. Through the thinning trees, more beautiful as they bared, the clear chilled sky looked bluer; on the cold ground the mincing feet of pigeons were rosier. People were more beautiful, more sad. My eyes were opened to the tragedy of an old man fiercely alone, chin leaning on his liver-spotted hands capped over a cane.

Adam came home each evening, his smile quick and tender. The table was set with candles and an arrangement — autumn leaves, pink pears and purple grapes, or flowers. I was rosy. We sat down each night to a feast. Oh my, oh my.

"Tell me what happened at the office."

"No, you tell me."

"But I have nothing to tell."

"Yes, my dear, but you make nothing sound like an evening at the theater."

We were cozy. We were snug. We were shy and delicate, growing toward one another.

It was sweet and short. His job ended. Pregnancy startled me. How could such an important decision have been made without my consent? It wasn't intelligent. In the poems we memorized in school every American was master of his (if not her) fate, and captain of his (if not her) soul. Pregnant, eh? Why not? I took it in my ignorant stride. Everyone would see me, the grown-up married woman, the young mother, wheeling her beautiful beribboned son.

I gave some thought to how I should announce the news to Adam. Should I appear with knitting needles and blue yarn? Stay in bed and act fragile though I felt ravenous and vigorous? I decided on serving up the news with the first course of a partyish dinner. I dressed up in my trousseau frock, put on my Roman coin earrings, thinking how much the handsome profile resembled Adam's, brushed my long hair, tied it with royal-blue ribbons that flattered its coppery color, and though with Adam "between jobs" we were counting pennies, I bought a few flowers for a centerpiece.

"Two places set but so fancy, are we expecting afterdinner guests?" he asked.

"Not guests, but expecting," I said, feeling witty and gay. "How do you feel about being a father?"

A wave of blood rushed up as far as his forehead, then sank, leaving a wake of murky green. A single dark, damp furrow pressed itself across the curve of his dry upper lip. "Are you certain?"

"I missed two weeks."

"Let's hope it's a delay."

I felt as if I'd struck my elbow a sharp blow. The room receded in a cone of intensely bright light at the bottom of which a small figure refolded his napkin.

"You haven't told anyone, I hope."

"I was going to tell my parents after I told you."

"Plenty of time to worry them."

"Worry? They'll be delighted to have a grandchild."

He shook his head, not like an American saying "no," but

up and down, rocking like a rabbi. "Don't be a child. They reasonably might worry about how I plan to provide for a baby without a job."

"You'll get a job soon. You are bound to . . . a man of your education."

He put on a false smile. But his head never resembled less the Roman on my earrings. It was tilted forward as if a hard punitive palm were pushing against it. "You are a dear child; also, God willing, a fortuneteller. But with returning veterans getting preference it isn't going to be easy to get placed. We won't despair, will we?" His bitter mouth belied his words.

"Despair? Who me?" But there was a sharp contraction low in my groin as if I would expel what was there if I could.

Every morning he left the house before eight to "see people."

He came home every evening more drawn, his hair seeming blacker, his skin paler, his thin nose beakier. He inquired after my health in a stilted way, clearly disappointed to hear of no change "for the better." There was an end to kisses and compliments. He sat reading. From behind his newspaper a continuous column of cigarette smoke would rise. I sat in my matching armchair giving way to a dreamy lassitude, closing my eyes the better to sense the underwater currents in my womb, the pressure building in my breasts.

One evening from behind the want ads he said, "I met a fellow who worked in the same insurance office I did. He hasn't found a place yet either. He told me his wife has had an abortion . . . They know a doctor from the old country." He lowered the newspaper. His face was sallow and pinched. He looked as if he had walked all night in cold rain. "Hunger is bad for children, my dear. I . . ." His voice broke. "You may not remember, I happen to. It's a crime to bring a child you can't properly feed and care for into the world."

"No one starves in America." I said.

"No dear, nor in books. It is not a problem Shakespeare takes up in *Romeo and Juliet.*" The newspaper trembled in his hands. He folded it and laid it on the arm of his chair. For a second I wondered who this man was. He rested his head back. The oyster-white film of unshed tears gleamed between his lowered lids. "Think about it," he whispered.

How could I not?

I thought about it; about my sickly brother Reuben, about myself as a puny, asthmatic child. Adam had a point. A good beginning was every child's birthright.

Waspy rumors buzzed in my head. What was an abortion other than illegal and dangerous? Menace shrouded the word. I had never had a gynecological examination. In my youth such a thing was done only in the dark and terrible hours, when midwives had failed. I tried to imagine what an abortion would be. In my wildest speculation I did not envision my "privates" being forcibly invaded, the embryo scraped from my womb.

"Goose," my mother pooh-poohed. "Educated goose." She harrumphed in that coarse way I couldn't bear. "Too much brains, too little common sense. The father's daughter. Only it's not so bad for a man to be a *Luftmensch.* So your husband doesn't want the child! Big *so.* Who do you two think you are to fight nature? You're young, you're healthy, you're married. You get pregnant. So it's too soon? That's true. It would have been better to enjoy your youth a while longer. So, complain to the authorities. He's not happy about it? Whooo Whooo. News. It's not convenient at this moment? A child is for a moment? When was a child convenient? To the king of England it's convenient. Adam has no job? What's the matter, he'll never get a job? You have no money? Whoever had money? Women bear the children and take care of them. Men make a living. You think your father and I planned children? They came, we took them. I wish I had had a dozen like my mother did. You were inconvenient, so your father didn't love you? You know another father who has his daughter's shoes made to order, who buys her silk robes? He wouldn't die for any of you? On the street he wouldn't let a child go to play the wind shouldn't blow on it.

"Adam is scared. That's all. Men are always scared. That's news to you, too, my stupid daughter? Those poisons the druggist gives to bring it off, you can be sick your whole life from them. And from abortions, don't talk. Some butcher will scrape out a baby from you like you're a garbage pail! Even you wouldn't do such a crazy thing. Filth! Filth! I don't want to hear from it."

She slammed the door behind her; Daniel-Boone-conservationist in sequins, off to a bar mitzvah.

I was determined to make a distinguished record for myself; perform as ably in the role of a wife as I had a daughter. A good daughter did not contradict Daddy or worry him, because he worked hard, loved us and demanded only what was for the best. A disobedient child or wife could hardly expect to be loved. Was I imagining it or had Adam already withdrawn himself? In sleep he no longer curled around me; he tossed and rolled to the far side of the bed. (It did not occur to me that he was clotted with self-blame at his failure to provide "as a man should.") Should I do as he wished? I had had no practice in discovering what I wished, no skill at all in fighting for it. In marriage I was still aiming at an A in conduct. Almost in a spirit of adventure, I agreed.

The abortionist was a beautiful woman: Slavic features, obsidian eyes, a straight back and a profound alto voice with a rolling Russian accent.

"How are you about pain?" She tapped a silver and ivory

letter opener against the glass top of her ornate desk. Her elegance exacted my bravado.

"I don't know. Like anyone else."

"You look as if you don't know. I prefer to work without ether, it's safer for us both." Her breath bore down significantly on *safer*, taking me into her confidence. It was for my own good.

"Will it be long?"

"No, but it will seem so. You rest afterward."

She opened a needlepoint folder and studied a calendar.

"No ether, then."

Her head was turbanned in white surgical gauze, whiter than the white maquillage masking her austere face. She reminded me of my Aunt Giselle. I was hypnotized in her presence, almost honored to be there. My voice came out childish and obedient. "Just as you think best."

"Tuesday at two P.M. One hundred dollars now. Remainder of payment when you come back."

I had been prepared, and handed over the cash. The white starched coat crackled as she slipped the bills into a pocket.

"Come this way." She led me around rooms other than the one by which I had entered. "Someone is in the waiting room."

The apartment gleamed. Polished furniture. Bibelots, porcelain and silver sparkled from tables and cabinets. The Hudson shimmered through heavy lace curtains. A huge dog shook off repose and, haunch against the doctor's thigh, moved as she moved. She bent and scratched it under its slavering maw.

"Friendly?" I asked, my hand poised.

"Not very."

She undid a series of locks and chains on the door. "Tuesday at two. No one may accompany you. Have a woman friend wait for you on Riverside Drive at four. Do *not* tell her the address or my name."

Fresh from high school, I had only girlfriends. Adam would wait in the car.

Apprehensive, bemused, I walked along Riverside Drive, pounding my feet heavily (you never can tell when strain will bring on the blessed curse). I tried to reproduce the burred roll of her speech as I marched.

I can't altogether blame Adam. He hadn't a clue as to how I felt about an abortion since *I* didn't know. How could he guess that in the womanly part of me I was an ebullient ignoramus? I sounded competent and acted it too. I had developed the bossy air of an older sister. I talked with bookish authority on every character in Shakespeare. I was considered clever. I had earned a word of praise from my celebrated father-in-law when I said I thought rabbis were mistaken to grant a man divorce if a wife's cooking lacked salt; that it was simple to add it, almost impossible to take it away.

The night before the abortion Adam was more disturbed than I. He walked the floor, smoked one cigarette after another and seemed to hold himself rigid against tears. He looked so despairing I felt I had to comfort him. "Don't worry, a doctor is doing it. How bad can it be? Other women have had it done before me." He held me to him, rubbed his unshaven cheek against mine, then kissed me on the forehead. "You're a good girl," he said. I had my A.

The room smelled of someone else's blood; bloodstains on the doctor's white skirt; a bloodstain on the gauze around her hair as if her woman's hand had rested at her forehead in a sudden access of pity. But no, under her starched straight skirt, the slope of her loins was tight; the stiff coat stood away from her breasts as if they were hard wax. My arms manacled to a table no wider than a coffin, legs in leather straps against steel, fire hissing under the sterilizer, fear set me shivering like a wet insect.

"Behave yourself. Hold on to these hard." She put two steel rings into my trapped hands.

"Other women do it," I said to myself. "Lots of women." I had a crazy hope that Adam would rush in and save us.

She was at my trussed feet. I shut my eyes. Her skirt rustled. The dog was panting in the room and I wanted it to get out but I didn't dare ask. Paper rustled. Thin steel sounds came from her movements at the sterilizer. Steel entered me, parting me, forcing me open.

"I'm injecting a local," she said, "this will hurt."

Hurt? What do you know about my pain: I am so me in it. It was stunning. My breath funneled inward and was sealed off by pain the way boiling wax seals off air in a jar; then it roared out.

What had I ever known of pain? This was the real thing. Boiling up in my flesh. Torture. Glowing embers. Bombardment of the senses. Burning. Tearing. Knives. Crushers. Extractors. Piecemeal.

"Stop. Stop."

"It's too late. Lie still, dammit."

I twisted. I tried to tear myself out of the straps. Screams were erupting out of my mouth, my head, my ears, "Mama, Mama."

"Shut your trap, goddam it. We have to knock the brat out; she's off her head."

An enormous witch ran in and clapped an ether cone over my face.

"The goddam bitch will have the police on us . . ."

The surgical instruments clanged. I receded from my screams.

I came to consciousness on a cot. By a ghost of light, shed through a transom, I knew it was in a narrow hallway. The stench of vomit and blood was me. Moans were coming from the room beyond, from a braver woman than I. I was too weak

124

to put my hands over my ears. From behind me came kitchen sounds. Running water. An eggbeater. Pain I could bear burned at me. I stirred.

The witch heard me. She brought a glass of strong hot tea in a holder like the ones we had at home. She loomed over me, immense, gray-robed; a bundle of keys at her waist, a contorted Christ on a coarse chain on her chest.

"Awake, huh? Thought you never would. Got to get you the hell out of here, they'll think you dead, whoever's waiting. What a coward."

I apologized. Weak tears. It was true, what this rough hag was telling me about myself: I was a coward.

"Coward," she repeated. Keys and cross clanked against the tray. "Anybody, even *Bachfisch* is allowed to make the fucken, make the fucken there; here they make the screaming, the crying."

The dog breathed in the odor of my blood. At her command, he followed her out. She wore heavy laced shoes, like a man I had seen arrested outside a ladies' room where he was masquerading as a nun.

On Riverside Drive Adam was asleep on the front seat of the car. I stared at my husband, the unconscious stranger, ashen as death. Wishing he were dead, wishing I was. Sorry and angry at him for what had been done to me; at myself for what I had let be done to myself.

Cramps were scorching tracks between my pelvis and my breasts. My cauterized womb felt as if crammed with broken eggshells. I would never be able to expunge the stink of iodine, vomit and blood or the brutal, surreptitious atmosphere. "Filth. Filth!" (My mother had spoken truly.)

I leaned against the car window and could not muster the will to tap on it; to connect myself again with this man, slumped forward, knees raised like a monstrous embryo. When he became aware of me, he leaped up. Relief brought life back to his face. He too had faded.

Gentlemanly, he opened the door. Gallantly, he assisted me by the elbow. He said nothing. (What was there to say?) He drove carefully, avoiding bumps, as if I were pregnant. I held myself from him as separate as possible, half nauseated, half crazy with horror.

He helped me into our bed. "A glass of tea?" I could not speak, my tongue felt leathery. When he put a spot of milk into the tea I could scarcely contain my gorge. When he held it toward me I avoided touching his fingers. My appetites had gone, with my strength, into a bucket. I felt like a charred log that would crumble and collapse into cinders and ashes at a touch. I felt vulnerable as a peeled egg. I felt there was a wild she-animal caged inside my skin. I had not known she lived in me, this creature capable of shrieking hysterically, of hurling a glass of tea across a room.

He cleaned up the mess without a word. I drowsed and slithered into a nightmare that went back to girlhood when I used to be sent out into the dark to find Ezra. Shrewd little underdog, he sensed my fears and revenged himself on my bossiness by hiding and not answering when I called. I was shouting his name again across a leaden pond that answered with eerie echoes. Dingy grasses strangled the edge and vile-smelling mist smoked off the surface, blanking out the tops of the snake-rooted trees. Ezra's face gleamed from under the water. It looked like the decapitated head of a marble statue. "Oh God, I didn't mean it," I cried and plunged into the icy cold.

I gasped awake and went into the bathroom. Adam seemed not to notice when I came out dabbing at my swollen eyes. Looking through me, he made me and my suffering feel insubstantial. I had never felt so frighteningly alone. I wished I could climb into my mother's lap and be rocked and sung to. But I knew I had violated something deep in her and I didn't dare talk to her. Jessica might have sneered, or mocked me. I would have been too humiliated to air the matter with a school chum. This was no schoolgirl matter. It was an animal matter and animals have no words. That may be why Adam and I could exchange none; because I felt like a sick cow and he looked like a beaten dog. Maybe the words we needed were the ones we'd left in the old country where they had been formed along with our milk teeth. Maybe we'd lost them in translation. Whatever pity we felt for each other, it seemed that *Herz, harts, coeur, serce* did not add up to a whole heart that could speak out in English. Like mourning figures on an urn we remained at a fixed distance from each other, silent, not able to touch.

*   *   *

Re-reading what I've just written it occurs to me that it is too *logical* to be altogether true. Even engulfing tragedies are sparked by the chaotic, ironic and grotesque. I've left out something for which I could not, at that time, invent reasons. But now that I have less confidence in the margin of free will allowed us by both biology and history, a memory insinuates itself. My first impulse is to let it sink back into the slime as unsuitable. But then, if I'm looking for myself, maybe that's just where I'm hiding. Anyway, one of the luxuries of old age is honesty past shame, past fear, and also past hope.

*   *   *

So there we were, Adam and I, with my physiology and his humiliation and only one bed. Late that night Adam crawled into it. I had my face to the wall, but I was still swallowing tears. Now and again a hiccup would bring up a taste like burned eggs in a rusty skillet. He lay down, as far from me as the bed allowed, and let a long-held-back sigh ease out of him. As we lay there the air slowly began to thicken. A kind of lethargy was easing my tensed muscles. I sighed too, turned on my back and stretched out. But exhausted as I was, I did not relax and drift off to sleep. Neither did he. I could hear his breathing not slowing into sleep. It was accelerating, getting uneven, heavy, a muffled catch in the outbreath like a whimper. His body was tensing. Nervous energy, almost palpable, was piling up between us. I too was breathing more rapidly. Suddenly we both groaned and rolled toward each other. We were coiled in each other's arms, chest to chest, legs interlaced, eyelashes touching, holding so close we could hear each other's pulses slamming.

No, it was not tenderness and sympathy at last, not shared grief or recrimination. It was no feeling I would have imagined appropriate or possible. It was lust. Mind-eclipsing, sorrow-obliterating, death-defying lust. He groaned with it. We moaned. We were wrapped in sensual flames more ferocious than anything we had yet felt. It was nothing personal. It had nothing to do with us, poor rational sufferers. It gripped us, shook us and governed us. Our bodies understood what our right minds would have rejected. At the moment it hardly mattered that a breach had been made between us that we would not cross in a lifetime. Our lips met.

Since then I have heard about people — strangers to each other — trapped in a fire, having been found coupled in the act of procreation; that in times of famine, as the death rate rises, so does the birth rate. If a primate is robbed of its nursling, it at once goes into estrus so as to conceive again, out of its normal rutting season. I could go on. Cut a flowering plant before it seeds and it goes on making flowers until it has spent itself. Reproduction is the species' desire and necessity; the species cares nothing for the individual's right to self-determination. Shakespeare may say, "Ripeness is all"; an overriding power says, "Reproduction is all." I say, "If you are lucky, you get grandchildren out of nature's scam."

*　　*　　*

My first pregnancy finished my confidence in nature's alliance with me. How could it have happened to me without my willing it? How could I have torn it from me without my knowing I didn't want to give it up? How could I be . . .? But, poor monkey, I was promptly pregnant again.

I concealed it, even from myself, until one morning I was overcome with queasiness. Adam could not help hearing me retching. When I came out of the bathroom he was greener than I, breathing heavily, mouth open as if he had been punched in the stomach. His gaze fixed on my bosom, where the blouse gaped at the buttons. He raised one eyebrow, narrowed the other and his lips formed the question, "How long?"

"I'm not sure. I've had two lightish periods." I faltered.

Adam said nothing at first shock. There were glances. His tart courtesy was a little tarter, his aristocratic demeanor more strained. The narrow bones of his face appeared more prominent. One eyelid drooped at an angle like a shutter on a loosened hinge. He ate little, in small reluctant bites. He moved around me without touching me, as if I were contaminated. He wanted me to understand him without his saying anything. One night, lying awake next to him, I was overwhelmed with pity for this frightened boy-husband and took him in my arms. We both wept. But I did not help him ask me.

Then, as they used to say so concisely before the scatological mode coarsened distinctions, "his bowels turned to water."

I made myself dumb and blind to his body signals.

He read aloud items from the newspapers. INFLATION SPIRALS. SOCIALISTS MOBBED. WOBBLIES BEATEN. PRICE OF EGGS SOARS TO 62 CENTS. WOMAN AND FOUR CHILDREN

FOUND DEAD OF STARVATION. RETURNING SOLDIERS SWELL
RANKS OF JOBLESS.

Fear forced him into the open.

"A child! What for? The army?"

"This war will end war," I said. (It had no number as yet.)

"Then it will be the only war in history to bring peace," he answered.

But it's hard to look supercilious dashing into the bathroom. When he came out I said, "Our son will refuse to go to the army."

"Much thanks. Police pack him off to Siberia. The mother is left to fend for the children and herself. I know how that is." He threw up his unemployed hands. "The world doesn't need one more *maudit Juif* for an Easter pogrom."

"America," I answered, "is not Russia or Poland. We don't have pogroms."

"In America the Ku Klux Klan will honor Jews with fiery crosses. American war veterans will lie down like lambs beside Bolsheviks, Pacifists, Socialists, Huns, Negroes and Jews. Peace on Earth? Don't you know any history?"

He sank into a chair.

"History does not have to copy history. I am not going to have another abortion." There! I'd said it. I sat down, folded my hands in my lap, waited for lightning to strike the henhouse.

He slammed both palms down flat on the table, then lifted himself slowly, his hands whitening under his weight. At that moment I was as frightened as a rebellious schoolchild facing the principal. I don't know what mulish defiance showed on my face, but he compressed his lips, thrust his palms out in a gesture that meant I wash my hands of this. "It's on your head," he said and strode from the room.

From the hall he said, "I have an interview in Providence. I won't be back—I wanted to run after him and scream "Don't abandon me!—until tomorrow night," he added.

I waited until the door shut before I let myself cry.

What to do? If I did not have an abortion my husband would leave me, or if he stayed, hate me. If I had another abortion why not another after that and another after that until I went crazy or died? Why wouldn't I get pregnant again and again as long as we were married and bedded together? Our inadequate birth control methods would go on being defeated by adamant nature. Like any weed I was packed with seeds that would insist on germinating, and growing full cycle. My husband would insist on uprooting each in turn.

My dilemma seemed to me unique and unsharable. I felt bitter toward my parents who had pushed me, denied my fears, given me no hint of what lay in store, who, in fact, kept the truth from me. There was no one to whom I could confess my shame and injured pride. My husband bewildered me. When he fell into bed after a day of futile job-hunting he lay on his back, tensed, arms raised above his head. If I moved my hand to slide it into his, he no longer closed it over mine. He gave me no opening into which to drop my hopeful remarks. When I offered them anyway I felt like a dog who drops a stick before a master in no mood to play. He slept like a feverish child, throwing the covers off, sighing. I would watch him, his pulses fluttering, his eyelashes quivering in fitful sleep.

Brushing my hair in front of the mirror, the sight of tears rolling down my cheeks surprised me. Was this musty fatigued sensation unhappiness? How could I, who had barely started out, be unhappy? My beautiful life had to be waiting around the corner.

I had been hoodwinked, that was clear now. I had been an obedient daughter, dutiful and bookish. I had acquired and expended the housewifely virtues I had been assured were my ticket to domestic bliss, though admittedly my ironing left something to be desired. I was willing to be a dedicated mother. I had done my best to be a cheerful helpmeet, as well as an obliging wife. I had overcome my reluctance to math enough

131

to go to the library and read up on Babbage and Pascal and Byron's daughter and the computerized jacquard loom, so I could be a companion, too. And though I could not understand what delighted my husband in machines that would carry out calculations without human intervention, I willingly typed his job summaries and applications. And I smiled a lot.

He couldn't find employment. Returning veterans had preference, and his specialized technical training was as yet unappreciated. There was nothing I could do for him. Tears of pity would rim my eyelashes when I saw how washed-out he looked. In sleep he would sigh and crawl into the curve of my body like a miserable child. Toward dawn he would stir, then move away.

I prayed for a foetal accident. All over the world influenza was flying swiftly, swiftly, death summoning the unwilling. Why did it spare me? Another lunar month ticked off bloodless on the calendar and I and it still lived.

So knowing myself a hopeless coward in the face of pain, disordered by my possessiveness for the life expanding in me, torn between anxiety and a sense of helplessness, and for various other reasons, obvious but not easily stated, I decided on suicide. An Aquarian, I decided on death by water.

It is hard to imagine that in one year of marriage — a socially approved marriage at that — a girl, barely nineteen, could seriously be brought to suicide, not in a state of adolescent imaginings, but in hard despair. The ambiance of diffused hopeful feelings, of generous youthful eagerness that had surrounded me had been frozen, each expectation chilled in the atmosphere of reality: the way warm mist forms ice crystals — at each upward soar, again chilled, frozen layer on layer, till the weight becomes insupportable and they crash as hailstones.

*

Late one icy evening I dressed myself for a watery grave. Between the idea and the acting of even a dreadful thing, there is so much physical activity to get through. Adventitious materials constantly intersect the main action. Little decisions break the tragic ascent. Like: what to wear? My taupe coat, broadcloth, lamb-lined, round nutria collar was too good for drowning, but it was a long walk to the pond and bitterly cold. If I went without a coat I would attract attention. Then, too, I needed pockets for stones to weigh me down, so that I couldn't struggle to the surface, reflexively, as I heard suicides sometimes do. I wanted to arrange to float, if it came to that, unbloated face up like Millais' Ophelia surrounded by flowers and reeds.

My modish plaid skirt, a fashionable six inches above my ankles; my petticoat, thick with ruffles that would soak up water and weigh me down; chemise, but no corset. A brassiere? Indecent to go out without one. No need for the peach satin blouse, a gym middy would do. Lisle stockings. I laced my shoes as loosely as possible to allow room for small stones. A hat? No. A hat would be telltale on the surface. If my braids flowed open, so much the more Ophelia.

At the last moment I was detained by the inexorable logic of physical details. I had to go to the bathroom. Pregnant women pass water more frequently. Tea kettle off. Water water everywhere.

At five-thirty-one I set out for the boat pond.

Door locked. Had trouble with the key. To take the key or put it into the mailbox? No fantastic letter of salvation. A circular advertising a course for secretaries to prepare for the time when employment would pick up. An announcement of a play to be performed by the high-school French Club. Why not leave the door unlocked so he'd know the bird had flown? He'd know soon enough. Would he be grieved or relieved? No need to devise drama. Leave a note? (It's amazing, this need to be accounted for up to the end.) Yet how was I to explain the

133

intricately obvious? I had already collected more baffling minutiae about my husband than I could put together. Anyway there was no point in trying to answer questions that had not been asked. It was not Adam's way to ask questions that led to ambiguous answers. He liked things to be exact.

I had chosen the hour and place with care. Mothers and nursemaids had already prammed or walked their children home to fathers returning from work. Hot-dog peddlers, sweet-potato vendors, balloon men, park guards, all had gone home — how blessed the simplest hovel — to children and paternal doings.

Niobe, here I come.

I clumped down the empty path, unsteady in my loose boots, my heart clumping along with each step, yet also suspended like a huge icicle over the pond ahead; my poor heart, so alone out there in the frightful solitude, catching reflections from a cluster of flickering lights at what I took to be the water's edge.

It was not quite the edge. Four lanterns hung from wooden barriers that had been placed around a main spurting water. Pickaxes and shovels lay on the ground. I stood in the pool of light, considering which way to approach the pond.

The men saw me some time before I became aware of them, four burly ditchmen around a truck almost invisible in the dark. If they had been speaking, I had not heard them in my absorbed agitation. They were drinking beer in preparation for a nasty job on the frozen pipe. The man closest to me leaned on his shovel and sucked air through his teeth. I was sorry for my uncovered bright hair. With my bulky coat and clumsy boots I might have passed for ugly, or too old to notice. The silence gathered around my figure like a chain. Then slowly conversation clunked out of it. Tough Irishmen. Rough Italians.

"Hey, look wha's here."

"Yeh, looka wha's here."

"What you know!"

"It's a pussy cat."

"Izza Klitty cat . . . pretty klitty cat."

"Wha's a pussy lookin' fer in the turrible cold?"

"Turrible cold. Fer a little pussy cat."

"Lookin' fer what? Maybe we got it."

"Yeh. Maybe we got it. I got it."

"Hey pussy cat. Here pussy. Here pussy. Here pretty pussy."

"Come here pretty pussy. We got cream."

"Cream yeh."

One of the hip-booted figures moved a step forward toward the ditch that separated us. There was a stirring among the others. One man slid off the front of the truck. Boot buckles grated on his way to the ground. All four men were on their feet, gathering themselves together toward me.

I could almost feel myself in the mud, mud sliding under me, me under their booted length, mud in my hair, over my face and if I struggled too much, finally mud stopping my mouth. There was the pond waiting; but before I could get to it, there was the filthy ditch.

I turned and ran. I ran for my life.

On the avenue newsboys hawked; men in bowler hats walked rapidly, darting between horse carts and Model T Fords; a young couple, arm in arm, studied a movie poster: *Daddy-Long-Legs;* a world of happy solutions. I shook my fist at the stars and swore, "This child will be born."

Should I have stayed? Should I have stayed and accepted the death suggested for me? Was it stubborn of me to resist death in earth because I had presumed death by water? Would I have run had I known what was to come of us, Absalom my son? For good or ill, I ran home. I was on my way to motherhood, not

135

once, not twice, but four times. Absalom, Ariel, Aaron, and Benjamin.

*   *   *

When I was a child God spoke to me through my father. But the grandly abstract theories he advanced about Genesis were made too painfully concrete when I couldn't get my first child born and I sided, then and there, with my mother. As far as women are concerned Creation is a botch.

My father adjusted the knifecrease of his impeccable striped trousers and settled himself more firmly on his . . . his quodlibet. (The most obscure word I could find for an abstruse argument.) "Considered profanely, Eve formed out of Adam's rib, in chapter two, clearly contradicts the pre-existence of woman in chapter one."

The rabbi tugged his silken gabardine firmly fore and aft, and blue eyes ahoy, forefinger testing heaven's clemency, ran into the high metaphysical wind. "According to the Hebrew text of *our* year 3860 . . ."

My father rocked forward before either the rabbi or Uncle Solomon could launch a rebuttal. "In chapter one Creation is accomplished. '*Male and female* created He them, in His own image, and blessed them and said be fruitful and *multiply*.' Yet in chapter two it is written, 'There was no man.' Then Adam is formed out of dust and Eve out of his rib. Clearly, gentlemen, no amount of exegesis can make sequiturs of these. There are two versions and version one is superior."

The rabbi shut his eyes negatively and waggled his clerical forefinger. "Are you postulating that God swept out one Creation like a housewife sweeping out *chometz* for Passover, then swept in a second?"

"No, Rabbi. I'm asking, since procreation is preconceived in

136

chapter one, what purpose was served in placing the moral burden on woman?"

My mother, setting down a tea tray, sang out, "Some gentleman, God! Putting the burden on women."

(My mother's irreverence was regarded as a hereditary taint on her father's agnostic side. Somewhere along her hard way — as her family's Cinderella, as a refugee, as an immigrant — she had shelved the imagination of significance. To her it was more shrewdly comic than tragic that, to get on with living, even a puppy taken from the litter, whimpering and shivering, must let itself be beguiled into accepting a hot-water bottle toweled with a wind-up clock for nearness of flesh.)

In the kitchen my mother mimicked: "Clearly, gentlemen, version one is no story. The whole week He's lecturing, Be fruitful and multiply, and nobody shows up. On the sixth day He makes *Himself:* 'Male and female in his own image.' Where can a story like that go except back to Monday? Get a plate, Arnie, I forgot to bring in the cookies. In the second chapter — what he did to women! But it has characters, things happen, there's a crime, there's a punishment. People got ashamed of their nakedness, and high time! Grownups running around naked like two-year-olds! Ach, poor Eve, pregnant and dispossessed. The first pregnant refugee. How could a father let her wander around in the desert? What's to eat in a desert — lizards? The Big Landlord had such fancy apartments He couldn't take in a child? Elephants, yes, whales, horses, yes, but children, no."

"God warned her," said I, Miss Goody Two-Shoes.

"So what child is perfect? *She* bit the apple and right away every creature in the Garden knew how to make babies."

"How did you make me?"

"I found you in a cabbage patch."

"Last time you said a stork brought me."

"You'll grow up, you have time to learn. So, whose idea was babies if not God's? He didn't have dust enough to make people? He got bored, He put the job on women. It shows you, Arnie, how careful a girl must be."

"Of what?"

"Don't interrupt me, listen. No matter what a man tries to talk you into, he'll blame you after if you give in."

"Give in what?"

She glared down her nose and went on. "Men will wag a finger of blame. '*She* made me do it!' That Adam, what a sissy. Your father would never have tattled. And curses! God should not have lost His temper. 'In sorrow shalt thou bring forth children.' I fooled Him. Cramps, swollen legs, pain. But sorrow? No." She gives me a rare hug. "That snake got his. That mischief-maker had to crawl around on his belly and eat dust. Hey I just thought of something funny." She laughed so hard cookies slid to the floor from the plate she was holding. She picked them up, her concession to hygiene a dusting-off gesture. "The snake was the first bachelor. God does not like bachelors, especially smart alecks who try to get between couples."

"What about lady bachelors?" I asked, thinking ahead.

"Don't worry, peanut, you'll fatten up. Someone will take you. There are no Jewish nunneries. You don't want to be an old maid, eat. Here, take this plate into the gentlemen. By God, if women had written stories."

In a nice example of life imitating art, my mother voiced the sentiments of Chaucer's Wife of Bath.

> *By God, if wommen hadde writen stories*
> *As clerkes han withinne hir oratories,*
> *They wolde han writen of men moore wikkednesse*
> *Than al the mark of Adam may redresse.*

Perhaps version one can be criticized for preoccupation with form and absence of feeling. But in matter of literary fact, it is the very model of a story that goes from beginning to end.

Linear. Sequential. Self-satisfied. The way God intended stories to be. "In the beginning" . . . day by numbered day down to "God saw everything that He had made and behold it was very good." What a moment for the Creator! Why indeed did He begin again? Could the critics have shared my mother's view, that it was a round-and-round go-nowhere tale, like my Aunt Giselle's campfire story? But, I should get my first child born.

*   *   *

My calendar said I was due. My belly was stretched to bursting. But labor did not commence. When I think that an elephant requires twenty-two months from fertilized egg to term! And where, outside obstetrical journals, has this martyrdom been sung? Volumes have been dedicated to love. Idylls to courtship. Epithalamia to marriage. But nothing to those weeks when you are a tangled circuitry of wires with false rumors and scrambled messages shooting to belly and brain — a pain here, a fear there. Those weeks when the child presses against the sciatic nerve or weighs on the blood vessels in your legs and they throb and swell and you wake and hobble around the cold floor to restore circulation or uncurl your cramped toes. Those weeks nightmares ride you breathless and leave you sweating and unable to stir because you are hiding from yourself the enlarging statistical possibility that you, who deserve a perfect genius, may by mere chance be bearing a mute, a mongoloid, or already carrying the dead. Or, insult of insults, carrying nothing. False pregnancy. Pseudocyesis. If it could happen to Mary Tudor why not to a commoner like me? If it could happen to a domestic cat or a dog, why not to me?

I retrieved every horror story I had read or breathed in with the gossip-polluted prurient air. What a relief when at last pain was followed by similar pain. I switched on the light, watched the clock and, though the contractions were still forty minutes apart, I called the doctor.

"Labor," she said. (Yes, *she* — a Russian refugee.) "Good, I'll meet you at the hospital."

But the pains stopped and I was sent home.

"False labor. Such things happen," my doctor said.

Days later the pains began again. Back to the hospital. Again the contractions faltered and stopped. No one was cheery and bright-faced about it the second time. The labor-room nurse did not say, "Well, sometimes that happens."

On the fourth day of on-off labor my waters broke. My doctor called for help from the specialist who owned the maternity hospital, Dr. Starobin. By that time I was dazed with fatigue and medication and fantasized stripping off the coarse hospital gown, getting dressed and escaping from the whole failed venture.

I wanted everyone to leave me alone, especially my husband. I felt ugly, smelly, itchy and freakish. The drama I had been imagining was petering out, a fiasco. The son I was going to put into my husband's arms, the male child who would carry on the great family name, appease my in-laws and my husband, was refusing to be born. Added days in the hospital, and now added expense of another doctor were further humiliation.

Adam had paced the waiting room, had drowsed downcast and embarrassed on the leather sofa, had given up on the third day and gone home to shave and change, had come back on the fourth. He was clean, freshly laundered, polite and repelled. When he kissed me on the forehead, I remembered seeing my father kiss my pregnant mother on the forehead, and thinking of a blue butterfly against a stack of laundry. No, Adam was no comfort to me. In fact, the shell of propriety separating him from my gross state made me feel like apologizing to him for not accomplishing the birth more discreetly, quickly and neatly. As any bona fide woman would have.

When I said, "Why don't you go to the employment agency? Maybe the baby will bring us luck and you'll find a job," he went off, relieved.

140

I wouldn't have minded holding on to my mother's hard hand but my parents had been urged to leave the waiting room. "You never can tell how long the first one takes. You will be called as soon as it is born," a kind nurse assured them.

Though I still hoped to live, I was prepared to die. I was also bored. I took a book out of my dressing case and as if ominous things were not happening to me, thrust myself into *The Sense of Beauty: Being the Outline of Esthetic Theory.* I was determined to shut out my consciousness of the stillness within me as well as the regular screams accelerating properly in the next labor room.

An odor of ether and a dry nasal sniff preceded the man who filled the doorway like a gentle elephant. Double stems of a stethoscope dangled from one pocket of his surgical coat, a book weighed down the other. Having no interest in describing my broken waters I once again focused on my page.

He backed out into the corridor, glanced at my name card on the door, came in again, scraped the surgical cap wearily off his large head, his hair springing out bushy in all directions. "Feeling well enough to read, Mrs. Arkady?"

I nodded, always polite, smiled minimally, and looked down again.

"Good girl. What is it?"

"Santayana."

"Santayana, eh. *The Life of Reason?*"

I giggled. "Too late. Though I don't exactly qualify for *The Sense of Beauty.*"

He chuckled and put out his hand. "Dr. Jeremy Starobin. I'm the stork, little girl," he said.

"Mr., or plain Storky?"

"Storky will do nicely."

He ambled to the chair beside my bed. Gave me ample time to take him in. A massive homely man, fleshy yet powerful; round mujik head, eyes small, but in spite of discoloration from fatigue, bright as birds in the heavy burl of his face.

He took the stethoscope from his pocket and held it for me to look at, slow motion, like a good pediatrician approaching a frightened child.

"It will feel heavier than the normal type but it cannot harm either of you. The oversized receiver picks up and amplifies the heartbeat even when the baby presents breech or lies transversely as in cross birth. Which is what is slowing things up for us." He bent over me, smiled a paternal, heartening smile, rubbed the metal on the palm of his big hand to unchill it before moving it over the sore taut mound of my belly, and listened without withdrawing his straight attentive gaze from mine. Listened. Sniff. Sniff.

"Dead?" I finally mouthed without breath.

He sat back heavily.

"No, dear. Tired, but the heart is beating." He did not drop his eyes. "You are alone?"

"So you see."

"We need your husband's permission for surgery . . . in case . . ."

"Why? I'm in my right mind."

"So I see. But you *are* legally underage." He cradled my cold hands in his.

My father would not have approved of those hands. They were large and workmanlike — very unaristocratic. The wrists were heavy and wide-boned, fingers muscular and spatulate like big clamps, nails pared close and straight across, the skin crinkled and bleached from scrubbing.

"We'll deliver you before long," he said.

I nodded without hope.

He picked up the phone. "Delivery . . . We'll take Mrs. Arkady in when you've scrubbed up again."

From the neighboring room scream alternated with groan,

but exultant and determined. Another woman doing her part well while I was letting everyone down.

"You are very busy here, aren't you?" I asked politely.

"It's been a busy week. I need one minute's sleep," he said, closed his eyes, and on the instant plunged into deep rest. Exactly sixty seconds on the bedside clock, and he snapped alert.

"That was precise." I said.

"Part of my obstetrical equipment." He reached for my pulse. "Now lie back and try to relax. Everything is going to be all right."

I knew that couldn't be true. Weak pains straggled through me, but I could scarcely moan. I had nothing left with which to meet the sluggish contractions. Cold sweat ran down my breasts and belly.

His broad fingers probed my pulse and held. Steadied by his calm, by the stethoscope resting on my belly and connected to his ear, I swayed into sleep as if I were riding on an elephant.

Suddenly he dropped my wrist, scooped me up, blanket and hospital gown flapping, and, holding me close to him, loped down the corridor with unruffled speed, calling, "Delaney . . . O'Rourke . . . Emergency . . . Emergency . . ."

Bells rang, metal clattered, nurses surrounded me. They fastened their eyes upon me, the eyes of death. "Casey," he said, "ether." An ether cone fumed down on my face. "Count one, two — " I tried to resist. I wanted to be there when it happened. A woman's whisper twanged, "Doctor, I don't hear the heart." Bats with muffled faces screamed my fears. "Count . . . three, four."

Tumescence. Merciful heavens nothing but tumescence? A woman runs a terrible risk. Remember Mary Tudor. After her pleading for copulation, after her swelling and her broken waters, after her agony in public places, the screaming and the crying, only the dry rumor of midwives verifying, "No son,

143

woman and queen, no son." O Hail all Marys. Mother I need a friend, be near me now and forfend . . . five.

What's the use of pleading, let me be there, let me be aware, anything better than nothing . . .

"She's asleep, doctor . . ."

She sleeps, my lady sleeps.

Retrieve . . . retrieve . . . mama papa wanna gimme luv-luv lullay away baby spit-up drooly spittle-specked soft stool powdered bottoms . . . Linger awhile heaven-hungry to the stars lovely asunder luminous for spacious skies . . . far away from dreams of thee . . . No no not Hannah thee. Flutter from me erotica . . . lepidoptera cecropia great spangled fritillary . . . o glide in me unfathomably . . . slide out of me a fish . . . pubic. Cry covert menstruant. Pry secrets from rock. Scratched graffiti. Earth words geologic. Wicked consonants unvoweled. K-ss. Lodes of s-x. Buttressed. Buttocked twixt schists of bedrock. Trap rock. Crushed thick gravel speech. F-ck. Why cannot we like cocks and lyons jocund . . .

"Open your eyes, my love. It's a boy."

NoNoNo. Flying away on a bear rug, riding on a pony, holding on tight to my cousin Jessica as we are sleigh-drawn by my uncle Joshua who turns to approve us through snow-fringed lashes. My father swimming with me past eel grass and minnows, out into air my mother and aunt, screaming as I gag, fall into silence. Plunging through time on a pogo stick carved by my woodsman grandfather.

"It's a boy."

In the long petrifaction cell by liquid cell blood fossilized bones calcified tears crystallized to stone these are pearls that were my eyes. Cold. Fool's gold in my mouth. Cooled volcanic dust, thou art, art dust . . .

Stone tears dragged me very deep down. Too deep to come up alone. How long I lay. NoNoNo never to come up.

Jeremy was masterful. He reached down for me. "You have

a son. You have a son. You have a son." Steady pressure for resuscitation. "Breathe in . . . out . . . in . . . out. You have a son. A son. A son . . ." Warm mouth at my stone ear. Warm tears on my numb face. "You have a son . . ." Redolence of ether. Sniff, sniff. "It's a boy. Listen to me, my child. It's a boy." Hand triumphant on my pulse. "That's right. Come on. That's my good child. Come on. Open your eyes. Open your eyes love . . . You have a son."

(Jeremy, my dear old friend and physician. You are no longer waiting with me for any miracle of birth.)

Again the nurses were bringing the newborn children to the mothers who waited, breasts tender with milk. Again the baby trolley trundled past my door without stopping.

I rang for the nurse. "Why don't I get to nurse my baby?"

"Dr. Starobin's orders. He wants you to rest."

"I'm rested," I said.

"The baby is not," she said. "He's in the special nursery; he has a touch of jaundice."

I let out a scream, and before I could cover my mouth, a second one.

"Would you listen to that?" She swept out of the room.

Tears were still oozing out of my swollen eyes when Jeremy came in on rounds later that night.

"What's this I hear about crying? After you've been so good."

I broke into sobs.

"Come, child, you are entitled to a few tears," he said soothingly. "But not so many. Think how lucky we've been. No damage to you or the boy, only a few forceps bruises.

"He's got jaundice." I hiccupped and wept harder.

"Nothing; he'll be pink as a new mouse in a few days."

"Never." I shook my head hopelessly.

145

"And why, madame doctor, this diagnosis?"

"He's going to be a mongolian idiot like Hannah's brother."

"Oh Lord." He sat down on the edge of the bed and rumpled my hair. "Who is Hannah and who is her brother?"

I drew the sheet over my face.

"Come out of there," he commanded.

Meekly I obeyed.

He moistened a washcloth with ice water from the pitcher. "Here now. Cool your eyes, so you can see to read. We're going for a ride on the elevator up to my library."

He rang for a wheelchair. Ten days in the hospital followed by a period of Ming-vase fragility at home were the usual terms of a ladylike *confinement,* as it was called.

The top floor of the building was high-ceilinged and chilly. We passed unoccupied rooms, mattresses turned back, shades drawn. "My private floor," he said. "I'm attached by bells and buzzers but we try to keep patients below."

He wheeled me through a large room, spacious but impersonally furnished — a hospital bed, chair and dresser. Books and several telephones were crowded on a white enamel bedside stand. In the adjoining library bookshelves rose from floor to ceiling; red and gold medical volumes covered one wall. From the others, names leaped out: Darwin, Dickens, Shakespeare, Schopenhauer, Goethe, Tennyson, Heine, Hazlitt, Disraeli, Zangwill. Books lay about on the broad desk, on the leather sofa, on the floor. A copy of Pepys' *Diary* lay facedown on the armchair.

"Lots of waiting in my work." He patted the book in his pocket. "I don't leave the hospital if a patient is in the final stages of labor, even if she isn't mine."

"Lucky for me, but don't you have an assistant?"

"Certainly. And I do try to get home to have dinner with my children, but on many nights I stay here. The hospital is my responsibility. We have a fine record, the best. Let's find *M* for mongolism." He lifted out a red tome."We'll check it out together, but first I'll telephone down for the exhibit."

He stood beside me, a tree-trunk of a man. "Special nursery." He laid a steadying hand on my shoulder while he spoke. "Maggie, bring the Arkady baby upstairs to my apartment. Of course I remember he has jaundice. Bring a nursing bottle."

I was soggy with tears and anxiety.

"Here we are: mongoloidism, mongolism, also Down's syndrome. 'Regardless of race, oriental characteristics . . . yellow skin, slant eyes.' Ah! Here we go: 'One. Distinct skin fold in the inner corner of eyes. Two. Broad nose. Three. Thick tongue.' — this one's important — 'Four. Single crease in palm. Five. Head lolls. Six. Shallow grooved brain . . .' We won't need to take the investigation that far."

The elevator stopped. The metal gate clanged. Footsteps echoed on the terrazzo floor. I broke out in a sweat. Dr. Starobin took the bundle in the blue blanket from the nurse and exposed the little face.

Absalom's skin was faintly yellow but he did not look in the least oriental. His head was a shapely oval like Adam's. His eyes were deepset like my father's. He had forceps marks and scratches on his forehead. A black-and-blue bruise distorted one eyebrow.

"Would you look at that nose, Mrs. Arkady — if you can find it. Would you call that a broad nose?

I let out a long quavering breath.

Jeremy prodded the cheek. A pink kitteny tongue flicked in and out, "Or a thick tongue?" Searching for a nipple and finding none, the round light eyes opened wide, the forehead wrinkled in outrage. He was adorably responsive. We all laughed.

"Whew. Better not keep him waiting for his grub," Maggie said. "He's got a terrible temper, that one."

"Look very closely. Do you find any skin fold in the inner corner of slant eyes?"

"No, I don't. I really don't."

"Now Maggie, try to flatten his fist so Mrs. Arkady can read his palm. Watch. She's having a hard time getting it open. See how he grabs her finger, grabs the blanket. That's it, my boy, grab. That's what we like to see, high-voltage energy plus greed. The real gifts. They come with health and intelligence. There."

The palm was triple-veined and moist as a rose leaf in the morning. "Now watch this, so you can rest assured Dr. Starobin's hospital does not starve its babies. Watch him. Three days old and he delivers his orders, *Give me my bottle, now.* Observe, mother, how lightly nurse is supporting his head. Do you see any loll in that neck? If you are satisfied, Mrs. Arkady, that this athlete is not a mongoloid, Maggie will take him back where he belongs."

Jeremy touched my cheek much as he had the baby's. "Smiling again. I didn't think you were the type for a postpartum depression."

He sat down on the arm of his chair. "When I began to specialize in obstetrics I couldn't tear myself away from the nursery window. So much is defined at birth! It went against my medical training to believe it. The baby nurses would say with complete assurance, 'She'll have trouble with that one, colicky and tantrumy.' Or, 'That's a bright lad she's taking home.' Each birth includes a year of postnatal care" (we both smiled) "and my records showed the nurses were most often correct. It's unfair how much is determined. As a physician and a socialist, I began with a very optimistic opinion of the power of environment. I've come to have more respect for the inherent."

"You mean nurture is unimportant?" I said defensively.

"Of course it's important. And since we're on the suject of nurture, Mrs. Arkady, I'm hungry. Shall I have a midnight supper brought up for us, or do you think you could get to sleep now?"

"I'm too excited to sleep."

"In that case, let's make you more comfortable." He fetched a pillow and blanket from his bedroom, set them on the sofa and put his arms out to me. A moment of surprise, then, a child who has been longing to be carried, I let him lift me. He carried me to the sofa, tucked the blanket around me, then relaxed in his black leather chair.

"Who was Hannah?" he asked.

Thus we began the conversation that continued for the better part of our lives.

*   *   *

Hannah and I were best friends, thick as thieves from a day in the fourth grade when the whistling wind of possible failure shivered my moral assumptions about my honor. While I was sweating to memorize the multiplication tables, Hannah was manipulating Avogadro's number. "If you take six point zero two times ten to the twenty-third power . . ." Tempted one day by the vision of her perfect subtrahends and minuends I let my too acute glance slip through the sightline she made of the angle of her elbow. She didn't stop me. Her door; my sin. (I had weighed my father's disapproval of an imperfect grade against God's disappointment in me. My father won handily. "Only eighty in arithmetic today, my daughter? And where, tell me, are the remaining twenty points?")

Poor Hannah! Born a girl. So long as she had been an only child her luminous intelligent gaze had been encouraged in the masculine realm. (Her uncle Solomon used to test her with Kabalistic conundrums. "Such a head wasted on a girl.")

Suddenly (Sarah surprised) a son was given; Hannah had a brother. There must have been momentary rejoicing in whatever ghetto of heaven was allowed the Jews that year. The sage had a grandson to carry forward the wisdom of the ages. Rich in Talmudic lore, Uncle Solomon (one of the regular disputants in my father's parlor) had a nephew to instruct. Hannah rushed me home to see the baby.

"He has a big head," I reported to my mother.

"Newborns look as if their heads are too big."

"He's yellow like a Chinee."

"Jaundice. In a few days the yellow goes away."

Not if it's Down's syndrome. The rest of the family turned yellow instead. Hannah, Uncle Solomon, along with its Mama and Papa, one by one, were wrapped in yellow silence and disappeared from congregational view.

I was in the seventh month with Absalom and though Adam continued to be melancholy and unemployed, and we were borrowing to live, my thoughts flowed smooth as water slipping through a hand in the wake of a canoe. Will it be a boy or a girl? Gorgeous or merely beautiful? A genius or merely talented?

A carriage was coming toward me, wheeled by a woman whose coat hung open. The buttons dangled. Her hair was stringy, unkempt, her skin oily and sallow.

"I'd never let myself go like that," I thought, "a baby is no excuse."

And then I saw it — a bull-calf dressed in a boy's suit; long trousers and jacket. His head lolled, his slant eyes rolled meaninglessly, he dribbled. A blubbery idle drone made a bass continuo. Almost abreast of me I saw it was Hannah, wheeling her brother who had grown into this . . . this . . . miserable calf, with a sidelong expression of placating and pleading. She passed me, wheeling with one hand and picking at her scalp with the other. She did not see me. Her eyes were downcast in the habitual avoidance of those who are constantly prodded by stares.

Fear grabbed me so that I almost wet myself. I waddled home. In the bathroom I stood over the bowl and vomited until

I heaved bile. Then I lay down, shaking, trying to salvage my wrecked confidence, my hand tender on my aching belly where the flesh was rising in sympathetic bubbles. I willed my mind not to dwell on Hannah, plucking her scalp, the sore bald spot shining around a bloody scab. I willed not to remember how her mother's weeping had become a whimpering; how they wrapped her in a tight blanket and took her to a "rest home for her nerves." Or how Uncle Solomon, a bewildered bachelor, pitted his earnings against the ignominy of his sister being abandoned to a "crazy house." Each in turn eaten up, sacrificed to the yellow calf, lost to their own possibilities, sucked into the vortex. The lone survivor would be wheeled after Hannah's coffin. (I hate myself for thinking of the old Jewish remark about killing a healthy chicken to make soup for a sick one.)

I became obsessed. I tried to pry out of everyone everything about abnormal birth and prenatal influences. Like a superstitious traveler who professes no religion but bows down in every church, I worshiped in museums and libraries, concentrated on portraits and models of the beautiful, the brilliant, the successful, the famous. I shut out dwarfs, avoided late Goyas and gargoyles; listened to Bach, not late Beethoven; memorized formal lyrics; contrived crafty questions about rumored taints, about an uncle's convulsions, my brother's palsied head. Were mad spinsters locked away in attics? I read Mendel, studied green peas, knocked on wood, threw salt over my shoulder, wished on stars, prayed myself to sleep and woke shuddering.

A terrible agonized pity for the imperiled life within me began to dart in and out of the days like blackening silver threads among gold ones in a tapestry. In superstitious dread I kept my terrors locked in me. (Adam had not, meanwhile, become a sympathetic expectant father.)

To everyone's dismay I cut my hair. I said it was too hard to comb now with my heavy belly to lift and that later I would not have time. But it was a secret bargain with the powers that be.

151

"You have one of mine already. Don't, parent gods, don't revenge yourself on this baby. Don't punish me for having been a docile wife then or a rebellious one now. Don't harm my baby."

It came to me that Bluebeard, Genghis Khan, Nero, the Whore of Babylon, Medea, were not fictions on whom one closed the book. No, all the murderous, gun-slinging, knife-wielding gangsters, torturers, bullies, fiends, all the wicked of the earth and their victims, all the bums, beggars, drunks, had been babies some girl had carried in her, day after day, hour after hour, through the dazed ninth month that goes on forever, because the cord is never wholly cut.

*　　*　　*

Once in Perugia:

It was 1949, after World War II (another example of addition that subtracts).

After a precipitous return from San Gimignano, where I had gone to see the picture of martyred St. Sebastian in the Mayor's tower, I was hot, dusty and tired from the bus ride and I sank into a seat at a sidewalk café, on the steep slope diagonally across from the clammy unbeautiful cathedral. It was late afternoon, perhaps a half hour before the dapper masculine day would begin and the tables were still unoccupied. It seemed to be the Healing Saints' Day. Hordes of pilgrims were coming out of the cathedral. Down the steep flight of steps figures seemed to be falling into a Bosch-like scene for the *Triumph of Death:* the lame, halt, blind, noseless, chinless, limbless, the withered. They dragged, hobbled, or were carried — genuflecting, away. Urged on by sextons, a wrung-out matron wheeled her skeletal mate down the incline, a bewildered mother shambled across, supporting her palsied child, each enclosed in the loneliness of those whom nature has humiliated. A bell tolled. One of the pair of bronze doors swung closed.

A dignitary appeared in the cavern of the doorway, his ca-

152

daverous face and burning eyes at odds with his ornate ecclesiastical vestments. Seen from below he looked like an ascetic saint ascending. He tilted back his head and drank air, wiping his gaunt face as if to wipe away the day. (Is this what the desert lions were for? Is this what it was all leading to?) His ringed hand shook as he mopped, then dropped limp to his side. This day was over at last. But not quite.

Something was crawling toward him from behind; a creature on hands and knees. As it reached him, it fumbled for his hand, grasped it and glued slobbering lips to it. His Venetian Elegance recoiled, recovered, made a sign of blessing and tried to pull his hand away. Kiss. Kiss. The sign of the cross once more. It was no use. His Eminence struggled to pull away, the monster held. Like most monsters, he was strong. A sexton and a priest ran forward, disengaged him and led the bobbling creature away. A dishevelled woman was running toward it, adjusting her black skirt. *"Deo Mio. Son andanta a lo latrina. Un momento solo. E mio, è mio."*

Call it what you will — the silver cord, the umbilical cord, momism — it does not have to be imagined. It does not exist through the transformations of artist or analyst. It is an implacable physical reality.

Absalom, Ariel, Aaron and Benjamin: they have revealed to me the mindless tenderness that persists through anger, despair, even twitching repulsion.

The maternal instinct, in fact, cannot be imagined. Colette says it is born complete, fully armed and bleeding. Sociologists, not only male chauvinists, agree the race's survival depends on woman's self-abnegating, tender dedication. Biologists have claimed it inheres in a pinch more or less of magnesium. Whatever its source, I was unprepared for maternity, for what I have come to think of as the tragedy of Motherhood.

I don't mean the drudgery, the 365 days a year — day-in, night-in — on duty. And frankly, divining my night's fate by observing excrement was always disgusting. My lips are sealed about sandbox society, crayoned walls, playing Monopoly and even waiting until they've been bathed, fed, bedded down before being free to go to the bathroom, close the door and decide among a bath, hysterics or reading a book. That's all part of wanting to do the best you can so they'll be well and happy.

What I was unprepared for, and never learned to bear, was the hate. I've read Freud, and Frazer, and Frankenstein, and it doesn't help. I thought *my* children would never feel the vast repulsion that compels each thing created to reject whatever created it. To me that was theory. I planned to be the perfect mother, unambiguously adoring and therefore adored. I would nurture their tiniest talent, cherish them as individuals, be a confidante and friend. How could they hate me when I planned for them to be safe and happy?

I was feeding Absalom his lunch; a bit of expensive lean beef, freshly scraped by me. He spit it out. Babies do that, but this was different. He didn't tongue or dribble, he spewed with fury. I'd say he snarled. It was a Saturday. Adam had offered to let me have a few hours off at naptime while he was working in the living room with an amusing man from his office. I had fed the men lunch and I wanted this child to finish his so I could say nitey-nite, and go out, anywhere, to the library, to see a Charlie Chaplin film, walk at my pace, out by myself.

I scooped the beef off the bib, put it on the spoon, saying, "Now, darling, eat your yummy beef." Again he spit it out. I pushed the food back, he spit it out, his eyes electric with rage. I pushed the food in, he spit it out. Maybe he just didn't want to eat, but it was also a contest. "Eat it," I commanded.

There was a sudden hush in the living room.

Absalom picked up his lovely Peter Rabbit tripartite plate

and hurled it. Meat, spinach, applesauce and china flew. Blobs of food spattered onto my clean skirt and blouse, my fresh stockings, shoes, the scrubbed floor, my hair, my cheek. "Waaah!" He had the nerve to bawl.

I glared at this cannibal baby who was swallowing me and spitting me up; his screaming mouth with food dribbling out of it, his fat neck and face sticky with food, his octopus arms flailing, his fat, carry-me feet kicking . . . and I lifted my slave hand and smacked him on his fat arm.

There was a sound like a receding wave. Then he let his breath out . . . "Waaaaah!" His cries filled the air.

Adam came into the kitchen. "I hit him," I said. "He's being bad." There were my finger marks on his baby flesh. Adam picked up his son, who buried his head in his father's collar and sobbed piteously. The man in the next room was standing by the window trying to look as if he had heard nothing. I couldn't imagine how I was going to walk through to put Absalom into his crib. I moved toward him to take him but father and son retreated, clinging to each other.

"I'll put him in for his nap after he quiets down," Adam said.

I began wiping up slop, determined not to break into sobs.

"Bad. Bad." Absalom whimpered. Father and son were regarding me, the omnipotent ferocious female of every man's helpless infancy, with the same hard stare of hate.

* * *

I took up the subject of hating mothers once with Jeremy, when I had had a bad day with my children. Arie, my flower, whose every gesture seemed to me a work of art, had put on an expression that had fangs when I intervened in a quarrel she had been having with Absalom. And Absalom, my adored Absalom, had looked at me as if I were the enemy of his universe, then picked up a Wedgwood bowl he knew I treasured and hurled it to smithereens.

"Did you hate your mother?" I asked Jeremy.

He snorted into the telephone. "Way back, when I was young, loving your mother was quite the fashion."

"It's a lost art," I said. "Hating mothers is mandatory now. Freud made it good for the children's health, and all hell's broken loose now it's out in the open."

"Jews have had bad luck with their gods. We didn't need Freud and his guilt. Enough already with Jesus. We are always convalescing from the guilty accident of being born, like bastards, into a world community that wishes we would drop dead. It would have been happier for us if Christians had adopted the Gnostic heresy . . ."

"Which I happen not to know about."

"No one is guilty. *Birth* is the expulsion from the garden of the womb. Birth is the origin of all sorrow and antagonisms."

*   *   *

We have waited for births, Jeremy and I, and—over the long years of our friendship — a death here and there, too. It often happened that our conversation would be interrupted by a signal from the labor-room floor.

Usually after a delivery, in his bloodstained whites, trailing ether (the odor always clung to him), vibrating with strain, he was exultant. "I never get over the miracle when everything, yes everything, goes well." At rare times he came back upstairs frenzied. "I never get over the outrage. That effort. That immense chunk of life. One trigger cell goes wrong and it's worse than wasted, much worse. One tick of the organic chronometer goes out of phase and the mechanism never synchronizes. In a world full of imperfection, why demand perfection of the embryo? It's monstrous!"

He was shouting from his dressing room into the library where I had been reading while waiting for him to come back upstairs. A nurse who had brought tea shook her head in sympathy with his distress. Obviously, it had been a bad day in the delivery room.

"Lovely fortune in your tea tonight, Mrs. Arkady." She peered at the leaves circling in my glass.

"My destiny looks sparse. Only four small leaves."

Jeremy came in slipping his stethoscope into the pocket of a fresh surgical coat, his hair bristling after his shower like a rain-drenched silver shrub. "If it's children you're talking about, I insist the four you have are a sufficiency, Ariadne, a great sufficiency."

"Nothing to fear, Jeremy. There are four leaves in my glass and you know how dreadfully precise oracles are."

"My Irish witches can foresee a heavenly future in tea, palm, by conversion to the true faith and, lately, in Tarot cards. Isn't that so, Casey?"

"You're making fun of me, Doctor. There is a sermon in everything." She fluffed out, starch-stiff, gum-shoes quick-stepping on terrazzo.

"Have you thought of serving Chinese fortune cookies, Storky?"

"Tell me what you want and I'll have one stuffed for you."

"I want it to read 'You are destined to be loved by a tall dark man of *substantial* means.' "

"You need a fortune cookie to tell you that?" He drew back from his remark at once. "Remind me to tell Adam about a project that might be coming up, having to do with research in numbering chromosomes."

"What's a chromosome more or less in the family?"

"Mongolism, it seems." He wrung his hands, dropped them heavily onto his knees and rocked himself; a mourner chanting Kaddish for what should not have been born.

*   *   *

Monstrous births. They hover on the horizon of my memory. A single word, an image, and they are drawn to me in a straight line as if they had my number.

A small incident can conjure up a shape that links itself to my circumstances. On that terrace in Perugia where I was sunk in quite other losses, the sight of a defective child activated a cloud of dormant guilts, like the swarm of moths I once saw flare into emergence when a log they chanced to be in was thrown on a fire. I was outraged then too, that instead of flying outward and away they hung on the heat beating their way toward the flames, ordained, by some idiotic genetic mischance, to contradict the law by which the species survives. "Why, Storky? Why?"

Only last night I wakened to the haunting image of Hannah wheeling her brother toward me. I got up from my chaise where I had fallen asleep. The landscape glowed pearly as if snow had fallen. Not a twig rustled, not an owl called. The light that had pierced my sleep was from a yellow moon cutting its way through an ice-clogged sky. The cry that had wakened me was mine.

I stood at the window fumbling with my memories. On the musky terrace a girl in bridal gown appeared and disappeared into a rank garden through which exiled ghosts drifted. A few notes of a song descended like petals. A receding figure — oh, my darling daughter, my Arie — blew a kiss. Can it have been to me? Did I hear "thank you, Mother" or "damn you"? A boy's voice, Benjamin's, mocked a radio: "Who knows what evil lurks in the hearts of men? The Shadow knows! Ha ha."

And Mistress of:

"My lord, she may be a punk; for many of them are neither maid, widow, nor wife."

— SHAKESPEARE

DANIEL AND DINAH were on the terrace, lying head to head, a pair of long-haired ginger cats dozing among the flotsam of a Sunday *Times.*

"Today's newspaper gives me the jitters," I said. "It reminds me of my youth. Phooey. What are young people going to do about jobs?"

Neither of them stirred. "You hear, twerps?"

My grandson lifted a sheet of the paper from his face and squinted up without opening his eyes. "Down with the work ethic. Up with welfare."

Dinah yawned. "My brother is always concerned with the big issues. What *did* people do in those days, without social security or much welfare?"

"Went on the bum, panhandled, squatted with more fortunate relatives, or starved. (I did not say what Adam and I did.)

"You mean squares like my old man panhandled?"

"Lay off about Dad, will you, Danny. Not too bad bumming up here in the dacha."

"You two talk about the work ethic as if it were mercifully on the way to extinction, like polio."

Heavy breathing answered me. "Crippling poliomyelitis!" I repeated.

"Wha' dat?" Dinah purred and opened one eye. "Granmaw, is it all right, I borrowed your white sweater again?"

"Yes dear. Who do you think will pay the national debt, Daddy Warbucks?"

"Who he? He who?" They said together on outbreaths.

"Whoo hee hee whoo. I got donkey grandchildren."

"Poor Granmaw. Feelin' quality, gotta put up with us white trash." Dinah rolled on her side and squeezed her face into a fatuous smile.

"What about making a living?"

"Now dat's serious talk. You mean nobody gonna take care on us? Not me pappy, not de goberment, not de granma?" Danny whimpered. Both of them sat up and begged.

"I could sell my fair white body," Dinah said.

"Are you kidding? You're over thirteen, my dear sister. You got freckles on your nose and I know for a fact you got 'em on your knees. Where is your capitalist know-how? You're too old for the street and no man is buying what he can pick up for free."

"Sad and true," Dinah said. "Reading Colette has raised my expectations: those jewels, those gowns, those lessons in deportment. Everybody had a rich lover then, I betcha even Grandma!"

"It is well known that parents don't have sex and grandmas know nothing about lovers," I said. They both laughed comfortably.

"The professor has had an insight." Danny pursed his lips, hemmed and hawed, then said solemnly, "We are going into business with you, Granmaw. Real creative . . . like . . . man

. . . I mean you make the best hot chocolate in the world. We'll open a stand on the Canadian border. We'll get skiers, honeymooners and draft dodgers. You can't beat that for a hot-chocolate crowd."

"Count me out." Dinah sighed. "I am retiring from adulthood. I want to stay at the dacha with Grandma and run a stand by the gate like when we were kids. God, I sound sunstruck — somebody change the subject."

"Right." Danny slipped his arm tenderly around Dinah's shoulder. "Thanks, Grandma, for putting me on to Biely's St. Petersburg."

"I hadn't suggested it as a model, Daniel. I do not approve of explosives."

"Take that up with Nixon, old lady, and I'll support you all the way."

A car horn beeped. "Tennis, anyone?"

Danny sprang to his feet. "There's Uncle Ben. Coming Dinah?"

"I'm going to sit here on the floor and mope."

"You mean wait for the Vincent creep to telephone. Sick."

Dinah gave a nervous little shiver. "I guess you've figured by now, Grandma, my present input is not resulting in output."

"Can I help? Maybe design a different flow chart?"

"I've tried sequential, indexed sequential, direct access . . ."

"The mechanism can do only so much, my yellow flicker. Maybe there is hopeless disagreement between the systems."

"Christ, why can't I get it together? I'm twenty-six years old. I don't know what I want to do. I don't want a career in the family computer business even though Uncle Benjamin is a doll to work for. No point going on with a Ph.D. in philosophy or literature. The colleges can't occupy the tenured staff they have. At my age, my mother had Danny and me, was already serious about being a painter. You had it all worked out, a husband, four children. It's not as if I'm trying to be different. I'd be delighted to conform."

*   *   *

What a luxury to be able to conform. I would have adored a red, white and blue childhood complete with maryjanes and dance classes — the childhood that I had watched from behind glass, skating by, skirts billowing, arms entwined. I had aspired to every American-made model: Girl Scout, cheerleader, class flirt, gymnast's mascot, prom queen — but I had remained class grind, a flustered greenhorn. The role of Mary Pickford, everyone's sweetheart? I never had a chance at it. Pola Negri? Vamp? Jazz baby? Whizzed past before I tried for them. When my opportunity came round I grasped it. I would be a perfect American mom.

Leaving Jeremy's hospital, my mother carried Absalom. She tugged at the baby bonnet, pulling it down to cover the forceps bruises still visible on his forehead.

"Let him be. He's handsome enough, Mom," I said.

"He has to make a good first impression on the world," she said, giving the bonnet another tweak.

I was clinging to Adam's arm, feeling weak and uneasy on my feet, despite the added days in bed Jeremy had decreed for me. He must have left word to be called because the receptionist said, "Doctor Starobin will see you before you go."

"A real doctor," my mother said. "A blessing your lady called him in." She cooed over Absalom.

"My lady is also a doctor."

"By you she can be a doctor" (under her breath), "midwife."

Jeremy stepped out of the elevator, aura of ether and his sniff sniff distress signals coming off him like steam pressure. He said, "Mrs. Arkady, telephone if you have any question. Any bleeding. Any discomfort. Try to rest. I don't want you to rush into activity. You and the baby have an appointment in four weeks. Come earlier if you feel any discomfort. Bring the baby if you see anything that troubles you." Sniff. Sniff. "Don't look anxious, I don't expect trouble. He's had jaundice and a hard birth. I want to keep an eye on him."

"I'll bring my wife and son, if I may, on a Saturday afternoon. I can't thank you enough for everything, Doctor Starobin. We are much more than financially indebted to you." Adam's slight bow included the baby. "We'll begin taking care of our bill as soon as we can."

"If you've paid your other doctor, forget about mine. One delivery bill is enough for a baby, even such a big one. I come with the hospital." (Spoken like an institution.)

Sniff. Sniff. He pulled a thickly packed envelope from his pocket. "For the baby," he said, "a little gift from me." He handed the envelope to Adam, who turned it over to me.

It was not a *little* gift. But as the teen-age mother of a son miraculously saved from death-by-drowning and death-by-maternal-asphyxiation, I was able to perceive Jeremy's gift as a third miracle, one that would save us from death-by-starvation.

"Extraordinarily generous of the doctor," Adam remarked. "To what do you attribute it?"

"Just shows what a good doctor he is," I said. "He knew exactly what the patient needed."

"You made it clear, I take it?"

"No. Maybe our doctor said we couldn't afford the extra days of hospital or the private room he ordered for me."

"Perhaps."

"He's a saint," I said.

"Not to look at."

"He is homely. But one forgets that, talking to him."

Adam elevated an eyebrow in a supercilious exasperating way.

"He's a wonderful conversationalist," I said. "And an omnivorous reader. He has a big library — not just obstetrics and child care, but politics, philosophy, art, history, fiction, poetry . . . He has books sent from England, too. He brought a stack of the latest ones to my room. Douglas' *South Wind,* Joyce's *Portrait of the Artist as a Young Man,* Shaw's *Prefaces.* When he went on rounds he'd sit down awhile and we'd talk about them."

"I can see you were not bored," Adam said drily.

Absalom was a husky boy. In a few weeks the forceps scars were scarcely visible and he was following the proper chart of development for a genius. I diapered him too often, curled his golden floss around my fingers too many times a day, worried over his turds, picked him up and cuddled him at every squeak, woke often at night to listen to his breathing. I dedicated myself to my career. When Absalom made a perfect score on his checkup, I was prouder than I had ever been of any 100 percent on my report cards.

"Good. Good. Good. Couldn't be better," Jeremy said. "I can't say the same for you, Mrs. Arkady. Your red cell count is low. Begin adding a bottle of formula a day to the baby's feeding. If your weight loss continues you will have to stop nursing. Are you eating enough meat, eggs, fruit?" He stopped and answered his question with a question. "Has Mr. Arkady found work?"

At the desk the nurse handed me a sealed envelope. "Doctor says you are to take this. Your next appointment is in two weeks."

When I opened the envelope at home I found Jeremy had repeated his green miracle.

I waited for Adam to say something when the rent bill was not slipped under the door. He said nothing. He was no cooler to me than he had been, no less courteous, no less amiable to the baby.

Why didn't I say straight out, "Adam, Doctor Starobin loaned us the money to pay the rent"? Maybe because there was nothing straight out about my relationship to Adam. Did he say nothing because he was too humiliated at not being able to provide? Was he signaling, "You brought this situation on us, you can solve it any way you like"? Or was it partly, as Shakespeare, our expert on human ambiguities, has said, "It oft falls out, to have what we would have, we speak not what we mean"?

On each visit Jeremy repeated the miracle. (If a miracle is repeated frequently, cause-and-effect relationships should not be hard to discover.)

Fresh fruits and vegetables filled the ice chest. More expensive cuts of meat appeared on the table. There were candles and flowers again. Was I taunting or goading? Was it resentment or dammed-up anger?

"And how did the doctor find our crown prince today?" Adam asked.

"One hundred percent perfect. He's promoted to applesauce." I waited. Adam did not ask about my health. I volunteered. "Dr. Starobin says my blood count is still too low. I'm to eat rare beef and liver."

"You are feverish, Mrs. Arkady. You are inviting influenza. There *is* an epidemic. You should be in bed. My car will take you home. I'll send food down from our kitchen. Don't get up any more than you must."

One night Absalom ran a high fever. He twitched. His breath rasped. The baby manual warned of convulsions. I grabbed him, threw my coat over my bathrobe and telephoned Jeremy from the corner pharmacy. "It's over one hundred and four. I've heard there's polio around."

"Alcohol sponge, aspirin, call me back in one hour. Take my private room number."

"I can't. I'm in the drugstore now with the baby."

"Where is Mr. Arkady?"

"He's in Hartford. He has a few days work at an insurance company there. He won't be back until Saturday afternoon."

"Get into a taxi. You can both stay on the top floor until you are recovered."

"I have no taxi money."

"I will wait for you in the lobby."

It was easy to accept books. "I've been reading this and thought you'd be interested." "Let me know what you think of this." A telephone was installed. "Read that line again." "Call me any time."

We talked on the telephone at all hours of the night while Jeremy waited for some woman's pangs to accelerate. "There's my bell. Call me back in half an hour if you're up." (Jeremy and I were poor sleepers, Adam was not.)

Delicacies? *Peu de chose.* "You sound tired, Ariadne. Absalom teething? You need some chicken soup. I'll send the porter. It's Friday and the gefilte fish smells good, too. You like apple or prune strudel?"

Theater tickets? "The labor room is full, I can't possibly get out to see the O'Neill play. Go for me, you can tell me about it. Adam doesn't care to go? Take Jessica or your mother. I'll send the car."

My wardrobe improved. "I don't like your cough, Ariadne. Your coat is not warm enough." (Ah, after all a touch of *La Bohème!*) "One of my grateful fathers is a furrier who would prefer to pay his bill in trade."

Very shortly, our accommodations improved too. "Get an apartment with a room for the baby, some place you can talk

166

to me at night without worrying about waking Adam or the baby."

We talked. What did we talk about night after night? Practically everything. Heredity and environment, classical unities and Russian formalist criticism. *Tristram Shandy.* T. S. Eliot and variant readings of Job. Probability theory and unicorns. Surrealism versus symbolic logic with its universe of interrelated classes and established hierarchies. We discussed morals, chess, families (mine and his), children (mine and his), the weather, Marx, the birth rate and famine, Kabala, bird migration, fortunetelling, Freud, chicken soup, the League of Nations . . . Perhaps it would reveal more if I were to list the subjects we did *not* discuss: money, spouses, sexual deprivation, silence. Money, fear of hunger, love, chronic despair. Money, marriage, fear of abandonment, ecstasy, the sensual odor of tropical fruit. Money, happiness, breasts (apart from mammary organs), loneliness, unhappiness, money. In our nonstop conversations we skimmed over our depths like a pair of figure skaters on the frozen surface of a pond.

Months passed. A year. Jeremy's casual green miracles kept appearing. Another year. When Absalom was two, Ariel was born. She, too, was forcibly delivered.

"A boy and a girl, both breech births, alive and undamaged. I can understand your wanting two children, but doctor to patient, Ariadne, you shouldn't have any more."

The post–World War I Depression was forgotten. Adam's career prospered. He made a name for himself at calculating risk factors in industrial insurance and moved upward in the ranks of respected actuaries. The Veterans' Administration appreciated his company's ingenuity at computing pensions, disability payments and insurance. Always interested in calculating machines that would require no human intervention, Adam invested in a manufacturing company.

Jeremy continued openhanded. "Adam, don't let a little capital stand in the way. Penny wise, pound foolish, you know." Or, "Adam, if you think the device is worth exploring, take it to my man, he's used to making up special instruments for me. Share the patent? Nonsense. No, no, leave me out of it, Adam. It's yours."

And Aaron was born.

"Why in the name of God you insist on being an earth goddess, Arnie, with a pelvic cradle like an undernourished adolescent, I'll never know."

"I'm a career mother and mothers have to have children."

"You're not a mother unless you have one every other year?"

"Storky, actually I do it so I can stay in the hospital for a couple of weeks and eat supper at midnight with you and talk until morning."

He put down his fork and knife . . . Sniff . . . Sniff. "In that case, couldn't we manage it more directly?"

"You mean we can all move in and live with you?" I laughed.

"Well . . ." He withdrew the remark. "With so much baby experience, I could use influence and put you on staff as a baby nurse."

And the miracles continued. "Ariadne, take the children and go to Florida for a few weeks. Ariel's cough is lingering. Take this . . ."

"Take . . . Take . . ." as they write in medical prescriptions. *Pro re nata.* O my belated Santa Claus, inexhaustible father of my impoverished dreams.

When Benjamin was born Jeremy said, "Ariadne, my heart cannot take another one."

"What do you mean, your heart? Storky, don't you dare have anything wrong with your heart! I can't live without you. Tell me the truth at once . . . Is there anything wrong?"

168

"So long as you can't live without me, there's nothing wrong with my heart. In the seven years we've known each other you have had four children. *I* can't take another, and you shouldn't. Someone else will have to deliver the next one."

"You know you wouldn't trust anyone else to deliver it."

"Don't try me, child."

"Don't make remarks about your heart, then."

"It's a bargain, then. No more babies, no more remarks about my heart."

He came over to the library sofa and put his big hand around my toes. "You must understand the difficulties, my dear."

I sincerely did not understand his heart. Then.

One September day, on a leaf-viewing expedition with the children, I drove to New Hampshire. We stopped for a picnic on a meadow that sloped down to a hemlock-bordered pond. A shallow waterfall cascaded into it. The meadow was weedy with tall goldenrod and asters. Absalom set off at a gallop, hallooing as he ran. Arie gravely lay down and rolled. Covered with aster petals and pollen, she looked like a superior copper-petaled chrysanthemum. I followed Aaron, my shaggy puppy, who tumbled and bumbled after her. Benjamin was asleep in my arms. My eldest was peering into the resinous water in which the dark forms of fish undulated. He was, like most children, a deep thinker on matters of death and creation. "I saw a frog and a turtle. Did God make them, too?"

"So we are told, my darling." (I kept my opinion to myself.)

"Would He mind if I went fishing?"

"Certainly not, my angel."

"I want to live here," he said. "Can't we stay, Mom?"

Arie and Aaron echoed their leader. "Stay, stay, stay . . ."

When I saw the FOR SALE sign tacked to the white farmhouse nestled between two giant maples I let myself fall in love.

"It's too expensive," Adam said. "I've been putting cash back into the business."

We were having a late supper with Jeremy, and Adam explained, "Dial telephones will replace human operators everywhere. The telephone company is going to want relays in the hundreds of thousands and I'm tooling up. Objectively, Ariadne, this is no time for me to buy a farm, and at the end of nowhere too. I'm going to be too busy to get up there."

(Maybe money was tight, but surely not as tight as he said.)

"I love it, the children love it. Imagine being able to own a waterfall."

"Couldn't you bring yourself to love something closer?" Jeremy said.

"I love it madly, madly," I said.

"Ah love, in that case. I can't shorten the distance, but I can lay out the money," Jeremy said, smiling like an indulgent father.

I smiled like an indulged child.

And Adam? Adam shrugged.

We played our parts deadpan, like characters in a Buster Keaton comedy or a repetitious pornographic movie: pie in the face or sexual whipping wiped away harmless, the raped heroine innocent at each encounter. She learns nothing. The clown is beaten but his suffering is feigned. Bruises are wiped out with magic ointments. No one ages. Genêt's pimp is a love hero. Sade's characters are tireless, "After ten orgasms, I was as fresh as at the beginning." In pornography and parody no one changes.

If only I had had the consciousness. Old age is instructive, as diminution of desire is instructive. Two judgments are necessary — one in the heat of desire, and one after—as Tristram Shandy's father pointed out. And when it comes it's as useful as jeweled rings which no longer slip over calcified knuckles. What can you do with belated consciousness except suffer guilt and remorse or make a fool of yourself trying to pass it on?

*   *   *

The mother of four children was having dinner with Jeremy. We were in his library, two old friends, Jeremy relaxed in his chair, his eyes shut (they were bothering him already), I, reading aloud *Measure for Measure,* a brandy at each one's elbow. If only I'd smoked cigars! Who says a man and a maid can't be platonic friends?

"Read Isabel's lines again from 'were I under the terms of death' to 'ere I'd yield my body up to shame.' I love that impossible girl. Put her in a Jewish gabardine and she would pass as a Talmudist. A real *Luftmensch,* but I could listen to her talk forever. 'Ignomy in ransom and free pardon are of two houses: lawful mercy is nothing kin to foul redemption.' Ah, poor generous sweetheart. All that passionate intellect corrupted the moment she sets her feet out the nunnery door."

"In the Shakespeare course I'm taking everyone thinks she's a prig for sticking to her principles."

"What does an innocent girl know from principles? Theories. Practically in her nightgown she goes to fight for justice. She doesn't know the stinking world. She doesn't know herself or she wouldn't go near a nunnery."

"I don't agree with you at all."

"I don't imagine you would, my child." His laugh was indulgent and affectionate. "I'm all for honor but Isabel saves hers in a cheater's cheated deal with Mariana. I am not criticizing the deal. What choice did she have if she wanted to save her brother from torture and death? It's her level of consciousness that interests me. It's her high opinion of herself. *Her* skirts are clean. She can give the witnesses a blooded sheet the morning after she marries that arrogant monster. Mind you, she has a thousand virtues. She means well, when others are self-serving, including Mariana, but she is self-deluded."

"You'll have to prove it to me, line for line."

The intercom buzzed. "Another discussion that will have to wait." He picked up. "Yes Delly. Prep her. Keep Patterson on." He sighed. "Caesarian scheduled for later tonight. I am going to go and reassure my little patient. Pretty little woman; she's worried about the scar. And why not?"

"Dear Storky. You may be the kindest man in the world. No wonder all your patients fall in love with you."

"Fortunately for their families, they fall out of love as soon as they leave with their little pink and blue bundles."

"Some of us never leave."

"Fortunately for me. Speaking of leaving, why don't you stay over tonight and drive up to the dacha in the morning? Jessica and your mother are with the children."

(How uselessly I see you now, flesh and spirit rising.)

"Adam is calling for me later and we're driving up. I must be there. Truckloads of lilies are waiting for me."

"Not truckloads, my child."

"Don't be alarmed. They weren't expensive."

"It's not the amount of money that alarms me, it's the Napoleonic scope of your endeavors."

"I can explain."

We both laughed. He sat down on the arm of the sofa. "Tell Daddy how you *happened* to buy truckloads of lilies."

"It's like this," I said, putting my hand into his. "Last weekend I *happened* on a construction crew at a road-widening job near our turnoff. The elms were already cordwood and a steamshovel was scooping up the bank of topsoil matted with lilies, many of them in bloom. For a nominal sum and a case of beer the fore-

172

man agreed to back the trucks into my pasture road and unload there instead of two miles farther down at the town dump."

"If I'd only met you earlier, I would be another Rothschild," Jeremy laughed. "I could be a doctor and go into the lily business too. What are you going to do with so many?"

"First, I'll divide them and naturalize the slope down to the pond. I'm changing my way of life. No more formal gardens; paradise gardens only from now on."

"If it's a drastic change, Arnie, you'd better get busy and write out a clear statement I can read and memorize when alone. Have a nap, child, while I go on rounds; you'll need your strength for gardening."

*　　*　　*

Oh Jeremy, my ghostly father, I'm over seventy and you are long since dead. There's nothing I'd rather do than talk to you again; see your patient homely face, hear you say, "Turn up the sound, Scheherazade! Go on about the distinction between formal and paradise gardens."

I wrap myself in the academic gown you paid for. It was durable stuff and I use it as a robe. In memory of what eluded us, I ramble on, as if I could amuse you again.

Close your eyes, dear. Sit back. You can't see? Hold my hand. Pretend we old verbal lovers are among the formal ruins of a cloistered garden. The arched corridors, the straight paths bordered with medicinal herbs confirm a monastic pattern of willed order. Think of it as a way of life, an expression of one image of happiness. It came into being through people like my father, like Adam, and yes, like you too, Jeremy, who, by choice or temperament, set themselves against the world's menacing disorder; who aspired toward a happiness in which nothing extravagant, inexplicable or random should occur.

173

When I began to garden I tried to replicate this heaven. On Adam's graph paper I laid out herb squares and vegetable rectangles, each row straight as a taut string dictated. A nun (or my Aunt Giselle) could have paced the narrow walks, her eyes on heaven.

Whether medieval monastic, ancient Arabic, neoclassical French or skyscraper modern, the formal garden is an achievement in solid geometry. It expresses *Principia Mathematica* in floral logistics. Rectangles, triangles, circles, segments of circles are connected by traditional devices. The gardener states his plan, then submits himself to it. It is an enclosed system, like symbolic logic, sometimes reduced so wholly to abstractions that it dispenses entirely with vegetation as in a Japanese contemplation garden. It strives for expressive lucidity. Its restrictions are integral with its beauty.

For years I labored at formal gardening; I enjoyed my chessboard enclosures. But slowly I was drawn toward unpremeditated arrangements: the surprise of a wild blue flag gaining a foothold where the brook happened to slow at a curve; watercress taking advantage of the protective shoulder of a rock; wind-sown flowers in the meadow. I began to aspire to models of spontaneity, in effect to paradise gardening.

The paradise garden is an attempt to recapture Creation as it was gathered from the swarm of Chaos, then flung free of restraint or corruption, directly from the sun-warmed hands of God. The perfect Happening. The look of noninvention, of spontaneity, is central to the concept. No matter how artfully created, its harmonies must appear to enlarge of themselves, a continuous becoming, a randomness that yet unfolds. Ambling along, we should pause in pleasant amazement as an image that was left behind unexpectedly reappears and reverberates. Compositional strands must not appear purposeful, though they lead to where we chance on happiness in a secret glade, or stumble on tragedy mirrored in a dark pond.

Unfortunately for me, and perhaps for you too, those I came to love beyond caution or measure were paradise gardeners in spirit. Absalom, then Paul, and lastly Daniel.

Most of us (judging by myself) grasp at both, and try to balance between, leaping from binary simplifications to the spontaneities of the unconscious, searching for artful correspondences, drawing our inexplicable unresolvable griefs after us. Perhaps the effort, the passionate effort is all. In Genesis I and Genesis II, we see God Himself thought it possible to integrate both formal and paradise gardens, and made a botch of it. Where on earth is the synthesis?

When I woke, Jeremy was behind his desk, lamplight thickening his nose and deepening the folds of his jowls. A mohair coverlet was tucked over me.

"Did it turn cold?"

"Not really. But you were chilly . . . a little pale. Have some brandy." He poured, then warmed the snifter in his hands before bringing it to me.

"Was I asleep long? Were you back here long? Did Adam get here yet? Is it late?"

"No. No. No. No to all four questions. You look thirteen years old when you're asleep."

"That's because I'm a slow bloomer."

"True. But I'm patient. I am waiting for you to grow up."

(Did I hear that? Not then.)

"Why should I, with you for a father?"

"I'm afraid there's something to that," he said ruefully. "Well tell me, did we buy anything today in addition to the green Lillian Gish hat you were wearing when you came in? It is becoming."

"Yes. I sent a rug for this space between the sofa and your library table, a Persian. If you approve it, I'll match a warm color out of it for drapes; the room is getting too blue and intellectual."

"I'd still be dropping down on a metal hospital bed up here," he hesitated, "if it weren't for you . . . your attentions . . ." Sniff. Then, quite as if it were an afterthought: "Ariadne, have you ever considered divorce?"

"Divorce? That's practically an obscenity."

"From our background it is, but it is not unknown."

"What does a woman divorce? Her family life? Her children, their home, friends, school, pets?"

"I've heard of children who survive."

"Jeremy, can you picture me explaining to my father and the rabbi my grounds for divorce? My father, of course, is sitting barefoot in sackcloth and ashes since I've uttered the word. The rabbi says, 'Such a fine boy from such a fine family. Why?' "

I smiled at Jeremy expecting him to look amused at what I'd conjured up. He looked grave.

"I'm answering no, Adam does not beat me. No, he does not gamble. No, he does not run around with other women. No, he is not a spendthrift. On the contrary he never buys me anything, which is too bad because he has good taste."

"What other plusses does he have, Ariadne?"

"He is an eager beaver at work. He is the children's father. He is gentle with them. He's rather good-looking."

"I'll grant that." Jeremy sighed.

"Let's see, what else? He is well-bred, loyal, honest."

Jeremy looked at me quizzically. "The regular Boy Scout, eh?"

"You know what? I think I'd be pleased to discover that Adam is hiding a backstairs life, that he feels excesses of heat and cold he's ashamed of . . ."

"Like what?"

"Anything intense. Eating the backbones of canned sardines in bed. Sneaking backstage and smelling the prima's tutu. Having a *Blutsturz* over a boy tap dancer. Ferrying lepers like Julian the Hospitaler."

"Some hopes," he laughed in spite of himself. "You think Adam has no out-and-out sins?"

"No. Poor Adam. All his sins are of omission," I said. "I'm sorry for him. From one country to another, then one language to another, then right after we married, to be hit by a Depression. It took him years to make a secure place for himself, as you know. No matter how rich he gets he'll feel poor."

"He does have problems about money." (If there was acid in that, I recognize it only in retrospect.) "Dear Arnie, we were all immigrants but we aren't all depriving. Sorry, I guess I've had too much brandy," he said morosely. "Some of us enjoy giving. You have a sweet way of always bringing a little something when you come."

"Do I? I never noticed."

"I have. Cookies, an article that's relevant, a jar of your jam, a joke, flowers from your garden. You are overindulgent to your children. I suppose the same might be said of me."

"Both Aquarians, water carriers."

"We make quite a couple," he said. "Overindulgent father and mother with numbers of ungrateful children. Only we're not married to each other."

"It would be cosy," I said lightly. "But it would be incest. You've been a father to me since we met."

"That's because you were Rima-the-Bird-Girl back then."

"Bird brain, you mean. A grown-up married woman about to have a child which I couldn't do without your help. But seriously if I had thought of divorce, I couldn't have done it when Adam was down and out."

"Very high-minded." Sniff, sniff. "Now that he is up and about has divorce occurred to you?"

Still at a distance from his meaning, I theorized on. "How could anyone break up a family with four children? I couldn't

177

live with the guilt of sacrificing their well-being for, say, being in love."

"Let us say, being in love." His voice softened. He retreated into the darker side of his desk. "It *is* a moral dilemma, dear Arnie. One couldn't, in conscience, press a woman to a decision, could one?"

(Suppose he had come right out and said, "I can't in conscience press you, Ariadne, but would you get a divorce and be mine?" Would I have done it? I can't honestly answer yes.)

His head was resting against the back of his chair. I couldn't see his face. "I know you love your father, but do you think he behaved in your best interest in pushing you into marriage?"

"No. I wanted to go to college. But more than anything I wanted to get out of my smother-loving family into my own life. I didn't know I was being passed from the prison of girlhood to the prison of wifehood. Of the two, I prefer the wifehood one."

"Knowing your father's reverence for scholarship, any idea why he refused to let you go to school?"

"To him, Adam was a greater match than he had dreamed possible."

"For him or for you? Vanity!"

"Remember I had been accidentally compromised. I think he believed no decent man would marry me. And I believed him! He said I couldn't find a better husband in college. And what does a girl go to college for if not to find a husband?" My voice broke, surprising me with pent-up anger. "He was afraid the big fish would get away . . ."

I got up, walked around nervously, replenished Jeremy's brandy glass. "God, I was a blob of dough. I was stunted. I had never had an allowance, never spent a cent unbeknownst to my parents, never made a decision on my own, not even about my clothing. Elizabeth Barrett lived the life of an eagle in comparison to me."

"Why not go to college now? You've been taking classes at Columbia as it is."

"Those are extension courses, one evening a week. I hadn't thought of going for a degree."

"Think of it. I can afford another child in college. You might consider life on your own. You could teach, or write."

I thought I was changing the subject. "Jeremy, did I ever tell you the story of Adam's mother and the dumbwaiter?"

"No. Tell me my bedtime story, Scheherazade. Turn up the sound."

"Sit back, Storky. Rest your eyes."

"Married. Gleaming with bridewax and optimism. Adam newly unemployed, replaced by a veteran who had returned to his company. We had wedding present money and his savings, but Adam was anxious about money."

"We immigrants tend to be."

"Jeremy! Not you. You are generous to a fault . . ."

"Compensation!" He sounded somber. "Go on."

"We were in Central Park when Adam suggested we go to his parents' apartment where I could stir up an omelet for lunch. What with my family's health food prohibitions I had been looking forward to having a hot dog. Also I was uneasy about cooking in my mother-in-law's kosher kitchen. 'I wouldn't mind a hot dog' was as much as I permitted myself. I thought it would be un-grown-up to press my wish. 'An omelet is better for you,' he said."

"Sacrificing himself for you, from the start?"

"Well maybe he was thinking of me a little."

"Go on with your story, poor little bride."

"Adam's father opened the door, said 'Ah' in that vague scholarly way that looked through people, stroked his beautifully kempt beard and wandered back to his library.

"I knew enough about dietary laws to ask Adam to find me correct pans, dishes and silver for dairy foods. I made the omelet.

I never found out if Adam did or did not get his information reversed. His mother came in just as I was stacking and clearing. It was our third meeting — once before and once at the wedding. She took one look, became, well, an iguana puffing herself, twisting and turning her ash-colored head. Eyes retracted, eyelids hooded (she had invisible lashes), venom-shot she struck. She snatched the cloth from my hand, swept up dishes, silver, frying pan, even the salt and pepper shakers, gathered them into the cloth, and opening the dumbwaiter door, dumped the entire contaminated bundle out of her sanctified kitchen."

His big hand remained over his eyes. "I won't ask you what Adam did." His voice was sad.

"Guess."

"All right, I guess. Nothing."

"Correct. I thought he was too well-bred to make a scene in front of me and that he must have returned and had it out with his mother privately, because we did not see his parents again until Absalom was born."

"If that's well-bred you should have married a rude commoner, like me." He sat forward into the light. "That is a dreadful, dreadful story, Scheherazade, and it makes me very angry."

"You'll have to cut off my head then."

"Oh God, oh God," he groaned, "child, child. Where was your sense of self-preservation? Wasn't there anyone to defend you? A friend? Jessica?"

"At the time she was in South Africa, trying to live with her father. But you know how we are. It's too painful for you or me to be out-and-out angry. I ended by telling myself Adam was respectful of his mother."

"I cannot believe that you didn't quarrel with Adam about that."

"Believe it. Adam and I never, never quarrel. We wouldn't know how."

He leaned back out of the light. We both toyed with our brandy snifters.

"Ariadne, I would like to ask you a personal question."

"Feel free. It seems to be our night for it."

He spoke quietly as if he were fatigued by our foray into the personal. "Did your father ever ask you where the money was coming from for you to live, let's say, as comfortably as you did, in the years before Adam . . . was successful?"

"Not directly. I think he assumed Adam was borrowing from his father, a well-paid professor. We never openly discussed money."

"How well-bred you all are," he said. "How incredibly well-bred."

The receptionist rang. Jeremy picked up without opening his eyes. "Mr. Arkady on his way, send up tea."

Sniff. Sniff. "Arnie, before you leave tonight, I'd like a moment with Adam on business."

"Hiding something from me?"

He shook his head. "Isn't there a saying about the best place to hide something is in open view? Adam will tell you if he likes."

It could hardly not have been an experimental setup. Looking into the mirror to put on my new hat, I had to see the two of them. Jeremy had to have placed himself in the doorway between his dressing room and library. I saw Jeremy hold up a roll of greenbacks. In fact, he held up the roll like a magician showing he has nothing up his sleeve.

"I don't need it right now, Jeremy," I heard Adam say. But he leaned toward the money.

Jeremy thrust the roll forward. "If you don't need it, you won't use it. Add it to our account." He held it closer.

Adam put it aside, but with the back of his hand, so to speak.

"It's terribly generous of you but I don't actually . . ."

"Oh take it. Send our girl south for some sun. She needs to get away." He slipped the wad into Adam's pocket. It stayed. Father to son?

Jeremy glanced at me in the mirror, then led the way back to the library with the bitter and satisfied look of a doctor who has verified his earlier diagnosis of malignancy in the presence of a doubting witness.

It seems remarkable to me now that I did not cry out, "Enough."

I saw myself in the mirror putting on my Lillian Gish hat and buttoning my Mae Murray coat; and the hat did not burn on my head and the coat did not turn into a shirt of fire. There was a flush of guilt on Jeremy's face and a touch of remorse on Adam's pale one; but where was my retort?

Jeremy said, "Adam, don't you think that new hat is worth every pretty penny it cost? It's so becoming."

Adam took my arm. "Women's clothes are a mystery to me, but we can't deny my wife's looks improve with age."

Jeremy said, "Considering she's turning thirty, we can look forward."

He buzzed the elevator bell and waited with us. Sniff. Sniff.

"I'll call late tonight, Jeremy," I said.

"Any time." He closed the grill on us. "Drive carefully, son."

On the trip I could feel the money in Adam's pocket. There was a fluttering inside me, like something stirring in a cocoon. One of the stages in my slow metamorphosis from larval narcissism to consciousness.

There might have been salvation for all of us if only, if only I had been conscious enough to cry out, Forgive me, Father (either or both of you), it is a dashing and spurious style your daughter is practicing, acting out stock-shots that should have been edited out and left on the cutting-room floor. I am being light-footed as Irene Castle twirling toward Vernon, Leatrice Joy in her motor car; a heedless heiress; a coquette receiving far more than she gives; Clara Bow the It girl in a raccoon coat; Theda Bara the femme fatale. I am one of those Hollywood models your prodigal daughter should have debunked in her youth when Rudolph Valentino gasped at her cruise gown and, in shipboard moonlight, kissed her palm. You should have let me go to the movies with the girls. You should have arranged an American childhood. You should not have been an anxiety-ridden immigrant. You should not have been poor. Because I had a frightened and drudging youth I am corrupting my age.

If only Adam and I had known how to quarrel! But neither of us had been schooled in open combat. We had been trained to skirt those quagmires that we could not amiably negotiate. At times a swift spurt of feeling hissed up in us. But it sent us in opposite directions, as if we'd been surprised by snakes. Over the years we became committed to certain maneuvers, a few economical if not brilliant gambits. His. Mine.

"Objectively . . . Ariadne."

"What's objective about it, Adam?"

His face would take on the guarded tower position. Was he exposing his king? Should I trail my queen? After the opening, the rest of the game was predictable. Adam would wait, alert to the opportunity of an exit word which he would set down with finality. "We need say no more, Ariadne."

He would leave the room, the émigré passport look on his face, withdrawn between greenish cover, rebuttoning his English jumper-sweater in a kind of formal leave-taking.

"Let us call the matter a draw, Ariadne."

(Why not checkmate?)

My reaction was equally predictable. I would castigate myself for having made an issue. It wasn't nice of me. I'd bake a batch of cookies or whip up a special cake. When I had calmed down there was Jeremy to ring up and amuse with a bookish conversation. By then, if the issues hadn't been too volcanic I would go upstairs to our common bedroom hoping that Adam was asleep and the crisis would blow over. If I'd guessed wrong he might be sitting in bed reading, his fingers coding a noiseless tattoo of agitation against the blanket. Seeing his drawn vulnerable face would fill me with guilt at having upset him. Worse, a look of dislike or sharp disapproval would depress and humiliate me. Worst of all was a look of fear that accused me of being a mean witch, an unwomanly woman who had given vent to anger.

Sometimes I was too pained, or smarted too much at an injustice, or I felt too helpless and awkward to go to bed. I went from one child's room to another, adjusting a blanket, taking heart from the warm reassuring smell of healthy child, from a friendly cat or dog that lifted its head as I entered. Then I went to read in the living room, spending my unused emotions on some drama, like a spinster who goes to the movies to find release in celluloid fictions. It was a small comfort to hear the milkman's horse and see the chill watery light of new morning.

Early in our marriage, impelled by my clumsy nurturing habits and by youthful confidence, I had tried to reach out to him before he was lost in his silent Sargasso, becalmed perhaps for days. I quickly lost my confidence as I lost the struggle. I would lie beside him, sensing his silence hardening. I could hear my blood pounding as if I held an empty conch to my ear. To go to sleep he turned his back. It was a perfectly fine, manly back — muscular, lustrous — but if I were to write a book about my marriage, that turned-away back might serve as the picture on the jacket.

If I had had more wisdom, independence of character, a greater measure of self-awareness or tact, I don't think I could have amended the history of Adam's back. It was too private a story. Much as I've considered it in my arduous climb into my seventies, it has remained incomprehensible to me. At best I have a crude understanding of it.

I turn my back, it said, on everything I might love. I do it because I must. I turn from anything that might attract me or delight me and get me to care too much. I rebuff it in advance. I do not want to be loved because I was loved once and I loved in return and all was taken from me. Say it was war. It was the czar. It was honor. It was being Jewish. I was abandoned. I entered my solitude. I offer myself to that past. I don't mean to be cruel, but I am overwhelmed by any demand for intimacy and I will never again expose myself to the anguish of being abandoned.

Then again, why do I need to understand his back?

Whitehead puts the answer better than I can.

It is endearing, this human insistence on clarity, this clinging . . . that is based on fear, superstition as to the mode in which human intelligence functions. Our reasonings grasp at straws for premises and float on gossamers for deduction.

*   *   *

There is a smell of scorch coming up from the kitchen, pea soup I left simmering in case Danny and Dinah arrived at the dacha — as they do when they can — late Thursday night instead of early Friday. I scoop up a wastebasketful of false starts, rush down and shove the kettle to the back of the stove. As I pick up a handful of papers and reach for the lid-lifter my memories shift. My whole being is startled into a time change.

I alert, adjusting to the past the way a woman adjusts to a child's shift in the womb.

I am standing at this stove — a common black kitchen stove — lid-lifter in one hand, paper in the other, on the opening morning of the fishing season the year Absalom was nine and I was twenty-nine. Suddenly my father appears. I can hear his voice as if he were alive.

"A dacha in New Hampshire?" (Ah my sad father! How eased he was when his daughter the immigrant achieved a dacha in Golden America.)

"I sleep well, Ariadne, knowing you have a good husband, an ideal husband. I look at you, my blessing, four healthy children, one cleverer than the other, an apartment like *Gott in Odessa,* and a dacha in the country."

"We borrowed for it."

"In America that's how people buy. You borrow. You pay back."

(I comfort myself that my father, who, for all my resentments, I have never ceased to miss, had "too much brains and too little worldly common sense" to have imagined my tainted liaison with our good family friend, Jeremy. I value him and his good opinion even posthumously.)

"Such a dacha, acres, woods, a pond. And what you've made of it, in no time."

"Only takes money," I mumbled.

"An orchard like an *allée.* A vegetable garden like a chessboard. An Eden you put together, my daughter."

"You left out the biggest part, Father, my flower gardens."

"Since you mention it, enough already with flowers."

"You have a few Commentaries, Poppa, to prove the Lord walked in a vegetable garden in the cool of the evening?" (I

186

could see him shelving the topic for a debate with his Talmudic disputants.)

"A garden should be like a good woman with her children, pleasant to see but not for too much show. A few flowers, yes, but a measure in all things should be."

But soft . . . that light. Put out that kindly light. I have no doubt my father's ghost stalked in because I had offended his Mosaic Majesty by plucking the children out of school for the Gentile joy of a fishing expedition.

"A Jew goes fishing?"

"Father, in our Dewey days childhood is for children."

"Daughter, nonsense from Rousseau. Childhood is for learning to be human."

"You don't believe a child is good by nature?"

"No. I believe in original sin and foolishness. Civilization takes discipline and sacrifice. If Rousseau was naturally good, how was he able to abandon his five children to an orphanage? And why did he suffer from persecution mania?"

"Father, we are building Eden in this greenhorn's promised land."

"May it be for amen. God Himself tried twice and you see His results. Your theoreticians of Eden better study the Book."

"You put too much faith in the printed word. Don't you want your grandchildren to be free and happy?"

"You forgot Dostoievski's Grand Inquisitor? Free and happy are non sequiturs. Cossacks are free and happy, especially during a pogrom."

"Forget history."

"Will they let you?" He stubbed his cigarette impatiently. "You are the mother of my four grandchildren, but you talk like an innocent. We are foreigners here, as everywhere. Men, animals too, I believe, mistrust everything outside their milieu.

That is why every beast was given some means of escape. Man was given intelligence."

"It's a new world, Father. No more scapegoats."

"People are never finished with making them."

"We have the Bill of Rights."

"Tell that to the Strasbourg Jews."

"The world has improved since then."

"What else is new? All the wicked men are dead already? Arnie, this year Arabs massacred Jewish students in Palestine. The world did not make it its business any more than it did the Kishnev pogroms in 1903, or the murders by the czar's Black Hundreds, or Haman's expropriation plot.

"Oh Lord how long? Who knows what next year will bring on us. It will not be the Messiah. You, my American daughter, do you know about your *Numerus Clausus?* In Europe anti-Semitism was open. So-and-so many Jews to be admitted to top universities. Here it is done by gentlemen's agreement. A few counted seats for a few counted boys who don't look too Jewish."

"Token integration? Not in America."

"Your American cousins, my brother's sons, had to go to medical school in Edinburgh and Geneva. Granted in America they don't kidnap eight-year-old Jewish children for the czar's army but count the Jews appointed to teach in Columbia University or invited to join Morgan's bank. No one puts Henry Ford in jail for anti-Semitism."

I see him outlined against his wailing wall of tomes, an oracle about to dispense wisdom elliptical as proverbs. He lifts down a quarto volume. Now he bends to the lamp with it, carefully turning wheaty rippled pages, light from below, a half-curve on the lower part of his somber face, the upper part in deep shadow. His scarred forefinger passes down the double column of text.

188

"The year 1349. Plague spread over Europe. The Jews were accused of having caused it through poisoning wells . . . In Berne a number of Jews were tortured until confessions were wrung from them . . . They burned the Jews in many towns and wrote of this to Strasbourg, Freiburg and Basel so that they too should burn their Jews.

"If there were good men opposed, they did not prevail, Ariadne. When I was young the Jews had a bitter joke about how Russians and Poles would resolve the Jewish problem . . . 'It will be decided that if the Russians kill their Jews, the Poles will retaliate by killing theirs' . . . Perhaps under socialism men will not be such wolves . . .

"Ariadne! You have not answered me. At some Edict of Expropriation like the one that made my family poor immigrants, what will you take across the border, a fishing pole?"

The question remains. If there was so much against our going fishing, how did we get to go?

*   *   *

"Great guns! Little fishes!"

Toast cooled at the very lips as the Crown Prince slammed down the newspaper he had been scanning for an item to take to class discussion. Imperiling the cocoa-pot he thrust his head forward; boy-crusader in a helmet of brazen curls, fearless with the desire that our love and indulgence had empowered.

"Fishing season! Do you realize fishing season opens tomorrow in New Hampshire?" His eyes darkened like pebbles under a flow of water.

"My God, look not so fierce on me," I muttered.

"Where will *I* be? Guess where I will be."

"In school," his father said.

189

"Where?" Arie obliged, as usual.

"Where but in cooking class! Just what I need. Perfect."

Absalom's father scored a point by clearing his throat as if awareness stuck in it. (What instinct children have for the jugular of one parent or another when they need to divide and conquer.)

"It's a dopey school. They don't know the difference between boys and girls."

(Again Adam cleared his throat.)

"What is the difference . . . Yuk, Yuk?" Aaron's round face crinkled with small guile like pleating on the transparent water of a boat pond.

His sister slapped him, lightly.

"Don't do that, Arie," I chided.

Where I went to elementary school they thought of little else. BOYS ONLY. GIRLS ONLY. Gyms. Lunchrooms. Even on the stairs we were prisoners of gender, separated by steel mesh. But what is the reality of deprivation to the privileged?

Perhaps Adam would have preferred a Latin school, but he didn't say so. "You are aware this progressive school is run by flannel-breasted lesbians," he had commented after our interview.

"I don't need cooking. I don't even need school." Absalom's unreconciled voice stormed on. "I can go to New Hampshire by myself. Hitchhike. Catch fish and cook them. Make my own biscuits. Eat hardtack like sailors."

"You dassn't miss school." That was Arie, assistant wife, assistant mother, assistant enforcer of the law.

"Mind your own business, Miss Butt-in-sky? What do you know? What use is school to me? I'm going to run away from home." He shot straight up from his seat.

"Ask to be excused when you want to leave the table," his father said.

Absalom glared and bristled a " 'scuse."

"I'll go with you," said Aaron, not yet five years old and already a practiced conformist.

"MeMeMe take me," said Benjie, our youngest, and banged his spoon on his highchair.

"They are abandoning us in a body, little mother," said Adam.

"I'm staying with you, Daddy," Arie announced with a self-righteous inclination of her cameo head.

"Me too." Aaron shamelessly switched to his sister's side, leaving Absalom an isolated rebel, head thrust truculently high like a young stag posturing.

In his singleness and drive, in the clarity and intensity of his desire, our farm shimmered among our breakfast crockery; the white house, the meadow breathing in and out with thaw, the brook wild at release from winter, trout vibrating in every rock pool.

My first-born, my favored child, enviably free of the ordinary hopelessness that comes from learning what most desire comes to, emanated, in his young maleness, a kind of violent second presence, which in its narcissism, its inaccessibility, its aggressive masculine stance, had the allure of power.

"Gee I wish I could go . . . I wish I wish . . . Hey Mom . . ."

The voice of His Highness, the Child, challenges me to feats of placation. That voice must be part of the race's survival weaponry. Built in, like the upstream drive behind a salmon's fertility, it can shoot a parent back from the adult brine to the sweet source, the amniotic waters where maternal delusions of omnipotence bathe each embryo in perfect bliss. So, to confess it plainly, I, a responsible adult, surrendered us to my son's imperious will. I blurted out, "Your wish is granted, my son. Let's all go fishing."

Shock flashed through us all. Even me.

The man of the house stared at me, not with pleasure. Absalom closed his eyes, lids pulsing between brows and lashes like moths still folded and damp between brown hostage twigs. Then my reward. His lids fluttered open, pupils gone all to light turned to me dazzled with love as if they stared into the sun.

Adam took time to collect himself. "Your mother . . ." I was grateful for the capsule of courtesy in which he encased himself, though a look of distaste did slip through his defenses. "Your mother seems to have declared a holiday for us all." His mouth was so compressed it flattened and snipped off each phoneme.

The four children absorbed the drop in temperature. Four heads bobbed from father to mother like jonquils whipped in a fresh breeze. Absalom shivered.

I sat gaping at what had emerged from me. I reassembled myself as a proper wife and mother, yet I had a crawly suspicion that I had indulged Absalom, gained his favor — but not for his good. I bowed my head over my coffee cup to hide from the children's gaze. Shame flushed through me as I bargained with the future: "Oh Absalom, in a time of hate, recall this moment of our illicit joy."

Across our two coffee cups Adam and I looked at each other and looked away. I flashed a weak, placating smile at him. Disapproval puckered his mouth and eyes. As was usual in our compromises, each of us felt loss. We consummated our disagreement with a moment of pained silence.

Adam shook his head dubiously, then leaped over my affront and Aaron's tricycle to the telephone. He gave the operator his office number and, eyes forcing awareness on me yet mindful of the children, mocked with his special combination of polite emphasis sharpened to a cutting edge:

"My family seems to have contracted a fever. Yes, high. Hi-bernation fever. Proved contagious I fear. No. Not before Monday."

(I could hardly have expected Adam to rise spontaneously, lightheartedly, perhaps mischievously, to my imprudence. Yet, suppose he had — improbable doesn't mean impossible — suppose we had both gone Bacchic. What an example for our well-brought-up children, to have embraced anarchy together! It is another of those small scenes to which I return in moody hindsight.)

Good little Arie dabbed at her pursed red lips, breathing too quickly, like an overalert squirrel, Daddy's girl relishing the wife's disfavor.

"Aren't we going to school today?" she stoked, looked at me sidewise, blushed, and added placatingly, "I'll help with Benjie."

She patted Benjamin, her living doll. She undid his napkin, fastened behind like a seminarian's collar. He snuggled against her shallow breast and stuck his thumb in his mouth. "Don't lean all over your sister, Benjie," I reprimanded.

Brother and sister stared big-eyed and reproachful. Hansel and Gretel and the wicked stepmother.

"Arie, let him be," I began and stopped. What could I say to keep her from clutching her brother to her? "Don't be such a mother's helper; you're seven years old and already a matriarch. Go flutter, be a fritillary. Fly, Ariel. Don't be the one to cook breakfast for the gang; don't serve. Honestly, I tried not to do to you what was done to me. I didn't put Aaron or Benjie into your arms and say, 'This is your baby, love it.' I said, 'Phew, that diaper stinks!' and 'I wish he'd stop that screaming; he gives me a headache' and 'Don't mind the baby; go out and play.' I tried to stand like a rock between you and them, but you ran around it and picked up the big-sister, little-mother shackles."

It was my morning for chagrin. I watched her for herself and as she mirrored me, a tense, asthmatic child, already taking pleasure in saying yes to others' needs rather than her own. I wanted to say, "Don't be like your mother! Fly the coop!"

I began gathering up the dishes. Benjamin, the community

alarm signal, sirened off at the threat of being left boxed in his highchair. He tipped the bowl of oats into his lap before Adam could swing him down to where he could clutch at the knees of action. "Don't drop Benjie." Arie's breaths shortened.

Adam now embraced the event and organized it admirably. Notwithstanding he was a foreigner, he would have made a model movie cowboy. Like our native heroes, he did not enjoy concentrating on emotional subleties, but he rode action with boyish charm and cool good looks. "Action! Company: March! Every man to his post. Number one, Absalom. Get the luggage together while I get the car gassed up. Number two, ladies" (a heel click), "your talents at the lunch hampers. Number three, Aaron, I want to see a row of galoshes, two for each person, my boy. How many will that make? Show me when I return. Number four, Bee-Bee, find your bunny slippers, your blue blankie and your cuddly and set them by the door to wait. All right?"

Bee-Bee. At the naming Adam said, "Consider the postman, my dear . . . though I do not wish to gainsay your prerogative." (His language, like him, retained the tone of translation: ambiguities felt but inaccessible, true meanings lost with the original.) "Ariadne, Ariel, Adam, Absalom, Aaron . . . might we not venture as far as Bee? So Benjamin."

We basketed the larder, tucked children and gear into the big Buick. The three younger children bounced onto the back seat and Absalom slid into place between Adam and me.

Truants, we drove out of the time-clocked city, northward against morning traffic, through Connecticut's green and prescient spring, the season retracting as on a Chinese scroll rolled backward, to New Hampshire's brooks and buds glistening wet-brown as they swelled and broke from frost.

194

We arrived at sunset. Overhead a flock of migratory geese signaled. Outstretched necks and underbodies lit in burning-cross splendor, they flared down the sky and were quenched in the valley sanctuary beyond our pond. The upturned faces of the children were also caught in the glow. Dazed from the ride, they stood in a row, my four burnished angels, peering up in that nearsighted concentrated way, smiling their archaic smiles at wonders dropping from the sky.

"See de big boids," said Benjamin.

"Tomorrow will be fair," pronounced our eldest, "mackerel clouds."

"What do you make of those stratus fellows on the horizon?" asked his father, feeding his son's pride.

"A few early clouds. All the better for fishing."

They nodded manly and turned to unloading. By the time we had removed a few shutters, fired the kitchen stove, broiled supper, replaced a quilt birth-bloodied by a field mouse and warmed each bed with heated bricks, it was late.

I fell asleep to the plink-plunk of water dripping from the maple branches onto the roof and to the mating thrum of spring peepers rising, with the moon's rise, out of the mist along the pond.

We had been preceded by a propitious spring thaw. From roofs, trees, shrubs — every icicle trickled down its stem. To a steady ticking and crackling stunned molecules of ground water quickened and forced upward fissures through frozen soil. Every gully was a channel for the juices that oozed and steamed under a film of water. Freshets coursed seaward. One could almost feel male cell swimming to female cell, sense, in ways beyond knowing, desire locked to necessity — unlocking form upon form, rung upon rung (ontogeny — as every school boy learns — recapitulating phylogeny), in each evolution from monad to man lurking the possibility of mutation.

As I lay beside the man who sired the boy whose ardor for

fishing had persuaded us here, I wondered if at some watery arrest my husband's skin had acquired its amphibian trait of predawn chill, in which inhospitable climate I, in turn, had acquired the negative tropisms of an early riser.

I was mammal tired that morning. Also I was midmonth and didn't want to flare open like some pollinating morning glory. So as I shivered awake to his skin temperature's fall I grumbled, "Adam, you are as cold as a fish."

"Fishes, you will note," he answered in his neat alert way, "copulate and populate in cold water." And with eyes wide open he dived back into his deeps.

I blanketed myself within the covers. Behind my tightened lids a fireworks flower spiraled and exploded down a festival sky and sparks were extinguished in a violet, regulus of Venus, sea. As I succumbed to the sweet vertigo of sleep, my mother ear heard the stairs creak and the back door click behind the boy who had risen with the earliest birds and was gone to reclaim his brook.

It was his by right of exploration. For three summers he had dedicated himself to its mysteries; had magnified his fingers and toes in every scoop and rocksplash pool of the lively waters that foamed through stone pasture and juniper scrub of a land given up for barren, as Sarah, until the angels of internal combustion touched it and thrust it into eccentric fertility. Whereupon it conceived and bore a city folks' dacha.

I came downstairs to a kitchen that smelled of wet earth and fresh fish. On the sink board shone a mess of sunnies, caught, cleaned and delivered by Absalom, whom I could see on a rock below a cascade — a reed of a boy backed by a willow whose multiple trunk spurted a radiance of golden streamers.

I set a few lesser fish to simmer in readiness for a court bouillon to honor the trout of which I was confident. To quicken the fire I shook down cinders and ashes and from the kindling box picked a few shingles and a last summer's *New York Times Book Review.*

Heat seized the corner of a page. I watched it brighten, then pale and deepen to a brownness. Words swelled, bent backward, enlarged and wavered. The words *"In each of us there exists one novel"* hung a split second, glowed, crinkled into ash and fell. The italics are mine.

In each of us a novel?

A ray of sunlight feathered across my breast. (Remember, sunlight carries blessing, but not as a daughter may conceive.) Being so caught up, so mastered by the conception, I stood there, stove lid suspended in hand. Flames foxily leaping out of the hollow of the firebox caught the paper, and in the updraft blazed and singed my lashes and brows. In the protein odor of sacrifice I sickened. Everything went black.

Before my streaming eyes my life passed in a riffle of book pages, one closing on the other. Fire was eating steadily into them, rimming them slowly in black, creeping in from the margins, suddenly illuminating the body of each page in ash-cold lavender. And what did I see written? Nothing! Not a thing! Every page was blank.

What an incandescent moment! What an illumination! My entire life, cautious to the point of perversity, was passing in front of my eyes. It could mean only one thing. I was dying. Dying. It was written in fire. Not thirty years old and my life was a blank. I was as unalive as if laid out in lavender. A novel in me? There wasn't enough for a Mother's Day postcard.

What a denunciation! What an annunciation! A novel for everyone else? For me, nothing. You there, you oracle, you mouthpiece smoking out of the stove, you are making one hell of a mistake.

I've been a good, good, girl. Donned wifehood more obediently than my sweet Benjie puts on his snowsuit. Snap a picture

197

of me, in bed or out, and it will pass any customs inspector. My husband enters the male arena tended, clean-shirted, his mind freed of domestic and financial trivia, confident that his bed will be made, his excellent dinner waiting whenever he arrives. I am good to my parents (with Jeremy's assistance), my brothers, Jessica, my hard-pressed aunt Cassie. The family is the building block of society. Without my help society dissolves.

But it was I who was dissolving. What was left of my life was fly-ash sticking to the ceiling.

I quoted my father. "A wife is nothing? A mother is nothing?" I have brought four Very Important People into the world. I wash their starfish hands, smooth the wings on their shoulders; I send them forth loved, gloved, lunch boxes swinging, galoshes buckled, their hats over their ears. I never let a one of them go into a public toilet. You! Look at me in my kitchens, either one. Feeding, instructing, pleasuring. Yes, Arie, flour the cookie sheet lightly, turn it over and tap. Yes, Benjie, be fair, it is Aaron's turn to lick the icing spoon. Yes, my darlings, I will drive you to the duck pond to feed the ducks and geese.

Fire was hissing through the kindling, crackling, cackling at me. I tried to smother it with facts. Not even you can deny me those apple-green Sundays when spring came to Central Park, the seals breathing deeply in and out, water running off them in rivulets, the children exhorting them to gluttony. Arie, exultant in a blue princess coat, dancing as if her weight were being carried aloft by her orange balloons. And Absalom, oh Absalom! golden retriever of a boy — leaping up the stairs, flying ahead: "The polar bears are breathing smoke." Aaron, little peanut whistle piping where? where? Benjamin alert in the stroller, watchful, responsive as a folded leaf in sunlight. All of them sensing the spring and bringing it to me in their eyes.

Panic funneled through me. Fear shot up and out into the open the way fire that has been crawling through fissures undetected breaks through and envelops a structure in flames.

Smoke was filling the kitchen. I choked and coughed. A nausea unto morning sickness surged over me. The iron lid-lifter fell from my hand and tolled against the fire mat.

"Oh Christ. I must be pregnant again," I moaned.

Upstairs the children were scampering about on bare feet. They were beginning to quarrel. They needed breakfast. I set the lids in place. Put the kettle on. Watched a drop of water spit on the hot metal and sputter into perfect nothingness.

Nothing is perfect?

A Few Obituaries

There will be no other words in the world but those our children speak.

— GEORGE OPPEN

NOWADAYS I TURN first to the obituary column in the newspaper, which in the *New York Times* means I read from back to front. (My people have a long history of reading from back to front.) But in a small town, death, like birth, marriage and the weather, is still front-page news. So one Friday, when I pulled the gazette out of my RFD mailbox and saw the photograph of my neighbor's son, banded in black, I didn't need the text to tell me that Dwight Hansen added one more to the number of combat deaths in Vietnam.

Dwight was the boy next door. (Like his presidential name-sake, he was called Ike.) He and Daniel were of an age and had played together as little children, then fished together and later owned a jalopy jointly. He was the one who used to come by on his bicycle to check our house when we weren't there, fill the bird feeders, shovel a path through the snow if we were coming up in winter, and when he was big enough, mow the hillside meadow with a tractor-mower. A gawky polite young man, he had not grown out of blushing when he talked to Dinah. Ike seemed to be so lacking in evil intentions I thought he'd make a poor soldier.

Danny and I had sounded him out about helping him resist the draft. But he looked down at his shoes (he always wiped them scrupulously before stepping into our kitchen), brushed crumbs from his mouth with the back of his hand (the only immoderate thing about him was a capacity for milk and fresh-baked brownies) and 'lowed as how his country right or wrong could call on him. Anyway, he'd rather fight and get over with it than be cooped up in a CO camp or prison.

I walked around the house aimlessly picking up. (I always tidy when I'm anxious.) I watered the plants and carefully dead-headed a hanging nasturtium of its spent blooms so it would go on flowering. I stared out the window at two sparrows on a twig and when the female pecked the male away I realized I had been counting; he had trodden her seventeen rapid-fire times. There was a batch of eggs made sure! But what in the name of God would I say to Mrs. Hansen who had lost her chick and was past breeding? Take comfort from his bronzed baby shoe? Don't cry, the president will send you his posthumously awarded medals and you can frame them with the military commendations? The farm? You can will that to the state for a veterans' rest home.

Slowly I climbed upstairs to change into something morbid for paying a condolence call. On the stairway I straightened photographs, among them one of Aaron in his parachutist's uniform — a bombed church behind him, two building stones held meaningfully in hand — a snapshot that came in a letter after he was no more.

I would say Aaron looked handsome in his uniform, but in deference to my father I refrain. I remember my cousins, men who went to foreign medical schools, married first-generation heiresses of clothing manufacturers, then went so Valentino off to war. "They look handsome in their uniforms," I said.

"No man looks handsome in uniform," my father corrected.

Once in a restaurant I stared at a post-Korean prosthetic

claw, she buttering his bread, was caught at it and glanced away. "That's all right, ma'am" (Texas drawl), "I don't mind eating out of her hands."

I mind, boy. I mind very much. As the mother of one hero, and possibly two, I can't think of anything I mind more.

One of the few times literature was of absolutely no comfort to me was when the president's letter of condolence arrived. I called on Virgil, Homer, Dante to remember my fidelity to them. "Bring me a happier ending. Don't sing to me about the brave heroes yielded to dogs and vultures." (If there be among you those who do not understand what Patrocles is to me that I should weep for him, come see my Aaron's posthumous medals and military commendations framed with the president's letter. Oh framed. Framed.) He played his part in history, you say?

History! Down with history. Give me back my Aaron. If not for those Utopian grandiosities that spring up fully armed, dragon's teeth sown in the service of arrogant doctrine, Aaron would not have parachuted behind my cousins' line. Aaron would be married to a girl of ordinary bloom and be an academic and bring his two children to stay overnight while he and his wife went to a movie.

You think that's ordinary? Try counting them on the fingers of a mangled hand.

Sneer. Call it castrating. I, a matriarch, say take the world away from men and give it to mothers for a while. It needs to be washed, put to sleep, so the bloody mouths, the trashed limbs, the shredded nerves may heal. Give the damn thing back to us who salvage coffee tins, preserve unripe tomatoes, conserve orange peel, as ants carry off eggs because they are eggs. Stop the fighting. Stop the screaming, the crying. Put down your explosives. Everybody, into bed for a nap.

*

To pass from being to nonbeing takes a lifetime. To do so with style requires years of practice in becoming. (No one should die young.) It takes collusion to die your own death, to keep it from the hackers and technicians.

"Turn off those blinking machines," my father's eyes commanded. "Am I a man or a terminal cancer?"

Aunt Giselle died the death appropriate to her life. Wasting. Her flesh wasted, she dissolved into her skeleton. Her bones were buried in alien ground.

Aunt Cassie and my mother dealt with it, each in her own way.

Cassie disappeared from her son's house when her homeopath was dismissed and an M.D. was called who would inject painkilling drugs. She was found lying on a flat rock in a nearby park, wrapped in Uncle Heinrich's old coat, having breathed healthful pine odors to the last.

"When is a good time to die, do you think?" my mother asked her granddaughter, Arie, one hot summer afternoon.

"After Labor Day, after the children get back from camp and everyone gets home from vacation," Arie, her favorite, answered calmly, and went on sketching. "Grandma, doesn't the phlox smell like Mom's strawberry jam cooking!"

"On my grandfather's farm, when I was eight years old, I rolled down a hill with a little shepherd boy. We held our arms tight around each other. The hill smelled of strawberries. Then so did we." Strands of white streaking her strong black hair looked premature. Her emaciated hands lay idle in her lap, her wide wedding ring loose, held in place by the work-thickened joint.

"No, Arnie, I do not want exploratory surgery."

"Maybe they can take the lump away," I said.

"Not without taking me away," she answered.

"Can I do anything for you, Mama?"

"One thing, don't let them keep me in an icebox like they did your father. Put me right in the ground."

She began her fast on the Labor Day weekend. She did not break it.

The new science of cryogenics, with its spinoff techniques for freezing those about to die, will take away the finality of death. How will I read the newspaper with no obits? What will we do about Mother's Day — substitute visits to cold storage warehouses for cemetery treks? Where will we lodge heaven — in a computerized afterlife? When will a widow be a widow? A bereaved mother, bereaved? How shall we deal with infinities of losing?

It is certain that everything about it will be different from what we imagine, and not easier. Dying but not dead. Losing but not lost, like a person reported missing. Learning to live with a continuous parting, daily picking at it like a wound on which the scab is never allowed to heal. Waiting. Yearning. Grieving for ghosts on ice.

Where in life does death begin?

Theologically, is a homunculus a soul from conception?

Baptismally, may it be eligible for eternal life before emergence?

Legislatively, can the foetus be said to suffer murder?

This is a grave debate. It blazes between right-to-lifers and right-to-one's-own-lifers. It smoldered at first between Adam and me and, at the last, flared between Jeremy and me.

"Medically, it's considered a crime," Jeremy said. "My Hippocratic oath forbids abortifacients. When the nurses hold a newborn in their hands, I listen with them for the infant to answer for itself. You too must have heard in the first AAAH! that the being has already experienced . . ."

". . . has already experienced what?" I asked, defensive as only a person very much in the wrong can be.

"Creation and dissolution. It has arrived with Socrates' message: life is a lesson in death and dying."

"Socrates, I take it, understood baby talk."

He held up a subduing hand at my sarcastic tone.

"Say he learned it at his mother's knee. Socrates' mother was supposed to be in charge of parturient women."

"I bet Socrates did not acknowledge his source."

He smiled wanly. "I met you in 1919, Ariadne. It is 1945. It would be crude to end our long old-fashioned friendship in a modish battle between the sexes."

"Right, doctor." (Since the subject was abortion, I couldn't in conscience call him Storky.) "Is this cry supposed to be comprehensible in any language?"

"According to the Ebers Papyrus, which some scholars suggest was contemporary with Moses — presumed about 1550 B.C. — the child announces if it will live or die as its first cry sounds *ni* or *ba.*"

"Being Egyptian, I take it they were always prepared for a funeral."

* * *

Funeral. The word is like a bell that tolls for Absalom.

If only it had been Tuesday. But it was Monday. Washday. (Accidents in the home account for *achtung acht* percent of untimely deaths.) I would not have seen what I have seen if I had been using the mangle iron when he came home early from senior hockey practice. Had the churn and sump of the machine not drowned out the click of his key in the lock, I would never have shoved his door open with my shoulder. (My arms were full of his towels and underwear.) I would have knocked before entering as I had done for years, ever since he had said "just a minute please" at my step outside his room.

He had always had the modesty of a first child, and had grown up reserved in his personal habits, like my father. I had never seen him in the full manly nude and I took in at one proud glance the well-developed body, long in the torso, somewhat overmuscled in the thighs, rather like Picasso's young tumbler who leads a white horse through blue light.

"Pardon me, lovey," I said, and was half out of the room before I registered, among the brown fuzz on his chest, a sanguine smear; a raw red line of blood. Maternal panic. "Good God, you're bleeding."

Then just beyond his shoulder I saw it. As an endangered mole senses exposure and tunnels frantically downward, my mind tried for the dark.

I've helped deliver kittens, pulled porcupine quills from a silly spaniel's muzzle, dissected a lab frog, even skinned a rabbit, eviscerated poultry. I've read Edgar Allan Poe, seen news films, drained abscesses, yanked off adhesive tape, picked glass out of a knee with tweezers, had an abortion and, by design, looked at Magritte's painting of a mad girl drinking blood from a bird. I've snorted out of a Dali exhibition permitting myself irritated gentility at a still life of a dead mouse at the heart of a rose. And so much more! Picked slugs off tomatoes, dropped Japanese beetles kicking into gasoline, pried lice off a sick bird, prodded pieces of dead bird out of my wild flower bed where a startled owl must have dropped them. Why this alarm drumming through me? This resistance?

It was indeed a mouse.

There's nothing so irremediable about a mouse, is there, that I should grow faint and womanish at the sight of it?

This mouse was pinned down on a tray with laboratory expertise. The person who pinned this mouse down was practice-perfect at it. It was a white mouse. Bloodstained. Mutilated.

Headless, in fact.

There is a divinity that stupefies.

Instantly, milky cataracts dimmed my eyes, but the chemicals of unexpungable imprint burned on my brain, thickened my tongue and filled my mouth with metallic shock.

Still resisting the unspeakable, I worded with swollen tongue, "Biology homework?"

A sigh shuddered through him. His eyes, gray pools in sudden rain, rippled to darks of experience and resignation. With a look "as he had been loosed out of hell to speak of horrors," he waved his head from side to side. "No, Mother. No. No. No."

Then a burst of derision. Oh that sad derision aroused by our own failures, breaking out in scatology, "Shit! Homework? Shit. No!"

In an explosion of abrupt movements he snapped his switchblade back into its sheath, pressing it against his stained chest for leverage; twirled the knife once in a mockery of bravado, and dropped it over his shoulder. It clanged against the metal, and clattered onto the glass top of his desk.

Head held back high and handsome, he whispered, almost lovingly, almost conspiratorially: "There it is! You can't shut it out anymore."

"Shut out what?"

Smashing a toy that had frustrated him.

Teasing the dog until it snarled.

Coming home one night and finding the younger children cowering in their rooms, broken glass in the hall, the photographs dangling from their frames. "They wouldn't get to bed, kept jumping around. Drove me mad. Sorry." Little kids could do that to a sitter.

And much, much more.

"Now you know, Mother."

"What do I know?"

Still with his eyes fixed on mine he stretched out his arm, lifted a bath towel from the stack in my arms, and covered his nakedness. His fingers left a red stain on the white fabric and a smear above his navel.

"What do you mean I know?" Fellow conspirator, I also whispered.

The lift of his lips was at once contemptuous and tremulous. "Poor Mom. Poor Mom."

"Poor Mom? Poor Mom?" I repeated after him, as if I were under command to echo him.

"Poor frightened little Mom. Can't bear the sight of blood."

"Blood?"

"Can't abide violence. Mommy's golden boy got violence . . ."

"Why? Why? Why?"

He mocked my thin squeak. "Why? Why? Why? Because I like it."

"What?"

"You heard. I like it."

(Oh my life's savings! Lost. Lost.)

"Stop that, Absalom. Don't tell lies."

"Objectively, you are the one who lies, little mother." He mocked Adam's tone to perfection.

"You can't mean it!"

"Why not? I don't fit your pretty picture?"

"What picture?"

"Your family portrait. Your beautiful marriage. Us beautiful kiddies. Your perfect son. Me. I've had it! Play nice. Be good. Don't hurt. Don't hit. Don't hate. Be reasonable. Be Jewish. Me, I don't play nice."

I moved toward him. He moved backward. He raised his hand as if to strike me if I came closer.

How many simultaneous bits of information was he reading off my twitching face . . . fear, abhorrence, disbelief, disgust, pity, anger, regret for my arrogance, shock at my deluded pride?

Yet in spite of the mixture of disavowals, I was oozing toward him in a crushed exhausted tenderness like snail slime. Tenderness went from my body, heavily as through viscous fluids, streaked with stabs of lunar pain. "Oh my love, you don't mean what you're saying. You must be . . . joking."

"Lying again. Say it, Mother! I'm a monster. I can't help it. It comes over me."

Grief tolled back and forth between us.

"Don't talk . . . foolishness . . ." I whispered.

"I won't make trouble for you. I am going away."

"What are you saying? You can't go away. No, I won't allow it!"

"No? Not even if I say excuse me please?"

(He was nine years old again — and leaping up from the table to run away.)

"You're upset. It's an adolescent phase. It's nothing. Don't worry about it. You're making too much of it. You'll talk it over with Jeremy."

"I know all about me, Mother."

"You're no doctor. How do you know?"

"I know!"

There was this awful, quiet leisure between us. Time for creator, filled with desolation, to look away from her creation. Time for Frankenstein's monster to answer with hatred for his creator.

"Don't worry, I'll join the Marines. They'd love me like a mother."

Had he always had that ready ability to phrase with a knife twist?

"I don't want you to go away."

"Don't you though? Lying again. Tsk-tsk!"

God help me, what had he read out of me?

Suddenly he seemed to grow terribly tired. His glance swirled away like a seaweed island carried by wind, in concentric course around me, focused on me unbearably, negatively as it were, circling wider and wider in outgoing flight, leaving me in dead center.

A last glance of wild hurt eyes, pitying too, echoing helplessly that recurring scene in the parental drama.

"It's nothing to do with you," he said. "It's my life."

"It's mine too."

"That's your funeral," he said with scrolled mouth. "Your funeral."

And so it was.

After the event he did not weep, he did not promise a new start. He disappeared. There was no disorder in his room. His playing boots were side by side. His schoolbooks were arranged on his desk. One night he did not come home.

I checked with friends, with his hockey coach, with his guitar teacher. I called Adam in Denver. He happened to be out of the hotel. He picked up the message in his box the next morning and came right home. Together we went to the police station to report him missing.

"Don't worry, folks," the sergeant said, "most of them that runs away comes back in a week, ten days at the most." (What happens to those who don't?) "These kids from good homes, you know, looking for adventure. He's over sixteen, ma'am? We couldn't force him home if we found him. You could check the emergency rooms in the hospitals and the recruiting center. You say he's five foot eleven and an athlete? Could have lied about his age. They will . . ."

*

I went on with my tasks. There were three children at home. "Where's Absalom?" they asked.

They soon stopped asking aloud, but a pall of distrust tainted them. They closed ranks, clung to each other, saw less of their friends, and with instinctive tact brought none of them home, as they had until then. Aaron, my sturdiest one, returned from school subdued, no longer the exuberant friendly puppy. On his formerly serene brow a frown wrinkled, a tiny line. Arie, a long-limbed adolescent, went about with the shocked look of a betrayed sweetheart. She grew both more aloof and sharper to me as if to imply it was all my fault. When I put my arm around her to comfort myself and her, she stayed briefly and then politely found a reason for pulling away, like a cat drawing back in distaste. Benjamin lost some of his childish fat and looked taller. He looked less mischievous and more stoically Indian. A dimple he had in one cheek disappeared. "Hi, are you there?" he would call from the door. "Here I am, in the kitchen. Have some milk and fresh cookies." (I didn't ask him if he meant to be calling me.)

Adam lost weight. He suddenly looked every minute of his forty-six years. He canceled business trips. He came home earlier, some afternoons early enough to meet the children at school and drive them home. He played chess with Arie, built airplane models with Aaron and did math puzzles with Benjamin.

The children took to doing their homework in the living room rather than in their own rooms. After dinner we huddled together by the fireplace. We played records or kept the radio on against the heavy anxious silence. If the phone rang a column of prayer rose.

I plunked the strings of rememberings. Why not remain fixed at the trestle table in the happy light of spring at the dacha, Absalom frying fish at the black kitchen stove, wooly curls of smoke rising darker and lighter in and out of shafts of sunlight. "Who's for one more? Fresh caught, fresh fried . . . I have here

212

one more . . . going . . ." Arie, rosy and authoritative over her pan of buttermilk biscuits; Aaron, little boy blue in a tricorner newspaper hat, most admiring, demanding more fish, more biscuits, more; Benjamin popping raspberries into his round mouth, mischievously watching me not see. Why not? Have another raspberry, son. Dribble on your bib.

Yet it was not perfect there, either.

Walking with the children through the wet grass by the river meadow, Absalom saw the trail of blood first. "Something's been killed," he said.

Arie stumbled on the nest of baby rabbits, their eyes closed, mouths gaping for food.

"Their mother must have been wrung by a fox or a dog. She is lost. They have been left behind! They are hungry. They are lost."

"They'll die," Absalom said.

"What's die mean?" asked Benjie.

"Why did God let it happen?" cried Aaron.

"Silly! There's no god for rabbits," said Arie.

"If there is no god for rabbits, there is no god for me," Absalom said and stomped away, calling back, "You said there was, Mom."

Arie picked up the nest. Aaron held a piece of grass toward the milky-eyed babies. We tended all day. Doll blanket. Warm water bottle under basket. Baby formula eyedropper. But in the morning they were all cold. Bitter defeat. Tears.

In the pantry I shook my fist at the sky.

"So little, they just got here," Arie whimpered.

"It's unfair. They never had a chance," said Aaron, my Boy Scout.

I set the breakfast table and put on a bowl of fresh-picked raspberries. Tearful, the children sat down. Benjamin was the first to reach for a berry. Next, Aaron, tears rolling down his round cheeks, smashed a fruit against his palate and reached for another. Arie wept but also ate. Only Absalom sat, eyes wide and fierce, accusing me of falsifying everything.

Pain, I thought I had climbed peaks of pain and disillusion early in my marriage. But again, what had I known of pain? When Absalom left, I plumbed the depths of a more stony, enduring kind. In his continued absence, pain swelled in recesses I hadn't known were in me. Pain when surfacing from sleep like an exhausted swimmer panting for breath, trying not to wake up, putting off the moment of knowing once again he was gone. Refusing to let pain grip my mind totally before the defenses of consciousness could be erected. Keeping eyelids closed tight, then bowing to it, accepting his image as clear as if it stood mocking at the foot of the bed.

Once, when he was about ten years old I had awakened to find him staring at me. At breakfast he made a joke of it. "I'm doing a composition on how people sleep. Arie rolls her eyes white when I touch her. Her eyelids flutter. Aaron sleeps curled on his side or flat on his back like a baby, with his arms alongside his head. Guess what Mommy does? She tosses and groans and whacks her pillow in her sleep."

"Oh Absalom, what a story," I said. "That's not true."

He smirked. "Oh isn't it?" He looked ten years older and knowing.

"You left me out, you didn't tell how I sleep," Benjamin said.

"You sleep as if you were awake inside. Tallyho."

"Time for school," Adam said. But Absalom pinned him with a malicious grin, and a stare of cold steel.

"And Dad? Dead to the world."

*

Morning. Dragging myself from bed, trying not to moan like an ancient rag picker dragging a bundle, ugh, ugh, trying to breath regularly against the iron bar of pain between the breasts, trying not to bang the fist rhythmically against the forehead moaning ugh, ugh. Not looking in the mirror at the person who had failed to hold him; whose love was not returned; the mother whose son had looked at her with hate; the wife who must stop her muffled sobbing and go to the kitchen, grind coffee, cook cereal, eggs, toast muffins, set out the sustaining hot breakfast for the others; must push down the pain to its everyday level and get on with everyday chores.

In April a postcard arrived from the Tower of London.

"Very educational. Many beheadings took place here. Love A."

Thoughtfully, it had been sent to the country house. The mailman helped establish our alibi. "That fine son of yours studying abroad, I see. First time he's missed fishing season since you've bought. Probably he'll get back for hunting."

In May, another postcard: Gozzoli's Saint Sebastian, quivering with arrows. It was from San Gimignano, addressed to me. In July a third, also to me. Signed, "A loves A."

Then silence. Longer and longer silence.

In my despair I outdid myself at domestic chores. I cleaned and polished the apartment to a mirror glaze. I baked intricate pastries requiring close attention, at times all through the night. I would come to a startled consciousness out of a daze, as if I had fallen asleep on my feet, puzzled as to how the potholder came to be in my hand, my hand on the handle of the oven door. The slightest disorder unnerved me. I got out of bed to straighten a picture that hung awry. I had an inner monologue with a bath towel that resisted proper folding. Some days I spent in a state of apathy, until a moment of icy realization would catch me and clear my head, shrinking my nose membranes as if I had inhaled spirits of ammonia. I would pass from a tranced daydream to a state of terror, which again would slip behind me like a view seen from a train, before I could grasp it.

Adam and I did not talk of Absalom's disappearance. We waited. It was as if talking about it would seal it. At times I telephoned the missing persons bureau and talked compulsively to the unknown listener, reporting every detail as if it would chance not to end again on "That's your funeral."

My eyes were afflicted with his afterimage. If I looked up from the book I was trying to read, he would be on my retina, looking back at me, one eyebrow raised, the other eye wickedly, knowingly narrowed. Some nights I wandered barefoot from room to room and saw his outline glowing in the dark. He was ahead of me on the street. He was a shadow in the doorway. I went to the country house to escape and was sure it was he I saw setting off on the woodland path, with his gun. I ran after him, heavily, like an old woman. He became mist. Was that he night fishing or only fireflies among the reeds? Two figures were walking toward me on the road. I waved. One waved back. Close-up, strangers. The rise and fall of hope was exhausting.

I tried to recapture him, laughing. I came on him hugging his knees, stony and uncomplaining, his eyes shining. Had he been crying and I not noticed?

He had been so vivid. How was it he was fading into unbroken sadness? I remembered him passionately tying fishing flies. Had he been smiling?

He was gone. He who had been of and with us was gone. I had no other prayer but his return. If only he would come back, if only he would come back.

And Adam?

I believe in the reality of that man's suffering, for I have wakened him from his own weeping, his manhood limp with grief. I have heard him in his chamber mourning his carrion fruit, like old King David, "Oh my son, my son!"

We came to know those evenings of shared sorrow, neither of us putting a bite of food into our mouths. "Eat something, Adam."

"You eat something, Ariadne."

"With my mouth full how will I answer the telephone when it rings?"

We were careful with one another, as one is with people after surgery.

*   *   *

Where are the poets who have mourned with Jocasta? Where are the artists who have been moved to transfigure her grief at the loss of her newborn babe? Is the maternal instinct such a vulgar subject that it is good manners to keep it hidden? Ah, if women had written the stories . . .

Maternal grief is not confined to royalty. Unfortunately, my son, you became adorable to me in the pious sense. Morning and evening, in my prayers your name was on my lips. Sleeping and waking, you were not there. Burnt offerings. Memorial candles. Fortune cookies. Horoscopes. Followed clues. Put in ads. Read personals. Had faith in miracles and mirages. Denied. Despaired. Everywhere saw the son running toward the mother he was so self-righteously fleeing.

Everywhere, mothers looking for their sons. I would not have believed there were so many.

We hired a detective service. A clipping service.

From a Miami newspaper:

ITEM: Boy . . . swam ashore a week ago. Has no memory of who he is or where he came from. Appears to be about seventeen years old. "I sure would like to know who I am," he said, tears streaming down his cheeks . . . He plays the guitar. He has wavy red brown hair and light eyes . . . is five feet eleven, 160 pounds.

217

The officer I spoke to on the telephone told me he had already received more than a hundred calls from women claiming that from the description of the youth they were sure he was their son.

So it was that something I did not particularly want to happen happened. I became a tourist. During school holidays the children and I saw America. I read of a fishing competition in Oregon and at Easter we visited Oregon. During the summer the children and I toured the continent. I counted the quivering arrows in Gozzoli's St. Sebastian in the San Gimignano. "Very educational."

I thought I saw him through my hotel window, from a taxi, in a group of lounging bucks on the Spanish Steps. But it was never he. Someone reported seeing him in Pisa. I went to Pisa.

I was sure it was he entering the Leaning Tower and ran after him. At the first turning, I saw it was a young man who thrust his shoulders forward as stiffly and had the same Venetian color hair. On fire with disappointment, I stepped out onto the nearest viewing balcony.

Below, a funeral was in progress; a chamber of commerce, first-class funeral. A glass carriage, six black horses, white plumes fanning the air at each rise and fall of their deliberate flanks, a bobbing motion like water wings. Muffled hooves, muffled drums, almost inaudible the feet of the dwarfed mourners.

Descending slowly, stopping at each balcony level, I went out on the street and joined the spectators.

Clerics, sumptuously hooded and caped, the glitter and tinkle of religious emblems, shawled women crossing themselves against contagion. Down. Down. Rosa Damascene down in a chill of petals, down into the commanding mud.

The pace of the cortege is so slow I have time to gaze through the etched glass sides of the hearse.

It is a young woman. Snow White of the poisoned apple. She is small and still neat-faced from lack of living. Her gown is embossed with an all-over pattern like spider webs, white satin of low luster, stiff as if cut from tin. It stands away from her understated body as if not to touch her. Pressed against her, her ringless hand seems to hold a spray of white roses and a white moiré book, locked. Can a dead hand hold? Is she taking the secret of her novella with her, locked in her diary?

The hearse passes. Touch rosaries . . . lift up your hearts in triumph, bystanders, you have escaped this time.

How are we to proceed, if the cycle is broken, if the young press before their parents to their graves? There must be order, I tell you, even in dying.

A whisper follows after the hooves, the creak of wheels, the mourners, the priest's tiny bells. Clues. They gather. Murder? My heart clenches and swells quickly. No. It was suicide. The whisper gathers. Suicide. There was time for confession. Last rites. Saved. Crowned with all the idle weeds that grow.

Everybody begins to create a death for the corpse.

(Mock and postulate as you will, random death is more unbearable than a patterned end.)

There is only this little interval to dress her in possibilities which only last week were vast. I, too, go to find her.

Worms will not try that curious virginity? He let in the maid that out a maid never departed more? Pregnant? Betrayed? You promised me to wed? A fall from a great height. How many hearts fall with her? My brother Reuben, tell. My son Absalom, say.

219

My head was throbbing. I could not control my sobs. By-standers regarded me with curiosity — an American tourist carrying on as if she were near kin.

What's this? What's this I am wishing?

Would to God it were you, my son? Then I too would rest. Oh Judas mother! Be thankful for small blessings. There is in this crowd a mother whose son is smeared with this virgin's blood.

That son is not you, my Absalom. Nor are you the murderer pictured in this morning's newspaper.

The family was on the stand, two brothers, a sister and his gray-haired bespectacled mother. The mother touched her lips with her hand and then sadly extended her arm at full length toward the stony-faced defendant.

Nor are you the one who lay on the bar floor, eyes open, blood rusting in the sand. Would you believe that in our quiet neighborhood, minutes after the missing persons broadcast, three disgraced mothers, pretending not to see one another, arrived on the scene?

I elbowed my way in among the mourners. "Good-bye, child. Good-bye, child!" I sobbed. Some kind gentleman ceremoniously drew me out of the cortege.

My head was expanding with air. Air was fizzing out of my ears, out of a punctured balloon. I fled.

In the campo santo behind the baptistry the air was cool and smelled of cut grass trodden by tourists. On the walls the *Triumph of Death* was being restored. I myself was walking down a path, a bright new garden spade over my shoulder. I felt death running muddy into my mouth and nose. And I asked again, would it have been better for us, Absalom, there in the pond, in the ditch?

I will stand and shout, "Ladies and gentlemen, cultured

young men and women on educational journeys, the tour is abolished. Come home. Disabled veterans selling miracle medals and postcards to support future veterans, help! Help! I am a tedious joke walking. I have this garden spade over my good little basic black, and I am taking myself to a place where I will dig my own grave. Come back. Come back. It's years since I have cooked for you."

"An American gone loco." (How right they were!)

An English tour guide said, "A shame. A respectable-looking woman like you. Get along, dearie. Drunk in the afternoon! Go home and sleep it off."

The policeman, in order not to put an unpleasantness on the tourist scene, tucked me into a taxi.

*   *   *

When I began to travel, my impetus no merrier than to search for Absalom, he was an aberration, an early case of the pandemic. I searched secretly and by myself. Now there are societies of parents who have become Hare Krishna pilgrims. Not to Canterbury do we wend. No such luck! Like the sick who crawl to Perugia, like the shamefaced whose last hope is Lourdes, fanatic yet hopeful, old prospectors given up hope of a lucky strike but habituated to seeking, we are subject to mystical promptings that whip us on the search one last time. And one last time . . .

We became connoisseurs of communes, cognoscenti of mental institutions and addiction centers. Chevaliers of emergency rooms and police stations. Knights of storefronts and village pads. We have been to see, not the pope, but the gurus of Haight Ashbury, Amsterdam, Marrakech, Ibiza, Greek cave towns, the Spanish Steps, heroin Soho, New Delhi, the East Village, Vermont, Boston . . .

Absalom. It's years and your old mother still longs for indifference. Only indifference shows that one has given up some-

221

one. Your absence still anguishes and enrages me. I love you without illusions; I love deeply while I hate. I bargain with the gods. "Send me a sign," I pray. "Send me a postcard. Gods, send me a messenger to tell me you have arranged for my son to come to a well and find some Rebecca who will unload the caravans of his grief."

*   *   *

Do not think that after he left I did nothing but search for Absalom. No. Each child is an only child, not to himself alone, but to his parents; though every child does not tremble with the same lust to be gone. Nor is every child a figure adorned by a parent with tainted and sterile desires.

The drone bass of my life had to continue domestic. Daily I paid tribute to the ordinary tasks of dutiful daughter, exemplary wife, dedicated mom, conversational mistress.

I had to run off to search for Absalom as a woman steals time for a lover, loves him with one of her whole hearts, yet lives through the loss of him holding grief inside her like a vial of acid that must not be spilled to harm the children.

In my case I should say I learned to steal off to a lover through having searched for Absalom.

BOOK II

Perplexities of Her Sex

But we're not satisfied with what we ourselves have learned about the world and about ourselves. We're always waiting for a stranger to come and tell us something more. And "something more" means "the rest of it," and that's what we need most; we miss it. So go ahead stranger! . . . tell her what she herself is, beyond what she already knows she is . . . her life, her years, her great expenditures of self, what of herself is honey and what is gall on her tongue, the hunger she has, and the hunger she sees.

— ELIO VITTORINI

The Marriage Bed

The indecent spectacle was her own action beheld from the outside
. . . realizing . . . how infinitely repulsive the body of a life is without
its soul.

— VIRGINIA WOOLF

BLAME IT ON the weather again. Mini-climates impinging
on maxi-climates have upset my applecarts in a grippingly obvious way, not once, not twice . . . Weather, like a false but
passionate lover, has almost persuaded me I am the object of
its spontaneous storms. For me, blizzards blow. For me, skies
that are blank to the anthill crushed beneath some booted
hunter's stride, hang out festoons of snow and ice. If snow had
been hanging from telephone wires the first after-class that Paul
and I carried our coffee cups to the same cafeteria table, I might
have been alerted to danger, snow being a phenomenon that (for
me) combines crystalline order with the random violence and
absurd happenstance of reality. But autumn lingered well into
the winter while I was taking that course on the formal aspects
of modern poetry.

"Not another poetry class!" Jessica shattered an etude with
an arpeggio and sprang up from the piano bench. "Why not

225

politics or banking? Home economics would be better. There you might find someone to butter your toast for a change! How can you find a lover in a course like that?"

"I'm looking for my son, not a lover. At my age!"

"Your age is my age. Going on thirty-seven is supposed to be optimum time for wives to graduate to lovers."

"I didn't know there was a schedule. But if there is, you may be sure I will be late."

"Why don't you cut your hair and dedicate it before it turns white? Ariadne, you have the woman's disorder of fidelity. You finally creep out of the kitchen to college and you remain faithful to your dead high-school major. How boring."

"Boring!"

No doubt about it. Forms get as worn as content. That was the first thing the famous old poet talked about in class. Somewhere along the way he had gotten the idea that if he dressed like a racetrack tout — tattersall jacket, green suede vest, brass buttons — it would camouflage his vulnerability and his erudition, both of which were vast.

"Awright class, you want to get into this poetry game, you gotta empty your educated maws of leftovers. Start clean-boweled."

The bread-shaped ladies tittered. A young man sitting cross-legged in front of the rostrum snaked upright like a cobra to a flute. The man who looked like a severely handsome priest, the man who was Paul, scowled and sat back in his seat so hard it shook my chair as well as his.

"Let's get it over with. For next session write a mess of couplets or a love lyric in two quatrains. Just to make the game tougher, put 'em in a smooth skin. Nothing with a gritty shell. No X, K, Z, Q. Only soft sounds: F, H, V and vowels."

Paul, connoisseur of surfaces, leaned forward, amused.

"And after that, my jockos, not another quatrain or couplet out of you. Hear? We got a lotta good fellers out there proving those forms won't hold our content, they're exhausted, they have to be put out to pasture before they can be run again. Hear?"

For the opening session I had arrived early. (I've never gotten over being afraid I'll miss the boat and be left behind.) Precisely on time an exceptionally tall man in a somber black coat strode in, glanced around and took the empty seat next to mine. He nodded without smiling.

I hadn't the slightest inclination to be social. I was attending classes on Jeremy's insistence. ("You must stop running to find Absalom, Arnie. Listen to the doctor, my child. Go to school. Immerse yourself in work.") But what was I doing in a poetry course when it hurt me to breathe; when I needed to know how to bridge the chasm between what I had been given to expect of motherhood and the excrutiating actuality I was experiencing. I had thrown myself into reproducing family life on the basis of conventional models. I had wrested four children out of star stuff or primeval slime, or hurricanes, and clearly, they would not and could not reciprocate my love. They had their loves to attend to. My reward? I had found a capacity to suffer that I had not known existed. Philosophy is what I should have been studying. I was asking St. Augustine's questions now. What then am *I,* my God? What is my nature?

The man sitting beside me had a physical presence that was too dramatic to ignore. He had a high-strung horsey face — a long thin nose that flared out in fleshy nostrils — topped by a mane of glinting steel-colored hair that contrasted disturbingly with his coarse, intensely black mustache. He spoke with a slight accent; Swiss as it turned out.

As the term progressed we exchanged salutations, then a few comments, then, after class I joined him, among others, in discussion, then later to the cafeteria, later to the exit. Later, he accompanied me to my parked car.

"Good night, Mr. Donant."

"Good night, Mrs. Arkady."

Neither of us could be accused of plunging wildly ahead.

One evening I felt Paul observing me, his head toward the lecturer but his eyes peripherally on me. In the margin of his notebook, among inky doodles, I glimpsed a sketch that might have been of my profile. Our glance met but his eyes remained impersonal as the shutter of a camera.

Seasonable slush underfoot. I dashed along Fifth Avenue, muttering my list of errands: green peppercorns, a pair of lined gloves for Adam, a watercolor pad for Arie, Santayana's *The Last Puritan* for Jeremy (a reminder of our first meeting).

Out in the big world the Great Depression lingered, in spite of Roosevelt. Civil war was being fought in Spain. Lorca's death by Falangist bullets had been hued and cried. (I had cried, too.) Hitler's army had marched into the truce zone. Jews of the world were experiencing yet once again that despairing isolation at the world's recurring hatred of them. Daily the veneer thinned between French rationalism, German romanticism and official anti-Semitism. The Moscow trials had begun and the *cousinas,* grown old, sat wrapped in dark shawls of mourning for the dream they sensed dying in Russia's womb. "The same Rasputins . . . the same czars . . . the same Siberia," they cried.

But what I was pshawing and ptushing in and out of my mind was whether the sketch I had glimpsed was of me or not. In my behalf I can only add that an odor of romance lingered like cold ash in the world because Edward had abdicated a throne for the woman he loved.

So when Paul's hand shot out in front of me and arrested my flight, I was totally receptive.

"Mrs. Arkady, halt. You've already won the race."

He was carelessly dressed — black turtleneck sweater (badly laddered), a hand-knitted muffler (frayed), paint-spattered corduroys, and he could have used a shave. Still, he looked devilishly handsome.

"Aren't you well, Mr. Donant?" I asked.

"Do I look debilitated? I feel splendid." He twirled the end of his black mustache. "And you, are you quite well, Mrs. Arkady?"

"I . . . I thought since you were home from work . . ."

"Lord have mercy on us!" He had a pleasant manly voice that rose to a youthful tenor when he laughed. "You are a pillar of society. Dear madam, I am staying at home because I feel like it (no work ethic at all). Would you disapprove less if I said I was painting my studio?"

At his ironic appraisal a blush burned from my forehead down. "In that case you don't get a demerit," I rallied defensively. "You have a studio in the neighborhood?"

"It's more a converted tenement, but it has north light, doesn't cost much, and is convenient to my several breadwinning accounts. Come and see. I could rinse a cup and offer you tea."

Actually, I felt uneasy and shy, then silly for feeling so, a mother of four, one daughter about to enter the Boston Museum School, a son already out on his own in the world, you might say, if you were evasive.

Paint pots in the middle of the scruffy floor, a blue enamel coffeepot bristling with different size brushes like a bouquet of dried thistle heads, a stack of canvases seen from the smudged back, a closet, the door open, a tweed jacket, the black coat and a single suit visible, a grimy toilet seat up — towels on the floor, an unmade bed with a rumpled batik spread thrown over it, beside it a chair on which sat a clock, a used teacup and a stack of books. Out of paint's way was an excellent drafting table as neatly organized as a dentist's tray.

He put a teakettle on the hot plate, grinning down on me in a way that made me feel he was finding me ridiculous. "My method is clear, don't you agree?"

"Your desk is, in any case."

"That's the spirit." His laugh rose, clear and merry. "I work at home, and an organized desk is efficient."

"What do you work at, if I may ask?"

"A wide variety of things. When I came to New York from Paris, via Geneva, I designed type for a foundry. My employer had no objection to my not working at the plant and when the company shut down, I decided an office job would never suit me. You see how modest my needs are. I leave myself time to paint, take courses and invite my soul."

The sheer bravery of choosing a chancy life, of dismissing the need for secure income and respectable position in favor of pleasure, staggered me. Had there been a free chair I would have sat down in shock.

"Doesn't it make you anxious?" I asked and could have bitten my tongue.

He tilted his head and studied me as if *I* were the oddity. "No, Mrs. Arkady, boredom makes me anxious; I take only work I find stimulating."

The idea agitated me. Since I tidy when I'm uneasy, I moved toward the teacup, thinking to rinse it, then hastily put my hands in my coat pocket.

I believe he took pity on me. "I see my studio has disappointed you. Tell me what you expected."

"Let me see." I turned exaggeratedly silly out of embarrassment. "A vast skylighted room with windows from which we see the Eiffel Tower in masterly perspective, a column of draped figures, a large stand on which a model poses in brocaded Venetian velvet and jeweled snood."

"Tell me about the artist . . ."

"You are raven-locked, a touch of silver at the temples, you wear a toneless velvet jacket, a flowing cravat, pearl trousers. On the easel a heavily varnished portrait is rapidly emerging.

He picked up the whitewash brush and slapped it up and down a section of wall, vigorously. "Like this . . ."

"You've caught it exactly! Your eyes are fixed on me and I am looking at you heartlessly yet meaningfully . . ."

"Quite cross-eyed," he said, leaning close to my nose.

And that was as close as he came.

But after the next class we went together for coffee. And the next.

A week later he telephoned. He wasn't sure of my voice but I immediately recognized his. "Mr. Donant?"

"Mrs. Arkady? I have to take a blueprint to a contractor in White Plains. It's such a rare, crisp day, if you aren't elbow-deep in jam tarts, why not keep me company? We could drive up, have a walk in Woodland Park, lunch at a Greek restaurant I know, and be back before your little ones' tea."

I couldn't very well confess I *was* elbow-deep in jam tarts for Benjie's class bazaar, could I?

Winter was ice-deep, but breathing soft-nosed, stirring out of metabolic low. The summer pavilion was shuttered, nymphs and boxwoods wrapped in burlap, terraces and tennis courts impeccable under snow. A pair of German shepherd dogs loped across the frozen lake, their paws barely touching the water-filmed ice, positively waltzing, their tails waving behind their glowing beast genitals. They barked at the geese swimming in a widening black pool, snaking their necks, looking for hand-outs.

"I forgot the geese! How could I! For one hundred and two years I've been bringing stale bread and fresh children."

Paul groaned. "Halve it to fifty-one for my sake. That would mean only fifteen years to close the age gap between us."

I stopped dead. "You aren't a mathematician?"

"No. Don't struggle with that problem. I'll tell you my age. I'm thirty-six years old."

"You are younger than I am? I'm pushing thirty-seven."

"I'm pushing harder. I look older than you. I've lived a restless life."

"So have I," I said, with one silly toss of my head, casting a lurid glow on my straitjacket hours.

"Oh have you?" He gave me a sidelong, lightning dart of appraisal. "I would not have guessed it." Another look. The whites of his eyes seemed to enlarge. "I suppose one can never be sure."

Was this where it happened? As many times as I've re-trieved, scanned, reconsidered every detail of my tragic love affair — perhaps an observer would call it farcical — at-tempting to discover, rationally, where I dropped the in-criminating handkerchief on which Paul fabricated his exor-bitant suspicions, I've never considered this detail before. Was it *here?* Did I jeopardize his trust in me, or rather his trust in his judgment of me, in that moment of feminine vanity, in a desire to appear more seductive than I had any reason to feel?

A gander came waddling up, snuffling.

"Let's run from these beggars." I dashed ahead, assailed on all sides by images of the children.

"You run fast for a woman of such a great age. It's getting late. Let's eat before they stop serving."

It might have been better for me if I had slipped into the kitchen among the singing casseroles, the sizzling oils, among the Greek aunts, faint mustaches on their upper lips. There would be branches of sage and fennel, jars of honey with honeycomb; jelly glasses budding and building into yogurt. I might have come away with a recipe.

How censorious I had been of my mother's family, yogurt making, herbs gathered at the summer cottage to perfume teas all winter, stalks of camomile for hair rinse, sweet fern drying in bunches; my mother coming in from an afternoon among resin-seeping pines, a shallow willow basket on her arm, wood mushrooms exuding their nose-tingling peaty odor, bronze leaves in her loosened hair, pine needles clinging to her skirt — like as not, her shoes tied by their laces hanging over one shoulder, her whole being giving off the healthy tick-tock of a person in whom the physical clocks ran on time.

Mother, are you sure of my ontogeny? In your crossing and recrossing of borders you must have been terrified by a time zone. Something is wrong with my clocks. Too early marriage and children, too late love.

A few days later I met Paul as I was running up the steps in front of the Metropolitan Museum.

"Ah ha, Mrs. Arkady. Playing truant again, are you?" He stuck his arms akimbo in a schoolmarmish gesture that was hilariously unsuitable. "Explain yourself."

"Oh please, sir," I whimpered, daring to be playful too. "I'm doing my homework, sir, for a course, sir. Honestly, it's on El Greco."

"I'm glad you are a good girl. As a reward," he dropped his mockery, "may I take you to lunch?"

At the coffee urn the hearty Irishwoman greeted him by name. "Pleasure of your company again today, Mr. Donant."

At the table he said, "I like to paint these chunky Breughel types, lots of flesh, coarse-skinned, strong-featured. They remind me of the matrons who served at our church suppers."

"Were you religious, Mr. Donant?"

"Intensely so, until I was not at all. My mother was determined to make at least one of us a rock of the church. My full given name — I should leap up and click my heels — is Paul Matthew Donant."

"Rather a burden of saints? What happened to Mark and Luke?"

"Mark's middle name was Johann, and he pleased her by becoming an organist in our church. Luke was a girl, Elizabet."

"What did she fulfill?"

"Herself, I trust. She married and had children."

"And you, what have you done to please your mother?"

"Not much, I'm afraid. I'm a jack-of-all-trades." He looked down at his strong beautiful hands — sinuous and expressive as a mime's—"I like to explore a thing intensely, then go on to something else I don't know much about."

"And I," I said in a rush of openness that caught me by surprise, "I never let anything go. I save everything, even clippings of ivy, which is why my garden gets bigger every season."

He had not missed my forward movement. He flicked his mustache, cupped his chin in his hand and leaned forward with a pleased smile.

"I think a clerical collar would suit you," I said.

"My mother might have agreed, but not my wife."

234

My heart had absolutely no right to sink. I busied myself with the food on my plate. "Tell me more."

"I went to school in my home town of Rolle, became a day student in Geneva and bicycled home. I sang in the choir and at nineteen I married the beautiful soprano."

"Positively a myth. Did she remind you of your mother as well?"

He laid his knife carefully on the rim of his plate, bent his head and the whites of his eyes became conspicuous in a way that expressed displeasure. "I hope you aren't one of those women given to orgies of Freudian theorizing about sex."

I answered — boldly for me — "I am not given to talking about sex. I have no theories about it, Mr. Donant. And to date, I have always arrived too late or too early for any orgies."

To my surprise my sharp defense pleased him. An apologetic smile of boyish sweetness erased years from his face. He reached across the table and almost touched my hand. "I beg your pardon, Mrs. Arkady. I intended no offense. My remark, if I may explain it, comes from my annoyance at the fashion for titillating via psychoanalysis."

"I don't follow."

"I'm glad. You see I dine out quite a bit, and I get served warmed-over Freud with my meals in a way that quite takes away my appetite. I should have answered politely, 'My wife, from whom I have been separated for years' " (I had no right to be pleased) " 'did not remind me of my mother.' Mary was statuesque, blond, cool and undomestic. My mother was dark, intense about everything, small and, like you, a superior housekeeper, a devoted mother and an exemplary wife." (I had absolutely no right to be irritated.)

He rose.

"I have to finish some work. Before I go, let's look at a Manet. His surface interests me right now. It surprised me to learn that poets concern themselves with surface too."

"Transcendence interests me," I said. "El Greco. Burning away flesh."

"That's literary, not painterly. Most painters who aim for transcendence paint the way transcendentalists think, which I do not admire. Why burn away flesh? It's *the* thing to paint. It is all the innocent eye sees."

(A hell of a lot he knew about the innocent eye!)

Two women watched his departure — muffler, jacket, hair, long legs flying. Their mouths slightly open, they examined me with that candid slave objectivity women permit themselves. I winced at their estimate. No chic. She hasn't got IT. (I'd been married for over eighteen years and I knew that all too well.) We're younger, prettier, count her out. They walked ahead, their backs arched, their shoes, bags and gloves matched, two indulgently turned out women, sure of their right to be seductive.

Then it snowed! A light treacherous lovely film fell while we were in class. The roads were slippery and Paul offered to drive my car for me.

Adam was on the library ladder adjusting a speaker when we came in. "Hello little mother, were you a good student? I was uneasy about your driving." He spoke without turning.

"Meet Mr. Donant. He was good enough to drive me home."

"How do you do, sir, and thank you. My wife learned to drive late. Her reflexes are not conditioned to emergencies."

"Good sound equipment you have," Paul remarked, as if he hadn't heard. "What is it?"

"Tuner and amplifier Atwater Kent, Emerson speakers."

I left them and went to the kitchen (where else?). I could hear ". . . decibels . . . highs . . . lows . . ."

I sliced some cold meat and cheese, set rolls in the oven, put on the kettle and went upstairs to get out of my damp clothing. As I went through I heard Adam say happily, "What do you think? Isn't there a standing wave in the middle of the room?"

"Right you are, too close to the ceiling. Let's try lower." Paul was lifting books from the shelves.

When I carried in the tray both men gave me a glazed smile.

"Highs are too strong. It will give too much violin," Adam said.

"We'll be forced to listen to Koussevitzky on the double bass."

Adam chuckled appreciatively at Paul's quip. I joined for the pleasure of laughing out loud.

"Ariadne, what a coincidence. Mr. Donant and I are alumni of the same school in Geneva."

"Did you know each other?"

"No, he entered two years after I graduated. He's a mere boy."

From then on Paul drove me home after class and stayed. Adam working at his papers, Paul and I going over our notes, giggling over shared class exercises . . . you do a line and I do a line. Paul bringing Valéry, and translating freely, dictionary and thesaurus between us, one of my marvelous snacks, Bach on the adjusted equipment, Paul or Adam rising to change a record or throw a log on the fire, late news on the radio. Paul sighing, "Time to head out into the cruel world."

When the term ended we studied the catalogue together and agreed on another course.

When did the deception begin? And the self-deception? (I am always innocent until proven guilty.)

237

Locking the front door, Adam said, "A charming man. I wonder about his family life. He never mentions a wife."

"He has one. They met in church, she's older than he is."

He raised an eyebrow. I added, "A statuesque blonde."

"They must make a handsome couple," Adam said and headed up the stairs.

"I'll stay down for a while." (Not that he asked me up.)

A statuesque blonde. Nothing added. Nothing taken away. Like the rearrangement that goes on in the cells of a chrysalis. Into the pupal stage goes the crawler, wrapping itself in its own sticky emanations. They harden. The cells keep rearranging themselves. Out comes the butterfly; so delightful, Pieridae, satyridae, nymphalidae, oh Painted Lady, oh charming fritillaries, transcending criticism, transcending judgment of your voracious probabilities.

Adam's business was flourishing. War had spread over Europe and China, territories were being shifted on the map like chessmen. As Hitler, Franco, Mussolini, Stalin, Hirohito, Chiang Kai-shek became familiar names even in the tabloids, United States defense spending spiraled upward, and with it the need for sophisticated systems of information storage and retrieval. As Adam's business expanded, we entertained more often.

Paul became the extra man, the indispensable bachelor at our dinner parties. Adam's business associates appreciated Paul's technical background, which was sufficient to allow them to go on with their discussions without apology. To their wives he was formal and attentive without being flirtatious. Even Jessica, who guarded herself against intimacy with men by mockery, was pleased to discuss music seriously with him.

Adam usually invited Paul to stay after the other guests left. "Let us drink a stirrup-cup to my lady. The entertainment she arranged for our legates from Chicago surpassed her former excellence." Or, "My queen is lovelier than ever this evening, wouldn't you say, Paul?"

Like a reflex, Adam's compliments increased in the presence of witnesses. They struck me more and more as saccharine. Whether it was his increasing success, or a desire to be kind to me after Absalom's departure, at this period he became positively Arthurian, a parfit knight.

Amazing, how light conversation can weigh you down. There was nothing ostensibly wrong with "My wife can manage dinner for eight at the ring of a telephone. I don't know how she does it." To express displeasure at such remarks would seem wantonly hostile. But I felt my dinner churn. "They are so efficient. It would put us to shame, gentlemen, if our ladies ran the world." Or, "We rarely go to restaurants; my wife's cooking is unrivaled." Or, "Would you believe that my wife is the mother of four monsters, all taller than she is?"

My wife . . . my wife . . . my wife . . .

Well I was, wasn't I?

"You have such an appreciative husband, Mrs. Arkady. I do envy you."(Meaningful glances from wives, guilty grimaces from husbands.)

Or debonair as a carnation in a dandy's buttonhole, titillating tidbits brought out for visiting executives, as if one were to think of him as rather a sly, sexy fellow, putting on innocence like a dunce cap.

"I tell you the waitresses were scantily clad even for a private club. Running among the tables . . . well you might say . . . practically . . . Business you know . . . have to keep up with the competition's benefits. Ha ha." (Why laugh?) "Nice girls . . . Not too difficult to vibrate a man's electricity . . . to keep the image in the trade. Ha ha. Naturally it was only to be expected that when the girls scampered between the tables their bits of costume . . . hmm . . . hmm . . . veiling actually . . . became disarranged, revealing quite attractive elements . . . elements ha ha." (Why, oh why, laugh?) "Nothing to compare to our lovely wives" (a little guardsman's bow of the jaunty head, a boulevardier's flick at a nonexistent mustache) "I took out a cigarette and one of those fillies, no older than my daughter, if that, pranced over with a match and leaned, well, leaned right on me . . . they do like to tease, do their job well, ha ha. 'Now mind your flame,' she said. Everyone at the table laughed. I can't imagine why."

"Good night. Thank you — truly memorable dinner."

"Your husband is a Don Juan, Mrs. Arkady. I'd be furiously jealous."

"Oh we are never jealous, are we, Ariadne?" he said, one arm comradely across my shoulder.

"How fortunate for you both," Paul said, flushing darkly. "I am very jealous."

"No one would believe, to look at her figure, that this woman is the mother of my four . . ."

"Adam, please . . ."

Adam's cheerful face, my ungracious one. I thought I could see Paul coming to the usual conclusion: ardent husband, reluctant wife.

*　　*　　*

A snowy evening.

Zoom camera on a glass dome, the kind you shake so a snowstorm whirls around a compressed house. Focus on a man of schooled bearing, smartly dressed, suitcase and briefcase on the elegant side: Adam, in his middle forties, his figure compact, head and shoulders forward, walking briskly. A family man, one of a vanishing breed. Neither heat nor cold would stay

240

him from his prompt arrival at a sick child's bedside, though a woman's would dismay him.

That evening Ariadne *(c'est moi)* is doing her homework in the high-ceilinged parlor of their duplex; two crystal chandeliers, two marble fireplaces, one of them at a low blaze, two splendid cats picking their way from mantel to grand piano between ambushes of girandoles, ornately framed photos of children, two art-glass epergnes filled with dried flowers from her garden. (I am giving in to the impulse to distance myself from this scene in the impersonal person.)

As Adam enters, the cats leap down. They bound eagerly toward him but stop short of their usual slithering rubbing because his trouser legs and shoes are wet and sticky with snow.

Adam looks ruddy and clear-eyed. A Chekhovian Hans Brinker bringing home the silver skates. He shakes snow from his fur-collared coat, stamps elaborately, and since he has been in Cleveland for four days and three nights husband and wife exchange two wide smiles, a broad hug and a kiss on each cheek.

"Terrible storm brewing, I'd better stop over." He executes his gallant European routine between a bow and heel click, then adds, quite flirtatiously, "I continue to be grateful to sudden storms."

He says it charmingly. It should please, but the uneasy impression she has about his words is an absence of feeling. She hesitates. She has lately become aware of the nervous way she fills the vacuum between them with physical details.

"Your hair is wet. Your shoes. Better get out of your clothing. Have a hot shower. I'll bring you — what would you like — soup or chocolate?"

"Thank you, my dear. I'll have some of your superb hot chocolate. Could you render a report on our offspring, little mother?"

"Benjamin is sleeping over at Jessica's. She's taking him to *Aïda* tonight. Aaron has gone on a trip with his history club to celebrate Washington's birthday in D.C. There is a letter upstairs from your daughter who seems to be settling into college life fairly well." (Neither of them mentions Absalom.)

"Alone at long last!" Adam says.

But that seductiveness is for the living room.

In the bedroom she hung up her dress, and without comment stood with her back to him so he could undo her brassiere hooks, which he did, ending with a friendly pat on the back. Everything as usual. She held her hands under heavy breasts and mocked at herself when she realized it gave her satisfaction that they still shifted only slightly. (No fool like an old fool.)

He dropped his shirt and tie to the floor. He walked around, sipping chocolate, muddying the rug with footprints before he abandoned his sodden shoes and socks. He went into his bathroom to shower. She picked up after him, wiped up, stuffed newspaper into his shoes, and wondered for the hundredth time how such a meticulous, even overorganized man could undress as sloppily as a sleepy two-year-old. She told herself it was his small protest against a professional life that had to be exact to the nth decimal place.

She closed her bathroom door after her. Early on, Adam had indicated distaste for cosmetic details and she cold-creamed quickly, while her bath filled. She could hear him showering and humming (he *was* in an expansive mood) and sank into her hot bath, hoping he would take his time and not curtail her soak. But he knocked, opened the door and poked his head in. (Why bother knocking if you just barge in?) His hair was dripping wet, bouncing up in attractive ringlets, his face amiable and boyish. It was easy to see why the women in his office pampered him and why wives of out-of-town executives cooed,

"What a gallant husband you have, Mrs. Arkady," as he bowed over their coats, their husbands looking uneasy. But handsome is as handsome does, and a living room manner does not a marriage bed make.

"Still in the tub?" (Why ask questions that are not to be answered?)

He came in drying himself vigorously, clear healthy skin shining, his body robust and young for his age; broad shoulders, good legs — a little short for the long torso — only the slightest thickening developing under the ribs, unselfconsciously(?) rubbing his relaxed genitals and fluffing his pubic hair. He finished by taking one of her bath towels off the rack and wrapping it around his middle, glancing into the mirror (repeat of boyish hesitation) and reaching for her comb. "My hair is clean," he said for the (how many times is fifty-two weeks by, say, two times per week by going on nineteen years?).

She repressed a frown. The slightest rebuff could freeze Adam, and meant for a certainty *no sex,* as well as leaving her in the mean-spirited wrong. It amazed her how effective a control his lack of need could be. Or was it part of his plot to chill? He put down the seat cover, spread the second of her bath towels and sat. "I don't see Arie's letter."

He didn't like to look for things. "I put it right beside your bed lamp." (She cleared her throat as if the tightness in her voice had nothing to do with irritation.)

"How was your class tonight, little mother? I called from Cleveland to tell you not to drive to school when the radio announced a storm heading this way from Boston."

"That was sweet and thoughtful of you, dear." Really it was.

"I worry about your driving. You are not good at it."

"Paul drove me home." Paul, as it happened, was a temperamental driver, braking suddenly, dashing into openings, turning his head to converse, contesting each space.

"Sorry I missed him. I'm comfortable with him. It's his European background. Twenty years in New York and I still feel European."

"People don't transplant. I feel foreign though I came here as a little child."

"You never got very big." Gallantry again? Her hopes quite lifted.

"Paul is an attractive man. Probably he stands still while the ladies flutter round him." He said it with the smugness of a man who has never suffered from jealousy.

"I hadn't noticed it especially. Perhaps because his manner is so reserved and old-fashioned." (Had she been fluttering?)

"Any immortal lyrics?" he laughed. (Why laugh at what is not laughable?)

She circumvented the rankle his words left. "How was the Cleveland office?"

"They have a complex actuarial problem with the new department store account but I stole time anyway to go to a concert: *The Four Seasons* and the *St. Matthew.* A symphony orchestra is too big for the Vivaldi. I prefer it with a good chamber group."

"How was the Bach?"

"It sounded like a concerto for kettle drum and accompanying orchestra. We sat too far to the right."

"Who was we?" She asked it in the way of a woman who has not yet known the sickening pornography of jealousy.)

"Our man McAndrew, his wife and his wife's sister, who was hastily impressed into service." He said it archly.

"Did she suffer?"

"I believe she had a satisfactory evening."

"I'm sure you were charming." Was there a sharpness in her voice that he raised his eyebrow in the supercilious way she disliked?

She admitted to herself, it did annoy her that Adam was able to set up a parlor air of intimacy that promised more than ever evolved, certainly, between the two of them.

She rose from the water. Nothing in his gaze congratulated her nudity. He rose very friendly. He handed her the towel he had dampened. They might have been in the kitchen wiping dishes.

"I've got a few papers to look at." His mood *had* veered with his eyebrow.

She nodded, wondering how conscious he was of communicating no S-E-X. Were his little power plays and boyish intrusions tricks for making her tense? That was glamorizing him into higher consciousness and rascality than he had. Had he always had them and she not allowed herself to be conscious of them? Or had she been as afraid of having to act as Adam was to feel?

It was not that he was stupid. By no means. By inclination and career he had specialized his mind to take in and put out limitless amounts of precise information. He was an authority in his field. When he spoke he sounded firm and confident. But on personal matters he was silent or vague. By overendowing precision he had relieved himself of the necessity, and Ariadne of the possibility, of trying to express the inexpressible.

She picked up the towels after him, dusted herself with talcum powder, and still nude, walked out into the bedroom, braiding her hair. He was reading Arie's letter.

As she finished doing her hair, in the mirror she saw Adam glance up, smile (or *was* it a smile?) and return to his reading.

She drew on her long-sleeved nightgown and climbed into her side of the bed, too chilled to stay out of it any longer.

"Umm," he said. "Thermal! A hotel bed is drafty when you turn over."

"I'm not enthusiastic about sleeping alone, either." She moved closer, but there was no answering pressure. "I wish you didn't have to travel so much."

245

He was already enclosed in his reading.

She opened the Hopkins preface that Paul and she had been analyzing and tried to concern herself with outriders and sprung rhythms.

Adam pressed his nude back comfortably against her. In her accustomed position, facing away from him, she bent to her book. He adjusted his shoulder to her, and in silence they settled into the marriage bed.

Ruefully, she thought of Mrs. Shandy's "Pray, my dear, have you not forgot to wind up the clock?" Poor Mrs. Shandy. Did she too sigh for a month of Sundays? Did she, too, creep sleepless from bed, her spouse so excellent a sleeper he didn't miss her? Did she think of herself as a sex fiend?

A womanly lifetime ago, there had been such rage of deprivation in her, furies pointing shame as if they were Aunt Giselle flinging open the bathroom door to catch her dreamily toying in the bath.

Slowly she had gathered her data. No she was not a sex fiend. She had no sex appeal. After all, had she not been voted "girl in the class last likely to marry"? Surreptitiously, she read the cleaning woman's tabloid. "Peaches says Daddy Browning . . . unreasonable demands? forced? Police raid double love nests. Elinor Glyn's *Three Weeks* called obscene. Indian Guide Wife's Lover; husband accused of crime of passion. Companionate Marriage. Incompatability. Policeman charged with multiple rape!" Overheard in a tearoom, "My husband pesters me. Men are pigs." "You know how it is when the affair is over. The only cure for one man is another."

Where were these mythical men? Where was the one who longed for her? At last, the explicit information! Where else but in her father's library, in the Mishnah on Duties of Marriage according to Eliezar. Now hear this, Adam: *Every day* for them that are unoccupied. (Unemployed is also unoccupied.) Twice a week for laborers. (Surely Adam could be considered somewhere in between.) She had come to terms years ago. Sex was not a matter to discuss.

Adam patted her lightly (over the blanket) and switched off his lamp. "Good night, dear. A busy morning ahead."

"My light disturb you?" she asked in her usual polite way. And in his usual way, he was already asleep.

When at last she turned out her light, he wrapped himself about her without waking. She fell asleep to his calm breathing.

Toward morning she rose to consciousness of his hand searching its way in brief preamble and before she was fully awake he had mounted her in silent, direct assault. For reasons lost in the past they did not attempt to kiss. Drowsy as she was, her senses rushed to meet him, her nerves having learned a kind of prison economy.

Speak to me. Why do you never speak to me?

His eyes were closed. Were stag movies reeling behind his lids? Was he embracing some ideal sexy woman through her? Ariadne also kept her eyes closed. Separate but equal, they courted prompt release.

After he rolled off her he said, politely, like a boy who has had a candy bar, "Thank you."

What could she answer but "You're welcome."

She held her breath. He said his two words. She said hers. He was asleep again.

She lay staring at a slice of light knifing between the drawn drapes. It was 5:45. She thought of getting up and baking a cake, but there were no children in the house to be pleased at breakfast. There was the spring rose catalogue to look at. She could go on with the poem she had been writing. Plan a superior little dinner for Adam's next clients, say, poached salmon, sauce verte, soufflé Grand Marnier. Anything to get out of bed. She wondered if Adam had a study correlating

247

high efficiency in housewives with low sexual activity in their husbands.

He was perspiring lightly like a child who has fallen asleep after its bottle. In a peripheral way it occurred to her that his maneuver had something of the deviousness of an infant feigning lack of appetite, traducing its mama into feeding it, at the same time playing on her anxiety about urging him against his will, a drama, perhaps more satisfying than food, of getting pleasure while protesting it.

Vertiginous as if treading down unevenly spaced steps of a steep staircase, ignoring internal pressure slithering like loose gravel between my heart and my mouth, I reached the kitchen, and the telephone Jeremy had had installed so we could give way to the impulse to converse at any hour — he awake to his solitary situation, I, to mine.

"Jeremy," I said, "speak to me."

"Pick a topic — any topic."

"How about successful labor."

He was wide awake at once. "Natural is successful. Natural labor is one where the child presents by the head and is delivered within twenty-four hours without interference from midwives or obstetricians."

"That leaves me out," I said.

"I'm afraid it does. But fortunately for you, medical science, in my person, has progressed. If you've ever seen the armamentarium of a medieval accoucheur — knives, crushers, extractors, comminutors — you wouldn't want to think of anything being extracted piecemeal."

"Where did Adam and Eve learn how to deal with cord and placenta?"

"Serious minds have pondered the question, my little dear." (I had made a fortuitous move.) "Jean Astruc, a Pentateuch scholar, is officially credited with having asked how the first couple came by a knowledge of midwifery."

"I can hear the imminent father Adam crying, 'God! Help me! It's a prolapse of the umbilical cord.' "

"That's my Ariadne, judging the primal parturition by her own."

"And you not there to help. I don't see how God trusted anyone else. It might have required turning, or forceps, or podalic version, or a symphysiotomy, or even Caesarean section. How am I doing, Jeremy?"

"Head of the class perfect, little scholar. You get an A from me on your science report. Add to your list, Apollo rescued Aesculapius by performing Caesarean section on Coronis."

"No wonder he became a doctor. And I have one for your notes from *Tristram Shandy.* Hold on . . . Let me read it to you . . . 'Your Julius Caesar who gave the operation its name, and your Hermes Trismegistus who was born so before ever the operation had a name; your Scipio Africanus, your Manlius Torquatus . . .' "

He laughed, as usual, delightedly. I laughed with him, but on my face I felt the sepia sweat of self-disgust.

*   *   *

A beaded curtain parts. Strands of beads tingle against each other and swing back from my father. It is the father of my thirteenth summer, dapper in a beige suit set off by a perfectly laundered, blue and black striped shirt, straw hat set slightly aslant on his auburn hair, a cane tucked under his arm, and in his gloved hand a package wrapped in gold star-brocaded paper tied with silver cord.

It is Saturday, the day he stops work at noon and customarily brings home something from the big downtown world, so I have been waiting at the door, bathed, hair freshly washed, impatient.

When he sees me a smile flicks the corner of his bright mustache. He removes one chamois glove and closes his bare hand over mine.

In my memory we proceed down the corridor, passing from shower of light to dark to light, resonant with emotion re-strained at the brink. Together we enter the parental bedroom. My mother stands in the humbled light of that homeliness her parents, her sisters, and in turn, we, had bestowed on her. Her eyes are shrewd as a peasant trader's. Her strong hands tug at the frayed bathrobe scant across her ninth-month belly. Through green shutters, sunlight oscillates bars across her high-beaked nose. She bends her head toward him, her long black hair swings in one motion, heavy as a plush drape. Faint odors of onion and soap linger about her. It is afternoon, why is she not dressed?

"Tired?" he asks.

"Very heavy."

My father kisses her on the forehead, brilliant a moment in his blue and black stripes against her towel robe, like a butterfly on a basket of laundry.

"How are you, Abidah?" she asks him, tentatively putting her arms up toward his shoulders. But he has already turned from her and is holding the ornate package toward me.

"For my Topaz. I had it made for you." Thumb and forefinger twirl the end of the stiff mustache, his special gesture of excitement.

"So what's new about that? When does your princess wear anything you don't have made for her?" My mother coughs and blows her nose.

I put the package on the carpet and sit down to it cross-legged. It is too beautiful to tear open at once. Looking up at him, I see two of myself mirrored in his eyes.

"Open it. Open it. Don't be a baby," my mother's voice booms. "Let's see what your father is spoiling you with today."

Customarily the offering is a general one — a curio, a tin of Dutch hopjes, an illustrated volume, a few unusual flowers. I feel the awkwardness of a birthday child opening gifts in front of others who stand empty-handed looking this way and that way to hide the gleam of jealousy. If only it were my birthday, so that she could grant me the right. I wish he had brought some gift for her too. I hesitate.

"The paper is so pretty," I say.

"Slowpoke, open it already!"

(We are of two schools of gift-openers: she a tearer, I a lingerer.) I fumble with the silver string, then undo the paper without tearing it, roll the embossed sheet into a scroll and wind the string round it.

"Even the paper is expensive," my mother says. "Save it for wrapping another present."

Inside is a different paper, tissue sprinkled with silver stars.

"It looks like it lived with the other paper," I say.

"Sharp-eyed kitten," my father says.

There is nothing more to do but lay the package open. I expose folded silk. It ripples in and out of bronze, copper and gold like a brook in sunlight. I lift it. It spills astonishingly like water through my fingers.

"It looks like it cost a fortune," says my mother.

He laughs. "Watered silk. But don't you think it matches the color of Ariadne's hair?"

"Not really, but what is it aside from expensive?"

I guess, in a way hoping it is not something for me. "A Spanish shawl for the piano?"

"Try it on, little princess. And promise me never to wear a Spanish shawl. Leave that to your cousin Poppy."

"Something you don't like about my cousin's child?" I have never before heard my mother rasp so at my father.

"Poppy is more Spanish-looking, like your father. It might suit her coloring, but not Ariadne's."

My father lifts the silk from the floor. It takes the shape of a robe.

"Let me see you in this."

(If Joseph had been a girl, his father might have made him such a coat.)

I unbutton my blue smock and stand in my cotton underclothes. A shiver bumps goose flesh over me. He helps my arms find the sleeves. Butterfly wings flutter against my arms and neck and legs. He lifts my damp hair and spreads it over the back of the robe.

"You see," he says, as if that were what it was all about, "it catches the colors in her hair."

He turns me to face him, and bending over, ties the gold tassels. Against my skin, they feel like a cat's tongue, rough but feverish, like his mustache as he brushes a kiss against my cheek.

"Isn't she a flower in that?" he asks my mother.

I would like to run away and hide. I want to escape without looking at my mother, but I can't.

Her cheeks are mottled red, the faint acne scars, dead white. Around her thin lips the skin is drawn into puckers, pale green and white. Her eyes are black, her lids narrowed. She is not looking at me at all, but through me, at my father.

"Abidah." She thrusts me aside and exposes their secret life. "Have you lost your mind? What are you making of that child? She is thirteen years old, you are buying her things for a . . . *whoor.*"

The word splashes like a stone into a pool. My father blinks rapidly, a film like a bird's nictitating membrane chills his glance. "Wife, you forget yourself."

A tear drips off the end of her nose. She yanks the frayed robe over her belly and trudges out of the room, away from me, away from him. The bathroom door bangs shut. The key is turned in the lock.

252

The sound of bath water smashing into the tub does not immediately shut out the sounds coming from her.

A senseless cry wells up in me. "Don't let me win, Mama. Don't let me win . . ."

*   *   *

Would my mother, whom I loved far less than she loved me, be pleased at my humiliation? No, she would grieve. (We live in a maze where men, women and children are all hostages to one another.) I am certain that had I called to her one moment after she slammed the door on my father and me, she would have crawled out, dragging her pregnant weight through gunfire or flood to defend me.

Still another memory was beating to be let in, like a loathsome night insect flapping itself to death against a screen. Adam's smile in the mirror.

What I had glimpsed, blanked out, stored and now slowly retrieved was the frightening, even unbearable expression that whipped across Adam's face and disappeared like a snake in the perennial bed. I had seen it before. By chance, the door ajar had caught that sneer on Aunt Giselle's face and, pierced by the look, the humbled figure of Uncle Joshua.

It was not, to say it again, what one had expected. It was not what they were telling me from the literary supplements: Alexander Woollcott going to the theater in scarlet-lined opera cloak. Why not with me? It was not F. Scott Fitzgerald dedicated to one of those sacrificial butterflies with a poisonous taste.

They were telling it from the tabloids: better to be Peaches foibling with Daddy Browning than to be me. They were telling it altogether other in the movies: Janet Gaynor fresh as morning glories. Greta Garbo, her amorous reefs below ice, the surface like a catastrophic iceberg about to wreck John Gilbert, a sailing vessel dipping from the waist. They were telling it from the miraculous radio. But Vaughn deLeath and Jessica Dragonette, crooning so their strong sopranos would not shatter the crystals, were not celebrating my kind of awkward numbed desires.

Where was the one who longed for me?

I want my marabou. I want to recall things that other women have desired; borrow every shape to find expression.

Where was the one I longed to be?

*   *   *

The mention of marabou brings my granddaughter, Dinah, to mind.

She flashed into my city apartment looking thoroughly disheartened. She was dressed in slicker-yellow plastic and both color and texture were too much for her skin. Mind, she's lovely, but her charged feelings are sensing their circuitry: a shadowy tension line on the left side of her mouth —just where my father showed his — and a thin array of ghosting around her eyes, like striations that mark certain blue violas. When she's troubled I still find it difficult not to cradle her in my arms as if she'd bruised her knee, but failure has taught me to restrain my maternal delusions of omnipotence. I watched her going through her childhood ritual of examining and smelling the jars on my dressing table, and dabbing perfume on her ear lobes.

"Do you use moisturizing cream, pussy-Kate? Take a bottle. Take mine."

"You're a sexy old lady."

"The Lord giveth too late and taketh away too early," I said. She flicked a smile on and off, clopped across the room in

254

those squat-heeled hooves they're wearing, threw open the window and stared darkly down on the avenue. Fumes of bus fuel flapped in like wounded crows. A sheet of my manuscript blew off the stack beside my typewriter. Another one of my beginnings hit the dust and skidded under the desk. She banged the window shut. Her dress crackled like a fuse about to blow as she squeaked onto my larkspur velvet chaise.

I was throbbing in unison with her, but open sympathy disconcerts her.

"Go sit on a brown chair," I said. "I can't stand that yellow on my chaise."

"Repellent, isn't it? You'd better get dark glasses, it's next year's look."

"My vote for woman-hater's frock of the year. A prince would need an alpenstock to climb that glass mountain and find a girl's waist."

"If a girl isn't at ground level, she can forget it." Dinah stuck her lower lip out in a worried pout.

"Why not, whatever it is that hurts, spit it up in Grammy's hand?"

"Won't do any good." A tear dewed.

I handed her a tissue. "Salt makes runnels along the nose. Why don't you lie back on my couch. We could play beauty parlor. Or you could talk. Would you care to relieve my mind of one concern? You aren't pregnant again?"

"No, I'm on the pill. But if I were, I wouldn't have another abortion."

"What would you do for a husband and the child for a father?"

"I'd bring it up myself. You don't have to be on welfare, black or raped to be stuck with the job. Some of my privileged friends are doing it, and not because they want to displace men, but because men are shedding fatherhood."

"Will you please fight off motherhood until you find a man

255

who doesn't shed? Don't go radical chic now. Can you imagine your father? His son a war resister, his daughter a fallen woman and his mother-in-law a bleeding-heart peacenik? My poor Arie would be nailed to the cross, he'd bar the door to you, and I'm getting on for diapers, even disposable ones."

She glanced at me with a surprising amount of uneasiness, more than half as if to say, "You wouldn't shut me out, would you?"

"To Grandmother's house you can always come. But you'd have to train the little bastard to carry milk toast and a perfect rose up to his great-grandmother who wants a go at her typewriter. So you and Vincent have come to a parting of the ways?"

"It's my third serious breakup."

"Isn't sequential monogamy the 'in' thing?"

"I've had being 'in.' I hate bang-and-thanks-and-run. My brother may ask, 'Why make a pretense of emotion?' but I can't take the backlash. I'm past dating. One step from the meat rack. Will he buy? Won't he? If I'm ever going to have legal children, I'd better get to it."

"Watch that old devil, biology. Big families are going to be unpopular unless there's another plague that reduces the population by nine-tenths."

"I want affection, love if I can get it, marriage, children — a permanent r-e-l-a-t-i-o-n-s-h-i-p."

"That's backsliding if I ever heard it. You are going to be sent to a sex clinic for indoctrination, and sentenced to watch X-rated movies!"

"That's another thing I've settled for myself. Pornography makes me feel like an angry ice cube. I don't want instructions on how to be a champion baller. They can burn *Screw* magazine and the *Kama Sutra* and the *Village Voice*. I don't want to know how others do it. I'm original. But don't let's tell Danny or we'll get a lecture on freedom from erotic frustration and full sexual expression as inalienable rights and why act as if going to bed brought on love. His brainy kind are worse than the junkies who really don't give a damn about sex."

"Listen, my yellow flicker, before you throw out the whole messy revolution bear in mind it popularized women's right to orgasm. Before it proper females were supposed to bite their lips and suffer their husbands. Sex as pleasure was for sluts, sirens, Delilahs, Jezebels — vampires who killed off men. Medical opinion concurred. For a woman to enjoy the sex act would damage her womb and endanger her unborn children. If fear and guilt didn't stifle her urges, clitoral surgery for nervousness was recommended. I don't mean in darkest Africa. The mutilation was done in the United States by bona-fide surgeons in the twentieth century."

"If I can't go back and I can't go forward, I guess I'll never marry." She jumped up. Sorrow slid off her like small rain from birdfeathers.

"Don't enter a cloister this minute, my village Cleopatra. Toss your card back into the computer-dater. It won't cost you a cent."

She pulled her hair back and compressed her lips. "How would I look as a spinster?"

"Lovelier than ever. Just a wee bit sharp. But why not disregard the question for a while and think about a career. A couple of children are no lifetime occupation anymore. Say you give nine years to raising two of them to school age. A life expectancy of eighty or more leaves you half a century to feel obsolete. I had four children in the days when homemaking was *the* honorable profession, yet at thirty-five I felt as relevant as a middle-aged Buick; too old to be useful, not old enough to be a classic."

"My mother always knew she wanted to be an artist, and I don't know what I want."

"Not everyone does. Has it occurred to you that there is

257

merit in work per se. I mean just providing for yourself?"

"I should get my father to arrange a marriage for me, with a rich Mexican general or a banker . . . Was yours arranged?"

"More than suggested."

"I'd settle for a darling like Grandpa. He was a peach. I still have the dollhouse he built for me. You had everything, didn't you?"

"Sho' thing! Love is a thing that can never go wrong — and I am Marie of Rumania. Right! Darling, go do Yoga or something that rushes the blood to your head. You sound like an oncoming wave of conservatism."

"Don't worry, I won't succumb. If I weaken, Danny will save me." She glanced at the watch that lay on her wrist like a melted cookie. "Oh Lord I'm late for the demonstration! I'll have to dash to the U.N. Plaza to see that my brother doesn't get himself trampled by a cop's horse."

She dropped a kiss like a sunflower seed. "Let's you and I marry, we'll wear contrasting marabou . . ."

Brightness flew out of the room. Woodthrush calling through the fog, "Good-bye, love, good-bye, see you Friday."

When did the woman who "had everything" get around to marabou?

From Cinderella to Siren

How light we are, now that we are changed to birds.

— WILLIAM BUTLER YEATS

IF ONLY I had cast my horoscope I might have gone to the library, or hanged myself by my aunt Giselle's pearls. Of course there were portents. The earth was supposed to be in bud. Cardinals were in full courtship colors, but flakes as large as bird shadows soared on variable currents, shaking a feather bed of snow over patches of ice.

At the front door a gust tumbled a plump drift down on us. Paul stuffed his gloves into his pocket and brushed snow off my cheeks and eyes.

"You've been crowned," he said. "I can see you in a Renoir hat, covered in white silk roses." His hands created a quick curved shape over my head and alighted briefly, but barely. "It would suit you."

Lurking under his remarks of visual authority, behind restrained judicious observations, there was a note I thought was more personal than gallant.

"Paul, your shoes are soaked," I said. "You must take them off. You'll catch cold."

My voice faltered at his raised eyebrows and glower. "Spare your concern, madame. My mother let me out to play by myself some years ago. Allow me to pull off *your* boots."

When he kneeled, I had an impulse to press his head against my breast. I thrust myself back against the wall. "I'll make us a hot drink right away," I said.

He took his time, making remarks of mock disapproval. "Such wet feet. Naughty. Playing in puddles. Just as I thought your stockings are wet." He stood up. "I look forward all week to our after-class evenings here. Poor bachelor me. Lucky Adam. He's not in?"

"He will be soon. He's late now. Why don't you light the fire? Traffic from Boston must have been slowed by snow."

"He has to travel a great deal, doesn't he?"

"Yes, but he likes it; likes being in motion. He's coming home tonight and plans to leave for Chicago tomorrow."

"Now I will obediently light the fire *and* take off my wet shoes," he said.

I retreated to my kitchen where I could concentrate on my instruments and incantations. Bitter chocolate melted. Milk heated to a purfle. Vials of vanilla and almond unstoppered. Genie rum released from bottle. Limoges pot heated, bowl heaped with whipped cream, grated chocolate whisked over.

I bore the silver tray (mirror polished) to a low table by the fire. Swift, practiced, everything under control.

"As your husband frequently remarks, you are a genius." He fingered the footed cup with its medallion of cloud-banked cherubim. "A still life by Chardin. Ariadne, you must be the last perfectionist."

"Actually I am just holding on to the slippery past for the future. My grandmother's spoons, my aunt Giselle's cups."

He sipped. "Madam . . . this potion . . . this aphrodisiac . . ." (the word fell weightless as a snowflake) ". . . cannot bear the same name as the brown sand I scoop from a tin and mix with hot water and condensed milk."

Joy went through me at the vision of him alone in his studio. I masked the gleam under housewifely reproof. "How dare you compare this . . . aphrodisiac . . ." (not so lightly).

Steam swirled around his eyebrows and moistened his blunt lashes. His mustache was flecked with froth, his mouth heat-reddened. "Adam is right, your chocolate is better than any we had in Switzerland." (He was certainly conscious of Adam's absence.) "I must ask Adam if his class also fell in love with the headmaster's wife. We were, man and boy, infatuated with her."

"Infatuated! Adam?"

"It was required, a tradition. Someone had introduced a copy of Beerbohm's *Zuleika Dobson* to the school and it was rumored that she was the fatal model. Unlike her legendary namesake, Potiphar's wife, the headmaster's wife resisted *us* — en masse. I had a comparatively light case."

"Odd. Very odd."

"It is odd that Adam and I should meet, isn't it? Odder still, through you."

I was thinking more of the oddness of Adam infatuated.

"How did you decide to take a poetry course?" I asked.

"On impulse. I was in the library researching William Morris designs for a wallpaper job when I chanced on the announcement. In Geneva, at school, I learned nothing about English poetry beyond Shelley, Keats and Wordsworth. Voilà. It should be a lesson to purposeful planners like you. My only regret is our class meets only once a week."

"I can make chocolate for you any night," I said casually.

He was at once uncasual. His cup halted. His eyes narrowed. He was always surprising me into rethinking my own meaning. Was I putting him into the position of handsome bachelor en

261

garde? I retreated. "I keep a double boiler of it simmering on the back of the stove. Adam, my boys and their friends are addicted. May I add some hot?"

He held out his cup. I poured, heaped a dollop of whipped cream, handed back his cup. His head was still tilted questioningly.

Inexperienced as I was, could I not have intuited where this was leading? I didn't.

He turned his wet socks on the fender and wriggled bony toes. "Soon time for me to leave your rum-soaked haven. Sorry to miss Adam."

"He will be in soon." I shivered.

"Cold?"

"I guess so. My skirt is damp, also the wool is beginning to smell like wet sheep. I'll change into something dry, if you don't mind."

He stretched out by the fire.

I should have saved the watered-silk robe my father gave me when I was thirteen. Or better still I should have owned something more attractive than an either-sex camel-hair robe. Damp hair coiling and snapping under the brush, I considered myself in the mirror, hesitated, and at the last firmly rebraided my hair.

He was asleep, his length disposed Greekly, one strongly modeled hand in a loose fist. I sat so I could look at him without staring him into wakefulness. Firelight whisked over his face, vivid, and self-possessed even in sleep.

I didn't know how long he had been watching me from under slit lids, but when he saw I knew, he sat up, reached out and gave my bare foot a little tickle.

"You remind me of my sister Angie, camel-hair dressing gown, walking up and down, reciting irregular verbs, her braids swinging out stiffly every time she made a turn."

He held my foot and studied it as if it were a disembodied

262

cast. "Very few people have lovely feet. Donatello feet. I'd like to sketch yours."

(Had I recalled from childhood how my parents' seemingly objective discussions burst apart to reveal fierce dichotomies, I would have recognized conflict behind his references.)

The telephone rang.

"Yes, Adam . . . You can't? That's too bad."

Paul stood up and stoked the fire. In the pier glass I could see his face turn uneasy, his eyes stony. "Paul and I were concerned." (He relaxed one notch.) "Yes, we did get in a little late." (Another notch.) "It was icy here too. Yes, both boys are sleeping at friends'. I'll tell him, yes I will, I said I will. Yes, Adam. I will tell him you said to take care of me." (Paul's expression turned grim.) "Then you'll stay over, see Arie, and leave for Chicago from Boston . . . Give her a kiss for me. Until Monday night then . . . Good-bye . . . take care . . . keep dry."

Paul was as stiff as the poker he held. I bent over the coffee table and fumbled for a cigarette. "Adam says he hopes to see you next Thursday after class. He called before we came in . . ." I smiled, denying the feeling that Adam had put me in a humiliating position.

"He also said . . .?"

"He'll go to Chicago from Boston."

"Come, Ariadne, did he actually recommend that I take care of his wife?"

"You know Adam's manner. He means there's a storm."

"What does that mean?"

"Oh I don't know what Adam means. The stairs might be icy. The car stall." I parted the window drapes. "It's still snowing." He stood behind me, looking over my head at a sanding truck crunching past; a pedestrian bent against the wind, using his umbrella as a cane, and stopping every few steps to hold on to an iron-rail fence.

263

"It's dangerous out," I said, trying to put aside my exasperation.

"Your husband puzzles me. Isn't he jealous?"

"You've heard him say that neither of us is jealous."

"I assume that's dinner-table nonsense. I know he is aware of your womanly charms, I've heard him . . ."

"Embarrassing, isn't it?" I felt badgered, even menaced, by Paul's persistence.

"Somewhat public for my taste. I don't believe Adam intends it, but it disconcerts me. To an observer, it might imply I am not a man capable of being susceptible to an attractive woman. Perhaps he has some odd notions about me." The idea pricked him as soon as it was out of his mouth. "You might even have conveyed them . . ." His scrutiny was edged with suspicion.

"Perhaps Adam thinks I'm not capable of attracting . . . Oh Paul. What could anyone possibly say to deny your obvious . . ." I stopped myself. "Does a man have to be jealous?"

"Yes. It's built into the male animal."

"Then Adam is not a male animal."

"Jealousy is innate in a man's bones. In mine, I'm sure. My father once struck a policeman for excessive courtesy to my mother. I respect Adam and like him, but I would never invite another man's attention to a woman, certainly not a woman of mine."

"I find it embarrassing."

"*If* that's true, why not say so to Adam. Since you don't object, he might think he's pleasing you."

I couldn't blurt out to Paul that to Adam any act of self-assertion was regarded as hostile. I couldn't have explained what I hadn't perceived: that to communicate my wishes required more sense of self, more assurance of the worth of my wishes than I had. "It would seem so picayune . . . so ungracious," I said.

"You baffle me. You aren't talking about a guest, but your husband. You both baffle me."

All the same, I felt a rush of gratitude to Paul for corroborating feelings I had been ashamed to admit to myself.

"You say you are a jealous man? That's funny. I think of you as formal and restrained." I said, turning away, and flicking my cigarette into the fire.

"Have you found my restraint *funny?*" He needled the word.

"No, Paul. *You* baffle *me.* You find meanings I don't intend. I think of you as reserved. You, like Adam and like me, different as we all are, were brought up in the strict European manner. I would think you know what I mean." I busied myself with the tray. "All I am trying to say is that I can't remember feeling jealous about Adam. He's never suggested it about me, and we are married close to twenty years. I have envied some women's situations, or looks or style — a social twinge. But the murderous jealousy that Shakespeare attributed to Othello, if that's what you mean, that's for the theater. I wonder if it exists."

He tossed his head and nickered. "Well, that puts me in my place, madame. I can't blame you for that reproof. It was impertinent of me to remark on a personal situation between husband and wife. I apologize."

He began putting on his socks. Anger sparkled off him like a Fourth-of-July firewheel. I found the crackle of it amazing, and not unpleasant.

"Please, Paul, why are we talking about this? Why don't we go back to our schoolbooks like good children. The weather has changed so often today it may stop snowing before long and you can go then."

"It is blowing hard." He put his feet on the fender. "I will be a sheep dog by your fire . . . protect you as your husband directed."

"I'll freshen the chocolate, you freshen the fire."

"*Frisch, fresh, frosch . . . frisch weht der Wind . . . der Heimat zu . . .*" His true-pitched tenor took over. To the melancholy resonance of Tristan I glided the tray to the kitchen.

We were stretched out alongside each other, feet to the flames, heads and books in a pool of lamplight, when the chimes rang twelve. "Chocolate is finished. I'm warm through from the rum. I'll add another log and leave you."

I rested my head facedown on my arms. "Yummy, I smell like a chocolate rummy."

He sniffed deeply. "Yes you do."

He shifted ever so slightly so that we were yes-no touching. My nerves drummed to attention. Against my arm I could hear my pulse, circulation uneven as if constricted, then released, blood pumping frantically, limbs growing larger than life-size.

He lay very still. I was about to edge away from him as if the touch had been accidental when his bristly mustache brushed my cheek; his breath stirred in my ear. "My dear . . ."

His voice was so faint it might have rocked from out of deep sleep.

"My dear," I sang back to him.

As in the lunar curve of dream, the secret we had harbored in candid daylight floated between us. As in a dream, in the childhood of love, we lay cheek to cheek, without biographies.

But we were not children. We were two adults wrapped in the hard cocoons of our moralities. There began this trembling as of moths emerging from somber dormancy, clinging to their protective coverings. Throbbing with fear, we hovered above the volatile lure pouring out its sick sweetness between us.

He must have recognized it as carnivorous. He sat up, away from me, to give me time to return to safety, I suppose. I saw him cover his face with both hands as if he were praying into them, contending alone with dangers which in my ignorance I did not understand. I closed my eyes knowing that he would turn to me soon.

I was still lying eyes closed when he drew me to him and cradled my head in his arms. He held me so, rocking and comforting me as if he were sorry for me. Then his mouth sighed over mine.

I was suddenly breathless, but his mouth held me under, waiting for me to recover, and gratefully I was breathing, my mouth against his. Slowly, as if he sensed my record of defeat, he kissed gently for a long time before he took his mouth away. I lay in a trance too heavy for exuberance.

I must have been moaning because he began to whisper words that could have comforted a child. "It's all right, baby, shh . . . shh . . . sweet . . . honey . . . doll . . ." Honey and cream words. His hands went on amplifying . . . his kisses dropping at every junction. Each kiss a shock. Each shock mounting. Small waves, gathering to greatness.

"Ariadne . . . Ariadne . . . Ariadne . . ."

He threw my robe and gown from us. His clothes after them. We were naked in the firelight. He made noises I had never heard, like an animal suffering, a kind of broken whinny. ". . . Open your eyes . . . Look at me . . ." I obeyed him. His face was ferocious. It sent sparks of fear through me. He shook his steely mane and darkened over me.

He was lying next to me. The roaring had subsided, leaving my mouth tingling. His arm was across his eyes, his breath hissing a slight steam through his nose, his mouth soft under a smile.

"You make a lot of noise for a woman your size," he said and drew me against his chest. With his free hand he reached for my robe and covered me. "Rest," he said, but by the melancholy turn in his voice and the tension in his arm, I knew he was not drifting into sleep either.

The things women had omitted entirely from the coffee-klatch preenings! The awkwardness of finding her nightgown out of reach under the chair, feeling sweatily naked as she righted it and put it on while he groped around the floor collecting his underpants and trousers, and slid into them; the scathed sense that a barrier had been erected between them, something strange but palpable; the unexpected feeling that she would have preferred to withdraw for a time, be alone and reassemble herself.

"It's after midnight," he said, "still snowing and no one coming home." He studied her with an evaluating look that left her suspended and slightly apprehensive. "All right, you with the pigtails, are you asking me to stay over?"

Where would he sleep? Where would they sleep? The boys' rooms with their gear and single beds? Out of bounds. Arie's room, mattress bare, heat turned off, a basket of laundered curtains, a heap of clothing being sorted for causes? There was nowhere to go but the marital bedroom.

He, too, hesitated at the door. When he came in he sat in her chair, holding his jacket and tie in his lap.

"Here let me hang up your jacket." But she didn't want to open Adam's closet. "I'll get you fresh . . ." She stumbled. ". . . guest . . . towels . . . there's a bathroom there." She couldn't say "Adam's bathroom," so she pointed and escaped into hers. She visualized the exposed toothbrush, razor, robe, the intimate paraphernalia of another man's life. Oh the sermon of the inanimate.

When she came out powdered, and in her long-sleeved nightgown, he was already there, draped in a bath towel. She tried to think of something to say, but her mind bubbled up foam.

He spoke for them. "Why don't we go to bed?"

"Oh I'm sorry, you must be tired."

He pulled her to him. "Why must I be tired? I am not sleepy. I am not tired." He inhaled the odor of her throat and hair. "And you smell too clean."

*   *   *

My mother never taught me how to be a siren. From her I could not learn the feline coquetry of a cat, nor its seductive cruelty rooted in confidence. It was not given to her to communicate the grand conscious power of a sensual woman, nor the snow-queen frigidity of a Giselle, which goads some men to ferocity or, at the least, relaxes them into flirtation.

She was the very model of a Cinderella. She had animal vitality, ate when she was hungry, slept promptly when fatigue caught her. When she suffered one of her periodic headaches, she lay in a darkened room smelling of sour grass like a sheep dog, a vinegary herbal compress on her forehead. At the first easing of discomfort she would stagger up, check the household, and in her disheveled enthusiastic way, get on with her chores.

She never fluttered an eyelid in a stratagem of feminine weakness, never feigned coldness or affected seductive rage. Whatever innate coquetries a woman is supposed to possess in addition to her presumably maternal and domestic instincts, my mother didn't.

I don't imagine Cinderella simply removed her scullery apron, donned tiara and train and became intoxicating. Mother, chatelaine, matron, even queen, yes. But from Cinderella to siren is an eccentric uncharted course.

Perhaps one March day, spring, like a blue gas pilot flame flickering yellow-edged, waiting to ignite the brown fields, the children away being schooled to become rulers of the realm, the royal matron at loose ends, promenaded in the garden. Mind virgin, she watched earth unclench; saw small grasses triumph over snow, and on a black pine, yellow candles light a glade down which two lovers, line on line, melted together and became shade on shade, while on a pear branch two doves pulsing shook down images she had discounted as poets' incantations about spring.

She counted the children, and found again there was one missing. She considered turning the closets inside out for spring cleaning. There was no earthly reason to buy a hat. She had already spoken at length that day to her father confessor. If the agora had not been proscribed to women she might have walked there for animal comfort.

Her fairy godmother collaborated again. She sent a different kind of prince. A Lancelot. Not the Victorian knight of Tennyson's *Idylls,* but Malory's Lancelot; the Malfit, the badly made, the ravenous, carnal madman who raged in the wilderness infuriated with insatiable longings and unresolvable conflicts of loyalty, who fled and returned, fled, tried to rescue himself from his infatuation by other affairs, by marriage, by knight errantry, who returned, hating himself and her for returning, who appeared and reappeared until both he and she, worn out with years of erotic torment, fell wearily into abstinence.

Erotic torment! Infatuation! Insatiable longings! In my father's house men and women did not become images of worship or obsession. Radiance did not adhere to women. Even a figure of blandishment, like Queen Esther, was seductive, not on her own behalf, but on behalf of her people.

My father and Adam acceded to their sensuality modestly. Their perception of reality was not injured by sentiments of what should be. Their heads were not clogged with models that life was supposed to imitate. Whatever they may have differed about, they concurred with Spinoza that bondage to the passions is ignorance of necessity, and counter to freedom.

Distaste and disapproval outweighed the sense of tragedy when my cousin Naomi (I remember her gravurely) plunged all — crayoned frock, pink cheeks, bow mouth, yellow hair — into Luna Park Amusement pond when Aunt Sarah glared out of her pale Cyclopean eye, the other having been lost by a peasant's stone throw, and hissed, "No, No, for by my soul ye shall not give your daughters unto their sons."

To die for love, or to live for it, was an excess outside the pale. To break up a family for a love affair verged on gentile madness. A Jewish girl who had escaped poverty; who was a respected wife, mother, property owner; who had satisfied the family aspiration for material success *and* social ascent could not claim to be unhappy. That I lived at an emotional level where my conscience tormented me if I failed for one evening to provide a balanced dinner from soup to nuts for my family did not strike me or them as a summary of an impoverished life.

What I am trying to confess, shamefacedly, is that when my Lancelot climbed into my tower I proceeded in the only way I knew; domestically.

When I think of the trays!

When I think of *that* tray!

It was our first morning after. A Friday. A workday. He was asleep when I slipped from bed to repair the ravages of dissolution I was certain my face had acquired overnight. The face in the mirror was fresh and clear, with a little more color than usual and some darkening under the eyes.

At my usual high speed I set up a breakfast tray — pretty cups, pretty linen, pretty eggs with pretty bacon, pretty toasted muffins, pretty homemade jam, even a pretty bouquet: snips of carrot foliage and two red radishes scalloped into cut roses. (Ariadne the household queen.)

Paul was still asleep. My lover asleep in my marriage bed! He slept stretched straight out, one arm under his head, one hand on his chest, a crusader, lacking only, under the jutting toes, the submissive dog that symbolized a successful pilgrimage to the Holy Land. If I weren't holding a loaded tray I might have curled up at his toes.

"Paul. Breakfast," I sang out.

He stirred, stretched, sleepily focused on the picture of me in pigtails and tray and sat straight up. Expressions reeled across his face like speeded-up color film red, white, pink; shock, raw anger, incredulity, bewilderment. Finally overwhelmed, he lay back and laughed until he choked with breathlessness.

I stood there, Milady Lares-Penates, the damned tray in my hands, and watched his naked shoulders heaving, laughter churning out of his open boar-bristled mouth.

"What is so funny, Paul?"

He leaped out of bed, genital as a satyr. I averted my gaze. He lifted the loaded tray from my hands. Still shaken by bursts, he walked about looking for a place to lodge it. I pointed to the table between the windows.

"Now can you tell me, Paul, just what you find so excessively amusing?"

"It's only . . . only . . ." He struggled for the inoffensive word . . . "It's only that you are the most domestic woman I have ever . . . ever . . ."

Where I came from that was no insult. But he was from another hemisphere though he looked like a familiar constellation. I went aground like a mariner accustomed to steering by northern stars, trying to triangulate by Carina, Crux and Tucana.

While I flustered over how to avoid opening Adam's closet for a robe, Paul slid into his trousers.

"After breakfast, we'll get you out of this house." He announced it as a fact.

"Don't you have to get to work?" I asked, well-trained domestic.

"Is this milady's laundry day or do you have another engagement?" He slammed his foot down and bent over to lace his shoe. "I can take a hint, I'll leave. It had occurred to me in passing, we might spend this day out in the country together, a sentimental notion of mine. But if you're engaged." He was glowering up through his steely mane.

"I'm not busy. I'm not engaged. Darling, I'd love to . . ."

On this morning of all mornings, to be almost quarreling! Instead of taking me in his arms and gently kissing his obedient little girl good morning, there was a circle of rage around him, a ready anger. I seemed continually on the verge, or over it, of offending his sensibilities.

We ate in silence; rather he ate, because I couldn't swallow. A tear rolled into my coffee cup.

When he saw it a quick, vulnerable sweetness flashed from him, surprising me as it had the first time I had seen it cross his defended face. "Sorry, baby, I thought you were dismissing me. Maybe you are just dumb."

"I'm dumb," I assured him. "You can't imagine how dumb."

"Now eat your breakfast, honey baby. Heap the jam on your muffin. Stoke up. You'll need it."

"Why? Where are we going?"

"Away from here, anywhere so there's a bed."

Heat flared up my legs as if I had stepped on a hot-air register. "A bed?" I kept myself from adding, "in the daytime?"

"Unless you don't have time to go." His voice had that suspicious edginess again.

I went to him and pressed his head against my breast. "I want to go. I want to go wherever you go."

His hands slid over me. I bent down, noticing, but scarcely, my boldness, I pressed my mouth to his. When he let me go he said, "You want to go! Let's hurry. If we stay here another minute, we'll be back in your bed. Give me your car keys. Throw something into an overnight case."

"An overnight case?" I repeated after him stupidly.

"Are you making fun of me? Luggage, my girl, luggage, we must have luggage. Pack an apple and a newspaper if you can't think of a robe and toothbrush."

He hesitated as if he himself were confused by his agitation. He drew me against him, rocking us both, brushing my neck with his lips. "It will be all right, people-feeder, chickadee-feeder . . . birds do it, rabbits do it . . ." His voice was coaxing and furry. "What you don't seem to understand . . . is that . . . unless we work at it night and day, we're not going to catch up with these wasted months." He whispered the rest . . . "So we've got to get down to it. Seriously."

While he drove, one hand kept leaving the wheel, touching me as if it had a life of its own, except that it seemed connected to a tense forceful bodiness that oppressed him.

"I'd drive into the first field and get at you, if it weren't sloshy with mud and snow. You've been told before, but I'll tell you again, you have a perfect body for lovemaking. Narrow, but full-breasted . . . and a waist that's easy to get all the way around," his hand accompanied the words, breasts, waist, thigh, " and those long legs to wrap around and lock . . ."

I felt myself blushing. "No. I have not been told."

He snorted. "I forgot. You've never been told, you've never been jealous, you've never gone to a hotel, immaculate mother . . . I'm to believe . . ."

274

I was as smug, after the gift of myself, as an inexperienced girl. "You will in time, because it's the truth. Paul, you are my first love." I could not say "lover," a word tossed out by the "fairy" who laundered my yard of hair. ("They can have their hair set three times a week. It doesn't mean more than bridge clubs. But when they start with pedicures they don't have to tell me they have a lover.")

"Don't ever try to flatter me with lies, Ariadne."

"It isn't a lie."

"Please! We are both close to forty. Your husband is often away for days. You are a very attractive woman. Don't ask me to believe nonsense. It will be hard enough for me to be sure of your love from now on. I warn you, I'm jealous and possessive." (I hadn't a clue of what that entailed.)

"You can be sure," I said as if that made it a fact.

He drove without speaking. After some minutes he broke into a whistle so melodious, so joyous, it has endured till now.

Life had surpassed literature. What I had read about, imagined, felt deprived of, heard in music, sensed in the intoxication of certain weather, and assumed I would never have, had been surpassed.

"The birthday of my life has come, my love has come to me," I said to myself. I was a bride, ravished at last. An ignorant bride.

Nowhere had I read that a man may love, may adore, may lavish himself on a woman and yet never muster enough trust to overcome his suspiciousness, his resentment, his fear of being dominated to be taken into marriage, even a mystical one.

*

My education began promptly.

He slowed down in front of a country inn, then speeded past. "College kids here, it will be noisy."

We were past before I felt the barb. I busied myself with assurances. Parked roadsters blazoned with university pennants. He had made the obvious connection. But as every program operator learns, two bits of information fed into the computer reinforce each other.

"There's another place not too far from here. It is more private, but it may not be open this early."

Quite without time lapse a whip of pain lassoed itself around my chest. My breath crowded up the back of my throat and across the roof of my mouth in a growl . . . or was it a howl . . . aaaaaaaaahahahahaha.

His foot decelerated the gas. "What happened?"

"You've been there. With someone. I want to go home."

"Aaahaha . . . What do we have here? Now *that* sound I understand. Oh I like it. I like it very much. I recognize it. I made such a sound myself only last Thursday when I left you, Ariadne, with your ever-attentive ardent husband . . . eh . . ."

His scowl was an ugly mixture of pain and triumph. I backed away from him, my hands and feet went lumpy and cold, my heart burning as if a skin had been ripped off it.

He drove for some miles before he touched me. More miles before he whistled again.

He stopped at a general-store-post-office-gas-station. He came out with a bag of groceries. "Bread, cheese, chocolate — quick energy — milk, boiled ham, ginger ale . . . oranges . . . must have oranges for color . . . We certainly won't want to get out of bed today."

I bent my head to hide incredulity and shock.

"This is the place. Wait while I find out." As he was closing the car door he said, "I stay around Stockbridge when I come for the music festival."

I had to be content with that. And what did I expect the man to be? A virgin?

I watched him stride down the garden walk, take the entry steps two at a time, the severely handsome Reverend Arthur Dimmesdale himself, for whom I had willingly put on the scarlet A.

The housekeeper welcomed him, pleased not to be accepting a couple of dissolute college kids. I was appalled by his ease, flustered by my lack of it. *Daily News* reports of raids loomed, garishly detailed by clerks, bribed bellboys, cameras, sleazy detectives, and captured hotel registers.

He opened the car door. "Everything going our way" (whistle, whistle). "Luggage and groceries. I could carry you across the threshold but we don't want to shock madam."

"I told your husband," the woman said (oh that was what a man said), "the electricity is not on, but it won't take ten minutes for the gas heaters to heat the cabin. If you don't mind walking back through snow, it's clean and quiet back there: you can have a good rest."

She went on chattering while she lit the heaters, opened the mirrored wardrobe, showed Paul where candles and an oil lamp were kept. He assured her that he would not hesitate to come back to the main house if we required anything.

I stood by the window, looking out at the brook, splendid with thaw-ice riding the black water. I kept my face turned away so she wouldn't be able to identify me. At last Paul eased her out the door.

"Come here to me."

I stand unmoving.

He holds out his hand. "Come here to me, baby." His face is stern, he wears the formal face of early love.

"Come here," he coaxes and commands, "I'm going to undress you, it is time for bed."

Who me?

"You bad girl, come here."

I move toward him in fear and trembling.

What is this, fear and trembling? Who does he think I am? Who do I think I am? Who do I think he is? Paul. Corinthians. Kierkegaard. Ariadne. What are we all doing here together.

*   *   *

Shadows of pine and water slide along the walls and ceiling and flow over the man, the somnambulist who reappears, no matter how many doors I shut. He stands fully clothed, my sky-blue dress thrown over his arm, his weight resting more on one foot than the other, left hand in trouser pocket, a fell Sargent, head to one side, appraisingly as if sighting through a brush line; a spray of shadow leaves continuously sliding from ear to cheek, then losing itself at his surprisingly sturdy throat.

"I'm nude," I protest.

"Nude is for life-class. You are naked."

He tosses my dress onto the wicker chair of the cabin he has rented again and yet again only ten minutes earlier. "And you are blushing again because you never . . ." He leans forward. He flicks a thread off my belly, as if he were brushing it off an important porcelain vase. "Stand over there."

He stares unblinking, while he removes his jacket, undoes his tie and loosens his shirt collar.

I am following his gestures as if he were a hypnotist.

"If you need cover, princess, let down your hair . . . That body. Every time I think of that body sitting next to me buttoned up to the chin in navy blue, I want to make up for the

waste. I've got to spend serious time studying . . . Turn around
. . . You need to study too, you need to study idleness from the
ground up . . . with me . . . Turn around! I want to study
. . . Turn around, I said, let down your hair . . ."

I want to obey him. I want to do exactly what he wishes. Yes,
I'm frightened. My heart is knocking, my flesh buzzing. I am
a housewife. Mother of four children, twenty years with a husband, without once feeling this wild desire edging on fear. My
hands are moving without my will. I am drawing the tortoiseshell combs and pins from my hair. The coil loosens, slides
undone and slowly tumbles. Behind me he catches its fullness
on his face. He shakes his head back and forth, his rough
mustache scraping and tingling the small of my back. Everything he does seems full of freshness and catches me by surprise.

"I'm drowning. I'm drowning. What a way to drown!" he
says between kisses. His voice is abstract as a lament, muffled
against my buttocks. His arms are around my waist.

The sorcerer's apprentice has drunk of magic. I'm going to
wake up, rueful, on the kitchen floor with my apprentice mop.
I'm an interloper. My agitation is mounting. This is someone
else I assure you. My mind is attacked by his words. Four-letter
words, blackening at the edges. My legs are attacked. They are
being cast in plaster, the heat and weight drawing me down to
the ground. A death mask is being made of my useless legs. I'm
going to fall.

He knows my every thought. He will not allow me to fall. He
rises and lifts me in his arms. (You may not lift a mother so.)
I'm afraid of heights. My weight embarrasses me. Why have I
let myself put on weight? Why is my skin streaked from child-
bearing? Why am I not a wraith? I try not to stiffen. He kisses
me quickly, hurried rain on my eyes, my cheeks, my forehead
. . . My life is being drawn into his mouth through my breasts.

"I'm too heavy," I moan.

"Are you, baby? Are you?" Kisses. Kisses. "Are you,

279

dearest . . . ?" He rocks us from side to side. "Look at you . . . Look at us."

Two strangers are suspended in the wardrobe mirror. In its abyss, among quavering rhomboids, a grizzled satyr carries a drowned woman in his arms.

Look at them, bewitched! Lovers at their age! Shameless as aging Antony and Cleopatra. His hair is silver. She's no youngster either. Scandalous. Preposterous. I am this married woman, this mother, this fornicatress. It's a terrible mistake. What would my father say? Wait. Let me go. Have I prepared enough food for the children in case they come home from their separate dates? I must leave immediately and attend . . .

I lie in his arms, limp and odorous, limbs dangling, strength flowing away through my hair toward the dark pool of floor. Oh, Elinor Glyn, tell me, if my mother never told me all she should, how can I help it if I'm no good. I don't want to go on with this. I'm not strong enough. It is killing me. I don't want to seep out of my skin, my mind, to want to be part of anyone so much. What am I doing with this WASP, this descendant of inquisitors. He's dangerous. He's the enemy. I don't want to want him. I am a Jewish mother. I have no time to play. I make big family dinners. I read many books. I go to night school. I am an intellectual. Let me out of here. Only yesterday I was studying perception. I'm reading up on art. Visual perception in particular requires the illumination of the object. "Put out the light!" The eventual absorption of this light by the observer or observed increases the entropy of the system . . . Don't you understand, entropy, Paul. Entropy. And the mountains made low and the valleys into plains . . . Your New Testament. "Put out the light . . ." Color may be produced from pigment. It is then opaque and never achieves the transparency of colors evoked from light. I want to be in the dark. "Put out the light!" It pours through colored glass like burning icing, flowing

280

nougat, sick yellow and bitter chocolate. Off light, cook.

He does not hear me. He is listening to his own blood drumming.

I am exhausted. My head falls back on his forearm, my hair is waving like elodea reefs swept by alternating currents. "Put out the light, Paul, put out the light."

He whispers his secret. "I want to look at you . . . look at you . . . look at you . . . darling . . . We're going to walk Miss Goody Two-Shoes down the street stark naked . . . I'm going to paint twenty-foot pictures of you . . . everybody will see what you are . . . I'm going to paint miniatures so I can flash them . . . no more lady . . . no more housewife . . . everybody will know . . . look at you . . ."

Too much is clearly seen. Narcissus invented the mirror. It mirrors true the sight I see. I see the woman's face is crazed. A man is going out of control. No, he is in control, of me, his eyes never leave me. This man is not my friend. This is not the man who sat in the living room talking *plein air* . . . "I paint what I see." This man is unhappy. His expression is hopeless. His lips are drawn back like a ferret in a trap.

I want to comfort him. I want to waste my flesh away for him. I want to be terribly good to him. I want to make him happy. But I don't know how. I know nothing about sex. I thought sex was an instinct. My instincts have been shaken out of me by vacuum cleaners. I am a drudge. Cinderella always knew that in a castle she'd be a scullery maid.

What is a scullery maid doing in this prince's hunting lodge? I will lose him. I do not know how to caress his royal, buzzing, high-keyed arrogant body. I wish I were a trained Japanese courtesan. Why didn't I read pornographics? See filthy pictures? Spy through keyholes? I want to consign my body to his lust. I want to run away.

He seems to know this too.

He puts me down on the bed, but his knees grip my ankles

while he unbuttons his shirt . . . thumb and forefinger in apposition . . . button one . . . how the gesture compels my blood. The nameless bones of my pelvis turn to moss-covered stones submerged in the pool of rushing blood. And button two. Adroit Homo sapien. He reaches down and touches me. The pool is seeping. "Wait. Red. Genuine red . . . ha . . . ah . . . ha . . ." Can a wild animal laugh? Does a bristled boar laugh? Perspiration is beading the skin around his feral eyes. Light splashes silver butterflies over his bare thighs.

He leaps, his head almost touching the ceiling. Is that a shout? I am about to be trampled. My heart is racing. I give up hope. His dark head rushes toward me, and hot against my ear I hear a hoarse command: "Now give yourself to it."

Suddenly, there is nothing I need to understand.

Or so I imagined.

*   *   *

Failure of imagination is not listed among tragic flaws. Yet I nominate it for the number one spot. Wouldn't Lady Macbeth's enterprise have died aborning if her imagination had kept pace with her ambition? I imagined, if I imagined at all, that adding a lover to my orderly life would be an exotic embellishment on the order of adding a cage of tropical warblers to my houseplant window. I imagined "living in sin," free of routine responses, would be happiness. My smiles would be real. With my penchant for idealizing, and my denial of the specific, I was sure our love would inform every act and, as the verse had it — "life would be a glorious cycle of song."

And I had reason to think so. It was perfect. It was waltzing together, two hearts beating in three-quarter time.

It was incredible to me that bodies could be so knowing about each other. It was a revelation that a man's body would know precisely what to do — how, when, where to please a woman's body which in turn would follow secret orders to please his. (So that was what Hardy and Hawthorne were saying women gave up the world to have!) To be fed until sated, until the bruised mouth moaned "no more" and the delighted body slipped helplessly into half-sleep, and the last conscious thought was, perfect, perfect.

Physical love. Like one of those entombed seeds that lies dormant for centuries, then displays the magical ability to sense the appropriate occasion for breaking out of its husk; like maple seeds flying on their red samaras to a place of germination; in Paul's arms I thrust down roots, sped vines, and lavished my springtime in a burst of autumn bloom.

In the affluence of his ardor I had an immodest love affair with myself, queening it in front of the mirror, and seeing myself, not as Adam reflected me, but as Paul did. The full-breasted woman in the mirror *did* resemble a Titian, you might say. The small-breasted slender flapper of my girlhood envy was *not* the artist's favorite model. "Don't get out of bed, darling. I want to catch that gorgeous curve of flesh . . . a quick sketch. Five minutes. Keep your thigh like that, and your arm over your head."

Paul introduced me to dramatic play dress that began where my father had left off. "That high-button modest look couldn't be more seductive." Or, "Wear muted colors only, you are air, sky, essence. Nothing harsh should lie against your skin." "I bought this amber chiffon scarf for you, it brings out your golden eyes. I have never looked into golden eyes before." (For him, I had no trouble opening my eyes.) "That narrow cape enhances your natural elegance." "Let's buy you that school uniform with the Peter Pan collar; we can play bad kids in it." "Pull that pink petticoat slowly over your red hair. Hurrah! A burlesque act. Take it off, take it off," he chanted and clapped. "Get a white satin dressing gown with loads of marabou. Sure; and then you can sing, like Marlene Dietrich, 'Falling in Love Again.'"

"Me sing?"

"You have a sexy alto." For him I sang.

Each encounter with Paul was a rainstorm refreshing the dull sensory plain of my life. A walk with him was like flying:

"Listen to that autohorn: the opening note of Siegfried's horn solo. Papapa pam," he tooted. Passersby brightened. "That manhole cover! Straight out of William Morris. There's an exhibition at the Morgan Library, meet me there tomorrow afternoon." "Can you believe those peonies? Peach color of your skin, milady. Bet they feel and smell like it. I'll take two bunches."

"Two?"

"One for strewing petals over you, or you can take one with you if you think that's wasteful." ("I'll do a water color before you go.") Passing a bakery, "Yum. In we go! How about cookies and milk at my place?" A sudden dark glower, "I'll blind that bastard if he leers at you — or do you know him?" "Watch that man, he's going to turn around and pick up the girl in the Scotch plaid, he gave her the eye as we passed." "See. Walk ahead, I'll pretend to pick you up. You act furious . . . Attract attention. Then we link arms and scamper off." "See how unexpectedly the bright blue car beyond the green car seems to be closer." In front of a gallery window, "Don't try to understand the painting, enter it. Imagine the first stroke on the canvas; it determines the whole work . . ." "You look ravishing." "Let's cut across the park, the magnolias on the south side are breaking out." "Step into this phone booth with me. I can't wait to kiss you . . . What, blushing again?"

See! Hear! Feel! Run! Play! Jump! Fly! Fly!

Ah flying! Linguists say it is from this verb we derive the four-letter word, which in print has evoked swift and harsh penalties in the past; when spat, has brought on street battles that put the Montagues and Capulets to shame; yet when whispered can be a password to rapture.

Watching for him from the top of the museum steps (he was prompt, I was early) I was surprised each time to recognize him — somewhat forbidding, somberly dressed, black coat, dark suit — picking his way briskly through the crowd, avoiding contact, nothing revealing his wildness except possibly the springy lope. My wolf in priest's clothing. In ways he *was* like an animal, not greedy, only ferocious. He ate simply and lightly, sometimes fasting for no reason other than that his body told him to. He drank little, smoked only at the end of a meal, and while he was not punctilious about the state of his apartment, he was as clean as Dionysius, or a cat.

When he moved into a somewhat better apartment in our honor and gave me a set of keys, I was perfectly happy. I imagined he was too.

"I can get away this afternoon, Paul, are you free?"

"Damn, I have an appointment. Let yourself in and wait for me in bed. I'll rush back."

"We have too little time together," Paul complained. "Don't you dare fall asleep. When will you be back?"

"I'm not sure about tomorrow."

In a life that had always been circumscribed by routine, spontaneity and chance were exciting additions. But not to Paul.

"Stay, stay, don't go yet."

I would have wanted to. But I also wanted to go.

I needed to get back to my children, for my sake as well as theirs. I needed time to run the house, prepare dinners for Adam's business colleagues, coordinate the boys' pickup schedules, carry on my conversations with Jeremy (I hadn't mentioned Paul other than as a classmate and family friend). As for my gardening, I did not think ahead to the summer. Beyond all these I needed time to think about Paul and me. I wanted to have my hair washed for him, my nails manicured. I wanted to soak in my scented bath (in the forenoon now) to savor hours I had spent with him. Time to think of games I had never played as a child, or in sport as a woman. Time to reread poems we read together. "I wonder by my troth what thou and I did till we lov'd." Time to weep a little, thinking about the poverty I had endured till now.

When I came rushing into his apartment, popped a casserole into the oven or the refrigerator, filled the cookie jar, quickly remade the bed with clean linen, then hurried to get into bed with him where we made love until I leaped up and dressed to leave, how did Paul feel? That required imagination or experience. I hadn't much of either.

Paul had both. He lived at an opposite pole of consciousness from mine. He was always conscious of how he felt and expected me to know. His imagination, riveted to a paintbrush, would have made him a Bosch.

"I can't very well keep on coming to your house, Ariadne."

"Why not?" I said. "What possible excuse could we give to Adam, Jessica, the children? Even the cats would prowl around objecting."

"Why not? How in the name of Christ I could have become involved with a married woman!" he groaned, and moved away from me on the bed.

I found out why not, very quickly.

Our after-class trio became a rack.

Adam was no more effusively flattering in public than he had

been. But now every compliment tainted me with sexual innu-
endo in Paul's eyes.

"I refer the question to the art expert. Paul, don't you agree
my lovely wife resembles a madonna of the Umbrian school?"

"More Emilian in the face, Correggio perhaps. But her
figure . . ."

Paul, camera-eyed, sighted along his coffee spoon as if it were
a brush and I a nude on a stand. "Her long limbs more delicate
in relation to her torso, more lyricism, Venetian." Turning
derisively from Adam to me, to Adam, to me, his full carnal
mouth drawn back, his teeth showing, his eyes, their whites
enlarged, "I'd say Tintoretto." Adam fixed his bland polite gaze
on me, Paul his glittering, ferocious glare.

Between them, I was an object being crushed.

"Correggio, Tintoretto, Venetian lyricism . . . hear that, little
mother? If my business goes kaput I can put you on the auction
block along with your antique Chinese carp tubs and French
lead waterspouts."

Had I been a woman of action, the hot-chocolate pot would
have been hurled at one or both of them.

Did Adam suspect when Paul and I became lovers? If he did
could it be he was relieved to overlook what he secretly con-
doned?

That I could have imagined Adam capable of such intricate duplicity was measure of how quickly Paul changed my
vision. Whether my focus became clearer or more distorted
I can't say.

Paul lived in a state of exacerbated alertness. His camera-eye
recorded every detail. His imagination played over it. Probably
his own intoxication with women, with music, with ideas, with
art in all its forms, with life in general, made him aware of
sensual possibilities in every encounter. A nuance, a gesture,

287

served to excite his suspicion. Suspicion, fired by his own success with women, was easily fused into conviction.

"Mr. McAndrew," I said at a dinner, "will you have hot soufflé or cold Bavarois for dessert?"

"Madame, I would be delighted to take my desserts, hot or cold, at your hand."

Adam smiled slyly. I smirked. Paul crashed his chair back from the table. "Excuse me," he hissed. "I am indisposed." He charged from the apartment.

"You have had dealings with that old goat before or he would never have presumed. I saw you hold his hand too long when you greeted him. To my face! How did you dare!" He fulminated. He disparaged. He berated. "Does your husband also bill for your sexual courtesies?"

In Paul's glare the world was illuminated like a red-light district.

"Flirtatious! Not enough you have an admiring husband and a dangling lover. Seductive looks! Don't deny it, goddam it. I saw you, woman. I am not conveniently blind like Adam. Don't belittle me . . ."

Who me, flirtatious! Seductive! For that matter, woman! It could not be Miss Goody Two-Shoes in the button-up navy blue suit he was accusing.

Constantly he forced me to examine the meaning of my actions, piercing my emotional fogginess with accusations, which I denied as out-and-out nonsense.

Sleepless with exasperation I would pick over his scoffings and more often than not uncover a thin thread of truth — enough for him to weave into a noose. It could be that I was coy with male guests, in the flirtatious style considered appropriate to charming females. Smile. Smile. I had never asked myself if *I* considered it appropriate. I had absorbed it as if I had learned to read from "advice to the lovelorn" columns and screen magazines. Yes, Paul's question was pertinent, not impertinent as I had said. *Did* I think he would find me more desirable if an old geezer ogled me? I suppose I did. Granting that his censure was excessive, my dining-table coquetries could be as galling to him as Adam's inauthentic gallantries were to me.

Through Paul's magnifications I saw my relationship with Adam in another dimension. Having eaten of the apple, I considered Adam's dandy appearance, his well-kept aloof body, and it occurred to me that it would be simple for him to live a secret life. Did he? Incidents popped into my mind for review.

The night Absalom disappeared I telephoned Adam at his hotel in Denver. It was after midnight, even in Denver. He did not return my call until morning. "I went to a movie. Picked your message up in my box when I came down to breakfast." Paul would have assembled the name of the movie, the hours of performance, the time the telephone operator and desk clerk went off duty, checked the plot and if disparities were revealed, would have pressed a confrontation.

Adam stood by the kitchen door, a tray of sticky glasses in his hand. Why had I not said, "Adam, let us go to bed now"? I had said, "It was a good party . . . why not leave the dishes . . ."

I had seen him bend over her bare shoulder, her cape in his outstretched arms. I could not be certain that his lips had lighted.

"I'll clear," he answered, "just the dead drinks and the ashes."

He smiled up to where I stood on the stair clasping my evening shoes to me. I did not trust his smile though it was dappled in lamplight. The door swung closed, I never knew. Even so palpable a thing. I never was sure.

I had never tried to make sure.

Paul would have cracked it open like a nut.

Could it be, I wonder, that I had been, all along, as fearful of acting as Adam was of feeling?

"What's your hurry today?" Paul said, as I unlocked myself from his arms and legs. "Someone waiting for you?"

"It's late. It's time for me to get home," I said.

He watched me morosely, the new me, polished and perfumed from toenails to ear lobes. I moved slowly, vain of my body which had pleased us both. I felt a bit dizzy, my head light, the blood having been drawn from it in the long afternoon in bed. Languorously I got into the slinky marabou-trimmed robe and cute french-heeled satin slippers (his floor was too dusty for padding around on bare feet). Before going in to the bathroom I turned for one more look at the lean muscular body that had led me through miracles of lovemaking.

"I love you," I said.

I moved gingerly about his bathroom. It was, as usual, a mess. But I knew better by now than to offend him by cleaning it. When I got home I would have a luxurious hot bath — there was never enough hot water in his building — and perhaps a nap or a daydream about him before dinner. I had prepared dinner before I left and had written Katie, a domestic who came in the afternoons, a note telling her to light the oven at five-fifteen. Adam would get home at six-thirty. Benjamin and Aaron about that time, also. It was afterschool sports for them and then music lessons. Dinner at seven. I hummed, thinking of how smoothly I had arranged matters.

"Happy?" Paul asked as I came out.

I smiled and nodded. He didn't smile, but he was often dark and moody as our afternoons drew to a close.

I slipped into the naughty peach silk petticoat and put on the schoolgirl dress that amused him. As I was snapping the round white collar into place he asked, "Happy enough to hum?"

"Why shouldn't I be, having you?" I blew him a kiss.

"Why shouldn't *I* be, since you are leaving me free to amuse myself?"

"I'm sorry darling, come home with me . . ."

"Shall we just walk in together, holding hands?"

I hurried, not knowing what to do about his anger, or how to avoid it.

"I have to go home . . ."

He was still lying among the rumpled sheets, having made no move to get dressed and escort me to my car or drive me most of the way as he often did. It was getting late. It was going to be one of those difficult leavetakings.

"Why don't you stay in bed awhile and rest. Take a nice bath before you go out to dinner . . . I'll lock myself out."

"Straight thinking," he said sardonically. "Would you leave two dollars on my dresser before you go?"

"Of course darling," I said, fumbling in my wallet. "But if you're short of cash why two dollars? How about ten or twenty?"

He exploded in rueful laughter. "Oh never mind." He arched himself seductively on the bed and in a harsh falsetto delivered Theda Bara's line from the film *A Fool There Was.* "Come kiss me, my fool."

"Meet you at the Met day after tomorrow at twelve," I said, kissed him, and ran.

From Passion to Hang-up

"I am sorry, one so learned and so wise
as you . . . have still appear'd
Should slip so grossly, both in heat of blood
And lack of temper'd judgment afterward."

— SHAKESPEARE

WAKING FROM THOSE alternations the old call sleep, in that dazed moment before optic nerve and brain connect me to the sparse and wintry present, a scene coalesces out of long ago. Luminous as a homeland in a parable there appears our dacha: a peopled room, a glowing hearth, familiar figures bustling about. I felt strong as the brook released from winter; vivid as the trout leaping below the cascade. I had the illusion that I could enjoy, simultaneously, all the roles life seemed to be offering me: Adam could continue to have his efficient wife, the children their devoted mother, Jeremy his talkative companion, Paul his impassioned lover, and I, I could have them all.

*

My mother and Benjamin were clearing ashes from the fireplace and discussing the ritual of that ancient fugue of death and resurrection, the Passover.

"Why should I pray for next year in Jerusalem," Benjamin said. "I already have a homeland."

"So pray it for others who aren't so lucky. Put those wood ashes into a tub, Benjie. Your mother will want them for the lilacs."

"I want to live right here," Benjamin persisted. "I'm an American."

"God forbid you should have to explain it to Poles or Germans."

Aaron and Adam were in the background, stacking logs, white birch and black apple, their two sturdy figures curving to and from the wheelbarrow. In the foreground Arie at a long trestle table was creating an arrangement of budded willow twigs, white aconites and glossy ilex. A frayed shirt of Adam's fell plumb from her shoulders like an acolyte's gown, sunlight through a shelf of cranberry glass banding her in pinks. She was smiling faintly, a flower held out before her, her face fragile in the luxurious frame of hair that feathered in red-gold wings to her shoulders. Except for the color of her hair, she resembled Adam, as if, with daughterly certainty, disregarding any reluctance there might have been at her fathering, she had prized out of him his best details; the oval of his head, slender cut of nose, light eyes — level but not intimate — shapely yet unsensual mouth, and then had fired them into a kind of bygone porcelain beauty. She even had Adam's trick of creating a barrier by drawing back her head when spoken to, as if she felt crowded.

Aaron stepped forward with an armload of kindling. "Salmon have their homeland too. The government builds fish ladders to help them return to spawn in the fresh-water streams where they were born."

"You have to be a salmon to be repatriated!" Adam fingered the ridge of his nose where it had been flawed in a boyish, goyish, get-the-Jew hazing at a boarding school.

"Maybe Americans won't need a Jewish homeland, what do you think, Adam?" my mother said.

"Don't count on Roosevelt. He too will be glad to trade in his Jews."

"You don't trust him, Adam?" (Adam had taken my father's place as my mother's referential male.)

"The French won't lift a hand. The English won't. The Russians? The Poles?" He counted off on his fingers. "You know better than I what to expect of Poles. The Pope? It's his Christian pleasure to eliminate heretical sects. The Arab High Commission? The Moslem Council will be supported fully in their anti-Zionist activities. What have they accomplished in the 1936 Partition? A battlefield. The planet is not big enough to allow Jews a homeland."

Adam himself seemed startled at his emotion-charged tone. No one spoke until Arie drew attention from her father. "I side with Benjie. This is my homeland. I am going to get married right here."

Her grandmother alerted on her haunches like a woodchuck. "Married? You have a good boy, Arie?"

"He'd better be good." She waved a flower at Adam, Aaron and Benjamin. "Did you ever see such a gorgeous honor guard?"

"Never in my life," my mother agreed.

"Arie is not getting married. She's promised to me," Aaron announced, only half-joking, eyes and mouth rounded in the clownish manner he affected. At sixteen, he was almost as broad-shouldered as his father. And his expression behind a surface of directness echoed Adam's in its quality of something

295

gently withheld, something unreachable — even to himself.

On Adam's other side Benjamin glinted; handsome, veiled, tall for his thirteen years, straight-backed as my mother, with her narrow bronze eyes and tartar fall of inky silk hair. Under the clichés of boyish good looks flowed the raw blundering reality of power, and the quality that all our children seemed to possess, as if in retort to our timidity — a capacity to give way to extremes.

"We'll head the villian off at Eagle Pass . . . who knows what evil . . . the Shadow knows, heh, heh." His voice broke.

"You promised, Arie, and a promise is a promise." Aaron pushed the joke, on his face still apparent the child who had toddled into his sister's bedroom with teddy bear and bottle, who had perched on her bed watching her dress for school until puberty made her secretive; long enough to have shaped his desire.

"Hadn't you better have a talk with your son, Dad?" A half-flush tinged Arie's pallor, like the ripening of a Queen Anne cherry. "You wouldn't want to marry an older woman like me, Aaron."

"She promised me too, son. You know about women . . . *la donna e mobile,*" Adam sang, an arm around each of his sons, Benjamin leaning against him.

We all joined in until my mother's voice took it away and we fell silent before her excellence.

"We're planning on a wedding in July," Arie announced.

"Not this July, Arie? You can't mean that!" I said. "You've just begun dating seriously. Why not an engagement this year and a garden wedding next June?"

"For God's sake, Mom, Jethro and I have been dating all through high school. We want to get married this summer."

"Calmly, Arie," Adam said. "Your parents need time to formulate their congratulations."

"Dad, tell Mom we don't want a big fuss. *She* can go formal, wear lace mitts. I don't want a wedding-wedding. Jethro may marry me in the attic. I'll wear the queen costume Mom made for me for *Iolanthe.*"

"Take a bow, Mom," Benjamin said. "From Arie that sounds like praise."

"Little mother deserves praise," Adam mediated.

"Remember Benjie as a green pea vine?" Aaron said. "We pinned him in at the last moment and warned him not to think of double 'P.' "

"Remember those gowns for Arie's dance-class party?" my mother added. "Your mother and I sewed sequins for weeks."

"I hope they've been saved for my seven daughters."

"Only seven girls, Arie? And an equal number of boys, I presume. What are Jethro's thoughts on the subject?" He disengaged from his sons and stood in back of me, his hands on my shoulders.

"He loves children. Like you, Dad."

"Just like I said," my mother pointed the remark at me. (I did not remind her that what she had said was, "Goose, educated goose! So he doesn't want children. Big so!")

Adam, behind me, rumpled my hair, parent intimacy between us. "I give you my word," he whispered into my ear, "fourteen grandchildren will be easier than four children. And now." Adam clapped for attention. "Action! Go to it, men . . . and my lovely ladies."

"How many are coming to the Seder?"

"Not one, not two, not three . . ." my mother and I mourned my father together.

Adam checked the list in his hand. "Jessica driving Aunt Cassie, Uncle Heinrich and old Uncle Boris . . . How's your count, Aaron?"

"I get *not* twelve — with the set of us, *not* eighteen."

"Q.E.D., my boy."

"That Aaron has a head for numbers, like his father," my mother praised. "Don't forget the extra place. My mother, your great-grandmother, set a place *every* night in case the Messiah should feel like eating a little something. Or if not the Messiah, one of his poor relations. By her religion it was an injustice for anyone to go hungry. Arnie, how did your papa used to say it?"

"To correct injustice is everyone's privilege."

"No one seems to be exerting the privilege nowadays," Aaron said with adolescent severity.

"A fine boy, that Aaron, an idealist like his grandfather. Such a lovely family, such fine children, my daughter, you could be proud. May you marry them all off here and see your grandchildren enjoy this homeland."

"Amen," Adam said quietly.

We exchanged peaceful smiles.

That is all there is to the scene. And though Absalom and my father are greatly present only in their absence, it is a fragment that sheds light the way courting orioles illuminate a dark hemlock; the threat of cuckoos, cowbirds and hawks hidden in the nesting future.

It was a good thing we had set the extra place because Aunt Cassie brought a refugee, a young language interpreter who had spent enough time in a detention center to look ageless as a skeleton and to learn to eat gingerly, with small renunciatory bites.

At the Seder, Benjamin asked the four ritual questions. Adam, paterfamilias, answered them to everyone's satisfaction. We all chanted "next year in Jerusalem." The flames blew aslant dramatically when Arie opened the terrace door for Elijah. Then, the boys turned to questioning the guest.

"How bad was the camp?"

He grimaced, patted his chest as if he were checking his pockets while a stiff wind whipped his face, gave up the search and let his hands sink into his lap. "Difficult to imagine is how simple it is to be cruel. Ordinary people think of such things as, begging your pardon, depriving inmates of toilet paper. A comparatively mild torture."

Arie giggled spasmodically, picked up some plates and ran into the kitchen. In minutes she reappeared at the terrace door. "Anyone chilly? Shall I close this?" she asked nervously.

"Please sit down. I was going to tell a story with a hopeful ending."

I don't suppose I have it verbatim, but this is how it went.

"It hardly matters which of the enemy had taken our town. Russian, German, Polish, Italian — men with guns use them. If they wanted the shoes on your feet, they stopped you on the street and took them. It was the same if they wanted a woman. It was death to say no to them. They were kings and you know, *ultima ratio regum.*"

"Like might is right," Adam translated for the children.

"The forenoon of the day of which I speak, the officers billeted in our house ran out of wine. They ordered my father to lead them to the tavern, where they found that the tavernkeeper had disobeyed orders to leave all doors open, had locked his iron gate and run away. An officer took out his gun and shot at the lock. By chance, a bullet ricocheted and passed through my father's chest. They laid him on a tavern table and had him carried home. They were regretful. They told my mother they would eat elsewhere. When my father died, it was only noon."

The speaker's hand resting on the table began to tremble helplessly. He looked at it angrily as if it were an intruder's, put a spoon in its grasp and held it firm.

Uncle Heinrich poured wine into his glass. Aunt Cassie watered it from hers.

"May he rest in peace," my mother said. "May his death not have been in vain."

"Oh Grandma, how could it not," Aaron said.

"I am certain there is more to your story," Adam suggested quietly.

"Toward evening I went to the barn to feed our two plow horses and to weep in private. As I put my head against our lead mare's face, two horsemen galloped into the barnyard. I did not understand the dialect they shouted, but they made it clear they were commandeering our team.

"While I saddled up, the soldiers clattered about helping themselves to bridles, bits, a whip, blankets, my father's sheepskin jacket.

"The grizzled sergeant in charge handled the horses like a dirt farmer, with muscular open arm movements. At the barn door he passed the lead to his fellow horseman, stood up in his stirrups, and to my horror, lifted me, and swung me up into the saddle of our horse. My poor mother must have been watching from the kitchen window. She abandoned caution — she was still fine-looking, a slight fair woman — and came running out. Pleading that she had this very day lost her husband, she threw herself in front of their mounts. The horseman called for a guard who held her back with one arm. We rode off, me between the two of them, my mother wailing dreadfully.

"The way was through woodland. The sun sank. Sky and trees were one blackness. Though I knew every road for miles around, it seemed to me that the four horses were stepping through a strange, oppressive darkness from which we could never emerge. The road was ominous. Men on horses reared out of the dark leading riderless horses. When we rode out into the open a cold wind cut across bare fields. The older man took my father's jacket from his sack and threw it to me with a sound like a dog's bark. He made a gesture of wrapping.

"After what seemed like hours, we came to a large meadow full of the activity of a camp. There were small fires, ordnance wagons, tanks, and so many horses it was obvious little plowing could be done on the farms in our countryside.

"I could smell river and recognized that we must have come to the fairgrounds of a market town about thirteen miles from ours. The two men slid from their saddles and motioned me to do the same.

"I patted our glossy horses as if I had the power to reassure them. But their ears twitched and they snorted and lifted and put down, and lifted and put down, their fettled hooves.

"The two men disappeared, leading our team away. I thought of trying to escape in the darkness through the chaos of men, equipment, fires, guards, riders and uneasy horses. But almost at once my captors reappeared. They were leading two worn nags, and beckoned me to follow them. Slowly, step by step, through a thinning and darkening space that my fears made ringing, they crossed the camp to the river edge. The horses smelled water and quickened to it. They waded and drank while the men slapped water on their own dusty faces. When we began to retrace our steps I thought we were returning to camp. But at a siding level with the road, they stopped. The sergeant made a stirrup of his hands, signaled me to mount and the next I knew, I was astride one worn horse and held the lead of the second. Both men walked with me to the bridge, shook hands with me, turned me in the direction of home, and left me there with the two horses, to get back and somehow carry on with plowing."

*

Outside, as my father might have said, Creation had failed again. God had nullified his bond with Noah, keeping word of promise, but breaking it in spirit. He did not deluge earth with water but He had covenanted nothing pertaining to blood.

There we were, at table, steeped in the ambiguities of history, each in our own way reassured that the world would survive and recover; that the goodness of a few would always save us — when the telephone rang.

"It must be Jeremy," I said, "wishing us a messiah or two."

Adam answered the phone. "What a pleasant surprise, Paul! In the neighborhood? Join us for dessert and coffee. Oh, no need to ask Ariadne, she'll be delighted. Oh, I see, just passing through. With a friend? Ah, well, if you can't stop I won't ask if it's a woman. Yes, I'll give your Easter greetings. Have a good time." Masculine laughter.

Paul telling me he was passing through with another woman? From Jessica's look, I knew I had turned dead white. She was putting one and one together. I escaped to the kitchen.

I couldn't believe it of Paul. My beloved was mine and I was his. He had given me the keys to his apartment. He loved me, I loved him. He was so avid for me he couldn't be brutal. (Notwithstanding my anguish over Absalom I kept on reading from back to front with Paul — from fatal event to early warning signal.)

I broke out of the kitchen, sped down toward the pond. I heard Benjie calling, "Wait for me, Mom," and Jessica, bless her, calling, "Benjie, come play a duet with me." On the slope I had naturalized with lilies, swords of green were stabbing through. I ran under the curtain of willow withes, and across the sodded-bridge into the wood. (Of what comfort were the works of my hands to me now?) I plunged off the path, tore through the brush, briars tearing at my hair, puckering my dress, scratching my ankles. Cramps slashed across my chest and belly. I didn't cry, I howled like a sick beagle. I retched and retched again, until, hollowed out, I rowed myself to the middle of the pond where no one could see my stupefaction. I heard Jessica at the piano, Benjie's violin, Arie's flute. I sat in the blue dory muttering, "How is it possible?" until the boys came hallooing to the dock and said, "Folks want to say good-bye."

Paul had fumed about my going, and I had shed a few tears, but I had hugged his fury to me as a proof of love. He had been in bed, morosely watching me dress at the end of our afternoon, when I told him the family was going to New Hampshire and I would be gone for two weeks.

He shot up like a geyser, "Two weeks? Where does that leave me?"

"I'll write you long letters every day." I hurriedly gartered my hose. "Will you write me, darling?"

His bristled mouth gusted steam. His stalwart throat corded in fury. "No I certainly will not. Don't you bother, sweetheart. Fucking doesn't travel well."

Shock brought tears to my eyes. "I *have* to go."

"Have to! Have to! Who has the hots for you up there? The mailman? Sign here Mars. Arkady and let's grab a quickie . . ."

"Paul, that's crazy talk. What do you think I am?"

"I *know* what you are, milady. I wish I didn't."

"Don't be absurd, Paul. Come up. Join us. The whole family comes up for Passover supper. They always have."

"Passover supper is two weeks? Who do you think you are hoodwinking? Adam?"

"I have to go. The house has been closed all winter. It's the children's spring vacation."

"Who says you have to go? You can't be real, Ariadne. Where do I fit in your scheme? After the laundry, the cooking, the marketing, the gardening, the dusting, your friend the doctor, the children's dentist, their music lessons, your volunteer hours at the missing persons bureau . . . and let's not forget the jam tarts . . . ah, then you make afternoon time for your daemon lover, for patient Paul. Sure I'll come up. You won't mind if I bring an old friend. I hate traveling alone. Almost as much as I hate sleeping alone."

But not another woman! Who was she? Was it a hostess who titillated him with Freud? Was it the young woman he had left our table to greet in the cafeteria?

She was younger and prettier than I, a deerlike creature with a cloud of misty light brown hair shading a broad white brow and big brown eyes. At his approach she flushed deeper than the pink of her ruffled blouse. She put out her hand. He held it throughout their exchange, his stance perky and cocksure. On parting from her he gave a tweak to his mustache, and walked springily back. His face was a bit hectic when he sat down, his back to her. She left almost immediately.

"She didn't have time to be introduced," he said.

"A friend?"

"Someone I almost married."

"She's very pretty," I said, in as judicious tone as I could manage. "Why almost?"

"Her boss was too attentive, and she refused to quit her job. I broke it off."

I could see her pouting up at him; her mouth and eyes soft with love.

Had he gone back to her? If so, what could I do about it? Roam cafeterias until I saw her and mar her youth and beauty with hot coffee?

We returned to New York on Sunday. On Monday, after I'd gotten Aaron and Benjamin off to school and seen to food supplies, I raced off to Paul's apartment. I didn't telephone; I let myself in with my key. He was out. I put food into the refrigerator, remade the bed with the fresh linen I'd brought, washed a teacup and noted it was a single one. I told myself I was waiting only to fling his key at him. The telephone rang but I did not answer it.

Wherever he had gone with her, had he come back? Would he? Today? Tomorrow? He had no job that demanded his presence, he was free to come and go. Why did I know nothing of his life outside of what he spent with me? Had he taken his suitcase? I went prying, my vision suddenly acid sharp. The suitcase was there. His black coat and suit were hanging. He was wearing his tweed jacket. It could mean anything. His bathrobe was next to mine. My slinky robe had not been tucked discreetly out of sight. One satin slipper was lying on its side. I set it upright. I should pack my things, strip the bed, drop the key and leave. A woman with pride would have done so. I had no pride.

I smoked one cigarette . . . another . . . lit another from that . . . Hours passed. I was angry in gusts. Dropped back into anguish. To taunt me in addition to deceiving me! Brute! Boor! He was gone!

Footsteps. They passed. Two sets of footsteps. Panic. Suppose he came in with her? I hadn't thought of that. What would I do? Make a speech? Fling the key at her? Shake hands all around?

Would I ever see him again? Footsteps . . . someone taking the stairs two at a time. He dared to be ebullient, the beast. I wanted to hide. I felt as if I weighed tons and could not lift myself out of the chair.

His key turned in the lock. "Hah!"

How ugly he looked in his triumph, how like an angry horse bending its head forward before rearing back, his face foreshortened, eyes rolling.

305

Ugly or not, I wanted him. I could not live without him. I would never be able to live without him. I would never want to. I would rather die than go back into the cold of my past. (If he had asked me then and there to stay forever or go, I might have stayed.)

No sound passed between us. He closed the door and leaned against it, looking down at me from under his stubby lashes, his eyes hard as iron. Hah! He had won. I, poor kissing fool, hadn't known there was a contest. From now on I would wait for him. It was out in the open. However important I was to him, he was more important to me.

My cigarette went out between my dry lips. He reached into his pocket without taking his eyes off me, drew out a book of matches and lit one. The flame shot up. Desire flared up in me as he moved toward me. He lit my cigarette and somberly watched the match burn down. When it reached his fingers he blew it out, dropped it to the floor and ground his shoe over it.

Was that his message? Burned out? Tossed out? Finished?

The decisions were in his hands. I had done what I could. I watched him take off his jacket and hang it on the back of a chair. He pulled off his tie, placed it on his jacket. His fingers went to his shirt button. In the gesture I thought I was saved. But no. His hand trembled. He sat down on a straight chair.

"You have hurt me," I said, tearfully accusing (I pray God my daughter and granddaughter have more womanly sense). I had handed him a hook for his anger.

"That evens the score," he said bitterly.

"*I* hurt *you,* Paul?" (How can a pussycat hurt a king?) "How?"

"How? Our clandestine, spasmodic life hurts me."

I wanted to fall at his feet, beg forgiveness, comfort him for the sadness enmeshed in his anger.

"Darling, my darling, I love you," I said. Hope was soaring in me, that all was not over.

"Ah what do you know about love . . . Miss Goody Two-Shoes?" He closed his eyes. A rim of moisture gleamed on his thick lashes.

"I'll learn, let me learn . . ." I put my arms around him and held him to me. We rocked together in sadness until he raised himself and, with me clinging to him, moved toward the bed.

*   *   *

So it was that Paul became a vengeful and faithless lover, converting our state into one more heinous than an impure state of marriage. And that was the end of my dream of two love birds cooing in a cage among my trailing nasturtiums and geraniums. The cage was there all right. But I was in it, not as a love bird, maybe more like a hooded hawk that is released only for hunting.

What cunning Paul forced me to discover tucked away in myself! And hunger! And anxiety! The sheer technical difficulty. Public and private dissimulations, leading to greater dissimulations. Truth frittered beyond recognition between Adam and me. The fake and real headaches and appointments. The longer delays for staying up past Adam's bedtime, twisting old customs to new uses. The slithery shift into converting Absalom's bedroom into my study, then into *my* bedroom. And so much more.

The problem of time. Free time achieved through speeded-up routines. Running, driving too fast, one of Dostoievski's invulnerable maniacs and idiots in full surrender to passion, desperate between compulsion and shame — amazing I didn't get killed in the race to get to him.

To get to Paul I marshaled those household virtues of mine — efficiency, reliability and years of nothing-to-hide frankness. These now counterfeits were pressed into ruthless service, enlisting the cooperation of butcher, baker, cleaning woman, children, Adam, Jessica. Everyone was drawn into my falsity, responding to me as they always had, while my past structures warped and shifted. I no longer was sure of what was true. To get to Paul (I *had* to get to Paul), yet to keep the refrigerator stocked, liquor closet supplied, dinners on schedule, children's routines undisturbed, I became a Hercules cleaning the Augean stables.

My every successful maneuver had a cutting edge. While it gratified Paul, it reflected on my integrity and increased his jealous suspicions.

How they lied, women who confided love affairs that sounded like lawn-party flirtations in gloves and wide-brimmed straw hats. Nothing they had said, nothing in films or books or poetry prepared me for the mean hostilities of an illicit love affair. The duels, the rages, forced conditions . . . "If you don't come today, I will . . . Ariadne." ". . . What are you doing tonight, Paul? . . . Why can't you break the engagement if I can get away?" Revenges . . . "All right, if you must go to a concert with Adam, I'll go with . . ." Reconciliations. Quarrels. Feeling ourselves each other's enemy. Scenes. Flights.

Through my love for Paul, I viewed the world with a blood-shot eye. Did Adam have a secret life? Did Jeremy have patients with whom his relationship was not fatherly? Was Jessica's love life vicious and not shy and girly? Had my cool daughter been having sex with the clean-cut boy she had been dating? The past became suspect. Had my father and mother been happy together: she so robust, he so modest in demeanor? Had Aunt Giselle been a lesbian as Jessica implied? What about my daughter and Paul? After a dinner party one night when he had been there, I said, "You looked so lovely tonight, Arie, everyone remarked on it."

"Paul looked as if he had some interesting ideas about me, don't you think?" Was she watching me? How much did she know, my little fox? "He's terribly attractive . . ."

The natural world, too, changed its metaphors. In the city

308

my familiar end-of-day walk to the west waterfront became a death watch. The smoldering sunset hissed its slag into the Hudson. Sky clinkers flamed and were quenched. A flare of burning copper was covered by a final outpouring of gunmetal. The day died and all the darkness to my thirsty mouth was fire.

When I fled to my garden I was no longer an innocent, contemplating an Eden I was creating. Everywhere death was being hatched. The elm trees' death was carried in the eloquent ovipositor of a beetle, or already curled up in the telltale leaf; death in the stranglehold of love-vine doddering in amber beads around a bared twig. At the base of a flowering dogwood, three leaves and a tendril predicted the conquest of woodland by poison ivy. Armies of maple seedlings surrounded a squad of cedars. Along the pasture wall honeysuckle was scenting the air at the expense of wild azalea. In the meadow, daisy opposed buttercup. At the stream's brink, swamp iris competed with cat-tail, the water cattails marched against lily and reed. Under the waterfall turtles waited to pull down the new-fledged ducklings.

Love? Yet God in heaven, what was it if not love? I would have "walked barefoot to Palestine for a touch of his nether lip." My love for him would have supported me through the seven stages of the cross. I also hated him with an anguish that was swollen with gall.

There was no one with whom I could speak of my subterranean life other than Jessica.

"Paul's gone off again? Come to Greenwich and cry on my shoulder. I'll meet you at the station," she said.

She greeted me with: "Taken to wearing white, Ariadne? My mother's habit."

"I hadn't thought of it as a habit . . . maybe it shows I've taken a vow of chastity."

"Perfect timing at last," she mocked. "We can go back to

playing house together under the bread-and-butter bush. I'll let you spank me the way you used to."

"I never did."

"Naturally, you wouldn't remember." In the scimitar of her smile there was a sudden cold resemblance to her mother.

Jessica's friend was a pug-faced violinist (a bruise-colored welt under her jaw where the violin left its mark), cropped hair, and surprisingly clear blue eyes. She finished pulling off her riding boots with a loud slap against her thigh, and sprang up. She did not offer her hand.

"So, you're the Ariadne Jessica was going to marry when she grew up. You're a lot prettier than the gal she's got." She picked a cigarette out of her shirt pocket, ignited a match with her fingernail, stared, inhaled a deep drag, said, "You don't look like cousins to me," after which she exhaled the smoke through her nostrils, her head thrust back in an attitude of manly impertinence. She swaggered over to Jessica, ran her hand through the short black locks, gripped hard and said, "Behave while I'm out." The next words might have issued from any mother. "I'm going to market. Anything special you gals would like? We need anything, Jessica?"

Jessica had not moved. Fur lashes still downcast, flushed at the absurd display of power, fine face hairs tensile as an angry cat's, she timed her scratch. "Hurry back, my love, so we can perform another act for my cousin."

An exchange of glances. Death in the kitchen. Death on the back porch. Who needs crypts? Two lovers taking poison from each other's lips. Where is the music we each long to hear?

"Come ingest lunch, Ariadne! Good heavens, my mother was sickening! She never asked, simply, like your mother, 'Are you full? No . . . are you satiated?'"

"English was a foreign language, Jessica. She would have preferred being born to it, rather than learning it from a bilingual dictionary."

"She always had to appear original . . . poppies on the teacups when everybody was doing forget-me-nots and violets. But how can you be original if you always have to be right?"

"Nonsense on stilts, Jessica. Come down to earth. It's time to stop being angry at her; we're older than she was when she died, poor lady."

"As I've said before, she wasn't your mother, you can forgive her. I could never understand what you saw in her . . . or in her damned foolish story . . . with the campfire. . . ." She brooded over her bread and butter.

"What campfire?"

"On a dark and stormy night a band of robbers was seated around the campfire. You were the smart kid. Surely you knew no one sits out in the rain by a campfire."

She lifted her masked face. "Dearly beloved, now that we are gathered here . . . tell me . . . Aside from torturing me, what did you get out of that fool story?"

"Torture, Jessica? You can't have believed that. We were going to get married, right?"

(It was not my amputation so I moved ahead lightly.)

"Tell me a story, about yourself."

"You won't like my stories. Not your style. What do you want to know?"

"Why didn't you live with your father after your mother died?"

"I tried. I went to South Africa. He still looked like a corsair. His hair and mustache were blue black, his teeth square and white except for one gold incisor, but life was finished with him."

"Children think their parents are ancient at forty. Jeremy's age when I met him and thought he was decrepit. Your father was not much older than we are now."

"He walked with deliberation. After work he sat on a bench in his small garden and smoked his pipe. He had rented a piano for me, and I played until pale blue butterflies ghosted out on the watered path. By then, the wrinkled black 'boy' had cooked dinner. It was grim. My mother had frozen us both stiff."

"Goes to show. Being frozen precipitated me straight into marriage, as you may remember. Jessica, weren't there tennis-playing colonial young men and women about?"

"Proper white girls and boys were sent to the continent to school, so they wouldn't see their parents drink. In time I discovered that before my arrival my father had been in the habit of going to his fake English club, drinking his two whiskey-sodas, playing bridge and about once or twice a month, stopping over with the widow of a diamond worker who had also made the route from Amsterdam to New York to South Africa with the trade. I had brought him little, if anything. My presence had taken away the small pleasures he had put together. He tried, the old darling. He made a proper tea party. The Dutch hausfrau ladies came and looked me over. I was odd; a bad match for their sons. They shut me out. It was too late for him to become the father of a young woman. It was too late for me to be a daughter to a father or to become a proper colonial, giving orders to an ancient black 'boy.' If I'd stayed I would have suffered the common fate of children who feel unloved. I would have taken to drink. I asked to be sent back to continue my music studies."

"He never married again?"

"No, we'd both had it." She made a grimace.

"You can't live your life as a retort to your mother," I said.

"Yes I can."

"Jessica, come on, are you saying that you live with . . ." I waved my hand to include her situation.

312

"Oh Christ, say it, prude. I'm a lesbian." She picked the lemon rind out of her glass, nibbled at it and stared at me over the yellow ring, holding me in her mother's glittering stare like a reptile.

(In the Duc de Berry's book, *Les Tres Riches Heures,* the serpent is half girl, with breasts and long blond hair. She is wound about the tree and holds apples in both five-fingered hands.)

"It runs in the family. Remember the beautiful *cousinas* . . . man-haters, the lot of them . . . oh, the slavery of it . . . not for any man on earth . . . !"

"Don't judge others by yourself," my voice squeaked.

"Don't be alarmed, Arnie. You're maimed like the rest of us, but some women find their luck, men who never make demands. Weak men like Adam, like your father."

"You know what, Jessica . . . Shut up."

"I'm not through — weak as they are, those men manage to extort virtual slavery from women like you. My mother, at least, tried for more out of life than getting supper on the table, even if the effort killed her. Look at yourself, Arnie. You finally fall in love with a living attractive male and you have arranged to get stepped on all over again. *He* wants this. *He* wants that. What do *you* want?"

"Would you say you're better off?"

Jessica sipped iced tea down to where slurps came up the straw. "I think so. I'm often lonely, but not any lonelier than you've been with Adam the Silent, and I have a career. I'm not tied to relationships through financial dependence and children's needs. I don't have dishpan hands. I don't carry responsibility for half a dozen lunch pails and then apologize if the cucumber sandwiches get soggy. I don't, in fact, apologize. Arnie, have you ever counted the number of times a day you say 'I'm sorry? . . . I'm sorry the toast I made for you while you were perusing the newspaper is too light for your taste, Adam.

313

I'm sorry, boys, the movie we went to last night was not as good as the critics promised. I'm sorry, Arie, it is raining and you wanted to sketch.' I know you have a personal interest in working with runaways but at a job other people get paid for, you are a volunteer." She stopped. "Oh don't look so affronted. Anyway it's no question of being better off. I wouldn't have the emotional stamina for your life: you take tiptop care of a husband, children and two houses. You dash around like a maniac looking for Absalom. You are overattentive to Jeremy, your faithful friend, as well as Paul, your faithless lover. I don't pretend to understand about men, but I thought the point about lovers is that they *are* faithful."

"I thought so, too. The fact is, Paul is not."

"Why does he fly off?"

"The scenario is always the same. I get held up at home. Say, the repairman takes fifteen minutes longer to fix the refrigerator than I predicted. By the time I get to Paul's apartment, his eyes are rolling like Othello's. I'm frightened, so when he starts pressing as to whether it was the same repairman as did the washing machine last month, I blush at the implication or hesitate in order to be sure to have the facts correct so I won't be caught up in a detail I've forgotten. But he's condemned me in advance. Also, I'm a little vague about time, he's damnably precise. Sometimes, if I'm lucky, he reads my face and trusts it. Sometimes he says, 'How can such a frank innocent face be so deceptive. You're a menace.' He flies into a rage and storms out, leaving me sobbing. Sometimes he comes back in a half hour, calmed down. Other times he swears that he won't go on. He leaves for months, letting me know he's dating a young woman he will definitely marry, this time. He announces with conviction that from now on we must go back to being proper friends. He may even introduce his future wife to Adam and me."

"He sounds like a bitch to me," Jessica says. "Does he accuse you of ruining his best years?"

"I guess it sounds turned around but he prides himself on his directness, so doesn't consider himself faithless, but only as honestly trying to break out of an unbearable situation."

"I can understand that part, once," Jessica said, "but why come tearing back to begin again?"

"He simply arrives. He doesn't write, telephone or explain. He appears at the house, breathless. Or I'll find him waiting outside the museum and he'll take my hand in his and, without saying a word, lead me to the nearest hotel. We fall into each other's arms. I cease to suffer; right then, anyway. Afterward I ache as if the surgical dressing had been ripped from an unhealed wound."

"What do you suppose is in it for him? To me, he is not as good-looking as Adam, but he is attractive enough to pick and choose, as his conquests prove. I'm not trying to imply that you aren't superior and all that."

"Thanks for the small comfort, dear coz. It isn't his beauty that is persuasive. Feature for feature Adam is better-looking. And I don't doubt King Arthur was prettier than Lancelot. Paul is all extremes; too tall, shoulders too wide, expression too fierce and suspicious. He behaves badly. Adam is always appropriate socially, but beside him I get the disappointed feeling one has when the bath water runs cold and my mind wanders to whether I've added cat food to my shopping list."

"I could swear you are a goddess, and he should be content that you carry his presence like an amulet between your breasts. But Adam is the one who gets all your services. His routines are unaffected, his shirts are as beautifully starched as ever."

"Let Paul risk marrying a nice masochistic housekeeper, give her children that he works to support, the way Adam has."

"What's missing?"

315

"For one thing, love; obsessive, exhilarating, physical love."

"Ah yes. Very messy business, women in love. Someone always trying for the upper hand."

"Maybe Paul wants no hand. My dimly functioning brain knows quite well he is a bachelor not because *I'm* a married woman with children."

"You wouldn't break up a family for a love affair, but would he want you to go off with him?"

"He has said so, but I think he knew I wouldn't be able to do it. 'You will never leave your cozy bed and board and those children. You won't give up paying tribute to the safe and ordinary . . .' "

Jessica reached over and patted my cheek. "People beat the ones they love. I don't know why they do." Her palm felt warm and childish. "Have some iced tea. Sugar? Lemon? Would you say he still loves you?"

"I don't know what love means. This battle has gone on for too many years. He must feel trapped in it or he wouldn't have to keep proving he can get away. He'd go. You can't imagine the hate I sometimes feel for that man. It eats up all the passion. Sometimes I think I know how he feels when he's unfaithful. I wish I could run out and prove I belong to myself. With anyone. But he's made it impossible for me to consider the act of love as a loveless act. It's supposed to be divine to be possessed, but I hate the way he's seeped into me, the way he's under my eyelids when I wake, the way I talk to him when he's not there. Look for him. Wait for him. Expect him. See him in a passing car, going away from me on an escalator. I'm a regular Evangeline and I hate us both for it. But let him whistle and I come running. He has the whip hand, if you know what I mean."

Jessica grimaced. "Sounds familiar."

"I wasn't being personal about you. Probably the secret of

the bastard's success with women. 'The Gentleman Rapist.' What a disgusting hook."

"Women are going to have to grow out of that," Jessica said. "Once as a child, traveling with my mother, we passed a Gypsy whipping his wife across the bare legs as she ran ahead of him on the road. 'Why does he do that?' I asked. 'Love,' my mother answered. I thought she was being sarcastic. And what do you know? Arnie, any brute who promises to beat me stands a good chance of being loved. I'm vulnerable to the quality I hated most, domination. Maybe I should advise Adam to take boxing lessons."

"No use. No use. He and I would compete for most submissive."

"You said it, I didn't." She gave me her snake look. "Maybe you can explain why, since you are submissive and Paul has the whip hand, he is so tormented by jealousy?"

* * *

Old as I am, I continue to ask myself that question. Was it merely that he was a libertine, so overalert in matters of flesh that he registered and enlarged the smallest fuzz of sensuality, the simplest awareness of gender, into a full-blown bedroom farce? Or was he such a sentimental romantic that he had persuaded himself too many times that the woman he held in his arms was the ultimate, sought-after love of his life, and so suspected others of the same rise and fall? Or was he like a weasel, who, at the slightest trembling in the underbrush, surmises a trap and flees?

When I read *Othello* in high school it seemed to me a logical tangle, an error that ballooned into a tragedy, not a tragedy arising out of character. Had Iago not lied about the handkerchief, had the truth about the handkerchief come out a scene earlier, there would have been no torment of jealousy, no crime

317

of passion. It did not occur to me until years after Paul had gone, I don't know where, that Iago and Othello are the inside and outside of one person.

Othello, the man-of-the-world, the aging bachelor, who has known too many women in too many ports, cannot yield himself, cannot accommodate to an attachment that leaves him vulnerable to a woman's power. Iago is Othello's suspicion confirmed, his jealousy verified; jealousy that can twist any act into treachery.

A woman in love for the first time, like Desdemona, with a man who defeats and outrages her parental and societal censors, who penetrates her fantasy life, and thrills her with his dramatic intensity, is in no position to be clever in defense of her integrity. She believes her intensity and abandon are unique, her ardor proof of her love. Unfortunately her ardor is precisely what forms the basis for her beloved's distrust. Her loyalty is under suspicion by his past.

To Paul I was a married woman, avid, faithless, experienced at deceiving; a woman who never had the sense to say 'No!' And my husband was not riddled by suspicion that my sensuality might be as vulnerable to some other man's provocation any more than I was of his. Unpossessed, we are both unpossessive.

Paul's restless suspicion should have been portentous to me. But I had to run the Dionysian course to the end before I learned how being torn between desire and revulsion can impel one to shatter the attachment, to deny it, to prove one can escape bondage by leaping into some act of defilement.

Some men revenge themselves by flamboyantly confessing their infidelities, as if they were penitents. Some, more mischievous, drop clues, set snares to be discovered. Paul was both kinds. So while I was busy carpentering my dovecote and singing domestic hymns, "Hear, hear, dear Lord, come to this lodging I am building in my heart," I should have been reading portents. They were all there.

318

I should have read it in his shifting moods. (He was not quite Othello, he was more like Mercutio.) I should have said, "My Lord, I know a plague is on my house. The wound is fatal from your casual prick. My memories are bound to be obscene."

The Doctor Unfathers Himself

"Your sense pursues not mine; either you are ignorant,
Or seem so, craftily; and that's not good."

— SHAKESPEARE

"NO MATTER HOW dogged and persistent my effort, Jeremy, reality never turns out to be what it *ought*."

"Reality doesn't mind giving ground as much as you do, Ariadne. Maybe it hasn't read the same books."

Jeremy unrolled a sterile injection setup and peered at the needle; his newly useless eye covered with a black patch, his head tilted to adjust to the lamplight.

"You sound sharp tonight, Jeremy. What's the matter, does your eye ache?"

"Be precise. My uneye."

I watched him test and fail the needle, change it and draw fluid from a brown bottle. "Doctor to patient: Your buttock, please."

"Patient to doctor: Am I mistaken, or would a litmus test show you acid tonight?"

"I must talk to you seriously, my girl." He pulled the covers sharply back up to my chin.

"Spoken like a true father. You realize I've passed my fortieth birthday?"

"My age when we met."

"Really! Did you *feel* old?"

Hand cupped over the blind socket, he brooded. "I'm sixty and I don't feel as decrepit as I looked to you then — or now."

"You looked like the world's best father."

"You were a poignant child."

"I was the model of a seriously married woman."

"We were all seriously married way back then. Family responsibilities took first place." (Sniff.) "I suppose your relationship with Paul has shaken your convictions?" His question sounded remote, theological almost.

"No. It's verified them. Our situation is full of torment. When we're together, we are torn by imminent partings, by my commitments, by his jealousy. When he leaves, I die. With him I come back to life."

He sniffed. "A latter-day miracle. You should report it to the Mormons."

"Storky, when I told you about Paul I didn't expect you to applaud my behavior, but I thought you'd be pleased at my having found a little happiness, trammeled as it is."

"Let me address myself to a question on which I have more experience than turbulent affairs, your health. Doctor to patient, or old man to young woman," he spoke wryly, "you must stop these wild dashes in search of Absalom. Vitamins can do just so much. You're exhausted."

"*You* can say stop. Your son is married. Your son is safely practicing law."

"My sister's boy went to Spain to join the Loyalists. Boys of Absalom's age leave home. I came to this country alone at fourteen.

"I've never thought of you as a boy."

"I was, once."

"My boy was ill. He didn't know what he was doing. I should have thrown my arms around him and held him by force, if necessary. I've seen boys brought into the police station with amnesia. Don't know their own mothers. You aren't there to pump him full of vitamins and order bed rest the way you do for me."

"Ariadne, it is not a matter of vitamins. If Absalom becomes well it will be because he has found his health, not because you have found him."

"Oh Jeremy, that's so abstract and heartless. It's not as if he's gone fishing with the boys. Or eloped with a vamp. He is gone. Years! God knows if I'll ever see him again." Hysteria was popping up in me like bubbles from slime.

"Shh. Calm. No more tears."

"My son looked at me with hate. Do you know anything harder than to look at the face of a child who hates you?"

"Ariadne, sometimes you remind me of your late father."

"Is that bad?"

"Your father was a refugee and a Jew. We Jews aren't allowed extremes of feeling. Until Paul, I never heard you admit them in yourself. Adam certainly never did. Absalom knew he had them. He thought he would be despised if his murderous feelings were discovered. You discovered them. And, while we're on the subject of feelings, look at us, Arnie. For more than twenty years we have talked to each other as if we were voices on a telephone line. All mind, no body; you, the pet child, I, the indulged father."

"I don't follow you, my friend."

"Don't you really?" He glanced at me suspiciously.

"No. What's wrong with that? It's been lovely for over twenty years."

"Well, shall I say life refutes theory or physical reality has been introduced?" He walked away from me into the depths of the room. "Let's stay with you. Absalom is gone. As I understand it, so is Paul. You must rescue yourself. The only salvation I know is work."

"I thought being a housewife and mother was *the* great womanly work. What career do you suggest — basket weaving? I have earned an honorary Ph.D. in box lunches. My job experience has been chairman of the P.T.A. bazaar committee, president of the garden club, and volunteer on the missing persons telephone line. Doctor, I am a forty-year-old housewife with no training, a vacant marriage, a malformed love affair, a missing son, a married daughter and two sons well on the way to being grown. Where do I go from here?"

"I'm not minimizing the problem. More mothers fall into melancholia from feeling superfluous than from menopause. Get your degree and teach. Or settle in and write. You once quoted someone saying there's one novel in every one of us."

"I never thought I'd hear you prescribe art for therapy's sake."

"Unless you work at it you can't tell if it will be art for art's sake."

"Freud's formula for salvation is love and work."

"I am in no position to speak of love."

"You! Father on earth. If not you, who? Getting us here, caring for every waif that comes your way . . ."

"Arnie, I am a half-blind doctor with too large a practice and too many dependents."

"Among which I may now count myself?"

Only his accelerated sniffing betrayed him.

"Jeremy, if I didn't know you all these years, I would say you are in search of a quarrel."

"You might say I am overwrought."

"Is it your eye?"

"No, not my eye."

He looked more crumpled and tired than I had ever seen him. His skin seemed to have soaked up ether like a coarse sponge.

His usually open, candid face was marked by irritation.

"Are you sicker than you are confessing? You are not permitted to get sick, dear Storky," I whispered. "You have to deliver Arie of my first grandchild."

"I can deliver with one eye."

"Should you take a catnap? Should I read to you?"

"Talk to me. Pick a subject." He shrugged. "Discourse about eyes."

"I can try. Sit back. Relax. Turn up the sound . . . In the matter of seeing, the *I* is the lens."

He was asleep.

The eye worries me. I tell you again. I have not confessed to you the trouble I'm having with Paul's Eye.

"I paint what I see," he said. Then I saw her too. Cried my eyes out. Or to speak of Manet, master of the moderns, the Innocent Eye. The hell I say. If you want innocence, don't look for it in the Eye. The Eye of the beholder is immensely prejudiced.

You, my dear Paul, are many eyed, like one of those jeweled idols explorers steal, not knowing they will be cursed to death. I found in you the red eye of love, the green eye of jealousy, the self-righteous eye of a false prophet, the roving eye of a rake, the mirror eye that reflects only the self. I detected those other eyes that mirrored you: sloe-eye, slit-eye, slant-eye, adoring, admiring, blind with tears. Too brief, your faithful eye, before it became an ireful eye.

> *Now do I drown an eye unused to flow*
> *And weep afresh love's long-since cancelled woe.*

Jeremy sighed in his sleep.

O, best father I ever had, they've taken away your bad

eye. Does a seeing eye wait for your unseeing eyes? Are malignant cells behind the glass eye, rushing you to glazed eyes?

Absalom, I kept my eyes open for you from day's eye to day's eye. Viareggio, Spezia, Pisa. . . . That's the way I got to be lying here, resting my rheumy eye. Apple of my eye, where are you now? Who put the evil eye on you, my boy? Where can you be, gazing with veiled eyes out of the tower of yourself?

Jeremy stirred. Sighed. Sniffed. Was wide awake.

"You know what, Jeremy? I continue to see what I have seen. My son, bloody. I keep waking to it."

"We are all bloody. Born in blood. I have delivered hundreds of babies and I can never reconcile myself to the injustice of the process."

"But it's also miraculous. To the woman it is always the first child; the conception which occurs mysteriously as sun striking fire through glass. You can't imagine the euphoria. Has no woman confided the deep-sea peace into which one slowly sinks, the dreamlike sensation of opening and closing to the rhythms of one's tidal fluids?"

"What I see at the bloody emergence is imperfection attached to the coiled umbilical cord. The slightest deviation can mean idiot, maniac, mongoloid, a child who gnaws at its own flesh, a child who destroys others. What has being born human to do with the idea of perfection? Or rational cause-and-effect? One child can take shock and aftershock; get kicked around, and grow up wholesome, while another, lovingly reared as Absalom, can be hopelessly mad . . ."

The words hurtled in from the periphery of my knowing. "What are you saying, Jeremy? Take that back . . ."

He was not a doctor for nothing.

326

"I can't, Ariadne. You must finally listen. There is nothing you or I can do about Absalom. Absolutely nothing. We do not know how or if nature and nurture operate together to generate malignant conditions." (He pointed to his eye socket.) "To name it *Schizophrenia* doesn't define it. Sometimes it shows up in adolescence."

"To accuse yourself or Adam is as rational as saying Cain became a murderer because his mother weaned him too early."

"Have you said it all now, Doctor Starobin?"

He sniffed, lifted the telephone and buzzed the labor room. Delly's brogue crackled through. "Quiet as an August afternoon, Doctor. This one won't do anything for hours. Two are due in. Catch your sleep. Bless."

"You've seen symptoms all these years?"

"A child is not a set of symptoms. And he was your child, my dear Arnie." His voice softened.

"But, he was more intelligent, more sensitive than the other children."

"You are idealizing again. He was also more moody, more combative and exceptionally aloof. Absalom was what he was, from the day I brought him forcibly into the world. He was never reconciled to being born."

"I must find him. Do you propose that I let him roam the countryside inflicting harm until they catch up with him and throw him into a snakepit?"

"You are overstating again. He may do better by himself. No one can predict the degree to which he may be roused. To some degree everyone enjoys hurting and being hurt."

"You don't believe what you're saying, Jeremy. I don't want to hurt or be hurt and neither do you."

"If you still believe that, you are being childish, or deluded. *You* don't want to hurt or be hurt! I won't presume to remark on who hurts whom in your relationships with Adam, Paul and me. But did you never pinch your little brother, then hug him,

327

did you and Jessica never spank, imprison, never entrap each other in sadistic games? Come now, Ariadne, what of the pleasure you take in exciting and denying?"

"Remember me, Jeremy? I'm the Jewish mother. What do I know about exciting then denying? In my marriage, I was denied. I hated the pain of it."

"You're sure? Dostoievski says we love life *because* it is pain and torture."

"Storky, I'm beginning to think you've become warped by hearing too many women screaming in labor."

"Maybe I see the first relationship as painful and bloody for mother and child. If the baby doesn't scream, we slap it until it does."

"Jeremy, are you back at Original Sin and the apple? Is it a woman's fault that the birth process is a botch?"

"No one's fault. It simply is. Every man and woman of us pushes out painfully. The first breath brings release from suffocation, and it smells of Mama and blood. The message is imprinted on the blotter-brain. We wash mouth, nose, skin, you can't expunge the smell, taste, feel of that mixture. Call it our first perversion. Who knows! Maybe we look for some of that blood relationship all our lives."

Agitation suddenly swept him to his feet. He rushed back and forth, his heavy trunk swaying like a tree in a strong wind. His skin oozed cold sweat.

"Surely in your years of coming and going in this place you have heard the pleasure within labor pain. Pain . . . and, aah, release." He made lashing motions. "I am gripped . . . a difficult birth challenges me. It is my arena. I enter the struggle in behalf of woman and child, of Ariadne and Absalom. I marshal my skills for a woman I may never have seen before, but with whom I share this dangerous encounter. She loves me. I love her."

Appalling overtones crackled about him as if owls whimpered in threatened branches. He was beclouded in storm, his pallor lurid, his living eye the moonlight at the corona's rim.

"The delivery is agony and ecstasy. Before she drops exhausted into postbirth sleep the woman reaches for my hand. She looks up at me. I am dripping, ugly — yes, I know I'm ugly — bloodstained, and she asks, 'Is it all right?' And I answer, as if I'd been entirely confident of the outcome, 'Perfect!' We separate like lovers." His voice rose . . . "Satisfied lovers!"

This must be a rage of dying, I thought. My dearest friend is dying!

He talked, and it was weird in this man of monumental build, in a voice that pitched higher and higher until it cracked like an adolescent's; as if all these years he had been hidden from me behind an oversized man, and now some passion of despair was flying him back to an unlived youth. His voice, gestures — a youth's, and a youth's ardor. "My dearest Ariadne, what rapture it must be to sink into love's pain and bliss . . ."

As suddenly as a wind drops a twig, his voice fell, "together." He drew his disguises about him. He dropped heavily, into his black leather armchair, his massive gray head like a damaged statue outlined in light.

I shook my head. "I don't understand you, Jeremy."

A fixed suspicious frown settled above his brows. "You are still toying with me, Ariadne, and that's not good."

"Toying with you? Because I've broken down in front of you? I've wept about another wild-goose chase after Absalom. I've babbled about my shameful mess with Paul; my desolate nonlife with Adam; my pyramid of failures and you, my dearest friend, turn yourself into a hostile stranger. Because I'm supposed to be always amusing? Or why?"

"I'll tell you why. You are a woman still playing at being my child." His voice was subdued but venomed.

"I don't recognize you, Jeremy."

"This is my night for turning from prince into frog."

329

"You're a stork, not a frog."

"Tonight, I am a frog. Tomorrow I'll do my best to be transformed back into your playhouse daddy. And you can be my bright amusing bird again, feeding me clever tidbits over the telephone."

"Jeremy, I can't believe you're mocking these years of our friendship. You terrify me. Your operation must have touched your mind."

"No, Ariadne, you have touched my mind. How can you be so stupid? I feel betrayed. Betrayed." His voice boomed. "You've confided in me, simply *told* me, *confessed* would mean some recognition of my feelings, that you are trapped in a brutish dishonorable love affair. You tell it to me, who has been tender of you these many years. Your extravagant behavior, your tears, have not been, as I thought, entirely for Absalom. I heard you weep for Paul. Because of *Paul.* No tears for me? He says he behaves like a rake because you won't get a divorce? Surely, you aren't childish enough to believe that. You love a Lothario, a womanizer, a bum."

I nodded. There was no point explaining that disillusioned love could possess and command.

"*I* asked you to get a divorce ten years ago."

"You did? Not to my knowledge."

"I did, though. Right in this room. But I loved you enough not to press you into conflicts. I thought of you as a woman divided between love for her children and a man. I believed I was the man. I gave up whatever comforts there were in my marriage. Used my work as a pretext to live in this hospital apartment you've furnished so attractively for me. The deprivation! The years, Ariadne! The Hippocratic oath does not swear doctors to celibacy. I thought we shared a moral stand, a mutual refusal to cheat and lie. Your adventure with Paul changes everything. It puts our years into another light. In the name of God, Ariadne, was it merely convenient for you to play at

330

daughter? What must I think? My dear, such questions assail me!"

"Jeremy, Jeremy. With you I saw myself as my father had seen me. A daughter. I saw you as everyone sees you: the best of fathers, a most loving father. That's how I always thought of you — fatherly."

"Not always. Not always." He was fixing me in a single ray, one keen eye, a hypnotist twirling a hallucinating mirror.

"Look straight at me, Ariadne. Do you dare? Do you dare say truthfully that you have not *known* my feelings to be *at least* as mixed as any father's?"

*   *   *

No, Jeremy, my newly opened eyes do not reflect the shapes you wish to see within your tale. In Sleeping Beauty's castle, you were never the prince tearing aside the isolating hedge to breach the spellbound years. No matter how I shift the scenes, your honest candid face bears no resemblance to a fickle Theseus — for whom I betrayed my household saints.

I've looked for your semblance in the dark corners where I played hide-and-go-seek with my boy cousins who found guess what for me. You aren't there either. I do not find you, Jeremy, where you said you were hiding. (I see us vis-à-vis fully clothed. Did you have nothing to do with that?) You are not connected to my sensual past so much as the clerk I chose to check my foodstuffs out, he cheats a bit, but he resembles him, that sweet-mouthed Irish boy who danced with me and one day called me honey. Sometimes the cart that automates the door rolls down the ramp too fast. I'm on the loop-the-loop on which that lifeguard hugged me safe. At that night's carnival he won a string of beads. I wore them till they broke and spilled. Theseus's forerunner: he laughed to see me cry. My dear, there is nothing about you that is eloquent of my Irish cupid.

331

Jeremy, you may command a mirror that will show me to myself so I may read the sins you say are written on my face. But all these years I've looked into your eyes and found me mirrored there, dressed in a child's disguise. Daily, your mirror must have lied. It said, "You are the fairest child of all!" And now you've shifted mirrors. The shadow of your sorrow has destroyed the shadow of my face. You see my wrinkles and wayfarer's wounds. You see me burning in my memories of Paul. You are changing everything between us.

"Memorial Hospital," Jeremy said. "August 29, 1930 — Remember the night your father died."

* * *

Alas poor ghost. His hour is almost come.

They had brought in their entire artillery for the terminal contest between their mastery and the carcinoma entrenched in my father's pulmonary swamp. His person was obscured by their ordnance — oxygen, plasma, glucose, green lights, red lights, charts, numbers, tubes. Tubes were deployed from his nose and mouth. Tubes issued from under the sheets. Bottles above, bottles below. Fluids added a sighing suspiration to the riffle of his breath grieving across the wreckage of his lungs.

Under those sounds lay the sedated patient. Nothing on his face, nothing on his half-closed eyes claimed those sounds. Parched, colorless except for the grizzled auburn hair and mustache, his skeletal body shrouded in sheets, a slight rise at the knee, another at the toes, he lay, his own sarcophagus.

The nurse looked up from her knitting. "Hot out?"

I put down my travel bag. "Very hot. Is my mother here?"

"She's resting. Doctor gave her a sedative. Strain on *her* heart all this . . ." She jabbed the steel needles into the yarn.

332

"I'll get me some iced tea if it's the same to you. Ring if you need anything. I'm Mrs. Grady."

I pointed to the patient's mouth. "Those sounds?"

"Not unusual," she said and escaped.

On the white folds of sheet an emaciated hand lay as if already adjusted to the tomb.

But it was not.

The hand trembled, tensed, spread like a relentless echinoderm gripping an oyster; five curved fingers strained as if to tear open the substance of his pain. He rolled back his lids, the eyeballs rolled after them. They focused dimly on me. He raised his forefinger. What admonishment, now, strict father? Let me hear! His mouth shaped a word. Nothing issued. Air rattled inward. He pointed to the battery of missiles and his forefinger moved right, left, in a gesture of negation. "Am I a man or a terminal cancer?" his eyes demanded. "Turn off those obscene machines." I stood beside him, and made a helpless gesture. His fingers accused, insisted.

"I can't. . . . I don't know how . . . They won't let me . . . Daddy . . . dear . . ."

A word, "pain," fumed slowly out of his mouth like steam beginning to spout from an eruption. A moan bubbled up, poured and overflowed. It kept pouring. It poured over me, over him, it poured over the bed, onto the floor, it flooded the room.

"Somebody come help him," I wailed.

I banged the bell. "Nurse . . ."

His cry rose higher. He writhed. All the pipes and bottles writhed and jangled with him. His eyes bulged, imploring.

I ran out into the hall. Miles of marble and no nurse in sight. At the far end a blue light and a desk. I sped to it.

A nurse looked up at me then down at her cards. "Please." She deigned a glance, a sour saint disturbed at her meditations.

"Mrs. Grady? My father's nurse . . .?"

"Mrs. Grady has left the floor. I will report to her when she returns."

I dashed back toward the room. An intern rounded the corner. "My father! Please come. He's in terrible pain."

He looked at me, from the ankles up, lovely woman stooping to unseemliness. "Normal for his condition."

Stethoscope swaying, he ambulated away. I shouted after him, "Dammit, do something. He's screaming."

"I'll inform his doctor when I see him, miss. Please be quiet in the halls, there are patients."

"What do you think *he* is?"

At the door, moans were still pouring. I forced myself to dive forward at a run, as into high waves.

The sight I saw threw me back, pinned me to the wall.

My father had thrown off the covers. Naked except for his bandaged chest, he was arched in a rigid curve out of which rose, fiercely erect, totemic, his vibrating phallus. From it, tubes and pipes ribboned away to an ambush of bottles that rattled and bounced in macabre celebration.

"It's not possible. Not possible." I grabbed the sheet. Threw it over him. But it skidded down the slope of his arced body and off, covering his face. I yanked it back. It slipped. Again I draped it over him. The sheet tented over the protruding organ, quivered and toppled to the floor. I snatched it up and flung it over him. He shook it off, again. On. Off. Naked, the terrifying giant of a little girl's guilty witnessing. I tried to hold the sheet down forcibly. I was on the bed with him, on my knees. I pushed down on the arc of his belly. It held firm. "Nurse. Help!" He twisted and fought me. I went wild with panic. The mother of four children was frightened out of her wits. IT was after me. IT dove between my breasts. IT beat against my bare arm. The hard naked member pressed against my cheek. My clothes were tousled, hairpins fell from my hair. He squeezed

334

me to him in a skeletal grip. I was tangled in his arms; legs, pipes, tubes. IT was smacking and slapping at me.

"Daddy," I sobbed, "Daddy, darling. Sweetheart. Lie down. Lie down. Let me go. No! No! Let me go. Please lie down."

Who would believe a dying man could have so much force? "Let me go! Let me go!"

A cry shivered through him. "Mama." His body collapsed, in parts, like a broken mold, and fell away from me back onto the bed."

"Mama," he pleaded.

"Mama," I joined his plea.

His breath continued its ordeal. "Mama. Mama."

I picked up the sheet and straightened it over his form.

Blind! For this people have been struck blind. Noah's heirs cursed into eternity . . .

When Mrs. Grady soft-shoed in, my goose-flesh skin had stopped prickling, the lunatic sensations were subsiding slowly like stirred sediment, clouding my emotions with somber and obscure significance.

In that domestic way of terminal-care nurses, she moved briskly, outside the stricken one's desolation. She tapped the bottles, adjusted a valve, noted the various fluid levels and placed her fingers on my father's pulse.

"Everything all right," she announced.

"All right? He's crazy with pain. Please, nurse, can't you give him something?

Mrs. Grady gathered herself together irritably. "He's as heavily sedated as his heart can tolerate." She recorded a reading on a chart. "He had the maximum dose less than an hour ago."

Again his groans rumbled over his bones and bruised concavities like mountain thunder.

The chief surgeon walked in, sultanic among his retinue, his face ether-sallow and anesthetized against imploring questions.

335

"Doctor, please, can't you give my father something to deaden his pain?" Stiff white coats rustled.

"I'm sorry, young lady. His heart can take only a certain amount."

"I've already explained that to the young lady, Doctor Samuels." Mrs. Grady's muscular lips moved ahead of her careful enunciation.

"His heart? Are you serious?"

Dr. Samuel's lips were pursed now, too.

From the patient a groan began low down and rose, wavering upward, remaining on the upper register for piercing seconds, before it broke and fell. The doctor and his court waited politely through the cadence.

"The patient may hold out for days. Perhaps a week. Perhaps we can keep him going for two."

Doctor, interns, disciples, technicians, turned and filed out.

"Why keep him going? Why don't you let him die quickly!" I called after them.

At that moment my mother stepped out from behind them. "Quickly? Quickly?" White face, red eyes, livid lips. "I'm in no hurry, Ariadne. I have time. Plenty of time. You go. Go home. You have your children. Your husband . . ."

Why didn't I fall on my mother's neck and weep, "Not only the wife is dispossessed. My father's daughter is dispossessed. Where will the perfect daughter be lodged?" What brutality kept me from saying, lucidly, mournfully, "Don't hate me now, Mother. We have both made him ours and been made his in thousands of joint becomings."

"Mama," the patient moaned.

"I'm coming, baby," my mother said, walking around me.

Mrs. Grady turned me bodily toward the door and put my travel case in my hand. "You've had a long trip. A bath and a night's rest will do you good. Come back in the morning."

336

"Shall I wait and go home with you, Mother?"

She didn't bother to look at me.

My footsteps echoed in the fake cathedral serenity of the lobby. Nurses and attendants smiled limpid Irish smiles. By what right were they putting on a musical comedy to accompany death? They were all part of an insolent conspiracy to deny that every soul in the throng was clogged with foreboding; that each of us, in part, had bowed to the idea of loss.

"Ariadne!"

For a moment I did not recognize Jeremy. "My child, what are you doing in someone else's hospital? Why aren't you in New Hampshire?"

He bent over me with that AaAh, open your mouth, alert. "You look faint, Lily Maid, are you all right?" He pointed to my valise. "Running away from home? Why didn't you telephone me?"

"Emergency. My mother called. I barely made the only train down. They operated on my father to find his carcinoma inoperable."

His arm went round my shoulder. At once he was all calm efficiency, interposing himself between me and difficulties. "Your mother should have called me to take charge. Perhaps we can move him. Take care of him better at my place. Easier on your mother. I'll talk to the surgeon. For the duration, why not use my family's apartment? It's closer to the hospital."

"Won't it put anyone out?"

"No, the whole bunch are out on the island. I'm due to drive out tomorrow, if no emergencies come in."

He led me back across the vaulted chamber. "Sit here while I look in on a former patient."

He whipped out a big pocket handkerchief, wiped my face, tapped my cheek and said, "Take heart, that's what it's for."

"Lucky the handkerchief smells of baby hospital, I hardly know you in your city suit." I tried to smile up at him but my mouth felt Novocained.

I closed my eyes, but instantly the image flashed on. What a wretched joke to play on a man. Merciless, self-perpetuating nature sapping a man in his last throes. Shaking him out like a dried pod.

"My daughter's room has its own bath. We'll put you in there."

A girlish room, photographs arranged over the single bed. Jeremy, standing beside a tall woman, full figured, not bad-looking at all. Jeremy holding a girl in his lap, the same girl with cats and kittens, the girl as Brownie Scout minus front tooth, smiling over a pyramid of cookies; in graduation dress, sweet-faced; with her brother, both of them holding tennis rackets; toys and pets — those signs of a free childhood; Jeremy's son and another young man, each of them posed, habited, in front of a saddled horse.

The Jeremy I did not know, husband and proper father, household man, was moving in and out of the room, bearing linen, books. "Some of the latest, Aiken, Hemingway, Thomas Wolfe, F. Scott Fitzgerald. Browse. Take off your shoes."

I slipped them off and rested my feet on a hooked rug, two cats snarled in colored yarns.

"My Rachel made that years ago at camp. Will you be all right in this kiddie coop?"

"Where else would I belong?"

"I'm running you a warm bath. There's a pajama top of mine in there." (He must still have been sleeping at home now and then.) "Don't try to unpack now. I'm bringing iced lemonade and a sandwich, also a mild sedative I want you to take. I'm going back to my hospital to make evening rounds, but I will come back and sleep here tonight, so you won't be alone. The noises you may hear later from the other end of the apartment will be me packing, but you should sleep through. I'll talk to you in the morning. Now a long quiet soak."

He kissed me on the forehead, gave me a comforting hug and sent me toward the bath. I followed his orders like a sleep-walker.

In the green water I lay listening to Jeremy's attending clinks and rattles. He put on a record. I heard him finish out "Star Dust" with Hoagy Carmichael, and whistle back from the kitchen with *Zwei Herzen in Drei-Viertel Takt.* Down the hall, "Blue is the night above me, blue as your eyes are blue." He sang in a pleasant baritone. Never knew the doctor sang. Did he dance? With his wife? With his daughter? What other aspects had he of simultaneous being that I knew nothing about?

Keeping the coiled arc of my father at bay, I tried to put myself back to yesterday at the dacha.

In the evening, as so often happens in the mountains, the weather turned violent. Huge clouds billowed up and tumbled across the sky as if tremendous parachutes had been sprung, main ropes dangling, lightning zipping down them, discharging their electrocuting power at whatever projected from the earth.

In a flash I saw Absalom gallop downhill, make a great stag-leap into the air. Head up, arms out, he was enclosed by a black sheet of rain, and disappeared at the water's edge.

I had seen him from my bedroom window, where I was undressing after a burst of gardening I hoped would catch the benefit of oncoming rain. I grabbed my robe and ran, shouting into the wind, "Absalom. Absalom." The soughing branches tossed and creaked. Giant elms waved like reeds. Thunder crashed. Lightning scorched the air. Streams of water flooded downhill treacherous under my bare feet. "Come back. Come back. Come back . . ."

When I reached the roiled water he was nowhere in sight. Every tree was a lightning rod down to his dear body; every pool a circle of fire. I slipped and slid. Water banged me against a ledge. It tore me away and sent me downstream with debris. Alder delayed me.

He was not on his special strand with its moon of white pebbles, nor at the deep pool where he had learned to lie so quietly, he knew the color of deer's eyes; nor had he been flung from his casting rock into the falls.

"Absalom. Absalom." His name was carried away from me in blue sparks. A limb crashed and toppled into the water like a dead body. I waded. I swam where I could. I climbed and clawed over rocks. My feet were bruised and scratched.

I found him.

He was lying prone on a tongue of meadow among orange devil's-paintbrush and black-eyed Susans, unhearing in the roar of wind and rain. I fell down by him, sobbing.

"Absalom, Absalom . . ."

He moved. He lifted his wet silk head. Water rested in his auburn lashes. Mirrors were suspended in his eyes.

"Hi," he whispered. "Hi."

Do you know what I did? Would you believe what I did? You've seen mothers do it when a lost child is found in a crowd. I did it. I slapped him.

Does that blow descend down our lives as certain angels are said to fall eternally from heaven? Wherever he is, does he remember that his smile changed? Fun or fury, masculine arrogance, boy anger, or something fiercer than either, he flung himself on me. We tussled. "Hit me, will you!" he mocked. He had me pinned down, my arms out on either side, our soaked bodies palpable. My son, water dripping from his hair, eyes wild, my Absalom gloated down at me and I gazed up at him, both of us wrapped in a mist of violent and fertile desires.

"I'm sorry, love, did I hurt you?" I asked.

"Terribly," he scoffed. "Kiss it and make it better."

"What a baby," I said. And I did.

Jeremy tapped at the bathroom door. "I'm leaving now. Don't forget to take the yellow pill, my child."

"I will obey you like a father," I answered.

The bed was made up. Covers turned back. The sheets received me. Tray and books did not withdraw themselves. You think it is nothing to see your father naked? Wicked daughter, long ago fallen in love with him. I assure you, pornographers, you must never let dreams take substantial shape, they must not be acted out. If you lie with your father, you will be cursed. You will worship strangers whom you translate into childhood saints. Oh the Lord shall smite you with madness and blindness and astonishment of heart.

I must have been screaming.

Jeremy was on his knees beside my bed. "Wake up, child. It's all right. I'm here. Wake up, Ariadne."

Pressure on my chest fixed me to the bed. I was immobilized. I could not unsolder my lids. Terror had fused them. Baritone groans honked out of my chest, as if I'd swallowed a horn. Jeremy slipped an arm under me and pillowed my head. "Breathe slowly, deeply . . . again, again, dear . . . in . . . out."

I was choking, my pulse palpitating in arrhythmic spurts. Perspiration trickled from me and turned cold. "It's all right, all right. It's a nightmare," he said.

"No. No. No." If I opened my eyes I would find I had become blind.

"Only a nightmare. Shh."

He stroked my face with one hand, pressing me to his chest with the other.

I didn't know I was weeping, but tears must have risen and overflowed like water surfacing on ice. At my neck the pillow was wet. I pushed it from me, turned away from him and lay face downward.

He began to massage the back of my neck, firmly, kneading at the cramped knot.

"Better?"

I could not answer.

Slowly the expression of his hand grew gentler. His strokes moved to include my shoulders. Smoothing. Soothing.

"Shall I leave you now?"

I could not answer.

He eased himself into bed. The first man other than Adam. Number now, one. I heard his robe drop to the floor. Caresses spread gradually from my shoulders down my tensed spine. Upward, downward, shoulders, spine, ribs, slowly, very gently, patiently. Kind. So very comforting and kind. His body's thrumming vaguely came to me, an engine warming up in a distant valley. His hand down my spine, rounded the curves of my back and upward again. Returned. Hesitated. Trembled. Rounded again. Large fingers traced the side of my breast.

His mouth softened against my ear, my shoulder, my throat. "Dearest . . ."

I could not answer. My body was drawn after him, an empty dory bobbing behind a schooner.

"Oh, my dear. My little dear."

When he folded me into his large competent embrace I let myself be enveloped. Nothing in me roused itself to protest his warm indulgent mouth, his big hands, his comfortable body.

Passive. Supine. I felt exhausted as if I had been towed half-drowned and beached. Everything very sad and very far away.

When he said, "Open your eyes, my love," I did not. When he urged, his voice heightening like a youth's, "Open your golden eyes," I could not for the tears.

"Love. Love. Love . . ."

From a great despairing distance, I released him to the climax of his possession with a few broken cries and moans. When he allowed himself to be overwhelmed I was hazily surprised by the ruthless totality of it.

I lay against his shoulder, collecting myself fragment after fragment, from this unfamiliar room, this inappropriate bed, from him, from Absalom, from my father, searching for myself as in a mirror shrouded for the dead.

Close to my ear was his murmur. "Love, love, love." But I was listening to my inner voice reciting: "Thou hast committed fornication."

"Are you all right?" he whispered.

"Perfect," I said, hardly knowing enough to know I spoke untruth.

The son. The father. And the father's ghost. What more could a woman want?

*　　*　　*

I was drawn back by Jeremy's "Ariadne, remember?"

I did not raise my eyes.

"My father died that night . . . I remember . . ."

Dignity forbade him to probe into what of him I had buried back there.

Shakily, we resumed the devices of our friendship. (Admit it, Jeremy, old friend, though we emptied the sensual with years of deprivation, in our talk, whatever the subject, we invigorated our ancestral existence.) We continued to speak on the telephone, two lucid conversationalists. We discussed the categories printed above the library stacks — Art, Philosophy, Politics, Religion, Literature. I discovered *Tristram Shandy* and gave it to him to read.

"It's a swarming chaos," he said of it.

"Isn't that what God used to establish order?"

"What Jew needs more disorder? We can't afford it in life. We don't want it in art."

(I'm sorry about that, Jeremy. I would have liked to present you with a minuet of a novel but it must await my more favorable transmigration.)

"Look at *Tristram Shandy* as a Jewish novel," I said, clearing away the wrapping paper from the cherry preserves I'd brought.

He settled into his chair and stirred his tea. "If you can prove that, Scheherazade, you get the Nobel Prize. Turn up the sound."

"Sit back, relax, Storky," I said. "In the first place Sterne's characters, like Jews, are under constant threat of dispersion, digression or restraint by the whimsical force that has authority over them. One foot on the stair, a man may be arrested for fifty pages. An edict of expropriation can dislodge and send someone slopping over the mud for chapters."

"Tell me more." He tapped an imaginary gavel. "The witness will proceed with her charming nonsense . . ."

"In the second place his sequences are like Jewish history: parody piled on absurdity. Large events place them in tragic-comic situations. In the background there's a big war in Flanders, but in the foreground is Uncle Toby's wound in the groin. It becomes a comic wound. It has absurd ramifications; it arouses the Widow Wadman's circumlocutions and pryings; it excuses Bridget's love life; it is the cause of Tristram's accidental circumcision, due to the window weights having been borrowed for the erection of Uncle Toby's toy fortification. It serves to reflect Mrs. Shandy's deprived sex life. There's no end to the laughter set off by impotence."

He shook his head and groaned in mock disapproval.

"See Storky, Laurence Sterne invented a form for our content. Our people, constantly robbed of the right to return to nests, thrust out of their improvised situations, kept from a homeland, subjected to interrupted family life, whose history is the longest chapter of chances ever endured ·by any people . . . Laurence Sterne writes for us.

"In summary, let us pray that our author, having condemned us to so much arbitrary displacement, will as amusingly hold us together in our joint themes of scholarship and sexual deprivation . . ."

"You win," he said.

The delivery—room signal rang. He stood up, put his arms out, dropped them. "Let there be peace between us," he said.

The door closed. Some petals from a stale bouquet collapsed and made a clutter on the floor.

His gesture, arms full of nothing, survives.

Tracing the Repeat

*Secondo che ci affliggono i disiri
e gli altri affetti, l'ombra si figura;
e questa e la cagion di che tu ammiri.*

— DANTE

And even as desire and sentiment
take hold of us
So do our shades take shape . . .

— MANDELBAUM (tr.)

"FRAME BY FRAMING". . . Daniel was declaiming at dinner (he does a fearful amount of declaiming), "for sale or surveillance, your dossier can be retrieved."

"Stop waving your fish fork," Dinah said. "I'm wearing Grandma's white blouse."

(Grown-up enough to count lovers and heartbreaks, and Dinah still likes to borrow my clothes.)

Daniel switched the fork to his right hand. "Must wave or it's no demonstration."

"Can they retrieve absolutely everything, boss?" She leaned

toward her uncle Benjamin. (Though I dislike her father's politics, I admit his German-Spanish mix is cool fire in Dinah.)

"They can get a print-out of practically every footprint: schools, charge accounts, bank accounts, phone calls, registration numbers, contributions, subscriptions, political affiliations — Danny, I'm sure they have you spotted — as well as plane reservations and probably any hotel, motel or inn register you've ever signed."

"Any — even a one-night stand in a tourist cabin?" I asked.

All three of them turned calm eyes on me; Grandma of the unrumpled sheets, clean hands, full cookie jar, emergency piggy bank. As for Benjamin: His mother? Never. He's an Immaculate Conception, or once only, for him. If the whore of Babylon had a son . . . and why not . . . ?

"Fortunately, these devices can only be fed questions to answers that are known. By the way, Mother, these quenelles really rank. What's your secret? I'll have another."

Three plates were thrust toward me.

"Leave room for the roast, gluttons. Don't you take time for lunch on the job? The way you eat when you get here . . ."

"No time off. Show your grandmother what comes of working around the clock at that manufactured prose. Give us a speech on loose morals, Dinah. More than three computer words in a single sentence and you win a free lunch."

"I prefer suffering the pangs of thwarted aspiration to interpolating with a Master-Slave Flipflop, or being the ultimate punch-out of an Improved Pulse-Steered Flipflop." Dinah fluttered her lids demurely.

"Pretty fair, duckie," Benjamin said. "I'd say you scored at least four."

"Neither has anything to do with the perturbations of being kissed on the mouth," I contributed.

348

"No score, Mother, unless you incorporate technical terms. Your turn, Danny. A political speech."

"The menace of information retrieval is at our bugged telephones. Resist Batch Fabrication. Protest being arrested as a Passive Component in a Microelectronic Device . . ."

"You've already scored. Now touch our emotions," Dinah said.

"Data are the death of emotions. For them I defer to Grandma. Take it away, old lady."

"How is 'the heart cannot thump for joy at discovering the precisions encased in a capacitor' . . . ?"

My grandchildren wowed.

"Now who is for dessert?"

Danny dropped his napkin. "I surrender. Let's walk dinner down to the pond."

"How about a few casts for bass, Danny; dessert and coffee later?"

"I'll row you guys around," Dinah said, "for the sake of my waistline."

I sat on the bench under the willow and watched the blue dory fade into the mists etherealizing the pond. The pleasant voices gradually lost explicitness and harmonized with the flutings of the evening birds.

A squirrel cautiously approaches. He noses, finds, raises humanoid paws and nibbles; lifts his head, defensively alert. Seems to fix explicit statuary eyes at me. He hears something ominous.

We are both transfixed. Something beats in the thickets.

We dash for cover.

*   *   *

Water breaks over boulders. A brook released from winter swells and crests, foams, crashes and roars past our woodland hideaway.

349

The seasons flood downstream. I am lying belly-down on a warm rock. Only my hands and forearms are still in sunlight. My fingertips ripple the reflection. Upside-down joe-pye weed fades in the resinous pool between roots of hemlocks that snake into the water. An orange is lying beside my head because Paul has put it there for color. It is the orange that appears nightly like the golden ball the frog retrieved and placed on the princess's pillow to remind her of the favor she owes. In the phoenix forever of this parable, the prince reverts to frog, the princess rakes the leaves. She is unhappy ever after.

On the near shore there seems to be a luminous torso, its pedestal ambiguous in green evening mists.

"Light's going too fast to paint anymore. Time to pack," Paul says.

Not me. I'm lying here on this rock forever and forever. The phoebes may twitter from the fir trees for all I care and the clouds collect over me till their round dead eyes remain black. Then let it snow.

*   *   *

It is not the peripheral nature of feelings that amazes me. No, it is the tenacity. Unbecoming as a garish postcoital flush on an old woman is this desire that can ignite in my decay like the smoldering fire of swamps, compost heaps, and rotting garbage. I'm old, by any actuarial table. I have a draft-age grandson; a granddaughter full of questions about how to live as a full woman, not shed biology, but not be defined by it. Yet I return to you, Paul, you who are phantom, voluptuary, cruel, even in the rotten residue of dreams.

Sometimes I wake, my moth-eaten marabou drenched in tears, my knees drawn up in the foetal posture of grief. I must have been back. We must have fallen into each other's arms. And when we lay separate again you must have said, breath steaming out of your carved mouth, "I'm leaving. I'm leaving. We're wrecking each other. I'm going to get married. I want a home. I want to know where I am at night, with whom I'm going to wake in the morning."

I admonish myself. But my past moves toward me and I move toward it. Why? Because you were my education, oh my snake, my darling snake. (No. I am not being phallic. These reflections are not indulgences, but surgeries.)

It was absurd theater for us to share the same stage. In the first place you and I were reading from different plays, so our actualities quickly ceased to be contiguous. We became discordant fictions, I living out mine, you yours. I cast myself as Queen Guinevere while you were playing Livingstone on a foray in the domestic hinterland.

In the second place, our forms did not match. Your form was modern, random and spontaneous. The Happening. And I was way back with old Fichte who defined the novel as the true form of an age of sin, homelessness and despair. I thought I was having a dialogue with a Faustian hero who would recover lost kingdoms with me. Paul, you never wanted to own *any* real estate, surely not the marital state. You traveled bindle-stick light.

You left a book we had finished reading on a park bench and I started back for it.

"Leave it for someone else," you said, "I don't keep books unless I'm certain I'll need them for reference." Then, mocking my prudence, you added, "I can always rely on your library if I need something on a Sunday."

Perhaps your most persuasive quality was the high Christian opinion you held of yourself (and I shared) accentuating your excellences but affable about your defects. Your prejudices were sacred to you, and for too many years, to me. Even your irrational jealousy, which you defended as intuition, or an observant intelligence, I considered seriously because you were so positive. You had an extensive vocabulary of fidelity, but you served nothing better than your own appetites, while I was all uncertainty and apprehension from my center out. I had a Jewish immigrant education.

What I know, I learned through partings. I had, and have, a problem separating myself from what I love. I hate separation. If it means anything, Jeremy had to rip each of my babies from my womb. For me, every meeting and every beginning suggests infinity. And I fell in love with you. You, student of encounters, have been my Ph.D. in partings. My third degree.

I'm not complaining. You took me to your unfrightened country. You were superior to the natives.

A walk in the park:

A couple of hoods menacingly fanning out toward us. You did not step aside, you gripped my frightened Jewish shoulder. "Aren't you afraid they'll harm me," I wanted to cry. You subdued them with electric current of your own violence. Gentile, lord and owner of your body, self-possessed, you dispossessed them. You demeaned them with a contemptuous stare and a sudden bristling dilation, red-eyed, the territorially assumptive male.

Without you I might never have seen that country of which you were a native. I might never have seen that land of vast cloudbanks and wild horses running, foam at the mouth. You procured my first papers. But it was not my father's land. I could never become naturalized, though with you I kissed away Adam's calm domestic kingdom and Jeremy's benevolent provinces, and the secure grave affection of both.

You were so brave I didn't realize you could be frightened of a little thing like a baby.

*   *   *

She had not thought of it as unplanned parenthood. She thought how their child would have long legs. Unlike Adam's medium-legged land birds, this one would wade the sea's edge like a rosy flamingo.

She said, "Paul, I wonder what our child will look like?"

(Old woman that I am, there are still scenes so humiliating I barricade myself from them by a change of person.)

He had just peeled the last orange in the grocery bag and he was feeding her. As his fingers brought each segment to her mouth, they stayed till she had licked and kissed them.

"Our daughter would look like you, I would hope. But not as pale as you now."

His face, too, was drained of color, with blue and brown crescents throbbing like bruises in the thin skin under his eyes.

"The beggar will have to go out with a clamming bucket." He kissed her throat. "Your flesh. Ummm."

He fell asleep, his head against her breast, his nose pressed a little to one side, a nurseling, sniffing slightly. She lay still, knowing it angered him to spend any of their afternoon in sleep. (Love had caught me too late for my passions not to be entwined with strands of maternal adoption.)

"I get all too much sleep without you," he complained.

She tried to see her wrist watch. His arms and legs tightened around her. "Stay," he murmured.

"It's time. I must go."

"You don't love me." He rested, his open mouth against her shoulder. "I won't let you. It's not time . . ."

"I have eight for dinner."

He groaned and flung himself away from her.

He sat up on the edge of his studio bed, naked, one hand still reaching back of him to touch her thigh, her knee, her belly. "Sweetheart, stay — just today."

She reached for her slip. On the dirty studio floor her toenail polish glowed . . . Ariadne, perfumed, polished . . . racing against time . . . pregnant.

Pulling on her stockings she noted a spray of broken capillaries in the shape of a bundle of dry twigs, and on her thighs the network of faint scars where pregnancy had stretched the skin.

"Paul, I'm quite serious. I'm pregnant."

"Good!" (Dear, that *was* your first reaction.) "You will be forced to run away with me and make an honorable couple of us at last."

And then he said, "Are you sure?"

"It might be a cold, or a heat, a change of climate, the altitude in your studio, the menopause . . . why not, I'm over forty."

"The menopause it is not."

In the car, driving her home, his eyes straight ahead on traffic, he said, "Have you told Adam?"

In the brief time lag between the rumble of his words and the lightning flash she said, "Adam has nothing to do with this."

"Am I supposed to believe that?"

"Yes."

"Do you lie to protect me or yourself, I wonder?"

"I don't lie."

"You are saying that to me, Ariadne, your lover, your fornicating lover, not your credulous husband."

354

"Adam has nothing to do with this."

"Ariadne, I was not born yesterday. Don't lie to me. You live in the same house, the same life, with Adam. I know the rooms. I know the beds. I've been in them with you. Don't you think I know what part I play? I'm milady's lover . . ." He spit out the phrases. "Adam's cuckolding friend . . . you think that's native, that I learned it at my mother's knee, or in Sunday school? I am the . . . the beast you keep hidden away and throw something to . . . if . . . if the children don't need you . . . if you aren't on a wild-goose chase for Absalom, if Adam doesn't require you to entertain clients. . . . True, you bring me left-overs . . . you bring me goodies . . . you bring me flowers from your country garden. You invite me to attend you there . . . You're motherly . . . you invite me to company dinners to keep up a front or is it to protect your flank . . . you're good, good, good to me . . . you are a kitten who never killed a mouse . . ."

He maneuvered the car aggressively through a snarl of traffic, his beautiful hands gripping the wheel, his adored face as white and taut as his knuckles. (A driver honked as he cleared by inches.)

"Don't you think I deserve some of that comfort, a home, a wife, regular meals, children? You think it's good for me to drag on for years being in love with you, a married woman? You think I wished it? Oh I've tried to get away often enough. The years my life has impinged on yours." He shouted each word: *"It has not been good for me."*

They were held up by a garbage truck. The roaring beside them was almost as great as the roaring within.

"Christ, Ariadne, even if it were true, I don't trust you . . . I would never be sure . . . You wouldn't be sure . . . Anyway what the devil are we talking about? You know damned well, and I know, too, you'll never leave that cozy nest, those overin-dulged, adored, tyrannical children, that loyal hard-working husband whose every move you can predict. You wouldn't dare to go with this . . . wild . . . me."

They drove holding their breaths in the charred and corrupted air. At the corner, where he let her out, cautiously, in case anyone should see them, he said, "Speak to me, Ariadne, say something."

You know what that forty-five-year-old woman said? Good God, I don't want to recall it. That woman said, "I'll see you Wednesday afternoon."

I'm not saying Paul was a voluptuary without a heart. I believe he loved me in his tormented fashion. I suppose at frantic moments he may have believed his fireside-and-slipper yearnings, envied Adam — husband, father, householder. But he was not a paterfamilias. He did not want to set up housekeeping complete with his babies. (How did an anxious homebody like me get a son who was well in advance of the modern fashion of forsaking, and a lover prematurely committed to noncommitment?) Perhaps he was caught, as the serpent was caught, in some obscure mesh of longing to snake between the daddy and the mommy, to sever their bonds. Perhaps not.

At times I find myself sympathetic. In a way, I *was* bad for him. Although I wasn't wedded to him, I was wedded to reality through my relationship with him and I catch glimpses from his point of view. Or it my grandchildren's view?

There was something prematurely modern about Paul. The keystone of his self-respect was similar to Danny's and other children of the sixties. "Telling it like it is" was almost a definition of virtue. Aside from some blindness in relation to his own reflection in the mirror, he was not afraid to look at anything. "If it exists, look at it," he would say. He would have agreed with modern painters like Arie, that the canvas must be wiped clean of false sentiments, and with Aaron that Hitler had gained power because the German people had turned blind eyes to the truth being enacted around them.

I think, partly, his affair with me undermined his faith in himself. It forced him to behave with deviousness. Distrust in himself spilled over into distrust for me. I believe some of his infidelities were motivated by the need to prove he was free to act openly in the dashing, spontaneous style he felt was native to him. He was a couple of decades in advance of the sixties in another way. He shared the relentless sexual ethic, whether he voiced it or not, of allowing himself to have everything, look at everything and of regarding cosmeticized views of life as the ultimate immorality.

I have continued to ponder.

*   *   *

Pregnant at forty-five!

A homesick fortuneteller, one of those desperate Gypsies who beckon from curtained storefronts, an indifferent tea-leaf reader, a nosy neighbor — seeing the abandoned dining room, the submerged kitchen, the marital sheets smooth as a morgue slab, the toys put away in the attic, the dressing table freighted with expensive unguents and optimistic night creams could have mumbled, "I see a pregnancy in your immediate future."

Adam and Jeremy, statistician and physician, might have pointed out that Ariadne, the gardener, was out of season. Practically any other would have been more timely.

Say, far back, at my special sign, frozen Aquarius. The air cold and clear, the sun shy of the zenith, casting clean elliptical shadows on the snow that fell in an erratic storm and suppose me *not* a virgin after my first night with Adam.

Or the opening day of the fishing season, the year I was twenty-nine; the meadow like a great bosom breathing in and out of hibernation, expanding and contracting under March ice, new green over perennial grasses rising to regeneration, Absalom fishing below a cascade, the children scampering in the room above. I might have had Adam's fifth child, with high school still to go.

Or, at my summer solstice, Jeremy's child, conceived on my father's last night, when frogs and toads (I know them well) plink and plunk their fortuitous sexy ensembles and swarms of tissue-paper moths accumulate like fly-ash on the screen. Would I have divorced Adam and married Jeremy?

Or, if with Paul, then in the first flush of autumn, when falling temperature and diminishing light trigger chrysanthemums into bloom; in the hour of our fullness; but not, like some grunion, drawn by tides of moon, to its own eclipse.

I, too, could have been an oracle. If I had gazed into my glass, and seen a woman divested of her last child, menopause closing in, a granddaughter on the way, I would also have predicted scenes nauseating as stumbling on a seagull rotting in a tangle of bleached seaweed, broken crab shells and rubbery testimonies of thwarted fertility.

"Bad timing if I ever saw it," Jessica said.
"I'll have the baby anyway," I said.
"Why not? It's a wise child. And if it is a duplicate of Paul and embarrasses you, I'll adopt the bastard."

For another month I told myself I couldn't give it up. I let myself be overtaken by the slow swoon warming up from my womb. Woke with my hands caressing my breasts, answering their growing tenderness. Paul couldn't change my mind, I told myself.

But he could. And he did.

Jeremy himself could not resist pointing out that the odds for bearing a mongoloid increase with the age of the mother. (To whom else could I have turned? I could find no one else who would have risked relieving me of it.)

There I was: forty-five, technologically unemployable, education irrelevant, but in shape: vital organs in function, metabolic rate high, estrogen level exuberant enough to make conception conceivable, with a greater life expectancy (according to Adam's actuarial tables) than the entire life span of a married female of a century ago, going home to a house, emptied like me, of biological function.

Inside, I could hear the telephone. The lock held.

By the time the tumblers gave, the telephone had stopped ringing, but I tracked across the floor and lifted the receiver. Hello . . . hello . . . whoever you are . . . speak to me . . . blblblaahh . . . blblblaahh beeped on the nothing air.

I collapsed on the sofa. The room stank. Dust puffed up and billowed ceilingward. I located a bowl of dead flowers.

The kitchen, too, lay under a dirty trance. When I turned on the tap there was a hollow knocking from the old iron pipes, a roar, then a brown trickle that gradually cleared. When I tipped the bowl over the sink, the stench of stagnant water brought tears to my eyes. There seemed no reason why I should stop their flow.

After a while the telephone rang.

"No there is nothing wrong with my voice, Jessica. I just haven't spoken to anyone today."

The bright stagey voice at the other end persisted. "You have someone with you . . . Paul?"

"I am alone. Couldn't be more so. Benjamin probably has his trunk unpacked by now . . . You know where the Pied Piper takes all the children? To Boston. There ought to be a suttee field right in the harbor . . . for used-up mothers. How do I feel? I feel like I look. Sepia."

359

"What's wrong with sepia? Wasn't that one of Paul's arty colors?" Jessica's affection has never precluded bitchiness. "Hold on, I'll light a cigarette."

She left me to reassemble the bits and pieces of my quavering identity. In the mirror the sepia woman wiped mascara from under one eye. The smudge made it look as if it had been blackened. She puckered her colorless mouth, examined each profile . . . some coarsening of the pores . . . good thing the nose doesn't alter much . . . bit of droop under the chin . . . too much bosom . . . well, Paul had left her immodest about her flesh . . .

Jessica picked up just in time.

"I'll call for you at seven, Arnie. Nonsense, of course you have to come, you promised. Analyze yourself while you're dressing. Freud did it and he was a mere man."

I stood at the window looking down on the familiar street. Complexities of time and space flattened like the trick books we used to find in Cracker Jack boxes . . . flip the pages, the figure races for home. From this window I watched for the children to come home from school, park, dates, from perilous and secret trials, from sudden confrontations with rowdy evil. From this post I endured the necessity of seeing each one go in turn; the years dictating departures until the youngest was also a receding figure on the expanding terrain of his own life.

(I should be pleased? It's natural! Semantics. Nothing but semantics! Am I a maternal duplicating machine? I'm not even pleased to see snowdrops give way to chrysanthemums. Horticulturally, baby's-breath may be perennial but I am not.)

Below my window, three little girls in summer dresses were jumping rope, their sunburned hair, their pastel skirts belling outward, then closing like lilies at sunset. Their mews and cries fluttered up through the stiffening sycamore.

A young man and woman strolled by preceded by two boys dreamily pedaling tricycles. Through leaves already stained with iron, light-stippled shapes moved through a Sunday of Seurats.

An adolescent boy reposed on one of the sooty lions guarding the opposite stoop. Book facedown on his chest, he watched a child hide behind the limestone beast, to be found by his startled mama. As I was startled, day after day, by each child in turn, for a nursery-school season, or until the ritual's mysterious gratification ceased . . . Though I be lost, I will be found.

Not that I wanted to repeat it: Arie, my work of art, lying against me like a tea rose, petal flesh translucent over twig bones or Aaron, my hero, sturdy arms akimbo, looking like an egg yolk version of Adam, on the porch roof getting the shutter job done, or whistling to hide his intention, accidentally bumping Benjie, the interloper, the family sweetheart, the scholarship boy. Or Absalom, my runaway, saying, "I'll never have another tooth fall out naturally. I liked that feeling when you could push the tooth back and forth and it would make a squishy noise and taste salty."

What will be my new game, now that I've come to the end of those thousands of rounds of monopoloy, monogamy, maternity, the compromised uses of matrimony? No I don't want to repeat it. But I don't want to be utterly alone. This tolling in a deserted house cannot be fulfillment of the womanly life.

They are gone, and it's a bloody letting go.

Paul was gone. Was it forever this time? Over the years we had put aside pride, put aside our ideas of virtue, but were held to each other with the persistence, obsessive, even disillusioned love commands. I had not yet bowed to the intolerable and put love aside. But the time had come.

I whisked mascara on my eyelashes. For whom should I

361

adorn myself? Adam in Cleveland? Jeremy in despair? The waiters? One of Arie's discarded beaux grown-up enough to play dotage with? I'll wear my dust-colored sleeveless . . . and jewels. It's a night for jewels, Paul.

You said, "Nothing harsh should lie against your skin; would you bruise a peony with metal and stone?" You have driven a stake into my gardener's heart . . . you have pruned me down to a stump . . . "Nothing should ever be allowed to detract from your golden eyes . . . my darling . . . wear colorless backgrounds . . . air, cloud, water, sky . . . you are essence . . ." How about clay, had you thought of clay you judicious brute? You bastard . . . you heart-breaking intelligent bastard. Tomorrow I'm going to buy a Mexican fiesta dress with huge red flowers . . . magenta on green . . . and a flowery bowery funeral wreath . . . no don't wrap it, I'll wear it. Take a tranquilizer? Write rhymed iambics? Auden said iambics are for satire and curses.

How shall I curse thee for whom I lost my childhood saints? May you become the bellows and the fan to cool a nymphomaniac's lust . . . may you have a mistress of numbers, one who counts and then recounts . . . may you have another (you will) . . . may she detail the exploits of her other lovers: leaving you with a bitter distaste, but hooked. (Do you have the consciousness, Don Juan, to feel much suffering?) May you know the melancholy that lies in wait for men who spend their substance on woman after woman. May you end your days in a seedy rooming house, with a milk bottle on the windowsill.

In lost love, every schoolgirl has Shakespeare to speak for her. Let him speak for me whose youngest is older than Juliet was when she died. What did you say, William? "But to the girdle do the gods inherit, beneath is all the fiend's." Wrong, the immortal fiend gets it all, head to foot.

I tell you the heart abhors a vacuum. To meet you in hell, Paul, is what I hope of heaven. I've drawn my grief through

362

numbers and it's just as fierce. Anyway you know what I think of numbers. German edicts scrolled on skin.

We need women poets to mourn our lives. Menopausal women to hot flush it away. Night-palsied women to speak for the inelegance of loneliness, the obscenity of loneliness, the crying at the mouth, drought at the breasts, at the gaping knees. Bring me to my knees, will you!

Burning! Burning! I incinerate in the fuel of unused love. It is not love that is the intolerable shirt of flame, but loss of it. I sink under the heaviness of no head resting on my bosom.

Hail to thee, Irish cupid, you called me a bitch. I have seen insolent bitches on beaches lolling against long sailors. They don't look as bad as Dad said they would. On rocks along their piers no pyre appears. Are they too riven through guts by spears of longing? No. There boys dive, girls leap into blue bays, while I drown in bays without boys or girls. I shall run down Dock Street, rouged spots under ravenous eyes, bad gull hoarse crying, "For God's sake, let me love."

Absentee children. Unpossessive bachelors. Come home.

Which one? Is it each one?

I am tangled in simultaneity.

Oh what a tangled web! The mother of my children was the woman obsessed with Paul. Both of me were twined and knotted and both were being drawn through griefs of parting.

I wish I could clarify the past as knowledgeably as I've just clarified the soup stock for the pot-au-feu, merely skimming the scum and strewing crushed eggshells. (The snow is good and my grandchildren, Danny and Dinah, are coming for the weekend with guests and it's a dish that can feed an indeterminate number at indeterminate hours.) But as Virginia Woolf has remarked:

363

A painstaking woman who wishes to treat life as she finds it, and to give voice to some of the perplexities of her sex, in plain English, has no chance at all.

If the intrusion of a housewife with slotted spoon and whisk casts a wholesome doubt on the suffering of an Ariadne awash on a Dionysian beach, it is because here also we have been lied to. Nothing in literature has allowed an Ariadne to grow up and become the bereaved Jocasta or the wailing Niobe.

*   *   *

In the restaurant Jessica shielded her eyes from the reflections duplicated in the right-angled mirrors. "I can't bear seeing me multiplied without end. On the other hand, it would be instructive for you to see yourself swollen-eyed and mauve green into infinity over Paul. You sit facing the mirror."

"You the family beauty at that."

"Not to *my* mother."

Jessica's glance skimmed away, flickering off and on like a candle in a drafty corner, her nail bitten fingers adjusting the collar of her white silk shirt.

"Looking for anything?" I asked.

"The telephone. I have to report in. Make mine an old-fashioned. Sweet." She grimaced apologetically.

Jessica lifted my icy hands and rubbed them between her warm ones. "Have you thought of psychoanalysis to help you bear this wretched year?"

"Psychoanalysis would have kept Aaron out of the army or alive in it? Or made me sterile? Or . . ."

"Look at it as a service. Viennese refugees are roaming the streets with couches on their backs. They need the dough. And it's chic."

364

"I'm not chic. Everybody tried God and where did that get women? Up in the balcony. Anyway, I can't stand the skimpy casting. Why name the complex for one runaway son? Why Oedipus? Why not the Jocasta complex for the bereaved mother? Or the Laius complex for fathers who want to kill their sons? Why not the Penelope complex for women with a disorder of fidelty? Or, my present company excepted, the Ariadne complex for girls who loved their mothers too little, their fathers too much, and are betrayed by their lovers?"

"Ariadne complex! Copyright that. Carry on Freudine. Tell me about her traumatic adolescence."

"What's there to tell? Daddy's girl, elevated, moralistic, a sexual nitwit, fearful as a Hawthorne heroine."

"Sounds like my mother."

Under the waiter's stare, Jessica dropped my hands, which had been cupped in hers. "You do look done in, Arnie. Another drink or shall we tuck you into bed?"

"I'd rather sip and talk. I don't want to prowl inside my life. Makes me suicidal."

"You can't do that. It is notoriously bad for the children. Look, this time you are definitely through with Paul."

"I don't know what 'through with Paul' means. We've torn it up and pieced it together so many times we could charade a patchwork quilt. But this last business is different. I'm used to his leaving, but it has always been in the open — 'Good-bye. I'm through.' This thing has changed me . . . I hope."

"Here's a tissue. Your mascara is running. Better keep talking about Oedipus."

"O.K. There lies Jocasta, the queen, her lover suckling at her breast, nine months to the day. She's maybe fourteen, fifteen years old. There stands the young king, knee deep in ransom, listening to the dreadful prophecy of a murder — his own. A voice out of a stone heart refutes the order of survival and damns the kingdom. What kind of heir is that? Get rid of him his counselors advise, and who am I to blame them? Laius, the father whose talent for loving has been appalled out of him by the threat of consequences so great they make a crypt of his kingdom, pierces the feet so the ghost cannot walk. But there is no propitiatory Kaddish that can lay to rest the little ghost. It lies nightly between husband and wife. There are no new heirs. The king goes forth lightly armed, relieved to meet the knife of the young wayfarer. As his eyes dim, he sees the son running toward the mother he is so self-righteously fleeing." (I tell you to see into the origin of perverse lust is to grow heavy with compassion.)

"So the son who has been deprived of his mother finds the mother who has been deprived of her son and they get married. How unlucky can you get?" Jessica said, wagging her head in mock mourning. "How awful sad."

"You can get what you think you wanted. Look ahead a few years."

"Already I'm hanging over the cliff."

"On the bed Oedipus yawns. He doesn't see the queen mother watching him in the mirror, so he has put by the regretful expression he has been wearing while telling her that kingly responsibilities will keep him from seeing her tomorrow . . . extorting mother-sympathy for the reassurance of it. She doesn't mind that too much. The woman as mother has never been free of the woman as lover.

"What she does mind are the signs. She has learned to be an oracle too. He looks fit. He's lost some weight. Is attentive to his dress. Clearly he is on the way to another affair, perhaps a lady-in-waiting — younger, prettier, frivolous — definitely not the maternal type. Soon a quarrel will fall into place to justify his withdrawal. Another cycle of sin and repent and be forgiven is getting under way.

"She wishes she could spend an evening with honest and luckless old Laius, whose quiet decency she has come to miss.

366

She would like to discuss Ismene's new tutor. She is tired of trying to remember to keep her shoulders back so her breasts won't sag."

*   *   *

Paul was stretched out on his studio bed, paint-spattered corduroys in a heap, his shirt tail in his coffee cup: "That was great, great, honey." After eight years his smile is still sweet and boyish. Why do I look away from it? "You know you are, and always will be, the lay of my life."

I can do without the comparisons. Even if he speaks true, I feel obese, downhearted, wary. What I am disgusted with is my own self.

*   *   *

"Ariadne, let's stop fiddling with this food," Jessica said. "Finish your drink and let's go. Would you like me to drive you to the dacha tomorrow, baby? I'd like to."

"No, I need to drag myself away from here."

"Good idea. Going to Mexico to see Arie?"

"No, Adam and I are due there next month. He hopes to have her affairs in shape so we can bring her back with us and she can have the baby here. I think I'll go to Switzerland."

"It's the wrong season."

"So what else is new?"

When we left, the street lay like a nightmare, empty under circles of lamplight and streaks of cold fluorescent bar signs. On top of an open garbage can a stray cat tore at a rib bone. Jessica led the way under some scaffolding. "The car is just a little beyond this demolition," she said.

We huddled together in the front seat. She drove, cautiously, avoiding a drunk who stumbled out between two cars. A man leaned despairingly against a lamppost and watched a blowsy woman reeling toward him from a bar. Two men wrestled silently out in the middle of the street. Better than being alone. More die of cold than of darkness.

"Tired, Jessica?"

She waved her fingers in assent. "Terribly tired."

"Will you stop for a nightcap?" I asked.

"I think not, I'll just take you home."

She waited, like an escort, until I unlocked my recalcitrant door. "Shall I see if there's a burglar under your bed?"

"If he has two arms I'll keep him," I said.

"Some joker. Call me when you get back."

*　　*　　*

Now then! Or was it now *and* then?

My true love (that is, I was true to him) said to me (a dozen times if he said it once), "It is the first stroke that determines the work. The moment the artist thrusts his brush against blank canvas the picture proceeds inevitably."

Such male autotheism! Such authority! It was beyond my maternal nurture. I could only adore it. Unfortunately, I kept equating the generalizations of concept with the specifics of precept. So more than love collapsed that last afternoon, when, still trembling with tenderness, my limp hand happened on a drawing pad that had slipped back of the pillows on his studio bed.

Me no Pandora, me Ariadne. It *was* open on a sketch from delinquent life. (Oh God it still presses me here!)

"I draw what I see. *Plein air,*" he had said.

I could see it too. (Had he meant me to? One can always arrange evidence.) There could be no mistaking the spent eyes rolled back on the bulge of black lids, the slaked mouth gaping, the appeased body dangling as from its own life line. They belonged to the housemaid, the young sloven with slack duster

368

and tautening belly who lurked below stairs, who throughout my stealthy ascent (why is heaven so high?) leered up my skirts through baluster slots.

(Oh you white-folks married bitch, you think you got something fancy under there.)

From under dome forehead and goat bangs her girl hate had for the last several months scarified my comings and goings.

I clung to the drawing. Screams shuddered through me. "Help! Murder!"

He ran out of the shower. Water dripped from him onto me. His hand was wet as he tried to mute my mouth. "Sh . . . Sh . . ."

"Murderer," I howled and crumbled. But not before I saw her face, elated and race-terrified, at the door.

"Disappear." He snapped at her. "She's trouble."

To me he said, *"You* don't sleep alone. So don't carry on. I'm only evening the score."

So he, she and I left.

She ran south, toting her half-white treasure under an expanding navel. I ran and had the abortion.

(Who would believe an old woman had so many tears left in her!)

Our lover had no trouble with beginnings. I see him as through a thin curtain, a lamp passing from room to room. I hear him establishing his new territory. "Modern art does not have a consoling function . . . As Artaud puts it (in French), 'I see it as an engine of destruction and disconnection . . . The theater of cruelty has been created in order to restore a passionate and convulsive conception to life.' "

Why not? If a male bird loses a mate he may immediately resume singing to advertise for a new one.

As for me, though I was sure I was carrying myself away with me to be deposited someday somewhere someplace (after all, I was only forty-five), by these tears I do confess the collection of feelings with which one falls in love is not retrievable, and not endless.

*　　*　　*

No one stared at me as if I were ineligible to belong to the human race. In fact, at the traffic stop outside the village of Voltaire-Fresnay a beautiful young man in a red sports car kept looking at me and licking his red lips. In fact, waiting for a table in the coach house inn (no doubt Mme. de Staël slept here and Voltaire did not) the headwaiter could scarcely contain his breathy Italian declension. He gripped his menus and lilted seductively, "Madame-a willa waita, or is alone-a?" (There's always a boy who loves his mother.)

"Come-a with me-a," he said, stripping me to the nude in one determined glance.

My mind is a swamp, from which I dredge, "Come!"

(Beside me on a bus, on my girly lap, a card is placed. Printed in a neat clear hand:

COME WITH ME
COME = ORGASM

Couldn't fool me, though. I had been warned by my parents never to come with strangers. A roll of piano music clutched for safety in my hand, eyes straight forward, I paid no attention to the rustling going on under the folded newspaper.)

In the mirror I watched the headwaiter carry his bulk lightly but aggressively away. I saw him return to my table too promptly, country muscles bulging against city jacket, lean over

370

me, his self-assured masculine head angled at attention, in mirrors, multiplied, and all the heads peered down my dress front.

"Room number?" His eyes were clear with intent. "You wish to order?"

"I'm not quite ready," I said.

"I like you take your time." His hand brushed my arm as he pointed to an item on the menu. "Very nice."

In spite of a green odor of cucumber wafting from him he managed to make me conscious of my arms, the clingingness of my dress against my breasts and, by the time he bent over me and filled my wineglass for the third time, an invasive current lapping covertly upward.

The dining room gave on to an immense silenced fountain; crammed from its basin up ascending tiers with scarlet geraniums, culminating in a copy of David's bust of Voltaire which peered out of the greenery, the foxy sneer caught in unrelenting marble, as if at that moment the buttock scene in *Candide* had come to mind. "You think all meals are edible? Then eat out of the seat of learning. Add it to your fool's inventory of permissibles. It is merely one more item to obliterate human distinctions."

The wicked head livened and winked a conspiratorial eye at me. The cobbles burned like scorched bread loaves.

A girl no more than seven years old wandered around the dining room. She stopped at my table.

"I like your dress," she said, imitating grown-up posture and expression like a spindly monkey. She had no child-face of her own, only her mouth puckered in an oral grimace sucking, sullen, insatiable, a perfectly unhappy nymphomaniac mouth. "My daddy knows the Duke of Windsor and Wally Simpson. . . . my daddy plays the guitar." She made a bubble-gum bubble and popped it. "He went to Majorca . . ."

My ever-ready maternity broke out in a prickle of placation.

"He'll be back soon dear." And as for me, I said to myself, I'm going to Rapallo to have tea with Ezra Pound.

I heard her at the next table. "I like your dress . . ."

A happy life does not elicit explanations. I can be an oracle, too. She is seven years old and condemned to repeat looking for her daddy.

The headwaiter's breath brushed my ear before he spoke. Black hairs flourished out from his cuffs and spiked the knuckles of his fingers. "Coffee and brandy in the guests' parlor, madam-a, I serve-a you there-a. There is excellent singers."

"Is it possible to have coffee later?" I asked. "I'd like a breath of air."

"Later. What you wish-a is possible." He brushed the tip of his tongue over his upper lip. He accompanied me to the door, opened it and bowed me out. I was startled by the sharpness of my sense of escape, and not certain that the constraint in my breathing was due only to the nauseating weight of oily odors from overblown chrysanthemums and geraniums. I avoided the open terrace and slipped into a side garden. I saw him come back, stand in the doorway and peer toward the lighted area.

(Truthfully, Paul, specter I summon, his figure does not compare with yours in its most casual attitude, resting your weight on one foot, hands in pockets, paint-spattered trousers, rumpled, worn sweater knit by some former girlfriend (always former), frayed shirt open at the throat too wide at the base for your head; or, waking to love again, an alabaster satyr alive in moonlight, your translucent twitching ears showing blood first. You are like one of those shaggy Dartmoor ponies with strong necks and aggressive muzzle faces, their temperaments pledged to undomestication, violence under their soft-lipped nuzzling. Warnings are posted where they herd: DANGEROUS TO FEED THESE ANIMALS. Like you, they do not remember how they ate bread from the hand. Like me, few feeders believe that when these beauties turn to range they trample the feeder under their hooves.)

When I returned, the lights were dimmed in the guests' parlor where a soprano and a tenor were in a crisis of pouring out their hearts. In the passageway outside the room, I leaned against the wall, weighted down with a sense of isolation. I barely moved when a hand eased itself onto my thigh. It lay there, its pressure increasing gently. It had a life of its own. It moved — up a little, down a little, forward over the curve, back and down. Breath on my ear. My cheek. Lost in the crowd. Invisible. Warmth, warm lips on my neck, on my shoulder, brushing my arm. For a drowsy second a tongue like a friendly dog's lapping. I was in some kind of Huxley feely film dreamily flickering toward its pornographic intention through leaves and water.

"*Dio . . . amore . . . Per favore . . .* Please . . . Come . . . Come with me . . . Come with me . . . *Bella . . . mia Americana . . .*"

Why not? He is asking me to stay. Granted he is not Paul but he is beside me, beside himself, asking me to tear off my clothes and fall into bed with him. This man whose blood swells against his jugular, whose breath is pressing his chest against his unsuitable suit, whose muscled arm I can feel purposeful across my back, whose fingers are pressing the flesh on my waist, his desire is toward me. He wants to take me, to hold me. He wants me to hold him in my arms, between my legs, within my thighs. He wants to pour himself into me. His wanting is entirely clear. He wants what he has wanted all evening. He wants the nearness of flesh . . . the nearness of flesh. I am alone.

Alone, you bastards, lover, husband, friend and sons too, you've left me alone . . . on this island sown with salt . . . my

373

flesh is all mouths and I want those mouths eased, kissed, bruised, fed. I want someone anonymous to take my hand and lead me. I want to enter an anonymous bedroom. I want to lie down in an anonymous bed in an anonymous room, a nowhere place, even a whore's hovel on the Ostia Road where truck drivers grind to a spontaneous halt. I don't want to know where he lives, so I won't find myself freezing in the snow in front of his place to see if the lights go on or off in the bedroom. I won't care where this peasant goes when he leaves me. When I leave here, he won't know where to send me one perfect spray of green lilies, one recondite quotation, one allusive card post-marked from a village where we picnicked by a brook. I won't think I see him ahead of me on the street. My eyes won't hunger after every arrogant back to see if it's he, cruising for me in front of the library, the concert hall, the galleries we've visited. He won't take my hand in his eloquent hand and lead me any-where, for I will be in another country and I'm already dead. I'll never plead. I'll never cry. I'll never die thinking I'm rock-ing him in my arms.

No, I will follow this bullock because he is anonymous and everyone around him is anonymous. If I open my eyes he will look anonymous as a pornographic, his spellbound face contorted, an ecstatic current from braced hooves to quivering ears.

I do not wish to converse. False words, words, words. In the beginning there were no words, only sounds, divided into day sounds and night sounds. With his lieder and her lullabys di-vided they the silences. Soothing *Stille Nacht* and then volleys of tarantara, tarantara in every square inch of me. And bon voyage and farewell forever and you have left me with sad ballads mocking the dawn, fugues of the peat-bog soldiers on afternoons of the faun when there should be improvisations and waltzes, dancing together, not, not the funeral march. Who needs words? To your deafened ears I still call with taped radiator whistles in the sleepless morning, vacuum cleaners in the afternoon, in the clinking cocktail hours, entering the cage of silence. Not for him these aberrations of farewells.

I want nothing said. I do not wish to confess my body to him. I want to lie worn out, weakened with plain lust. For God's sake hold your tongue and let me love. If you must utter, growl in Greek, in Hungarian, in Urgo-Finnish, in pidgin English. "I no spik English good." That's fine. I like you no speak English. You no understand me? Good. I no understand you. I no understand me. Does that even the score?

His thigh was firm against mine.

Lights. Murmur of applause. He lingered. "Later?"

"Later."

He bore the word jubilantly before him.

What's there in this that bears the name of love? Nothing.

After he left my room I gave the overseas operator Paul's number. I wanted to hurt him, demean my love so it would shrivel and die. I wanted to tell him I had evened the score. Hah! I wanted to vent on him the gall that was on my tongue. "You have driven me to it," I was going to say, "you idiot, you fool, you blind man, after the years of expenditure of self on you I have fulfilled your jealous accusations. I am a woman who has given herself to a stranger." And what was there of me to give?

There was only ringing on the empty air. And why weep over that? Didn't I want him to be happy, with someone else; a cozy wife who sat across the table from him morning and evening, day after day, through the rest of his life? Didn't I want him to sleep through the night, not get up and drive me home? Stay in bed, a warm body curled around him? No. I swear I didn't. I wanted him to be alone in a cold coffin of a bed. I wanted him

375

to find making love, so-called, as irrelevant and unsatisfying as I would find it from here on.

*   *   *

Now then? By what course, by what ambages, had Miss Goody Two-Shoes landed here? When she set out so gaily, was the course already set? How far back had the opening gambits been played? The first paint stroke been put on the canvas? Had I been deaf to the oracles? Unattended by my celluloid ear, had quasars been beeping to me from my outer Aquarian space? Suppose illumination had burned and howled from every bush, would I have looked? Would I have listened? Not likely.

One continues to feel innocent. Vamp till ready. The music is about to begin. The best is yet to be. So harsh on others, one continues to forgive oneself. No gouging out of eyes can shut out the sight, but why must the oracles be so terse, so fraught laconic? Why must we grope through the entire bloody maze in darkness only to be blinded at the exit? Why string us along to illuminate what's behind us? Are we put on to be each other's dumb show? To this day I go tapping around in the dark trying to retrace the path by which my father's daughter came to be in a bed I had rumpled with a stranger, in a hotel room into which a waiter had brought a breakfast I hadn't ordered, turning his face away to accord both himself and me the fiction of invisibility, trying to telephone a lover who had whipped me down all the nuanced avenues of infidelity.

I dressed and slunk away as quickly as possible, waving good-bye to Voltaire's head that peered out of the geraniums, as knowing and conspiratorial as it had the evening before. I crossed the border into Switzerland, and headed for Paul's hometown of Rolle.

*

In addition to being Paul's birthplace, Rolle's claim to fame is Mme. de Staël's ancestral residence, a gloomy ochre chateau to which that outspoken meddler would escape, stopping only to complain at Voltaire-Fresnay, whenever Napoleon advised her the journey might add years to her life.

Paul must have developed his spontaneities from stray mountain goat, or a Rousseauian strain that had slipped through one of his Calvinist ancestors. I could see no sign of their native noble savage in the citizenry. They exchanged salutations as if they were each handing the other a summons. A Teutonic policeman, who definitely looked predestined for his task, commanded the drab cyclists and somber taxis. Since I am not weather's darling, it was no surprise that it was raining icily. A punitive wind followed from Rolle to Geneva.

As if I had been sent on a mission that would be revealed to me when I arrived, I made my way to Calvin's cathedral. It was dark and inanimate. I climbed down wet slippery stairs into a café where metal tables and chairs were stacked and floors were being mopped. I ordered hot chocolate.

Fog and rain blanked out the lake. Flagpoles disappeared five feet above the ground. Mist made an absurdity of the famous fountains. A heavy-fleshed, broad-beamed waitress banged down the pot, slid the bill under the cup and scurried back into the warmth of the kitchen, leaving me, the out-of-season tourist, to freeze in the front room.

Sipping the hot chocolate (mine was superior) I remembered Paul saying, "I like those farm women, Mrs. Arkady, heavy-fleshed Breughel types like the women who served at our church suppers."

"And were you religious, Mr. Donant?"

"Intensely; until I wasn't . . ."

If the gods can send me a message smoking out at a kitchen stove, why not seething up on a multilingual bill under my cup?

377

Reality, as Jeremy pointed out, is not as exalted as I would like it to be. I reread the hieroglyphics of Paul's evaluating stare, the stare of a man who has tried many women and found them all wanting. Though I am no Monsieur Champollion and here was no Rosetta Stone to which I had suddenly found the key, glosses opened around me.

*　　*　　*

"Mary had been working in Geneva, living with her married sister. She came home to Rolle one Christmas and sang in the choir. She was a statuesque, placid blonde, the only attractive woman I hadn't seen every Sunday through my adolescence. The choir boy fell in love with the soprano.

"I was nineteen and a virgin, no great achievement in our Puritanical community. She was ten years older, but I assumed she had also remained chaste. I dreamed of asking her to give herself to me before marriage, but my upbringing was against it. I did a lot of praying for restraint. Had she given herself, I probably would have been too scandalized to marry her."

"My father and Adam would have felt the same way," I said.

"And you not?" (That evaluating stare.)

"I was good because I did as I was told . . . So, Mr. Donant, you married the soprano angel and you lived happily ever after."

"Rushing to conclusions, Mrs. Arkady. No. I loved her, was proud of my husbandly estate. But I wanted to know everything about her, my first woman, my wife. I began picking at her past, not suspiciously at first but out of interest. I happen to have an accurate memory for details and I detected disparities between dates, home visits and holiday trips."

"Most people are blurry about dates," I ventured.

"Not I," he snapped.

"One day a group of us went to Lausanne to the premiere of Honegger's oratorio, *King David.* That was in 1921. The per-

378

formance was given at the folk theater in Mézières. Mary suggested a restaurant, then reddened as she added, "I went there with a friend." Casually I confronted her. I assured her that all I cared about was the honesty of our future life together. Had I had any idea of the magnitude of possessiveness in a man I might not have persisted. She confessed to a love affair with her employer, a married diplomat who had gone back to his own country five years earlier. My rage caught me by surprise. I wanted to kill her. It was a matter of justice, as I explained it to myself. I had suffered needlessly. I decided that if I could even the score, I would be rid of the maddened feelings I did not recognize as animal jealousy. We would return to Eden.

"One forenoon I bicycled to Geneva and went directly to a café, the one below the cathedral, by the lake, trusting my instinct to lead me to a woman who would accede to my request. To my amazement, I found her almost as if waiting for me."

"Restraint falls mainly on the plain," I mumbled.

"She was a matron who had been shopping. Her packages were heaped on an empty chair next to her and the waitress who brought coffee and her bill was properly deferential.

"She was a type not uncommon in Geneva. Southern French, very like a Courbet, well-modeled flesh, with a good sheen and some pulverizations of pink. Her head was tilted back to soak up the weak sun cracking through the fog, and light outlined her slender long nose in a curious way, translucent as a wet fish spine.

"She was severely but expensively dressed as was evident to even an inexperienced bumpkin like me. I can see, Mrs. Arkady, from the way you dress that you understand the artistry of reticence. The charcoal of the suit you are wearing with the lead green of your hat; painters have died from eating that green."

His face above the black cowl sweater and clerical strip of white shirt was unflirtatious.

379

"She wore an umber brown herringbone suit, a fur neckpiece of three pelts, marten or mink, and a bishop's miter of a hat in a madder crimson. Draped over the chair was a brown cape lined with fur. I see her clearly enough to draw.

"I can't tell you how, from my background, I dared. It should have occurred to me that she might make a scene, that my reputation would be ruined, my family disgraced, my wife heartbroken, but I guess I was too enraged to be cautious. I sat down across from her. She merely raised her eyes, then lowered them to her coffee cup.

"I found myself drawn out of my rage into her, personally: the line of inky hair slicked like a Japanese woodcut into the upswing of her complex coiffure, the strong white throat thickening to the shoulders and already softening, the full bosom on which the furpiece rocked to her breathing. I said nothing. She said nothing.

"She lit a cigarette, a bit shocking back in the twenties, in unflapperish Geneva. She inhaled a strong puff. I felt as if she inhaled me with the smoke. Smoke whirled in her mouth, rode the square white teeth, and was released, fluttering veils over her ample lips, steaming out of her nostrils down the furrow over her upper lip almost as deep as the cleft of her chin. She sneezed suddenly and shuddered in her flesh, like an animal.

"She took her time — understood Valéry's rule of the hiatus — finished her coffee, her cigarette, put on her cape like a woman wrapping herself in a bath towel, gathered up her packages and handed them to me as if I were a delivery boy. She indicated with her head that I was to follow her. She walked, moving her weight from haunch to haunch on slender legs, like a splendid cow, and I followed — like a shepherd, I guess.

"We went to an apartment building overlooking the lake. I stepped over children's toys in a marble entry hall. She dropped her cape, led me through the ornate apartment, through a kitchen to a servant's room, and, still in silence, locked the door behind us."

"My children would have welcomed us at the door and invited us to play Monopoly." I said. "Then you went home, and lived equally ever after." I sounded gloomy and bitter, or was it envious?

"I wish it were true, Mrs. Arkady. No. It is not popular to think so, but I was punished, damned, I'd say."

He's certainly not going to confess he caught a disease, I thought. At the moment I disliked him intensely. "What was unequal then?"

"There was a worm in the carnal apple. When she let me out of the service entrance, handing me an empty package, my perceptions of women and sex were altered. She was not just a compliant wife. She was something else — a Delilah, a Lilith, a woman of practiced guile. She was possessed, yet self-possessed. She whispered to me, 'Find me again next week, wild boy.' I shook my head negatively. Wild? Not I. With dreamlike indifference that said, 'There are more where you came from,' she gave me a maternal pat, set me in the direction of the back stairs, yawned and closed the door."

"So you went on munching the carnal apple, worm and all. Your balance sheet balanced perfectly, and that was the beginning of your first affair."

"I approve of your censorious tone, but you *do* jump to conclusions, Mrs. Arkady. No. Orthodox systems like ours" (his hand on the table moved toward mine, he leaned forward earnestly, withdrew) "don't collapse quite so readily. I was a strictly brought up young man. She was, I understood, a siren of the most dangerous sort, the kind who turned men into beasts, a whited sepulcher, if you will, a false madonna, desecrating motherhood, veiled and fastidious on the surface but wholly given over to lust. That didn't keep me from being deviled by desire, worse than that, feeling murderous at the thought of other men with her. I fled into church, gripped the back of the pew and prayed. *Deliver me from temptation* was a text I came to know well. I sensed then and there the mindless torrents that can course quite by chance between certain men and women. I understood I could be wrecked, swallowed and spewed out by a woman. I felt threatened. I was afraid, I admit. I was horrified, not only at the view of myself she had given me, but at the ease with which a respectable married woman can deceive and betray all through a marriage, give her husband children that weren't his. I never got over that. A wife could not be trusted out of her husband's sight, or in it. I was not yet twenty but in one lesson I learned that, like most men, like Othello, I could be murderously jealous and would exact nothing less than total possession. I also realized there are people who are catalysts of a Dionysian kind. They consume others. They remain whole."

"Lords and owners of their faces," I said.

"Exactly."

"I didn't know her name or the house to which I had gone. With my visual memory I could doubtless have retraced our steps and found her but I never let myself go back. If there must be a moral to the tale, I was made immune in one shot to the postwar fantasy that sex can be a harmless plaything. Not for me, it can't."

"Some people seem to manage it," I said, thinking of my reading, as usual. He eyed me suspiciously. He remembered it.

"You know better, perhaps. I tell it so as not to appear better than I am." (Can't say I wasn't warned).

"Now Mrs. Arkady . . . touching on the Courbet. You see here, where his faith in his own observation breaks down? The picture fails there."

"Now that you point it out. I think I see it."

"Where the wrist blends into the forearm he painted what he *thought* he saw, not what he saw."

(And that, my dear Arnie, might well be the story of *your* life, your epigraph.)

"Next time, let's look at the Manet, shall we?"

Ah next time and next time. Hail! Six months and farewell. A month and farewell. And yet another quarrel. And another reconciliation. Days. Weeks. The mesh of years. The torn and mended, torn and mended mesh of years.

I paid my bill. (And how I paid!) I was ready to acknowledge my own damnation. Ahead of me there were the days; no day to come when I would not think of him. A day did come when I stopped wanting to stab him, stopped seeing him above me, his hair falling forward, perspiration dewing his eyebrows and lashes; when the hollow chambers of my being stopped echoing to the climax of his possession. No, I had not possessed him. Nor had I possessed myself.

Old man — (or did you, like Dionysius himself, remain young while I aged) wherever you are — last night, betrayed in sleep, I was walking by a brook released from sheet ice. It bent, broke, crashed and disappeared, roaring beyond our rented real estate. Unwillingly faithful, I stood in the sharp-shadowed moonlight and my tears fell and froze as they dropped on snow.

You called me, Paul, you said again, "Come to me, my best," but I could not move. What could we do in hell that we have not yet done to one another? My ghost, don't come back again.

Paul, you are the lidless one that slithers into the well, and shatters the glass surface, making conspicuous the pirate cobwebs when I look down hoping to see smooth sky reflected in country water. You are the gargoyle mocking me from the sill of the museum window when I think to see pigeons, iridescent, courting in the springtime sun. You are the maze in which my spirit scurries scampering for exits, trembling at dead ends, pawing at deaf doors as I smell the green grass of contentment beyond. You are the nakedness of which I became ashamed.

In Flagrante Delicto

The harvest is past, the summer is ended, and we are not saved.

— JEREMIAH 8:20

I WAS AT MY typewriter, wishing I could evoke a chapter opening heady as the brandy fumes coming up from the pantry where I had just moistened the Christmas fruitcakes, when I saw Benjamin's red Fiat Spyder gunning up the valley road as if it were a motorcycle. What's wrong with Benjie? Also, what can I improvise for his lunch?

Any legerdemain I might have surprised in myself went, flotsam or jetsam, down caverns measureless to man, etc. . . .

"When did you stop loving your wife, Benjamin," I asked, "or rather, why?"

"You keep trying to link occurrences, Mother."

" 'Why' was a respectful question in my time."

"You do carry on like an old-fashioned Maxwell Sorting-Demon, Mother!

(When Benjamin addresses me with that harsh condescension of a youngest son, the boy who had to make his way from family sweetheart to man of the world, I know he's quivering inside.)

"So your old-fashioned mother is a Maxwell Sorting-Demon — whatever it sorts. What's wrong with it?"

"What's wrong with it is that it's been proven nonsense . . ."

"We old-timers put a lot of energy into cause-and-effect. In physics, in art, not to mention marriage, we saw things bonded together with a hard edge."

"Sorry about that, Mother, you'll have to make do with our atoms and marriages held together by nothing more than the power of their invisible Coulomb forces."

Curious how, under pressure, he falls back on those over-developed intelligent and questioning defenses that have proven protective to Jews. He's American enough. Exuberantly physical. Daniel tells me his uncle plays a rough game of handball. (Yes Father, you have a grandson who plays ball as well as one who hunted with a bare knife.) Benjamin walked early. He would take a few steps, crow in triumph, then turn red, get down on all fours and crawl back to smack me, enraged either at having been set on his own feet, or at the difficulty of mastering uprightness. Yet he came naturally to the patient suspension that underlies mental accomplishment.

I remembered him, three years old, walking back and forth across the room puzzling over the way his shadow moved with him. Over and over, little Indian stalking his shadow, slowly, until he was satisfied that indeed it followed him on one side only.

"It's not that sad," Benjamin broke into my thoughts. "Put a good face on it, Mother. You would like me to give you details you can connect into a reasonable picture. Suppose I said, 'She was careless about the crystal.' Would that help? But to add

386

information would merely increase distortion. I would only destroy any information I *can* communicate by trying to devise linkages."

"What about trying for reconciliation with a structure of interacting details, my son?"

"Still reading our brochures, I see."

"Come on Benjie, we could go on with this oblique, brainy talk. I've picked up enough jargon to discuss probability theories and randomness on into the night. Obviously you came to talk to me. If I read your bits so far, it was your decision that you and Joyce separate. She is furious. She has gone off to her parents in Florida. Her outraged father is a lawyer which means the divorce will be an expensive, unsatisfactory mess. And you think it would be a good idea to spend the next six months in the London office while they cool off."

"You seem to have it all down pat. I'll leave after Arie's show opens."

"Would you care to tell me, so long as you're here, what, if anything, happened?"

"I'll get a drink. Sherry flip for you? Exactly when? Last Sunday. Guests were chattering in the living room; I was getting drinks in our bar. I'd taken a migraine pill, which I rarely do. My headache was gone but the inside of my head felt as if I'd smoked pot. Don't looked shocked, I smoke pot. Everything sounded crystal clear. From out of the conversation pit (how did I ever end up with a conversation pit?) a woman's voice kept breaking into other conversations with static. 'Fabulous . . . gourmet . . . finalize . . . sort of . . . love it . . . kinna . . . I mean . . . the vibes just turn me off . . . well children will do it every time . . .'

"It was nothing but noise. Pink noise. Imprecise, irrelevant, noninformation filling the air waves. It kept rising from the pit. 'Fantastic . . . super . . . campy . . . don't you love it . . . slenderize . . . boutique . . . microbiotic . . . yoga . . . groovy . . .'

"It moved in closer. It was right behind me . . . mechanical, shrill, one of those voices we keep feeding into the eight-array computer and rejecting because it fails at overtones. Saccharine sounds, like a talking doll, not a person."

"I know what you mean, giving the impression of absence of meaning." (I did not say it reminded me of Adam paying me public compliments.)

"Precisely. That noise came up behind me. 'Give you a hand, lover boy? Set them up, dearie, folks are perishing for drinks . . . Naughty boy, forgot to refill the ice trays.' It was Joyce! She rubbed her head kittenishly against my shoulder. 'One double Scotch for our neighborhood Burt Lancaster.' "

Benjamin was sitting upright on a straight chair, staring with narrowed Tartar eyes through his drink, which he held at arm's length as if he were trying to derive its formula. "A cube of ice slipped from my fingers to the floor. 'Butterfingers!' Joyce said, giving me a girly fingertip slap, then giggled to erase even that much anger. How can I tell if I might have preferred it if she had hit me, head on, with 'Damn you! Get into the scene, or out of it, you cop-out. They are your guests too.' Anything, anything *pure* if you know what I mean, anything that meant she sensed truly it was Joyce annoyed with Benjamin. We both bent down to pick up the cube. That is exactly where *it* happened. A pair of upside-down faces, her lovely hair fallen upside-down like, well, like a bundle of the best streaked mink tails, her wow cleavage wower than Li'l Abner's Daisy Mae."

"How can you tell if in one cleared headache you were sensing *yourself* so truly?" I asked.

He disregarded my interruption.

"I felt ice from my fingertips flow through me. I felt, 'This reel of tape is my wife and I despise her.' "

"You are sure it was an unambiguous print-out, my son?"

"Thank you for trying. I'm sure."

My grown son, handsome, a competent businessman, with all

our helpless taints to live out, staring beyond me at his jigsaw future. It was only for me to listen. It might seem to me his decision was too much in the modern trashing style — junk esthetics to blue-jean erotica — still, I could feel the raw truth. I, too, had been wounded by the laugh at what is not laughable. I, too, had bitten back, "Why ask questions that are not to be answered?" I, too, was mummified by charm masking habitual evasion. I knew well the futility of trying to mend by quarreling, by trying to expose guises that were meant not as masks for deceit (these would give hope) but were necessary for survival, like a rabbit's protective coloration. I could not say to him, "Benjamin, I know about rabbits." Rabbits have been able to devastate the continent of Australia.

What, if anything, happened?

It was sunset when I went back upstairs, and watched Benjamin's departure through a landscape made strange by patches of snow turning lilac. The red car appeared and reappeared. At the height between oak leaves, stiffened and charred bronze in the very motion of ranked defiance; lower, between birches caught in the cold intensity of dying, their stripped branches thrust into rigor mortis. Then he was lost from view between hemlocks netted in the thinnest shroud of snow.

Whether it was the splintering effect of tears, or a sudden gust, the numbed pond shivered into countless pavé mirrors just as a flock of geese plummeted out of weightless flight, turned earth-heavy and waddled to feed among ripened weeds. They hissed. They gobbled. Goose by gander, they bedded down among the blackening reeds.

I watched the sun burn out in blue air; the horizon swerve to meet its blood-red fall; the spectrum chill — lose green, turn indigo, the violet hues blacken in the first clear frost of stars. The moon rode in full. The geese, hallooing, rose and became again hollow-boned feathery flight, summoning, summoning — that summoning which the old pretend they do not hear, yet are inwardly rising to follow.

*   *   *

A dénouement!

Adam was in his study waiting for me when I arrived home from Switzerland. I wondered if he had arranged the scene: velvet-collared dressing gown Arie and Benjamin had given him for his fifty-fifth birthday, his well-groomed hair set off by a cravat of moody blues, soft black kid slippers that flattered his narrow feet, beside him a decanter of Scotch; in his aristocratic hand, not his usual sipping glass, but a tall Waterford tumbler. He was stiffly and elegantly soused.

"Good evening. What says the married woman?" But formal schooling being impressive as it is, he rose in greeting before leaning back, lifting his chin and eyeing me meaningfully.

It was too preposterous. After so many hail and farewell years, there lay a bundle of telltale missives.

I felt like a spectator, meditative, aware of the forms, at a distance from the situation. As soon as I saw the envelope with Paul's imperious India ink cursive, I realized I myself must have, if not arranged, somehow allowed discovery. For what other purpose could I have left it to be found by someone who didn't particularly want to find it?

Yet, if his emotions were inauthentic, why was he so dreadfully pale?

"If you denied it, I would not believe you." He waved, elegant fingers curved outward toward the evidence — a Mannerist saint exposing stigmata.

"I have not denied it, Adam, you never asked me."

That was unfair. An agreement between a gentleman and a lady is to be respected even if it is tacit.

I tried to think of an appropriate response. To match his I

390

should have sunk to my knees, Correggio's repentant Magdalen to Christ's *Noli me tangere;* Paul, in the background, descending hellward, a stricken angel. (I was still borrowing Paul's imagery.)

Ice clinked in his glass. His voice trembled. "You admit the charge?"

"As you've indicated, the evidence is conclusive."

It is always possible to rearrange evidence, as it is always possible to avoid seeing it. Over the years Paul and I had exchanged so many farewell, reconciliation and accusation letters that, a tisket a tasket, we must have dropped baskets of clues. His tasteless clues. My shrill ones. How had Adam managed not to pick any up?

Cold sweat beaded his cheeks. He kept cocking his head nervously as if he were loosening a tight collar.

"Adam," I asked, "tell the truth. Haven't you been unfaithful?"

"It is hardly a question you have a right to ask me. Objectively, if I say yes, I am a cad and a braggart and if I say no, I am . . . I am no less a cuckold."

The reproof valiant! Even at this moment when marital convention decrees there should be running between us, if not a river of blood, a dirty ditch of it, we were smacking at each other as through an old-fashioned feather bed. Yet, there was the pallor on his face and I could feel a chill moisture on mine.

Adam waited for me to say something. I couldn't think of anything to say.

"So you admit it?" he repeated.

"The evidence seems conclusive," I repeated.

Adam set down his glass. Just a shade unsteadily he walked to the door. For a moment it seemed as if he were after all going to take action; open the door and walk out into the night in his slippers, a distinguished-looking graying gentleman leaving his gray life behind and damning his graying discredited wife. Sur-

391

prisingly, he locked the door. What did he mean by that? He slipped the key into his pocket. We were locked in together. What was new about that?

He stood in front of me, his hand in his pocket, peering at me, an inebriated belligerence on his usually controlled features.

Did he think I was going to grapple with him for the key? Run away? If so, where? He swayed toward me.

Come on Adam, do something. Say something. Let's see what happens when you finally feel altogether righteously furious. Have you a gun in your pocket? A knife? If I have a choice, I prefer a gun. Stand back so you don't splatter.

What did I expect? A cleansing holocaust? A tornado that would spiral us up and away to be dropped in a bare place clean of past? Another beginning? An ending? Mrs. Arkady, if you want to die, don't expect him to kill you. Follow the example of Madame Bovary. Go to your husband's office and do it. Hang yourself with his computer tape. Or if you think you want to be free, whatever that means, get up and walk out yourself.

"I am not drunk," he said. "Ariadne, answer me truthfully if you can, have I not been a devoted husband and father?"

"You have," I answered not knowing what else to say that was any truer. My mind kept rolling questions into the empty space between us like snowballs packed on ice centers. And I a devoted wife? Do you feel how empty, though the feast seems great? Hear hollow ring on hollow? Have we shared each other's lacks? Paul, come back and explain negative space to me. Can you see negative space if it is not surrounded by defined areas of color? How can echoes resound through every hollowed-out chamber of my being if you are silent?

Why is it everything about Adam and me together seems so much more untruthful than the most antagonistic, tearing-apart moments with Paul. With Paul it is bloody. It is tormented. It has been ruinous to both of us. It's clandestine. We are ashamed of it. It breaks the heart of pride. Gratified sensuality has not brought peaceful sleep. We have carried it like a wasting illness; I have known diffuse, bone-aching fevers, freezes, pains; nights of boil, bubble, scum. But in its energy, self-love, self-searching, its fierceness, its insistence, even in its unhappy-ever-after, it penetrated the impalpable chaos. Even in its firm disillusionment, it balanced existence.

"My wife *in flagrante delicto!*" Adam shook his head, wonderingly. (Is that what it was? Even in this misery, my husband, can't we speak a common language?)

"How could you, the mother of four children?"

"Of the four children you invoke, Adam, there are only two who can answer."

"That was uncalled-for," he said, turning blue at the lips.

"I suppose it was. Delete it."

He turned and walked back to his chair, suddenly cold sober. "We have had twenty-seven years as man and wife, Ariadne. Four children. The making of homes and the difficulties of making a living, in good times and bad. We've had losses; terrible losses I might say."

The glass trembled in his hand. "Terrible losses . . ." His face thinned markedly, drawn with pain. He looked younger, as if he had been stricken with a wasting illness and years were melting away with the flesh. "Absalom . . . Aaron . . . Poor Arie losing her first child."

I saw the father of my children as he had been that Passover day, with Aaron and Benjamin beside him, bursting into song. Adam at Arie's wedding giving away our daughter, her bridal veil filming across his dark suit. Then, taking her back in divorce; going to Mexico with Jethro for it (she had asked her father to come), telling me afterward, tears in his eyes, how the "two children" clung to each other and wept when they left the courtroom with the final decree. Adam who with Jeremy had managed the sticky business of burying their week-old baby. It was Adam, not Paul, who had opened the notice of Aaron's death, grimaced and stood like a stone with hand raised while the paper fluttered from his fingers. Why had it not been enough? It was Adam who had gone with me to police stations, emergency rooms and morgues after Absalom's disappearance; Adam who had tried to protect me from the truth about Absalom.

I had been wakened by a rattle in the garbage pail. A raccoon, a rakish creature, looked up into the beam of my flashlight, nose up, a morsel in his dainty paws. In the dawnlight I watched him rummaging, then went back to the bedroom and told Adam. "Come see, it's adorable," I said. The rattling had become violent. The paving stones had become the color of grape mash, blue-black red. The pail was tipped and drumming. The drumming stopped, the blood still ran. The little marauder lay on its side, its pretty head out of the pail, its muzzle stiffly skyward.

Then I saw Absalom in the kitchen doorway.

"Dogs must have ripped it." Adam pushed me back from the window. "Go back to bed, I'll . . ."

Adam was addressing a question to me. "What do you think of me, Ariadne?"

"That's a good question. I don't know."

"I am outraged!" he said, but he looked, with his mouth open, like an inexperienced boxer who has been slugged. It was confusing the depth of pain in his looks and the skiddy surface of his words.

"Outraged father or outraged husband?"

"You omitted outraged friend . . . you . . ." His voice quavered.

"You what?" I invited, breaking the skin.

"I was under the impression he was my friend." Everything back under control.

"To keep the record straight . . . Paul was my friend when he came from class with me. He became a family friend. Who else does a married woman get to see but family friends?"

"You made yourself free, obviously. Paul is a pious fraud." He poured himself more Scotch. "A drink for you?"

"No thank you. You are drinking too much. It isn't good for your ulcer. You'll be ill." I said it out of wifely habit.

"Liquor does not go to my head," he said with pride, "but your concern does you credit."

"Oh, Adam. I've always been concerned." As Jessica had said, *his* supper had always been on time — not Paul's. What had he lost that he'd wanted?

"It doesn't matter now that it is past, but to satisfy my mathematical mind, just how long did this deception go on?" Adam pursed his lips.

Six months and farewell. Three months and farewell. A meeting and farewell. How to count? And not to count? "It no longer matters," I said, praying for it to be true, quickly.

He put the glass down on the table, without a coaster, and cast me a look of defiance. Ah well, any revenge is sweet. We're a long way from a crime of passion, Adam, so be my guest. One of the things I know is how to minimize alcohol rings. Why was he breathing with difficulty.

Just when I was almost overwhelmed with pity for the father of my children and about to ask him if he had heard anything new from Arie while I was gone, he said, "I see no reason why I should provide you with alimony."

At any rate, that implied a decision. He wanted a divorce. Quite right. Wipe the mess away. A well-to-do attractive male could do better for himself. I would settle into single-blessed grandmotherhood, God willing. Baby-sit for Arie — that is, if she came back home from Mexico and settled here with her new husband, and the child appeared as hoped.

"You can marry your penniless fraud, or get your old friend Jeremy to support you?"

"Jeremy? What has Jeremy to do with this? If you're short of money, Adam, why don't you go back and get more yourself from Jeremy? Or have you forgotten how?"

(Mirror, mirror on the wall! Oh, Ariadne, then was the time for words. It's disgusting to pick at old scabs.)

"He made it awfully easy to take," he said defensively.

"You took it awfully easily. What, may I ask, made *him* above suspicion as a lover?"

"He was like a father to us. Anyway . . . he was too honorable . . . and his age! His homeliness. You would never . . ."

Anger and guilt made me vicious. I hit him with it in the solar plexus. "Well, hardly ever . . ."

There we sat, two adults, parents, bereaved grandparents, climbing for protection into the make-believe daddy's lap again, and sucking our thumbs.

"What choice did we have, Ariadne? Starvation? I could not find work. You know I tried desperately. Having a child was *your* idea."

"I remember clearly," I said.

"Would it have improved your situation and Absalom's if I had killed myself?" His speech was slurring. "I certainly thought of it. If I had been insured I might have. Would you prefer that to a divorce?" He said the legal word, shook his head as if startled at it and withdrew it: "or separation." He fumbled with the silk scarf at his throat. His hand shook. "I have plenty of insurance now."

"What rot! Don't threaten me with large favors. Are you saying you took money from Jeremy for my sake?"

"Yes. And you?"

"You did it for me, Adam, and I did it for you and for the children. It turns out we were a pair of sensualists of sacrifice. Did you ever try to repay any of it?"

Our cases rested.

The prosecution wobbled to his feet. "I paid. I paid in humiliation. I do believe I am drunk." His eyes filled. *"In vino veritas.* Oh how I paid. I feel like killing myself. You know what I am? I'm a stingy bastard."

"Remorse is cheaper than cash," I said, wishing he would get behind his façade again.

"These profundities must wait on peristalsis."

His face was sweaty and drawn.

"Take a deep breath to avoid vomiting," I said.

"Thank you." He said his two words.

"You're welcome." I said mine.

Silence again.

"Do you want a divorce?" he asked, hesitantly.

It did not seem like a burning question.

"It's up to you," I answered, handing the decision back to him.

We both sat, feeling forlorn, considering our dreary boon companions: he, his remorse; I, my guilt.

Neither of us knew how to go on.

He was the one to break the silence.

"Objectively, Ariadne . . ."

Could he be joking, or was he sounding our worn-out battle cry? Was I supposed to respond with "What's objective about it, Adam?" so he could escape to bed, and leave me to go into my act. Would I make a batch of cookies? There was no one left at home for whom to bake. Telephone Jeremy? I was no longer free to do that. Have a lover's quarrel with Paul? If I were to break my resolution he wouldn't be home. My Christopher Columbus had doubtless sailed off to explore some azure-eyed Azore who had aroused him by a gesture, a scent, a way of pressing her lips together. He would be busy setting up his spike in new territory. From now on everything would be so astonishingly simple, now that I was uprooted from all routine situations and familiar responses.

Adam was talking to me. "Why not put the question in abeyance? Arie is expecting us next week. She needs us. There are legal matters to settle, hopefully before the child is born. You can go on to Acapulco for a few days' sun while I see to things in Mexico City. The reservations were all made before . . ." He waved to the letters.

"If Arie needs us." I picked up my suitcase, and went upstairs to unpack.

*   *   *

How had Adam been able to avoid discovering what was practically public knowledge? He had no right to his ignorance, damn him, as he had no right to leave me alone, even when he was with me, in the bedroom, in bed, and if it came to that, in me. Who did he think he was? King Arthur with his eyes fixed on the Holy Grail and his mind on the business of the Round Table.

There's a scene in the twentieth book of Malory's *Morte d'Arthur,* in which Modred and other politically motivated rebels force Arthur to confront the queen's long-time infidelity and to condemn her to judgment, which meant death at the stake. Is the king overcome with grief for her, with jealousy for himself? Not a bit of it. "Jhesu mercy says the kinge, he [Lancelot] is a merveyllous knighte of prowess. Allas me sore repenteth . . . that ever he shold be ageynst me. Now I am sure the noble felaushyp of the round table is broken for ever."

Poor King Arthur, forced out into the open, had to condemn

398

what he may have been inwardly relieved to condone. There was no advantage to him in lighting the fuse to the long, long trail of hints, rumors, winks, knowing smiles, clues, moody withdrawals, retreats, headaches and chills that would now explode his tolerable charmingly run citadel. If all he did in the queen's bedchamber is take off his armor, sip a hot mead and sleep the sleep of the busy man, who had a right to complain if his wife didn't?

Camelot did fall apart. But it was not infidelity that caused the fall, but the imminent fall that invited infidelity. It was something corrosive in the air. The generative and generational myths of the kingdom had been emptied of potency, as they have been again in our time. Valéry saw it coming. "It is over for now, the intensity of life and passion veiling itself, restraining itself, through a fine manner, through a very delicate form."

Why had I let it happen? I've had time to think about the mess. About twenty-five years. What had become clear was that no splendid issue could be expected. This was it. These years had not been preparatory stages, nor my acts promissory creatures in silk webs from which I would emerge with adult wings to fly into real life.

I don't think I intended to crush Adam with awareness of my relationship to Paul. I might admit some malice, but at the time I was not conscious I was using Adam to achieve several endings I was not able to enforce by myself, one of them with him.

Suppose years before this dénouement I had admitted to myself that Adam's elegant demeanor did not add up, that in his dinner-table stag stories and arch living-room gambits there had to be a provocative intention? Suppose I had refused to participate in empty rituals? Not accepted as a Platonic gesture his "Help you with your brassiere, Ariadne?" Protested outright his seemingly casual nudity, his invading my bathroom, exposing himself like a flasher, then withdrawing into his work only to pop out abruptly with: "Here I am."

Suppose I had let myself confront my own slowly emerging imago, recognized that my anger was legitimate, and given vent to it, acknowledging that Adam was using me as a voyeur might, in some unresolved and anxious game? Had said, out and out, that his ambiguous words and gestures were rousing evil emotions in me. Expressed my distaste, as Paul had suggested, for compliments in the presence of unwilling witnesses. "My wife. Would you believe that my lovely lady is the mother of four children?" While in the bedroom it was silent night, holy night.

Suppose, instead of evolving through Paul, I had already mastered a few rudiments, recognized that Adam needed to feel a woman was putting herself forward and that it roused him to rebuff her, and played his game. Such an elementary game it seems to me now: the maneuvers of a man still entwined with a boy's sense of wickedness. Fortuitously met, I don't doubt it has served as the matrix for passionate obsessions.

Suppose I had played flirtatious games as a girl and not been a stunted Cinderella?

Suppose. Suppose I had developed my own wings and flown clean away? Given a few hundred years I might have thought of it.

There is something radically wrong with the life span of Homo sapiens. If I were a sequoia I would now be a mere slip in my early seventies, with millennia ahead of me to get my tree-ness right.

Suppose — and I've supposed very haltingly and much too late — that Adam and I were not pushed into marriage merely by a chance snowstorm or by my father's petty fears and social ambitions.

Suppose Adam and I were drawn to one another in the amorphous logic of anxiety, our points of contact the immigrant point of noncontact: I, mortally fearful of action; he, mortally frightened of feeling.

(Most emotions are inexpressible, but I find the desire to explore them goes on unabated.)

Suppose Adam had preferred the isolation of the soul condemned early to solitary confinement, had not wished to know what was going on in me or anyone else? Had embraced marriage because he sensed he might be rescued from some forms of his isolation. He had learned to live like a hermit schooled in aloneness. But if there had been time!

* * *

In Acapulco, then, in a chic season, my life eroded as the Mexican landscape, I was a lone traveler dying of thirst in my own desert, with nothing left to drink from love's abundance. What had not been taken away from me, I seemed to have thrown away or lost. Chance underscored the situation, sending me incidents that appeared, like faded repetitions of a pattern in an interminable hallway. For example:

Picking through an English newspaper someone had left on a chair in the hotel lounge, an item leaped out at me.

AMERICAN YOUTH COMMITS SUICIDE

ACAPULCO: An unidentified American was found dead in his cell this morning, hanging from a noose made of his own clothing. He had been arrested the previous afternoon and charged with attempted assault and possession of a dangerous weapon.

The prisoner was reported to be between twenty and twenty-five, of athletic build, just under six feet, curly auburn hair, gray eyes. When arrested he was wearing a blue sailing jacket, white sport shirt and trousers. He was carrying no identification papers and refused to comment on the reasons for his behavior.

According to Señorita Ravis, a long-distance operator at the luxury hotel, Hi Roc, the young man had seemed agitated. She could see he was a foreigner and since she spoke English, she was

401

prepared to be helpful. He was neat and gentlemanly appearing or she would not have responded to him when he spoke to her. Then she saw the knife, an American switchblade. She screamed. He ran.

The arrest followed a chase by beach guards and a parking lot policeman who had responded to her cries.

It was not Absalom. But the message had arrived. Years, given no sign, it was time to say the prayer for the dead over this grave, too.

When I tipped the police attendant and left, it was still early morning.

The sunlight was tremendous. It had already agitated the cool air from the sea to the upper town. The final sonorities of a Mass were activating the market in the churchyard square. A coffin maker walked down a row of children's coffins — pastel pink, blue, pistachio — gilding brush in hand, freshening glitter here and there; a candy vendor passed a domestic touch over his pastille skeletons, skulls and other purgatorial sweets.

Death and resurrection being a continuous performance, the girl who stepped out of the funereal dark, quickened by the reminder of who and what she was — dust and ashes: immortal bride — wore an aspect that wooed like pollen: white veil petaled back over hair — Velásquez gold (the only gold left by the Spaniards) — face flushed, taking in approval like a good child in the circle of its family, a jewel, clinging to her father's arm.

Yet trust not your daughter's mind. For as she smiled, she scanned.

The previous day I had singled her out on the beach among a cluster of girls whose squeaks and small cries combined with the jibber of parrots and monkeys in the palms above them; again on the *zocalo* at the promenade hour, in native white, demure among courting youngsters. As she passed, young men lit up like phosphorescent fish, and spent fishermen withering on benches blessed their genitals with a caress. But her coquetry was directed at one only, a young diver.

From the dining terrace of my hotel I had watched her watch him — a pagan idol, a tourist sacrifice outlined in flaming torches — as he cast himself from a ledge between two cliffs to meet the onrushing sea at the precise moment it hurled itself over rocks dreamed by a suicide.

Later that night, drawn to my window by moonlight of a strange pink luminosity, and held there by the melancholy roar of surf far below, I became aware of a rustling beneath my window. Bougainvillea and coral vine stirred. On the white garden wall a human shadow moved, broke from the leafery and solidified on the cobbled street.

Barefoot, wrapped in a white rebozo, crouched low, like a young cat, all electric, Juliet waited. In white trousers and shirt, also barefoot, Romeo stepped out of an archway.

They stood transfixed in each other's gaze, two enormous white insects that swayed toward each other, vibrating, leaning on the lovesick air. Before their lips touched I turned back into the dark room.

The moon sank, leaving the sky to the alien stars of the Southern Cross. I made a chaise of two chairs and settled at the window. Night insects subsided. Mists rolled in and turned milky. Sleepless in the burdensome odor of jasmine, lemon and coffee blossoms, I heard the hurried pad of bare feet. A gate grated open; banged shut. It was the diver. He stalked through the garden, and trailing clouds of fury, bolted into the archway and was gone.

On the church portico I recognized him again. I had seen him frown away a bunch of flowers, disdain a candle, threaten a dog in his path, rebuff a young man with a flung-over-the-shoulder response before he leaped the stairs, came to an uneasy pause and leaned against a column as if his body were an encumbrance. He glittered with sleeplessness and rage.

When she saw him she turned blind radiant.

She had a smile, how shall I say, I've seen it on my daughter, I remember the shape of it on my own mouth — of sweet smugness, of innocent boldness after the early gift of the lips. I let you kiss me so you are mine forever.

She scattered hectic glances and flutters at him, ducking her head in birdlike courting motions. Good morning my own true love. She made little hopping steps, holding on to her father's arm, yet pushing him forward, as if saying, "Here is my father, ask for my hand." She blinked, gaped, her mouth open, and while her face and gestures cried out "Behold the child," womanly sensuality eddied around her, waiting to take her shape.

Instead of answering in kind, he grimaced, drawing his features into a false face of bones and sockets. Oh if looks could kill . . .

She arrested herself in mid-flounce and fell into a figure of grief not unlike a child playing statues, arrested in one of those postures that looks operatic at a funeral — flowers clasped to her, eyes too wide, mouth open as at the end of a scream.

Drops of perspiration beaded out onto the boy's tautened skin. Suddenly he raised both fists and shook them into her face, a chimp menacing his tormentor from between the bars of a cage. Then (oh treason of the blood) publicly trapped in his vigor, he doubled a local gesture into an insult, dropped both hands over his groin and stomped away.

(Oh, my Irish cupid. Banal as it seems, my heart sinks. Memory skids me downhill. My face burns to an old slap.)

A red stain flowed up her throat and spread over her cheeks. When it paled back she seemed smaller. She shivered and turned waxen like a fruit tree that has put out its first bloom and been caught by hard frost. The extent of damage would be known slowly, embodied in the shape of her erotic conscious-ness as a tree embodies shock in its annual rings.

I fled the portico, mocking the tears that burned my throat. Who was she, bruised girl in white, that I should weep for her? In the car I wept for the child of my fourteenth summer.

I left the curve of phosphor bay behind and ascended the arid mountain drive toward Mexico City. Late in the afternoon, I stopped at a *posada* of adobe and salvaged tin. On a terrace that hung over a gorge between two scarred knuckles of mountains, I lingered over a cup of bitter coffee.

In my state of disturbance, points remote from each other seemed to connect, closing me in, as in fairy tales, forests spring up in imagined footsteps and close behind the traveler, trapped as if character had materialized. For all the illusory years of struggle through thickets of daring and surrender, it seemed I had merely described dots on the transverse of a series of con-centric circles, wandering as lost souls are said to wander, through mazes and terrains blasted by natural disaster, return-ing, more lost, more tired than ever, to my isolated beginnings.

In the siesta sun, solitude stretched slack and fearsome as a rope ladder dangling above the chasm. Above and below were cliffs. Boulders lay helter-skelter among spent lava spills, an eroded planet out of which bristled an infrequent tequila cactus. From the crevasse rose the dry click of insects.

A pebble slid. A dry slow monster, mounted on a rock, swiveled its head like the gun turret of a tank. It seemed unbe-lievable that here creatures should be fruitful and multiply; birds build, iguanas breed, snakes, desert rats find shelter; mountain lions descend these crevasses to find water far below where the purple torrent slits its own valley.

Overhead vultures ranged in wide-winged flight, black against unrelieved blue. Beneath the shadow of their flight pattern silence fell. But blood would be shed. They too would have their way. Black wings planed, circled, rode currents of air and spiraled at last beyond range.

Under the emptied dome a bird called. A small sweet call like a first drop of rain. Again the bird. It became important to know if it was a solitary bird that had called, fluttered to a new position, trilling again. There it came again, with the pure animal tenderness we impute to it. Back and forth. A call, and, yes, an answer. Closer. Now both together. Silk threads shuttling across solitude, weaving a fabric of uncorrupted sensual assurance. It was as if I held the hollow-boned birds throbbing in my hands like shapes filled with warm ash.

(Jeremy would say I am still idealizing.)

I will go home to my garden, although it is November and I'm late for the chores of the autumn equinox. (But then, I've never gotten my timing right.) I will take up tools. Much must be pruned to master this everyday dying. I've been unlucky in love. The infatuations of my lifetime have wasted themselves like drops of water that sizzle off a hot stove. Literature was that rich muck in which my expectations developed. From literature I derived those fictions, those imitations of life, which, with the gravity of a child at play, I used to master reality. I have misconstrued everything.

From this day forth I give up searching for the idealized son, the loving husband, the adoring lover, the wise and selfless father. To the best of my ability I also discard the idealized self, that collage pasted together out of other people's expectations and affections. Good-bye, Miss Goody Two-Shoes. Good-bye, aggrieved wife, bereaved mother, heartbroken lover. Whatever the play was about, I'm not acting in it anymore. My costumes go back to the storage room. I am alone on a struck set. If I had my written part with me, I'd chuck it down this chasm. I have just switched off the ideational light of my life.

What next? I don't know how, or if, I can shape a life out of this dust. (Only God managed to blow a soul into the material.) But like the hermit whom ravens have fed, I must learn to be alone. (I suspect togetherness is another bill of goods we've been sold and everyone has to learn to bear isolation.)

Snow will fall. Juncos, within the naked mesh of viburnum, like quarter notes chirping in windblown cages, will fluff their small feathers trying to keep warm. What better can they do but sing and puff themselves; they are, like us, their only insulation. Where can we go, who are assigned a widening net of twigs to meet the grave necessity of snow?

*   *   *

Here, too, the scene requires a postscript. For all my determination to find myself in solitary confinement, I doubt that I could have entirely forgotten that Arie's baby was due at Christmas and I'd be back on family duty, at mothering and grandmothering.

BOOK III

The Link of Nature

Some men are born great. Some men achieve greatness. But women have greatness thrust upon them.

— ARIADNE ARKADY

And Grandmother of:

Responsibility is the navel-string of creation.

— MARTIN BUBER

THERE'S A ROBED figure pacing the terrace below my window. It is caught, ignited and quenched with each passage into and out of the stained-glass light from the stairwell. Heavy mist coiling earthward adds to the sensation of looking down through broken roof beams into a ruined chamber in which a tattered tapestry billows and subsides with the wind.

The party's over. Daniel and Dinah's guests have long since gone home. It is the birdless hour before the brown horizon is divided into earth and sky by the rekindled ashes of dawn. I've been writing for a long time yet I'm still groping for a way out from my center to a continuity. If I could extricate a belief in the significance of my actions and their interaction with others, I would be willing to settle for any coherence, even a coherence of failure. But perspective has gone out of scenes. In my memory everything appears on one plane: that tranced, Utopian plane isolated on medieval tapestries, the goriest scenes of martyrdom and battle calmly transcending their brutality.

The robed figure holds an object that glows faintly. No, it is

411

not Absalom returned, switchblade smoking with blood. It is not that despairing priest of Perugia, because if it were, I would be the monster crawling on all fours to kiss his hand. If it's Daniel, it could be a bomb he's holding. The figure lifts the glowing object to its mouth. Attenuated smoke slowly twists from it. A faint odor of tobacco rises as my father seems to read:

"Every day a robed figure presented the king with a perfect fruit. Courtesy demanded that he accept it, but the courtier who received it tossed it contemptuously into the treasury where it fell to the bottom and rotted. One day, the king's playful monkey leaped down into the pit, returned with a fistful of rotted fruit to which clung precious jewels. This is to say, my daughter, that in each ordinary day a jewel lies hidden. Do not make the treasurer's error and throw it away."

The match strikes, smoke spirals upward. "Now off you go to bed, my little Topaz. It's late."

A voice calls, "Isn't it lights out time for grandmothers? May I bring you something?" It is Daniel.

"No thank you, dear. Time for you too."

A burning cigarette arcs into the blanched grass, a glowworm out of season.

For all my enthusiasm about beginnings, I confess that faced with telling how I became a grandmother I hear myself muttering, "How to go on. God how to go on."

I would only have to call out to Danny and Dinah to have immediate physical evidence that I am indeed a grandmother. Not once . . . not twice . . . not . . . but I won't count that one.

"Wouldn't you have a big family, if you had to do it over?" Dinah asked, as we were clearing dishes after the party.

Danny immediately mocked it into a cause. "The question of

412

large families, even intrusive families, must be submitted to computers."

"GIGO," my darling granddaughter said. "Bet you don't know that one, Grandma. It's computerese for Garbage In–Garbage Out."

Danny was undeterred. "Look at it this way. Suppose we developed a midget strain of people to solve the population problem. If a one-inch shrew contains total mammalian possibilities, we could give up basketball or lower the basket and go back to large families. What do you say, Grandma?"

"I would take all the grandchildren I could get," I answered, lying through my capped teeth.

*   *   *

It was a Saturday morning in May. When the mailman honked I was dividing chrysanthemums, thinking how many years of gardening it had taken for me to learn to be ruthless, excise the worn heart of each clump, discard, not crowd the bed with every dubious possibility but to set out firmly only stocks vigorous enough to fulfill their cycle with bloom.

"Postage due, Mrs. A. Air mail." He flapped the envelope from the truck window.

"Real spring day," he said.

"One of the best," I answered.

"Your lawn looks great, what do you feed it?"

"Chicken soup."

We both laughed. I couldn't possibly have intruded slow-release fertilizer into our ritual exchange.

I reached for the letter, saw that it was from Mexico from Arie, and tried not to react as if it were bordered in black.

"No bad news I hope?" He waited in case there was something he could trade down the road.

I gave him what he already had. "My daughter. From Mexico," and slipped the letter into the pocket of my smock. To get

413

away quickly I went back into the house by the front door.

"Dear Mom"

A nettle of anxiety stung at the "Mom." Why not her habitual "Dear Mother" or her new-fangled more aloof "Ariadne"? Why was the child in her fumbling for the parent in me? Halfway down the page there was the word, swaddled, "pregnant" (I groaned). "Ricardo and I hope to be able to get through the legalities for a converted Catholic marrying a divorced American Jewess, and get to New York before the baby arrives. If we can't, you might be thinking of a chic winter holiday . . . the baby is due around Christmas."

Nothing so direct as "Come, I will need you." Still the same Arie. Rushing into intimacy and rushing out again, scornful in advance of the rejection that might follow. "Oh excuse me, am I interrupting? . . . never mind, it's not important . . . later will do . . ."

Pregnant again? Bless you my brave daughter. I would like to pray or light a candle, but I don't know to whom. Certainly not the wrathful God of Genesis who cursed Eve doubly: to bring forth in sorrow, and to bring forth a murderous son. If the new age rejects reason and embraces faith as we have been warned, women could do worse than to enshrine that votive females, deity of childbirth, the Mater Matuta.

The father of the pregnant unbride could wait to hear the news until Sunday night when he got back from his business trip. Poor Adam. Daughters should have some imagination for what doting fathers feel. He'd probably fly down to Mexico and try to grease the wheels with American dollars.

Jeremy would want to know. He would be at his Saturday office hours, his waiting room like a dockside, throbbing with women loaded with babies. I telephoned.

"Doctor," I said.

"Doctor me no doctors. Anything wrong, Ariadne?"

"Nothing, Jeremy. I'm coming back to the city. May I stop by tonight? Will you be at the hospital?"

"Where else would I be? You are all right? You don't sound it . . . I'll see you when you get here."

I went back to the chrysanthemums. I'd put them in for Arie's wedding to Jethro, and in the years since, the beds had tripled. I had hoped she would choose a June wedding when the garden is at one of its peaks. "You'll have to wave your magic wand and it will burst into proper bloom, it wouldn't dare not," she said, snippily.

"How about four weeks earlier or three weeks later when there's a blaze of bloom? Why just the end of July? I'll have to interplant mums and annuals."

"Oh, Mother! Don't nag."

"Even the phlox is slow. The woodchucks got the early growth."

Her eyes brilliant, her equivocal mouth shaping itself in her father's sardonic set, she carried herself out of the room, shaking her head like a tousled chrysanthemum, mumbling to herself, "Fuss, fuss . . ."

Anyone who has tried to contrive a perennial border that blooms continuously from March through October in our tempestuous New England zone knows what formidable alternations of submission and attack shape the character of a gardener. Year after year one bows to premature heats that force bloom and wreck the color scheme: to frosts that arrest or obliterate. Optimism and enthusiasm are tempered by experience. Not everything in the catalogue will grow. The beginner does not believe that she must discard, thin, clip, burn, tear out the spindly, the diseased, the unwanted. But knife in hand, the chastened gardener evaluates the potential of each cutting,

415

dealing with weakness before the scion has drained the parent stock; learns it is necessary to condemn the inadequate to compost.

At that point, fear I had been fighting got the better of me. I got up off my knees, heeled in the remaining chrysanthemum cuttings and walked down to the pond.

The pond lay in its vault of hemlock and willow, blue sky poured light directly down. Looking into the water I saw myself mirrored, faded and pale. I could be drained of my remaining substance as simply as by stepping back I removed my image. I threw myself onto a flat ledge face up into the light, surrounded by shadowless trees.

Listen You up there in charge of the gift of life. I'm not fit. You've made a horrible mistake. Here's the rest of my ticket. Give it to someone who wants it. But this time, leave my Arie alone, you bloodthirsty maniac!

I must have lain there for hours because when I started uphill toward the house, gleams of sunlight were receding westward along the floor of the woods. At the far end of the resinous tarn a pair of Canadian geese flapped their great wings and lifted themselves with only a muffled mew. Until this weekend unmuted clarions had preceded their takeoffs. By their silence I knew they must have begun nesting. "And to you, too, blessings. Blessings on your innate wiliness. May your silent ordeal defeat the competing wiliness of eagle from above, turtle from below and fox from under your wing." God send me a sign.

I ran past the terrace where Arie, her bride dress filming across Jethro's groom suit, had blown us kisses full of promises. Promises! Promises! For what grandchildren shall I retrieve the picnic glade behind the pasture wall?

The oppression in my chest increased until my heart felt

pushed up high as if by a ninth-month child. O Lord, you are hard on mothers.

Arie, what do you want of me? What is your message? Do you want to risk having this baby? You must be frightened, my child. How can I help you? For one person to be able to help another in such an event, a whole constellation of things must come right. How much do you suspect? How much do you know? This too must remain ambiguous. Did I succeed? In the name of the mother, the daughter and that baby's ghost — let me believe that I once succeeded.

When I left the house the windless dark was sweet with Hail Dianthus and Farewell Lilac. The music of the night, faint as if borne on bars of moonlight to my solar-trained ear, was a perfect orchestration of motifs and lunar rests. Coming up around me from the grass, Fowler's Trilling toads. In descending order: Leopard frogs on the moist hillside, chorus frogs from the meadow. Hylas honking their horns in trees. One-two-three and rest. As it should be.

From the wilder shore boomed that passionate solitary, the old bullfrog. Barroooomm Barroooomm. Very evenly. Now all together. Sostenuto. Rare sostenuto. A tremulous whistle, low, low, rising to a screech owl call, descending with a whistling fall. Hooo. Hooo. Over the river and beyond the woods, to Grandmother's house we go . . . A whippoorwill added three chuck-chucks. Good night, sweet *Caprimulgus vociferus.* Angels attend us. Are you telling me that all will be well?

The next instant the truce was broken. Tic. Tic. Tic. Tic. Tic. I was no longer a citizen, but an interloper, an explorer who, having informed himself of a few stock rhythms, suddenly apprehends a baffling tattoo riffled out by unseen jungle drums. In his flimsy shelter he feels his insolent flesh crawl.

Tic. Tic. Tic. Tic. Tic. No crescendo. No diminuendo. A

mechanical continuum that would crackle until for its reasons it could go off like a time bomb and blow up the world.

Tic. Tic. Tic. Tic. The sounds came from a huge maple between me and my car on the driveway. Tic. Tic. Tic. Steady as rain. But in a clear sky a gibbous moon waxed.

Tic. Tic. Tic. Tic. I switched on my flashlight, played the light on the nearest branch. I could make out nothing but young leaves. Tic. Tic. Tic. And then I could! Each leaf was criss-crossed with yellow larvae. On true and false legs they wormed and reared and sloped. Over, under, rising or falling, on each leaf each blind gorger chomped away. Tic. Tic. Tic. Tic. As if all each one knew and all it needed to know was one truth, that its life depended on the next bite. Like a curtain they swung on silk threads between leaves. They were swinging around me — against my mouth, my eyes, my ears, into my hair, on my neck, hands, underfoot.

Arms flailing, I swam through tangled air toward the car. I was webbed in worms, assaulted by them. Worms stuck to the handle. I had to break through their slick to open the door. They were shrouding me. Nauseated, I started the motor. Raced it. Stalled. Jolted again. They were all over the window. I turned on the windshield wiper. A mess of them were squashed. I was blinded by their gluey trails that slimed the pane. I backed out of the driveway, panting with the effort to control retching, whimpering no, no, no. Ninth-nerve convulsions eased only after I was speeding along the highway.

"I'll walk upstairs," I said to the porter. "Don't ring for the elevator."

The corridors were empty, the proud new fathers departed having left cigars with other new fathers who also, ad infinitum. The hospital was enclosed in its night shift; mothers bedded down, blue night bulbs slipping identical beams through doors identically ajar. Floor nurses like sea captains concentrated in cubicles, a cone of light on entry cards from which lifetimes of certificates, visas, passports and horoscopes would surge.

On the third floor you knew you were in the critical core by the twitching in your nostrils. You entered a heavy atmosphere fraught as the rim of a sleeping volcano; a malodorousness compounded of ether, Lysol, ammonia, iodoform, blood, diapers, rubber sheets and brown soap. Behind glass doors sterilizers blinked red lights; formula ingredients boiled and bubbled; racks of bottles jiggled over steam. The formula kitchen separated two nurseries: One, dim, overheated, suffocatingly quiet, for prematures and other weaklings; the second, brightly lit and bustling, pink and blue baskets arranged in businesslike rows.

Through the second nursery window I could see Hennessey at her routines; babies still on the trolley that had carried them back from their mothers and the ten o'clock feedings. Undiaper. Let it kick and squall, good for it. Wash the parts. Male and female created He them and that's that. Gauze on the healing umbilicus. Flip, flop, over and under, there you go, sweetie.

The infant arched his back and screamed. Hennessey made a mouth at the boy, a tender little mockery at his lustiness, before she picked him up and stuffed a bottle into his mouth. At once he began sucking strongly. When she tucked him back into his basket it was with a smile and a pat. Have it your way!

That's how it was going to be for him.

I watched a nurse lift a pink bundle off the trolley, a girl limp as a rain-soaked peony, soft petal hands half open . . . take-it-away-from-me-if-you-want-to hands. She fluttered eyelids at the washing and closed them at once. Nurse's arm under her back, the whole hand to support the head. Slow. Slow.

That's how it was going to be for her. The nurse teased the lips with a nipple. No response. She patted its cheek. It sucked, abandoned the nipple and slept. In the next basket a screamer who had emptied one bottle was making motions with his lips, screwing up his face, turning red with complaints. She brought a second bottle, which he immediately began to suck.

Ask and it shall be given thee.

But not always.

In the dim nursery Molly accepted the sick, the weak, the premature, the unfit.

From the delivery room, voices; unhurried. That meant post-delivery.

The door swung open and a nurse with a blanketed bundle in her arms soft-shoed toward the nurseries. By her spraddled gait I recognized Delly — Jeremy's right hand. Twenty-two years ago, when I was with my Aaron, she already had the beginning of that spread.

("Now bear down like this . . . from right here. Gently, it's not a wheelbarrow we're wanting you to give out with.")

She cooed into the bundle, "Shh, now you're here you'll have to put up with us." Then she saw my figure against the window.

"No visitors on this floor please . . . oh, it's you, Mrs. Arkady. How are all the big and little A's?"

"Busy tonight, Delly?"

"Slowing down. Spring lambing almost over . . . One more tonight but you never can be sure."

From the labor room a cry soared, robust and even jubilant, on three notes like those that might begin a Hugo Wolf song. Delly checked her watch.

"Contractions getting close. I'd better settle this bundle before the next one arrives."

Again that cry.

"Sounds like she'll be no trouble," I said.

"Ah, if they were all like that. Normal. What a blessing it would be, God's will be done . . ."

She gave me a straight look. How much guesswork had

gone on behind those eyes . . . eyes that fix you in a Catholic phrase . . . ?

"I'll tell Doctor you're here. Will you go down to the dining room and eat?"

"No, I'll wait in his study."

She swerved around me. Passed the formula kitchen. In the first nursery Molly looked up.

Keep going, Delly. Don't go into that one — go to rough-and-tumble Hennessey. We would see a sign.

Hennessey took the bundle and the card. Delly stood by as a twig arm was lifted, a circle of tape removed and identifying beads braceleted around the tiny wrist. Delly checked her watch. Hennessey cosigned the card. Official. You're here, boy, and you're normal.

*　　*　　*

Arie's first pregnancy had been wrong from the start. She puked and mewled and wilted from conception to delivery. Labor went on and on.

I worried at Jeremy the second morning.

"Aren't you afraid the baby will be injured? Does she have to go through what I went through with Absalom — why don't you do something. Maybe a Caesarean?"

"She's not doing much yet, Ariadne. I know it seems long but the baby is still up high. It's her first . . . sometimes slow . . . you know. The contractions are not close and regular. A Caesarean isn't indicated . . . and it mars . . . be a help, dear. Take your two men away . . ."

He put on a big voice, one arm on Adam's shoulder, the other on Jethro's. "Why don't you take these nervous fathers to the dining room and get another breakfast? Never lost a father yet . . . or a grandfather. Arie will take her time. Don't worry. The baby is big and strong. Get to your offices. Ariadne will stay, she'll call you the moment . . ."

He made that nervous sniffing sound.

That night he forced birth.

When he came up to his study to tell me, his surgical suit clung to him wetly. Ether drifted heavily from him.

"Why can't I see him, Jeremy," I said.

"Tomorrow maybe. Come on down to Arie, she's in recovery."

I stopped at the bright nursery window. Jeremy walked ahead. "He's not in there. He's with specials," he said. "Forceps."

Wrapped in blankets Arie lay, still etherized, sick odor flowing out of her. Her eyelids were double dark and sealed, her insurgent hair damp streamers of tangled seaweed, pale, drowned.

Jeremy leaned over one side, I over the other.

"She's not helping," he said. "Open your eyes, Arie. Open your eyes, child."

"It's a boy," I whispered.

"Open your eyes, Arie, love, open your eyes. It's a boy."

"It's a boy," I repeated.

Her eyes rolled under her eyelids, a catatonic who hears from a great distance.

"It's a boy . . . it's a boy . . ." I held her hand. It was cold. I kissed it. "It's Mama," I said.

Her eyelids crinkled. She made a shape with her mouth. "Mama."

"Louder. Darling, louder. Speak to me. It's just what you wanted. Tell her again, Jeremy. Tell her again."

He squeezed her wrist. She opened her eyes and looked at him. Sniff. "A boy."

A corner of her discolored cracked lips trembled upward in a smile.

422

"A big boy. Tell her, Jeremy, a big boy."

"Yes. It's a big boy."

In the hall he was all professional. "She'll be all right now. Let her rest. No visits till tomorrow evening. All of you need a night's sleep. I'll have the car take you. Go home now, Grandpa, Grandma, Great-grandma, you too, Jethro, she'll be all right." Sniff. "Good night ladies, good night gents, see you tomorrow. It's snowing, be careful."

At the front entrance I said, "I'll be right back, I left my book upstairs."

Jeremy and Delly were outside the doleful nursery, her back was to me. In the dark glass I saw her reflection as she crossed herself. Jeremy threw up his hands, palms out, homely Semite with a despairing face, protrusive eyes staring down a long perspective. He looked ancient. Knees bending, saggy surgical pajamas flapping, he walked heavily, sloping forward.

"Jeremy, will he live?"

His eyes were wet. He did not speak. Looking into his silence I saw that I had failed to ask the right question. He was wracking himself to find the answer that would lead to the question.

"Perhaps we should wish that he does not."

The next day Arie was strong enough to protest. "Why can't I see the baby?" I had dry-shampooed her hair to get the stench of vomit out of it. She was sitting up, green-pale and weak. "I haven't seen him."

"They showed him to you in the recovery room, when you came out of ether."

"I don't remember. Anyway I can feed him his bottle." She plucked at the breast binder." (No, I don't want you to develop milk, Arie.) "He's a great big baby and you've both had a hard

423

time. He has a touch of jaundice. It wouldn't be good for either of you for you to nurse him . . . the next one. Listen to the doctor, honey . . ."

The floor nurse brought in a bouquet. "Mmmm lovely flowers." She exuded false cheer.

Arie repeated her question. "Why can't I feed my baby his bottle?"

"We do what the doctor says. We don't want to expose him to more infection, now do we . . . ?" She was backing out of the room.

"I won't know him when I take him home."

"You'll know him. Doctor says you will both stay a few days longer to get your strength back. You'll be glad to get a night's sleep then, won't she Mother?"

"How is he today?" I asked.

"Beginning to take nourishment."

She popped the thermometer into Arie's mouth, found the pulse on the girly wrist, primly concentrated on her timer, jotted her findings and vacant-smiled herself out of the room.

I read the card in the flowers. "Healthy wishes from Aunt Cassie."

"How did you keep the witch away?" Arie asked.

"I barely restrained her from coming to advise Jeremy how to care for you and the baby. I told her she could come on the eighth day."

What I had actually said was "Awful news, Aunt Cassie, the baby is not right."

"Is it a weak heart?"

"No, head. A mongoloid."

There was silence.

"Does Jeremy say it will live?"

"I'm afraid so."

*

424

"You can feed him today." The nurse propped the baby into his mother's arms. "Support his head." She hurried out, eyes busy on the floor. (How everything turns away from disaster!)

Jeremy stepped in and stood next to me. Our hands groped together.

Arie touched the bruised places on the puffy forehead. "He's full of hurts," she said softly.

"Those welts will heal. Forceps babies . . ." Jeremy's voice trailed.

"I was no good, darling, was I?"

The baby screwed up his misshapen face.

"Feed him before he howls," I said, "I can't stand babies crying."

We all laughed. Ha ha sniff.

"Must make a good impression on your grandmother." She cooed and placed the nipple at its lips. It began to suck greedily.

"Little pig. You're strong. You've got a funny face but you're adorable . . . isn't he Mom . . . ?" Did I imagine a note of uneasiness?

"Here's his father, ask him," I said.

"Don't come too close, Jethro, you seem to be getting a cold. Your eyes are streaming. I said the baby is big and strong, but not handsome."

"He looks like a Chinese coolie. If my son is big and strong he can support us early. I'm tired in advance." The young father laughed. He had the same fatuous expression on his face as other fathers.

"Is his skin going to stay yellow?" Arie asked.

"A touch of baby jaundice . . ." I heard myself repeat my mother's assurances about Hannah's brother . . . "In a few days the yellow goes away." Unless the rest of the family catches the color instead.

*   *   *

425

Reality had again failed to meet the least that could be expected of it. Like an innocuously romantic young lady, I had imagined that in grandmotherhood my life would be elected to glide along sleigh tracks in a relationship of parallel beauty — age and events — across appropriate fields of peace and wisdom, lustrous as quartz fish-scales artfully tipped in silver and gold by sages with smiling eyes. Like Catherine the Great I would pass through an unwounded foreground of silver bells, pennants, hats off, applause. Kept from me the maniacs, murderers, mongoloids, the monstrous births that tug at infinity. Transfigured into loving children licking Halloween candy, those threatening mutterers from whom it would be useless to beg mercy.

(If not mine — oh God, what a terrible journey — if not mine, then whose?)

It's late. In the room behind me, a stack of yellow paper lies beside my typewriter. I have been writing a set of scenes through which I move like a superstitious sleepwalker, putting a hand out and withdrawing it again, from a cup in which pellets of poison wait to be dissolved.

Looking out the window at the five A.M. sky I feel I am diving free of earth, through water blue as air, or air blue as water. Surf, combers, phosphorus waves, spill around me. Stars flow past, into my open mouth.

I go back and put my arms around the typewriter. I'm sorry, Father. I can't explain how your obedient daughter became part of so many scenes so ugly, so forlorn.

*   *   *

Aunt Cassie sat by the bedside, hunched, a blackbird, bright-eyed and beaky.

"Neither rain nor sleet," I said when I saw her. "How are you?"

"How should I be?" she said lugubriously.

"You look well."

"I'm not." (Nothing of that night compresses. Every frame hangs on almost without motion like a bad home movie.)

Jethro came in coughing and wheezing. "Bitter out," he said. Cassie roused herself. "Don't go near Arie. If she catches cold she's liable to get milk fever."

"I have to be healthy for two." Arie blew her husband a kiss. Her hands looked wax-papery.

"Have you been drinking hot lemonade and scraping grapefruit rind?" Aunt Cassie missed no opportunity to practice medicine.

Jethro wiped his streaming eyes. "No, would it stop my eyes from leaking?"

"Boric acid will. I'll run to the drugstore next door, get some. You can wash your eyes right here before you go home." She hopped up.

"Golly, Aunt Cassie, not out in this weather."

"I love rain and snow. So does Ariadne. Always has . . ." She was on her feet and on the way out.

"I'll walk you to the entrance." I followed her out of the room.

"Jeremy showed it to me," she said. "What a future for a young couple!"

Jethro was sitting in the one easy chair with his eyes closed. Arie's bed had been lowered and she was lying back on the pillows. The bedside light had been pushed aside, so I couldn't be sure she had been crying but a handkerchief was balled up in her fist.

427

Neither of them spoke.

From the corridor, the party air of a maternity hospital breezed in and died. "Beautiful. A boy . . . A girl . . . like my mother . . . like your father . . . In my whole life . . ."

Adam arrived carrying a package. "I brought us a puzzle to play with, Arie, a five-hundred-piece toughie. Just as well. I met Jeremy and he says he wants you to rest a few days more."

She managed a smile for her father.

"Also, I brought you a letter from Aaron. He wants you to send pictures of the baby. He can't get leave from basic training camp."

"I'll read it later," she said, "after you go."

Cassie returned with supplies. "Swallow this yeast in honey when you get home, Jethro, you'll feel better. I'll get the eyewash ready."

Cassie opened and closed cabinets looking for a jar in which to prepare boric acid solution.

"Use my teacup, Aunt Cassie, and for goodness sake stop rattling."

"Jethro, there's an eyecup and solution on the sink," Cassie called from the lavatory.

He did not move.

"It's warm now, Jethro."

Arie groaned.

"Tired darling?" I patted her arm.

She snapped it away. "Oh, Mother, don't nag."

Jethro went into the lavatory.

After that we sat in silence until the visitors' bell rang.

A nurse poked her head into the room. "Doctor says family come upstairs and have tea with him before going out. He'll be up after rounds.

"I'll hobble home," Jethro said, "and put myself to bed."

"Don't forget hot lemonade and grapefruit rind."

"Have a good sleep," Arie said gently.

"You too, dearest, try to rest." Their voices were careful, as in a sick room.

"I'll stay till the baby's fed," I said.

"Meet you upstairs, Ariadne," Adam said, briskly, but his eyes were red and puffy. "See you tomorrow, Arie. I'll come early and we'll begin work on the puzzle. It will take us all week." He looked at me, compressed his quivering lips and left quickly.

The nurse put the baby into Arie's arms. "He's begun to gain" she said. "He's had an increase in his formula today. He moves in with the regular guys tomorrow morning."

"Would you rather I fed him tonight?" I asked. "I remember how to do it."

"I *am* tired," Arie whispered, and gave the little monster up to me.

The face I stared down on was swollen and undefined, like a pig foetus puffed up in formaldehyde, except he was alive and his loose rubbery mouth was opening and closing with the insatiable snapping motion of a fledgling cuckoo. Every ugly detail of it was clear: Down's syndrome. The mongoloid eyes with the distinct skin fold in the inner corner, the broad nose, thick tongue and, behind that yellow forehead, sure as the skin fold, the shallow grooved brain with its I.Q. of thirty to forty.

As soon as the nipple touched his lips he gulped and sucked.

"Hold it, boy, you'll swallow the world," I said, and adjusted him in my lap.

Cassie leaned over us. She picked up the little fist, opened it and traced the single crease on the palm. When her gaze rested on mine, it met my despair.

The child went on sucking. Then for some reason he stopped and gave a sharp cry. Gas probably. No hope of anything serious.

Arie stirred. "Maybe the bottle is too warm, it felt hot to me."

"Right. I'll run cold water over it."

"Let me do it," Cassie said.

"No, you hold the baby."

"Ssshh, my head is splitting."

When I shut the door it was so as not to disturb Arie with the flow of water. But as I reached for the faucet the cup of boric acid solution moved into my field of vision where it grew larger and larger until it blocked everything else from sight.

I turned on the cold water.

By what right?

Would a glass of boric acid, drunk neat, kill this adult? Just because I think I can't bear it?

That was the wrong question. It was not whether I could bear it, but could Arie bear what she had borne?

Not my business?

Says who?

Should she bear what she had borne? Should she put by her years, her palette, her brushes, her training, her talents, and dedicate herself to becoming like Hannah's mother?

The cup of boric acid stopped floating and settled down on the sink edge, a quiet cup of boric acid solution next to a box of powder. I picked up the box and read the label. I always read labels. DANGER. KEEP OUT OF THE REACH OF CHILDREN. NOT TO BE TAKEN INTERNALLY.

The picture that passed before my eyes was Hannah's pinky mother turned yellow, wrapped in a strait blanket, carried out to a waiting car, my last view the top of her head, picked sores in bald red spots.

I slipped the nipple off the bottle, flushed most of the formula down the sink and the remainder into Arie's bathroom glass. The tiny telescopic lens clear in my aching head focused on me pouring that formula back into the bottle afterward. I shook

430

boric acid powder, as much as it would take, into the eyewash in the cup, and stirred with the handle of Arie's toothbrush. Boric acid does not dissolve readily. I pressed each dry resistant particle smooth with my fingers, thumbing it against the glass. It mustn't plug the nipple. I dribbled in hot water, trickled the mess carefully into the bottle. Shook it furiously. Mixed with the formula I had left in the bottle, it looked bluish, as asp milk might. ("Dost thou not see my baby at my breast?") What lacteal bliss awaits my grandchild?

"Mom," Arie called wearily, "the formula will be too cool."

"I know, dear. I'm out of practice. I cooled it too much. Now I have to reheat it. Sorry."

I was burning. My body was a taper, my fingers the flame. My face in the mirror was a prisoner's. I would be in solitary with this deed, forever. (To sin, repent and be forgiven is a Christian luxury.) Do you know that unnatural vices are fathered by heroism? I won't ask you to forgive me. Don't look, this is too difficult for you, Father. Keep out of the way, sweetheart. The last flicker of being a child has just gone out in me. I am much older suddenly than you ever were. You are too young for me to speak to. Go row your boat gently down the stream. Go whittle your hopes. Take a walk with the dog while your daughter brews. You are about to lose your first great-grandson. Good-bye.

My throat kept stretching tighter and harder, a wooden box between my head and shoulders, a container for tears. Prepare a face. If I ever smile again, the smile will have to squeeze past this block of my throat. It will cut my mouth like splinters.

Tears ran out of my eyes and burned dry. Burning with rage, I held my fingers under a stream of cold water. Rage ran down into my fingers and steamed back up my numb arm, through my wooden throat, and through the crushed box that was my chest. There was so much rage that had I cut my fingertips and let my blood run out, hot geysers would have spouted. Rage would be

431

left burning in my dead flesh. If they burn me in the electric chair, ashes of rage will heave up from under the quicklime. If they burden me with stones and drown me for a child murderer, rage will rise out of me like bubbles of gases from rotting muck.

"Mother! The baby is whimpering."

"I come . . ." Not "Mom," distancing me with "Mother."

You up there, what do You expect me to do? I am by no means valiant. I hate to touch anything squishy. I'm squeamish about worms. To catch slugs in the garden I put safety collars at the base of plants or put out lids with beer to trap them. I don't ask it of myself to smash them. I feel gut nausea. I've done my part. Why must I take this leech you have adhered to my child's breast and tear him off her? She had just stepped into the water, how could You? You disgust me. You terrify me.

You see how it is with me. Who was it who decided that my education is to come by partings; my discipline by separations? What am I getting out of this but another good-bye? What souvenir is this to replace hope, the womanly aspiration, grand-motherly expectation? Is it my maternal fate to learn how it feels to be left with blood on my hands? Who the hell do You think I am, Lady Macbeth? (The voice of my bitter education said to me he must be killed.)

I rinsed the cup, put the box of boric acid powder into the wrapping paper Cassie had thrown into the wastebasket and slipped the package into my bag with Arie's soiled nightgown, ran hot water over the bottle to be sure nothing clung to it.

Jeremy dearest, you won't forgive me, but the doctor can't be the father to the child forever. The time has come for the girl to become mother to her threatened child. I can't trust you to do this for me, too.

"Slowpoke!" Cassie reached for the bottle and I surrendered it. She stuck the nipple into the incubus mouth and at once it

432

began to suck. I watched the yellow cheeks puff in and out. Hands folded in my lap, I watched the milky level sink.

It was so quiet in the room, my daughter dozing lightly at the far end, we two gossips tending the new baby at the other end, the sound of sucking, a nurse on rubberized shoes going by in the corridor, a last visitor on the stairway, the sound of sucking. The clock in the hallway. Tic. Tic. Tic. Tic. Chomp. Chomp. Tic tic tic tic.

Did I only imagine he stopped and squirmed?

"What an appetite!" Cassie marveled.

Arie said, "He's such a good eater they're putting him in with the regulars tomorrow." Was that pride building — and hope?

"He'll swallow the bottle and all," I said.

Chomp. Chomp.

"How old is Arie?" Cassie whispered.

"She'll be twenty next month. I know. Older parents . . . usually . . ."

"She's always been delicate, like your father's family . . ."

The baby stopped sucking. There was less than an inch left in the bottle. I reached for it. "Why don't you burp him and I'll warm this just a little."

"Let me do it."

"No, I'll do it," I said too loudly, and yanked the bottle from her.

"You two carry on like nervous spinsters. You're spoiling him rotten. Big as he is I'll never be able to manage him myself." Arie had raised herself on her elbow and was watching us, a maternal glow on her peaked face. "I think he looks less jaundiced today, don't you, Mom?"

"A little, dear. That goes away."

How much *did* she guess? Everyone is so adroit at self-deception. My friend Hannah used to say "I think my little brother is improving. He looked at me quite intelligently this morning." Absalom had to hand me my heart before I admitted the evidence. Paul had to draw me a picture.

I washed the bottle thoroughly, letting hot water overflow in it. I pressed every grain of residue out of the nipple, then poured the formula I had left in the glass into the bottle, rinsed the glass and returned Arie's toothbrush to it.

"Here, give him to me, it's my turn," I said, and lifted the bundle from her.

"Don't fight, Nannies," Arie said, "you can take turns holding my dolly. I can see I'm going to have too much help."

A pulse throbbed in the thin skin at his forehead. I pressed my finger on it as if that would stop its action. His breath puffed in and out of his broad nose. My heart felt like suet in a net. "Come then and take this last warmth." He sucked strongly.

Would he begin to scream horribly? Would the nurse be able to tell? Would they pump his stomach and save him? How long does it take? Time is relative. This is forever. Everything is relative. Dilemmas are relative. One may choose to die by refusing to commit an act necessary to a loved one's survival, or kill the sense of self by committing a dreadful act.

Would it be awful for the poor little cannibal? Would his last sensation be pain? How much could he feel with his low-grade nervous system?

My grandson went on sucking.

"Was your mother here today?" Cassie asked.

"Jessica drove her here this afternoon. She brought stewed prunes for Arie's bowels. Jeremy told her not to come out again in this weather, promised he'd make chicken soup himself and spoon-feed Arie . . ."

Cassie smiled.

434

"He's so good to the whole family, what a friend," Cassie said.

Look what I've done, good family friend. I swear, if it comes out, I'll confess. I'm grown-up now. It's all over with Romeo and Juliet. It's finished with Antony and Cleopatra. I can read Lear now.

"Is she taking care of Benjamin?"

"Benjamin is probably taking care of her. Or she's beating him at chess."

"Cheating probably," Arie mumbled from the bed. "Grandma hates losing."

Who doesn't? Seconds dropped like water from a dripping faucet.

Plop. Plop. Arie dozed. Sighed. The baby closed its slant eyes.

Was he changing color? In a burst of panic I put my hand over his open mouth and protruding tongue. Breath whiffled out of his porcine nose. Warm and wet. If I suffocated him would it be faster? Would it show? He turned his head away from my molesting hand. A muscle cord tightened on the neck, the neck with the built-in loll. Give up, boy, I'm bigger. My course is set. If this doesn't work I'll have to push you off a cliff, and quickly, before my child's love gives you nine lives!

Cassie was watching me. She shook her head resignedly. "It would be a mercy if he got sick . . . they are subject to pulmonary infections," she whispered.

I've passed you too, my radical aunt. This is my stand against cannibalism. I've shot past Mercy Falls and am being carried inside a barrel over Niagara. Good-bye to you too, dear, dear Jeremy. I'll miss you terribly. I'll be so alone. So alone. There are not years enough left in me to make an honest enemy like you.

It was Delly who came in for the baby.

"What's the doctor doing without you in delivery, Delly?"

"I'm just helping round up the lambs. It's Hennessey's night off and we're short-handed. Molly checked in with a cold and Doctor sent her home."

She held up the bottle. "Piglet, not much left for nurse."

"He's fast asleep," I said. "He won't give you any trouble."

"Bless the little man," she said.

Why could I not say amen?

* * *

"*The* screaming! *The* crying!"

"And everything must agree in gender? So much attention to sex! It's worse than the boys' locker room," Aaron complained.

I leave to scientists the explanation of how old memory cells stumble to attention and file out in their own peculiar order. I have scarcely recovered from encountering myself as a freshly bereaved grandmother, only to find myself in the flick of — the screaming, the crying — with my late son Aaron, who is studying German. He wears a parachutist's uniform. *"Das Leben,* life, is neuter? There must be some logic in German gender that I am not getting."

"The life or *a* life. In English one may speculate on life and death, man and woman, love and longing, but not in German. Nothing is polymorphous or relative, nothing is free of objectness."

"No meandering off with your mother, Aaron, if you are to memorize the prepositions governing the dative case," Adam said.

We hoped the war would end before the boys of Aaron's year were sent over. We hoped Churchill and Roosevelt would bomb the rails to the concentration camps. But Europe and its civilization went on being carried away on Hitler's cattle cars. Aaron went. We never had an opportunity to go on with the conversation.

The screaming! *The* crying! Oh those revealing, uninnocent

436

definite articles, rigidly possessed by their declensions; their nouns weighed down with thingness like guard and prisoner casting shadows on one another. You might think them merely linguistic residues like shards found at the mutilated feet of caryatids. But in German every construction is encased in objectness.

For some weeks after he was reported missing I was haunted by a bizarre physical craving — like a pregnant woman driven by a relentless desire for, say, raspberries in midwinter — to continue the conversation about definite articles. I had a sharp illusion that if I could do so, Aaron would be found alive. (Needless to say, I suffered from the suspicion that I was being punished for the murder I had committed.)

When the news of Aaron's death came, Jeremy took me in and let me lean on him. He was like one of those trees lumbermen call *wolf* trees, so vital they twist their thick trunks to regain light when obstructions have cut off access from the original direction.

There were our wounds in the foreground; his unfathering and my ungrandmothering. We tried to act as we always had — distancing pain by laying on intellect, masking and anesthetizing suffering by debate and analogy. Quarreling in the tradition of our forefathers by formal arguments. The blood seeped through, of course. Sometimes it spurted through our defenses.

He sniffed and cupped his hand over his eye patch. "Speak to me, Ariadne, say something distractingly literary."

"Would you say that Raskolnikov was ridding the world of a couple of old bloodsuckers?" (I had slipped right into blood.)

"Better try for a safer topic, Ariadne, that one won't do."

(Where could I go from there but, "Would you, Alyosha,

consent to be the architect of a social edifice built on the body of a child?") "Your turn, Jeremy," I said.

"If the species is to survive," he began, "science must impress on us that everything impinges on everything. A new ethic, if not a mythology, must arise, based on data. For example, one drop of botulism bacillus dissolved in billions of gallons of drinking water can infect a city. A single drop of blood is composed of more molecules than there are people in the world. No wonder Lady Macbeth couldn't wash it off her hands."

Back at blood again. We both groaned.

"Would you be willing to concede that what seemed cruel or anarchic, Jeremy, might be logical within a larger system?"

He heard the note of pleading in my voice. "My poor dear, how can we tell? We can't trust people to invent an ethic in relation to their own convenience. You have seen what can happen when an individual embryo deviates from the race's norm; when, as the textbooks say, ontogeny fails to properly recapitulate phylogeny. May it not also be true on the only moral plane we know?" He hardened again. "No, Ariadne, I do not concede a larger system in which murder is forgiven."

"I don't expect forgiveness, since I wouldn't withdraw my act if I could. Can't you understand I think it would be *im*moral to allow Arie to be sacrificed to a hopelessly deficient child? It's like that awful joke again, about a Jewish mother who killed a healthy chicken to make soup for a sick one. What kind of morality is it to kill off the young and healthy in war, or spend society's best resources and energies tending the sick? No. No."

"You are willing to make a judgment as to who shall live? Perhaps no Jews? No poor athletes? No eccentrics? What about the Symposium and Phaedo, transcendent reality, life essences, did all that become Greek foolishness to you, Ariadne?"

"It isn't that theoretical, Jeremy. To keep a defective child alive we must intervene with nature. Left to nature such a child would die. Chickens, stupid chickens, don't let a sick rooster procreate. They peck to death the weak and unable."

"So now we are to model civilization on stupid chickens?"

"I don't think of myself as outside nature. In my garden I thin out what comes up spindly, I snip side buds, thwart excessive fertility by pruning. I have the obligation to nurture what I have brought into being, including my child, and not to burden the world with it. In my garden I use traps, sprays . . ."

"Your garden has misled you." He stood by me, his big hand patted my hair. "You are shouting, Arnie. Better for your nerves and mine if we stop disputing this." My old Doctor Mirabilis put on his white coat. "Time for rounds." One hand on the door he asked, "Any word from Arie?"

"She writes that she'll stay in Mexico after she divorces Jethro. She may go to art school in San Miguel de Allende."

*   *   *

I would not have believed it, but as far as I know, Arie is the only one of my children who has fulfilled the cycle of bloom. When she married Jethro and gave up art school, she seemed slated to become one of those dabbling, tyrannical beauties who has too easy a life. But a random genetic fallacy, a flaw of numbering in the chromosomes humbled her. The chemistry, or alchemy, of grief, working on her depths, brought new possibilities to the surface. Arie is a wife, a mother and a dedicated painter. Ah yes, such satisfying grandchildren!

We were on the terrace — Adam, Arie and I — (a daughter is a daughter all her life). Adam was recovering from surgery and Arie had come to help in her loyal Casca-like fashion. Sour. After three days of moody weather dragging at Adam's stitches and keeping Arie restive, they were both tired. Now the sky was where it ought to be — very far away — and father and daughter were beginning to lift, too.

439

"Things are going very well at the office without me," Adam said. "Benjamin has a good grip on the essentials. We can be proud of our son, little mother."

"Takes after his dad," Arie said, "which should mean you have no excuse for hurrying back to the office before you're fully recovered."

"Arie is right," I added. "Get your strength back. Benjamin called to say he would be here Friday, so you'll have the weekend to go over matters and advise him. Someone remind me to ask him to get the dory back to the dock. It's floated down under the bridge. Our neighbor, Ike, went for bass and didn't tie it up well. He asked when Danny and Dinah were coming to stay. Oh gosh . . ." I groaned. They both looked up.

"Are those my pink water lilies I see floating free on the pond? Dammit, the muskrats must have snipped them."

"The least they could do is eat the evidence," Adam said.

"You're funny, Dad." Arie laughed appreciatively.

"The mailman says they store the roots at the bottom of the pond. I've never been able to prove that. Maybe if I row out when the light is straight overhead I could see."

"Not in the sun. You're no spring chicken, Mother."

"No dear, I'm not, thank goodness. I'll be fifty-five come Aquarius."

Warm air was rising and bearing odors, pollens and streamers of white-winged geometrids. "If those moths all give out with eggs there will not be a green leaf in the county next summer. I'd better spray." I regretted the remarks at once.

"You really should sell this place. It is too much responsibility." She relented a bit. "Except it's home to Danny and Dinah. . . . You should not be drinking the coffee black, Dad, let me get you some hot milk." (Sometimes Arie reminds me of my aunt Giselle with her edicts.)

"I like it black, dear. But Ike and I want to know when the children can come."

"Just what the doctor ordered, Dad. Two wild Indians! I don't know where they get their energy. From Mother, I bet." Her tone was not admiring. (It gave me a turn reminding me how my mother had loomed.)

Adam intuitively tried to mediate the tension between us, a tension that rose without either of us willing it. "Fortunately for you, her genetic bundle, as she calls it, includes her energy." He smiled. "Objectively, Arie, anyone would consider *your* energy remarkable. Am I mistaken or were you at your easel when I came down for a cup of tea after midnight?"

"I've gotten a late start," Arie said. Then she blushed at having revealed so much.

"Why don't you bring the children here after July camp?" I asked.

"Good thinking, Arnie," Adam said, "they can keep me amused until school opens. We guys have a playhouse to finish."

"No carpentering for you, Dad."

"I'll supervise while they do the hard work."

"Won't that be too much for you, Mom?"

"They aren't too much for me. They seem to have a tacit understanding of when I may turn dangerous. I'll work them to the bone, picking berries, making jam with me, when they aren't building with Grandpa. Daniel can help me dig up the tulips and divide the iris Siberica by the pond. He's strong for nine and he likes to garden with his grandma. You and Ricardo go to the seashore. Maybe Provincetown. You might enjoy taking some classes too, with Edwin Dickinson or Hans Hoffmann."

"I think you're milky in the filberts, Mom." The mother of my grandchildren suddenly shone like a teenager again. "The whole family accepts your offer." When she saw I caught her look of gratitude her glance skimmed away. She put down her embroidery. "Sit. I'll go pick the peas before you come to your senses and change your mind."

Her beauty still took me by surprise. Not seductive herself, she evoked the idea of seduction and violation. Even in this heat she looked cool as a corsage in a florist's refrigerator.

I watched her pass through a bank of Hemerocallis in all shades of mahogany, yellow and orange, until she broke into pointillist dots. The sun was so brilliant the Father Hugo roses faded with her, whiter than white butterflies. How delightful, how exquisite she is and this is, I thought. It is a limited triumph over chaos and isolation. But it is not altogether nothing. Something has been made by me.

I remember the next moment with the dazzling clarity of light cutting through lily blades, perhaps because I had never heard so much from Adam of fear and feeling. He threw his arms wide as if he wanted to embrace the light, the scene, me. "I want to live!"

His hand made a gesture that would have been a caress on my cheek if it had reached me across the table. "I want to live . . . with you . . ."

". . . with you . . ." I answered . . . as if there had never been a plot beneath my skin, as if I were not crisscrossed with tunnels, as if half a century had not severed me hourly from my innocent start when out-and-inner parts rang like one bell . . . "with Benjamin . . . with Arie . . . with Daniel . . . with Dinah . . . our whole family."

He sank back, and picked up the office papers.

It was the best I could do, honestly.

The gate to the vegetable garden clicked behind Arie.

*   *   *

Too bad. Just about when we were getting the hang of living together — not in an imaginary realm, succeeding or failing in comparison with fabricated existences — but each in our own

442

isolation; just when we were quite prepared to have things go badly and had developed the fortitude to accept our malformed, stunted natures and to hobble along together, he died. I trust my father's Zohar-Kabalism proves out hereafter: "that soul continuously reborn, continuously improves."

Adam died as he had lived; alone and in an adopted country. I saw him last in an airport. He was on his way to Israel, where he had become involved in creating a computer-training program. I was walking beside him toward the passenger gate when an involuntary sound welled out from deep inside him. Whether success, losses, the pressures of illness and passing time had opened him to his emotions, the sound was like ice breaking up.

"I wish you would come with me, next time," he said.

"I think I will," I answered.

Passersby saw a distinguished white-haired gentleman hook his cane over his arm, the better to take a haggard-faced woman into his embrace.

Nothing Is Perfect

What I should like to write is a book about nothing; a book dependent on nothing external, which would be held together by the strength of its style . . . a book which would have almost no subject, or at least in which the subject would be almost invisible.

— GUSTAVE FLAUBERT

I AM AN OLD woman sitting in my garden, newspaper in hand, bird-glasses at the ready. It is a morning in May. The bees are rising and falling in the flowering raspberry hedge.

The nesting silence is broken. From nurseries in the eaves, shrubs, trees, reeds, the clamor conveys that the young have emerged from their shells. Open beaks must be stuffed and stilled, stuffed and stilled. Voracious hunger of the hatched drives male and female to the task. From light to dark, parent wings dive, curve, dip, scarcely pausing in the portal-to-portal supply line. The courting wings fray and tatter. That's all right too. It's the season for that.

There are alerts and alarms. A squirrel to chase. A jay to harry. The caw of a flock of marauding crows sets up a commotion in the reeds and on the pond. I hear the mallard. I know her. I have spied on her secret early swims, and now that the

445

ducklings are hatched, on her clever teaching and huddling. She is flying low. She makes a sortie, a circular flight, quacking softly. It sounds imploring. I put aside the *Village Voice* and adjust binoculars. I watch her find one duckling and lead it to the shallows under the footbridge. Again she circles, lamenting. She finds one more. Again. So it goes. I count with her into the afternoon. There are two who will not be found. At dusk she is lamenting still.

The calamity goes unnoticed. A slight shift in the balance of nature.

The *Village Voice* is folded back on a description of a commune being investigated by the Boston police on the complaint of parents who have lost grown children to it and of neighbors who accuse it of deranged practices and child abuse. Its chief, alleged sultan and torturer, is a sinister guru of over forty. The picture shows young women dressed in attic-salvaged velvet, lace assemblages and some scabby, wolfish little starvelings, none of whom look like my grandchildren, I think. For that matter, how would I know what Absalom looks like?

Had it been Absalom it is possible I would not have recognized him. Who can recognize anyone from civilian life among these thankless macrobiotic starvelings masquerading in identical shaven skulls and pigtails, these jiggling skeletons uniformed in saffron sheets and tee shirts, begging for "bread" on the infectious technological sidewalks. No, I will not drive to Boston to have just one more look.

I do allow myself to imagine you, Aaron my son. You have become Dr. Arkady, professor of comparative European literature. Why not? You always had a flair for languages. You have developed chunkiness with your degrees and the academic life. You've come for the weekend to the dacha, with your family.

You enter on prepositions that take the dative case. Now you are *auf dem Pfad.* I wave at you as you come *durch meinen blauen Garten.* (Blue is very becoming to your fair complexion.) Now you are *gegenüber* the far wall of delphinium, *zwischen dem veronica, bei dem carpatica* and now *entgegen* a cove of blue lupine and columbine. You bend and pick a bell of platycodon and ring it. Your teddy-bear children, a son and daughter in the proper order — why not? — swim waist-deep through pools of artemesia and santolina, leap the lavender border and disappear, *auf Wiedersehen,* beyond the dark wave of juniper. "Your grandma and I want to chat," you say. How tractable are the dead.

You light your pipe. The tobacco is on the sweet side. "As you were saying, Mother . . . about agreement of modifiers."

There seems to be an odor in the air, reminiscently female, an odor of ritual blood. Mine, though I am long done with, done with the womb. It is faint but persistent, like iron-rust stains and unfulfilled desires. I confess that after the president's black news came, among my prayers — that you died quickly and without torture — was one: that you had spent manhood without constraint of modifiers definite or indefinite, before you leaped behind your cousins' lines, and that a child of yours lives. It's a gardener's morality. One flower, unseen, can verify the cycle and keep a variety from extinction.

"What are you teaching this term, my shaggy pony?" I ask.

"Robbe-Grillet," you say patiently. You were always patient. Suffered less from the uselessly brilliant intuitions that tormented Absalom and irritated Benjamin.

"Why are you crying, Mother," you would say, "we won the war."

"You call that winning?"

Robbe-Grillet? The German Zeitgeist has become our esthetic and our politics. To hatred, fear and helplessness the victims have added intellect! From the theater of cruelty, from

447

Nouvelle Vague film, no civilizing course can emerge. This is not the old-fashioned pornography from which, steeped in post-coital sadness, drained, aching, both sexes might wake instructed, refreshed and repentant, if even only slightly, as if what they had done had meaning.

Aaron would interrupt me. "The Marquis de Sade was French, not German."

This consuming of people is not the old cannibalism. There is no priest who sacrifices and in turn becomes the sacrifice. The warrior does not eat in awe the heart of the enemy, a frenzied logic in the knowledge that cannibalism has led before and may again, to consecrated cannibalism. From genocide we cannot come through merciful ambages and confrontations full of grace to a human answer."

Aaron would take his pipe out of his mouth, shake his head and say, "Still protecting yourself, like the good Germans, from the meaning of the Holocaust, Mom. You are still a Utopian." But he would look at me affectionately, so I can go on.

Robbe-Grillet! You are glorifying an obscene lifestyle that affirms the torturer and the death camp. See how he concentrates on objects with the ardor of a police interrogator. How he bombards the senses with vulnerable images . . . a child with soft hair, the nape of the neck . . . until the eyes swim, imagination convulses, the vision fills the scene excluding any detail that might allay terror; the way torturers pitilessly bombard a victim with light; the way a glowing tip of a cigar to a person chained to two rings set in stone dissolves the universe, the high compassion for its hungers, to a fiery point.

"Read all about it in the *Daily News,*" he would whisper as he faded.

Open the damned book on a sequence of images. His world: "woman flesh, exposing nape, subject of excessive command, slit thighs, ripped skirt, violent hand, tender slope of loin, leather whip, breasts of wax, iron manacle, dog collar, glowing

448

tip of cigar, vaginas parted wide forced open, two rings set in stone, prison, captive, chain, doomed. Long torture." Such savagery can never redeem the isolation against which we must continuously struggle.

His voice reaches me. Or is it my grandson's? "He's telling it like it is."

Pain. Unbearable pain is what our history has been leading to. Midwives. Mothers. Women artists. Monstrousness has been sown on us over and over again. Our wombs must refuse it.

*   *   *

Arie stood half in, half out the door.

"Mother, are you quite sure you don't mind our staying through dinner?"

"Be assured once more, Arie. Nothing to it. Salad and herbs from the garden. A cheese omelet. Dinah will whip it up — rolls and a cherry pie from the freezer, or fresh peaches and strawberries. I'd worry about you driving through traffic in this heat."

"Yes and it's too hot for you to have gone out into the garden. I saw you with your clippers. You shouldn't, you know. You are over seventy."

"I know, I'm no spring chicken . . . but the garden is overgrown." I sighed. "I don't mind the heat half as much as you do. Come out and sit down."

She looked wan, and, as usual, tense. Her toes (unpolished) gripped the sandal thongs like a runner poised for the starter's shot.

"Did Daniel and Dinah go off with Benjamin to play tennis? Ugh. I don't know how they do it, even at their age. Speaking of age, remember my friend Irene, the flautist? She's having another baby. She's forty-five — maybe forty-four. Can't be more than three years younger than I am. Her children are practically grown. The youngest is in college."

449

"Probably has a younger lover," I said, "and wants the baby."

"Mother!"

"Why not? A man can rejuvenate by taking a younger wife . . . start the family cycle over again. A woman can prove she can still get pregnant."

"Isn't there an increased danger of birth defect? Mongolism and such?"

"Statistically, yes." My heart ballooned up in my chest. Minutes ticked. A pollened bee hit a dephinium so hard it trembled. Did she know? Did she not? Would she probe? Now?

She perched on the arm of a wicker chair. "Whatever happened to Jeremy? He must be ancient if he's alive."

"He isn't. His hospital was closed. Neighborhood got dangerous."

"I drove past the hospital one day," Arie said. "That was years ago," she added hastily.

We looked away from each other, both attentive to the bees mumbling and bumbling up and down the overcrowded blooms like an old vacuum cleaner doing draperies.

"It was boarded up, a wreck surrounded by garbage and rubble. A section of the building had been broken open where the lobby used to be. Motorcycles and leather-jacketed toughs had commandeered it. Weren't you two very good friends?"

"I wish I had been a better one. From the time he delivered my first, we talked to each other almost every day, for years. Around the time you had . . . when he delivered your . . . first . . ."

"That was 1941," she supplied.

"He and I had a couple of serious differences . . . My fault . . . all mine. We patched them up and we saw each other after that, too. But then we had one we didn't patch up . . . and we weren't close after that."

"Do you know where he went after he closed up?"

450

"He never left the hospital. Molly told me."

"Who is Molly?" she asked.

"One of Jeremy's nurses . . . in charge of special cases."

She got up and walked to the door. "I must get back to work. I'd like more new canvases for my show, and November is not so far off as it seems today."

"It's too hot. Why don't you go for a swim?"

"Oh Mother, don't nag!" She slammed the door behind her.

I had been buying a Madame Alexander doll for Dinah, so it must have been fifteen years ago at least.

"Grandchildren keeping you busy, Mrs. Arkady?" and then in her straight tough Molly way, "We were mighty surprised not to see you at Doctor's funeral. Hundreds of his patients came from all over with their children . . . and you, such an old, dear friend . . ."

"Oh no! Oh no! . . ." The toy window blurred. "Why didn't someone call me? I didn't see an announcement. I must have been traveling. I always begin the newspaper with the obits. Was it in the Long Island paper? His new office must have been out near his daughter."

"No, he talked about that move but never made it. He never left the hospital," she said.

"I didn't think he'd just retire."

"I didn't say he retired. He never left the hospital, is what I said. Wouldn't leave, boarded up as it was. Kept his apartment. You must remember his apartment . . . He had his records and papers there. Said he wanted to write some articles. He'd never had time to write — always too busy in the delivery room." Molly let me have it straight: "That's where they found him, Mrs. Arkady, at the door of the delivery room. He must have been taking a shower. The faucets were not quite turned off. Maybe he thought he heard the emergency bell. You know

451

how he used to come flying. Ran so fast for such a big man. Took the stairs down. A bath towel was on the stairway. He was naked. Naked, Mrs. Arkady. Naked as one of his own . . ."

In my thin dream, Jeremy, it was a dream hospital, Presbyterian, polished marble and brass, wide stairways, nothing immigrant and up-from-poverty about it. But the cast was the same: hangers-on, unemployed cousins, the schlump your younger sister married, some friend of mine who needed a job. We were sitting down to supper. My place was set next to yours, but you were not there. "Where is he?" I became anxious. "Delivery room, I suppose." Your brother-in-law with the 20–100 eyeglasses went on chewing your substance. "Where else?" "Does he ever sit down to eat?" Your sister sighed. She also went on chewing.

I heard you say, from a high distance, "Come find me. Let's not play childish games of hide-and-seek. I know I said it's all over, go away. I meant I ache all over. The doctor has terrible pains, Ariadne, come and see me. Now or never. Come and see me now or never . . ."

I pushed back my chair and began to run. I was in my bare feet. There was so little nakedness between us, even that felt exposed.

In the dream I ran, bare feet slipping and sliding on the grand staircase. There were obstructions everywhere. My father in a top hat. A clown carrying a wedding cake, the tiered kind, with bride and groom dolls on top.

I missed the elevator on the second floor. Black cables coiled and vibrated in the open shaft. The next flight of stairs was narrower. It was slippery, fraught with menace. The corridor narrowed. Hospital beds wheeled past. I scanned them, looking for I don't know whom. Nurses carrying babies obstructed the landing. I made a sinister turn. I was in a ladies' room. A nun

452

had her back to me and waved me away in the mirror. "What did you know of sacred love?" she said.

The stairs became footholds like an Indian cliff dwelling. I am afraid of heights but I climbed, vertiginous. An elevator opened before me, enclosed in glass like a hearse in Pisa, like a shaky elevator in an old French hotel. It trembled upward. Sweat poured from me; ran down my legs. I had to make an effort to contain my urine. The door opened. I stepped almost into air; before me was a narrow cleft like a battlement aperture, far below blood-red earth, far above ice-blue mist.

"Doctor. Doctor." I called and from a distance you answered, "Doctor me no doctors."

I found you lying in an alcove small as a labor room, on a hospital bed, the metal showing at the raised back, the bedding slumped down into the center with you. Your bulk had decreased. You removed the oxygen tubes and pipes from your mouth and nose. They left wounds. "You are the only doctor I know. You know how to do these things," I said, and fell against you crying, "Doctor, doctor!"

You put your arm around me (it was still heavy) and pressed me against your chest. "Ariadne, you found me," you whispered.

Real tears soaked into my hair.

Everyone knows bad dreams are vanity. I was a bad dream. How *could* I have done it? Rather the question is, how *should* I have done it? Did you have nothing to do with it? Am I letting myself off too lightly when I say maybe you were sending some of the cut-off message? After all the gory hairy animality of lowing woman, calving, is it possible you were sending an unconscious message of clothedness to me? I proved not too difficult to undress. Father in heaven, forgive me, but didn't part of you want it that way?

Our last scene was preposterous. You didn't think for one

453

moment I was pregnant by Adam. You knew it was Paul's.
(That alertness to every state of being in the one you love.)

"Doctor," I said, "I'm pregnant." "Patient," you said, "how
long?" "Two months." "Not by your husband," you said. I
said, "I was raped." You said, "Did you tell Adam?" Same
question as Paul. "No," I said.

"According to Mosaic law it is not rape unless you screamed.
I would have heard you if you had screamed."

You sat with lamplight quivering on your jowls, hand shield-
ing your good eye. You said, mocking our formal state, "The
Hippocratic oath forswears abortofacients. I guess I am for-
sworn. I'll do the abortion, of course. Can't let the nurses know.
One of them might be religious enough to send me to prison."

Silence. Sniff. Silence. Sniff.

You put your big, benevolent paw down on the table. Your
eye took me in. The burning spear, as it came at Cyclops, could
not have glittered more. "After which, Ariadne, go away. You
hear me, do you not? Go away. You can't have everything."
The light went out. "Love must stop short of suicide." Ever the
good father, you added, "That holds for you and Paul, too."

Once in Sicily where I had gone with Arie to look at the
mosaics in Monreale:

The owner of a restaurant at a cash box. (Don't be offended,
Jeremy, a lot of cash passed between us.)

He was a big man, simian, heavy-lidded with high expressive
brows. Not at all the cut of the poor Sicilians who steeraged it
to the fruit and vegetable pushcarts of the new world. He was
one of those whose ancestors had come by way of Carthage and
the Norman conquerors. Heavy-boned, heavy quiet hands, he
sat behind a desk, a green light catching his jowls and big nose.
Too coincidentally, he wore a black eye-patch. Life often
overdoes.

454

A waiter passed a tray in front of him. He sniffed, without looking up. Another. A woman went by. His nostrils trembled. His flesh seemed to swell outward and enclose him the way an elephant might pulse in his skin, uncommonly still yet communicating total alertness.

Voices rose in the kitchen. Louder. Without a preparatory ripple, he roused into motion, like you, adrenalin-tuned even in repose.

Oh my dear, from the ruined tower all the bells rang. Hennessey . . . Delehanty! Emergency . . . And quite as if a bank of lilies hit by blazing sun had poured out sweetness faintly fetid with ether, I had the sensation that I was lifted and you were carrying me, still carrying me, to safety in your arms.

Timing, dearest Jeremy, timing is of immense importance. Don't you agree?

Arie returned with a propitiatory pitcher of iced tea. Fluttery as a moth beating against a lamplit window, she returned to the subject of Jeremy.

"He delivered all of us?"

"Yes, mine and yours, too." But why count now, child?

"He must have been a young man when you first met."

"Younger than you are now, Arie. But he looked like Methuselah to me."

"That's odd. I remember him as attractive, like a hearty Russian uncle from the country. But I suppose you and I prefer reticent formal types like Dad and Ricardo." She poured, slipped a sliver of lemon over the edge of the glass, pinched a sprig of mint, brought the tea to me, walked nervously away before she added, "Your friend Paul also made a very correct impression."

Considering your haughty, scrupulously reactionary husband, I thought, the apple hasn't rolled out of sight of the tree, has it?

What was she thinking, my princess, clasping and unclasping her hands and pacing — pale, feline and ravenous-looking with that alluringly icy presence that affects some men like glass mountains.

"Mother, how old were you when . . . your first . . . my brother . . . was born?" Arie made a shaky errand of putting our glasses back on the tray.

"It's all right, you can say Absalom. I haven't forgotten his name."

"You know, Mom" (the telltale child), "I still look for him on the streets. It's absurd to think I'd recognize him, but I visualize how a person I knew as a child might look as a grownup. One keeps . . ." She fluttered away, then beat her way back. "Would it be a relief to know he had died?"

"It's hard to imagine what I would feel. Long grief? Short grief? But to answer what I can, I was not quite nineteen when Absalom was born."

"My age when I had my first . . ."

At the collapse of reticence, my daughter, the bereaved mother, was suddenly filmed in sweat cold as that on the iced-tea pitcher. She picked up the tray. "I guess I will go for a swim." This time the door closed quietly.

Paul watching Arie maneuver her car into the driveway, and ease out, shapely legs exposed to the thigh; his eye more Delacroix than Manet. ("Manet's eye sweeps the subject, Delacroix's mind centers the subject.") Innocent objectivity was not his condition at that moment. I've forgotten why I had not been able to meet him, but being crossed had made him belligerent.

"Can't come? Must meet the handyman?" Minutes earlier he had arrived like an assault, a burning arrow. "Leave with me this minute or I'll, I'll run off with your daughter."

That's the kind of joke that is the death of an emotion.

How is it with you at night, Arie? Do you stare at the ceiling? Do you read in your twin bed while your conscientious Americanized husband, aloof behind his excellent spirits and consistent prejudices, sleeps in his? Should I wish you a formidable passion that will crack you and melt you and expose your core to yourself before all is wrenched from you? I tell you, everything is taken away. You don't want to die with the look of "Do not touch. It is forbidden." If you made a sound pressing your feelings into existence, would it be a howl of hunger? Is it painful to set so much into motion and then be unable to get at it, as if you were outside a glass window, looking in at a feast you had paid for, like Proust attending his own parties only by report?

Overhead, a sharp white trail crystallized behind an invisible jet plane, spread fake feather clouds and drifted out of high blue to streaked pinks and grays. A swarm of midges rose from the grass in a faint mist. A light sunset breeze picked up stray nicotiana odors and dropped them. Arie paced, casting a glance in my direction and withdrawing it.

Perhaps in relation to Arie I have also misconstrued everything. It is possible that she has, as they say nowadays, "found herself" in her work; that she has traded the warm sensuous gratifications of personal life for the boilings and freezings of art; that her impassioned concentration, her self-doubts, her

457

triumphs shut out consciousness of most of the outer world, in the way obsessive love does. Perhaps she never speaks of herself of her own accord because she has no need for the emotions of intimacy that I desired. As far back as I can remember, her reserves left me, at best, peering discourteously through accidental chinks into a darkness she had no wish to light up. Nor do I preclude the possibility that she and Ricardo are in personal agreement on how life should be lived; their common pact as stable as mine with Daniel and Dinah. It might well be that a formidable passion isn't of any interest to her. People like Arie, like my father, like Adam, and yes, Jeremy too, with an inherent or inherited sense of stringency — the kind an Eskimo might feel in a rounded white igloo, carving a piece of white seal tusk, duplicating a pattern of snowflakes resembling each other, infinitely, if only slightly varied — a way of life that can be thoughtful in its orderliness, perhaps elegant, but is also sparse. It may explain why Arie's show has canvases of white-on-white.

My daughter, grown woman, secret adult, I wonder if it strikes her as tragic that there is so little we know about each other. I am seventy-two and by now Arie is no spring chicken either, but I can't ask her if she and her father shunned intimacy and never desired it, or were helpless to achieve it. We have found no way we can see past our surfaces into the subterranean depths where a dead child and a cup of poison float.

*   *   *

The cork popped, champagne foamed and hissed as Ricardo ceremoniously filled our glasses. "*Bonne chance, ma chérie,*" he said, kissing Arie lightly on the cheek.

"One giant step for all womankind," Jessica saluted. "May you sell every canvas."

"If she does, she can dash backstage and sign a couple of blank canvases," Benjamin teased. "Here's to you, sis."

Arie lifted her glass. Was it to me? "Without whom . . ." she

458

said. Her mouth, so precisely like Adam's, shaped a blown kiss.

Without whom, eh?

She stood holding the glass as if it were a flower, the man's shirt falling plumb from her shoulders. She looked so much like the girl telling us she was going to marry Jethro, it was hard to think of her as a woman of fifty-two. (On that day, had I been a woman of experience or, better yet, self-esteem, I would have terminated the brief happy love affair with Paul instead of bowing to his lash.)

"Here's to Grandma, the 'vamp.' " Daniel said.

They all raised their glasses to me and beamed. Suppose they could see that haunting cup, that hissing potion I had dared to mix. Would they disown me? Would they say I had falsified everything in our relationships: grandmother, mother, cousin, mother-in-law? Would they recognize me, the confirmed coward who had lived a life of compromises dominated by fear amounting almost to perversity; the woman who could probably count on the fingers of one hand the number of times she had dared to act as a person of independent relationships to herself and others?

Suppose Paul happened to be gallery-hopping and recognized the name: Ariel Arkady Cordovero. (He had heard it once and though he rearranged details feverishly, he never forgot any.) Would I recognize the shapely soft mouth under a white mustache, the opaque eyes that could change from camera-shutter objectivity to rolling Othello frenzy? Would he appear in the nimbus of exaltation in which my memory surrounded him? And would he recognize me, a gaunt old woman who looked, as the grandchildren said, like a cross between a silent film star and the dean of St. Paul's?

A milky quicksilver curtain of fog had formed on the gallery window and beaded droplets ran around the raised letters, ORION GALLERY. The headlights of taxis and buses advanced and subsided in rippling waves to the stop-and-go rhythm of traffic lights. Shadowy walkers hurried past like fishes with phosphorescent faces seen through dimly lit water. Someone tall rubbed a circle of mist from the window. A long horsey head nosed against the glass, then swam away. What would I say to Paul? What do you say to someone you adored, to whom you said everything under the illusion you were skin to skin and from whom you discovered you were separated by a leather curtain of delusion; someone who might have been playing a part in Genêt's dream bordello; someone who left you feeling that you were a disguised streetwalker in a shabby barroom ballad that ended, "She was nothing but a fireship rigged out in a disguise."

Ricardo was making the rounds with another bottle. As he moved toward Daniel, who was hanging a picture, Danny looked at his father as if he could gladly run him through with the steel yardstick he had been using. Ricardo winced and swerved. Arie caught the exchange and made a forward step as if to hurl her body between the two. Ricardo gallantly smiled at his wife as if he had not been cut to the brain. It was the kind of courtesy I used to take for granted in Adam.

Benjamin peered at a canvas, then shook his head mournfully. "Dear me. Oh dear me. I see the future of art is in the past. You are sure we haven't hung the thing upside-down?" (Forty-six years old, shockingly white at the temples, he still teases his big sister, and she still adores him and takes it. Like chess pieces are we, each confined to our traditional moves?) "May I ask, love, how art arrived at nothing?"

"Rejection by rejection is how," Arie answered.

"All kidding aside, Arie, it's like an Ashby-Homeostat recording nothing but its own pulse recording nothing but its own pulse ad infinitum."

"*Nothing* is perfect," Arie quipped.

Everyone laughed except Ricardo, who looked as if he had opened the door on a roomful of people who fell silent at his appearance. (Poor fellow, born into Spanish, educated in French, married into English, the nuances of all three inevitably blurred.)

"It's a double-entendre on the word *nothing,* Dad." Dinah's glance trembled between father and brother.

"That is having its point blunted," Danny retorted, firing another shot at his father.

"There's nothing so new about it," I said, "Flaubert wanted to write a book about nothing over a century ago."

"Danny," Arie called, "get Uncle Benjie off my back. Explain why artists have dropped traditional subjects."

"About history, our guru Doberman says the past has no relevance to the future anymore. The world is the end of a sewer, a river of shit," Dinah added.

"Say ordure for Grandma, you creep." Danny put his arm around his sister's shoulder. "You know what, my sister has a fresh mouth," he said cheerfully.

"Danny," Arie called again, "snag Uncle Benjie."

Danny took his declaiming stance. "*Nothing* is not sexy, romantic or embarrassing. *Nothing* wipes the slate clean. *Nothing* is not full of lies about Vietnam." He glared at his father, who glared back.

Jessica, who was setting up the tape deck, called, "If you want some nothing music I've got a John Cage tape of silence."

"*Nothing* leaves too much to the imagination," I said. "I'm going to unpack the supper hamper and we'll all have a little something."

Danny continued to work at offending his father. "Not just Vietnam, it's the whole crock of enclosures we've been sold about sex, physical possessiveness, appropriateness, tradition, virtue, the work ethic."

"What happened to love, meanwhile, Danny?" I asked.

"I can imagine that you, Grandma, would be able to envision the possibility of human encounter so freed from enclo-

461

sures that any two people could sleep together on their own terms."

"When that possibility entered another man's mind about me, it proved catastrophic."

They all laughed, except Ricardo.

"How do you work this newfangledness? Walk up to someone in a single's bar, put a hand on a dimpled butt and say, how about it, honey?" I asked.

Ricardo gasped.

"Leave off the honey and you're close to the spirit of sex as a simple physical act."

"O eff off, Danny," Dinah wailed, "not that shit again. I want more than a quickie in a motel room."

"You insist on a pretense of emotion? I insist that sex is a simple physical act."

Obviously, not much has happened to Daniel from the waist down. I can't wait to hear what he has to say after his head has been instructed by his genitals.

"I find this conversation unbelievable," Ricardo said, and marched off.

"What do you say, Grandma?" Danny asked, his face suddenly sweetly earnest.

"She's not talking," Dinah said.

"What can I say, sweethearts? I only know what I know for myself. Sit we upon the highest throne in the world, yet we do but sit upon our own behind."

"So speak, oracle"

"Oracles are dreadfully terse, and they don't embellish, you know," I said.

They put their arms around me and made a whispering tent. (They were both taller than I.) "Speak. Tell us what you know."

"O.K. There is no *free* sex. Anonymity leaves a roaring emptiness, distaste, pornography and, if not boredom, brutal-

462

ity. Courtships without fondness are like lamentations devoid of sorrow. And the rest is silence until Thanksgiving weekend."

* * *

Sitting on the mourner's bench by my country fire of apple and birch, feeling myself old and uselessly wise, my ankle bones remembered the Charleston.

My grandchildren's dance party had moved to the terrace, it was Thanksgiving, but the night had misted in warm. Dinah and Daniel with other look-alike unisex figurines in unisex jeans, their unisex hair flying, were whirling and twirling in what looked like improvisations. They were not touching. Yet it would not be true to say they were unconnected. They were held together, like a group of Chassidic Jews, by intensity more than structure.

Was I only imagining that I could begin to recognize the outline of lost forms, like a modern archaeologist looking down from an airplane, discerning ancient forms? I was recognizing a step here, the traces of a waltz-two-three, the suggestion of a fox trot. Two formalists were facing each other in a moment of minuet. In a cluster of rhythms I could have sworn the instrumentalist was evoking the billow and dip of Irene and Vernon Castle cresting into the tango. An occasion piece. Miles Davis establishes a structure; the others get with it. Rather like Marianne Moore devising a stanza form that is held for the duration of that poem.

Once Jessica and I were watching Aaron, Arie and Benjamin skim over the lawn, swooping up fallen flower petals like long-legged nesting birds. With cries and flutters they salvaged what we had regarded as compost material: orange crepe-papery poppy, brown-tinged pink magnolia, darkening dogwood crucifixes, fallen stars of lilac. They flew with their treasure to a marble bench and, by some agreement, organized them.

463

"This way . . . no this way . . . it belongs this way . . . that's right . . . no, no, that's wrong . . . oh right . . ."

"Do you get their logic?" Jessica asked.

"It's beyond me, the order of the fallen petals."

The children must have known something we had only begun to sense. They came into it with the air they breathed. It was as if they intuited the exhaustion of the known structures, as if to them it was clear that in the arts the canonical texts were exhausted, as the tonal scales were exhausted, as the forms of our relationships were exhausted.

What will happen to form? What will happen to my grandchildren?

I won't be around to find out. Perhaps it seems more chaotic than it is. It could be as when Shakespeare was Protestant to the Catholic tastes. Forms will be reconciled. The substance of the canons will be melted down and fired with fresh impulses. Some great reconciler will reconcile. New forms will emerge. They will have to be abstract and serious enough to bear intentions and illusions.

What choice, my darlings, but to trust to the compost on the perennial bed?

How I Became an Un-American

I feel the link of nature draw me
Flesh of flesh.

— JOHN MILTON

I HAD CROSSED AND recrossed the railless bridges of alarm for Daniel so often during the night that I was relieved when the hands of my travel clock reached ten to five.

I don't sleep well in hotel rooms. I am overalert to the peripheral: the vibration of the nearby elevator, footsteps neither toward nor away from me, the resonances of the local speech. What is not peripheral is the discomfort in my pelvic area. It may be that I'm too old for restaurant cooking. I had too robust-and-burgundy a dinner with Daniel in a chophouse near the college.

I left him debating with a couple of earnest, soft-bearded classmates: "Production and distribution no longer have the labor value Marx attributed to them. Political power will collect around those who control the movement of information."

"That's what my grandmother here has been saying for years," Daniel said.

The young man looked my way and relegated me to my age.

465

A long-legged girl with unsoiled eyes loped toward us. Daniel leaped up. He'll be all right. I can leave soon.

I got out of bed and paced to ease my discomfort.

My window fronts on a scene with which I shall not grow familiar. As my father used to say, history is never finished with us. But I never thought I'd be sitting out the tag-end of mine in a foreign town. (Ever and always an unwilling tourist, I have found it necessary to cross another border.)

The sky is raw and untinged, almost colorless, like old ice thinning to where a faint translucence slowly intrudes itself, a steel ring gripping the horizon. Below the eastern brink a cold sun, straw-colored as a winter moon, has hammered a first blow that shivers crazed splinters of dawn and skids them across the white frozen clouds.

When has become Now!

I'm adrift on the ice floe of old age. My time is my own, God help me, all my own. What time? I am twice six and sixteen and twenty-nine and the sum of those. (Can that add up? I was never good at arithmetic.) Time past has caught up with future and become present. All mine to be compressed into a placebo to crunch at my end. What was, is fugitive, alas, as the years. I have the utmost difficulty in retracing events. I surrender to retrospections that lose and find me scenes with those I loved. On a word they yield to other scenes, offering me endless alternatives.

I'm tired. Tired of the maze in my head as I am at the sight of my half-packed suitcases. Tired of trying to invent an order for simultaneity. From now on I'm sticking to the chronological.

466

The fact is, I'm on the lam. Grandma is on the lam. It's not my fault this time, Jeremy. I have not run off into a winter wonderland to look for Absalom. You wouldn't believe what I'm doing now, my dear friend. You wouldn't believe that a gardener as experienced as I is transplanting in the dead of winter. It's a risk I felt I had to take.

How did I get here?

*   *   *

It was early Monday morning after Thanksgiving weekend when Arie phoned. "Hello, Mom. I'm not waking you, am I? I can call back."

"Of course not. I've been repotting Christmas cacti for an hour." (I get very attentive and cautious when Arie reverts to calling me Mom.) "Did you make it home all right?"

"Yes, the traffic wasn't bad . . ."

"Why are you up and speaking at the crack of dawn? What's wrong, honey?"

"Daniel. There's a notice from the draft board. He is to report for his physical."

"How is that possible? He has one semester to graduation and his grades are excellent." But I knew how. Too free with his speech. War resisters to the front.

"He won't go."

"Careful! Don't say anything incriminating on the telephone, Arie."

"Mother, sometimes I think you are becoming paranoid."

"The rest of America plays ostrich. Can't happen here! Not in America! Like the German Jews denying the evidence of Hitler."

"It is perfectly legal to go to Canada. You show your birth certificate and walk across."

"I don't trust our American legal eagle. Shall I drive down?"

"No, Mother. I'll come to you. I can't stay over, though. I called Danny and he's coming home late tonight."

My daughter pointed to the first paragraph of the *Manual for Draft-Age Immigrants to Canada*: "Young Americans are coming to Canada to resist the draft . . ."

"I'll check with the peace center. Maybe they have underground information on where he can slip across."

"Mother, do me a favor and forget that hay-wagon nonsense."

I took the pamphlet from her hand. "How about this? 'Prohibited Classes: Political Subversives.' Would you agree Danny qualifies? Or this heading in the table of contents: 'Try Not to Get Kicked Out or Sent Back.' Let's see, it says here: 'Draft-age Americans are often refused legitimate information and given incorrect versions of the law by self-appointed recruitment officers . . . Canadian-American consulate staff . . .' Fie fo fum, I smell bribed border Cossacks . . ."

"Maybe he can go up on a ski train. I'm sure they don't check a trainful of college kids," she said.

We were both silent. (Women, with their postpartum lives!) I waited for the end of her fingertip tattoo the way I used to wait for Adam's. Then I said, "It's an idea. But what will he do when he leaves the train, go from ski lodge to ski lodge?"

She didn't answer. I flipped through the pamphlet. "Listen to this: 'Even if the visitor *does* have money, the officers may suspect that he intends to stay permanently, if he is vague.' So it's no good if they suspect, eh? He's not welcome to just stay. Maybe the Canadian police get a few American rubles to hand a boy back."

"Mother, he can go as a tourist." Two tears escaped from the outer corners of her eyes, and lay like icy dew among the

468

delicate freckles darkening against her pallor. A chilled lily, moments before its blanched petals tremble and fall.

"No, Arie, not by himself. A young man who has received his draft notice is not just a tourist. He is an outlaw — wanted by the U.S. authorities. Until his status is settled he must look like a bona fide visitor, not someone emigrating."

(I did not mention my son-in-law, the Catholic, whose banner blazoned, *Not peace I bring, but a sword.*)

"It's premature to talk about emigration," she said, her voice small and hoarse.

"Women must never be premature," I said, aching to hold her in my arms, my mind scrambling for alternatives. (Mothers never get over the illusion that they should be omnipotent.)

She spoke my most unbearable fear and hers. "He'll disappear . . . He'll run away and lose himself."

"Oh no."

"Oh yes. Daniel has his father's temper and pride."

"No dear. Put that out of your mind. We can't let that happen and we won't." I spoke with a calm authority I did not feel.

"How can you stop him?" she asked, her voice hopeless.

"I have an old promise of his that he'll carry me piggyback if we have to make a getaway in his revolution."

"Mother, really, is this a time for your weird sense of humor?"

"Someone must cross with him," I said. As weightless as a parachute jump, I heard myself falling into a decision. "With an old woman like me it looks respectable. Even border guards trust their white-haired grandmothers. We'll go together."

"What are you talking about? Don't be foolish."

My poor daughter. Poor Adam's daughter, weeping behind her skittishness, pushing away intimacy, yet wanting to cling.

"Maybe the draft board made a mistake and we'll turn

469

around and come right back. We'll get out of the country and then we'll see what to do. In the meanwhile he'll register at some university. When the legal folderol is settled, or the war ends, we'll come back, if it's safe to do so."

She clenched and unclenched her hands — sinuous, dexterous as my father's. I thought, mother of my grandchildren, you must not fall apart. You must find the strength to take hold. "It says here, Arie, the best way is by car. 'There are retired army officers at Toronto and Vancouver airports who will count your draft status against you.' FBI-niks. Tell Daniel to get himself an international driver's license."

"You are out of your milky mind, Mother."

"No use getting angry at me, dear." I said it without criticism, viewing with her the long distance from a Daniel delivered — to where he lay blanked out in mud, in a low and dishonorable cause.

"Daniel will need a proper suit, a double-breasted dark blue."

"Neat and practical as ever," she said, as unforgiving about my efficiency as I had been about my mother's disorder. "Planning a farewell costume party," she asked in a voice bitter as stale coffee dregs.

"On the contrary. Trying to keep him out of a goose-turd costume. My chauffeur and I are going on a tour. If there are any questions we are on our way to Peru via Canada. I have a well-stamped passport to show I am an eccentric tourist." And I'll be damned (I did not say aloud) if another of our sons wanders off and loses himself from us, from himself, from the world. Not if I have to chain myself to his rucksack.

"I can't let you do that. And Danny wouldn't allow it, Mom. It's crazy."

(Ah, is it Mom, my child? Then between you and me it's settled.)

Women! You know why we haven't written *War and Peace?*

470

Because the generations are always tugging at our apron strings. We turn away from the paper to blow some child's drippy nose, while another child, anyone's — has crayoned bunnies over a scene we have written in passion's blood.

"Danny will chauffeur his grandmother on a Christmas excursion. No need to say anything more than that to anyone."

I said nothing about possible obstruction from the loyal citizen, her husband, the haughty scrupulous reactionary. I said nothing about families we knew who had emigrated to Canada with their young sons; nothing about her forebears who came to America with their sons to escape conscription; about sweethearts, mothers, wives, who went with their political men to prison or Siberia. I said, "You never heard of a grandmother going north with her grandson for his welfare? It's very American."

She grimaced. "That's racist, not funny."

(Dear God I try so hard with her and never get it right.)

"It's my chance to begin a new life."

"What's wrong with the one you've made? You plan to join the Royal Canadian Mounted Police? Run a hotel for conscientious objectors?"

"Not a bad idea. But I think I'll be a straight dropout. Express my refusal to go along with the system. Divest myself of material accumulation. Move with the impulse. Become a guru. I'm the age for a staff and a begging bowl."

"Come on, Mom, I can't stand your joking about it. How can you leave your garden, your friends, the rest of us . . . Jessica . . . Dinah?" A second set of tears watered the icy stain on her cheekbones. "What will you do in a place where you don't know a soul?"

"At last I'll have the solitude they say a writer needs. I'll write that novel I've been beginning over and over again. So far, events have not been conducive." (No they have not.) "I'll take my portable typewriter. You can lend me your waterproof picnic carryall, so when I cross the border my notebooks won't get wet if I sink into the snow."

"Excessively amusing . . ." Tears were flowing.

I brought her some Kleenex and put my arms around her. We both cried. Quickly and briefly. There was so much to do.

"You don't understand, sweetheart, honey. It's a favor, baby. It's practically the certain way of getting myself published. It's one of the oldest literary devices. You know I do everything by the book . . . I've always longed to have my life imitate literature. God, how I've tried. And it never has. Here's my chance. You see, you drop a manuscript into a customs house box, a desk drawer, an attic trunk, some latter-day Melville finds it and pouf!"

She shook her head at the madwoman, her mother.

"Hawthorne found *The Scarlet Letter* in a customs house, or was it a gable? Shakespeare never made up a story of his own, found them all. Goethe found *The Sorrows of Young Werther,* Laclos, *Les liaisons dangereuses.* It goes on to this day, especially in Latin America . . . Borges, Marquéz, Cela . . . All potpourris, collages. I have my first line ready. 'In the country of the collage the junk collector is king.'"

No. I had not struck the right note. She faced away from me, her forehead pressed against the cold glass of the window.

God it kills me to see my child cry. "Don't worry, Arie, love, I might be back by spring. The garden is put to bed. Jessica and Dinah will keep the house checked and in use. In the meanwhile you get the draft board to defer him, at least until June, so he'll have completed his academic requirements.

"Hopeless as it seems, maybe this suicidal war will be over by then. Get his father to see the practicality of that; of getting legal help so as not to waste his education costs. Lie to them. Tell them his peace protests were youthful idealism. Tell them he'll turn conservative, a young fogey. Use influence. Tell them anything. Fake a medical report, say he's a rapist, homosexual, a psychotic. Call the Pope. Pay someone off. Just get it done."

"Good God, Mother, you're simply awful!" she said and I guess she meant it.

Mothers and daughters! It seems more conceivable for a girl to become her father's mother than for mother and daughter to achieve that peace which passeth understanding.

I thought how my mother's ocean of energy had seemed to me inexhaustible and threatening, endowed with potency I could never match or evade, a force that circumstances could never drain, never exhaust in daily skirmishes, and that rose like the tide to meet events . . .

What did I expect, that my daughter would be made amiable and dulcet by anguish? Everyone would like to behave nobly in crises, but in the very act, awkwardness or pettiness overtakes us. The day of my father's dying, my mother walked around the screen just as I said to the doctor, "Why don't you let him die quickly!" Why did I not say, "Mother, you heard wrong. It was for his sake, not for mine!"? No, I let that barb fester in her. My father's wife was losing her bond with her earthly place and shape, but I did not fall on her neck and say, "I pity you. Pity me. My father's daughter is losing her father. Where will his perfect daughter be lodged?"

My fatherless daughter, I too wish Adam were here to help you. He might have, with more instinctive grace.

Arie paced, her head held slightly back as if to keep tears from spilling over, encased in chic, her coiffure petaled like a bronze chrysanthemum, her body tense, an unbroken shallow curve from waist to loin, her tight, short skirt barely rippling as she crossed and recrossed in front of me. "How, how, how? I don't know how to do any of those things. Bribe! I don't know how!" She burst into brief fire.

"Don't ask me how, Arie. Don't look like a candle that's about to be snuffed. Find out. That's how. We were all innocent once. If you manage, we'll be able to come back soon. If you

473

don't, I'll see him through until he's legally settled, in a Canadian school, and has made a few friends."

From the way the car jerked out of the driveway I could tell she was shaking with sobs.

As usual when I'm upset, I went about tidying. I cleared away scissors Dinah had used to trim Danny's hair, rinsed some cups and saucers, put away the chess set Danny and a friend had been using. I ran a hand over the sea of papers on my desk. At my dressing table there were still signs of Dinah's messing among my creams. I tightened the jars and wiped them. Dinah could come and visit me. How often? Jessica, my friend of over seventy-two years, would drive to Canada. How often?

On the stairway I straightened photos: Arie with her second husband, Ricardo, the stranger. My late husband, Adam, the near stranger. Benjamin with Joyce, briefly his wife, now a stranger. Children and grandchildren at various adorable ages: Arie in a tutu, Arie with her first prize for painting won in the children's division at the Farmers Market, Arie wheeling brother Benjie in an antique pram, grown-up Arie wheeling Dinah and Danny in the same pram. At the landing: Absalom at twelve with a string of fish, Absalom at hockey. Aaron, holding his 4-H blue ribbon chicken and his cat, Boxtop, Aaron on the pony. My sons whose hide-and-seek had grown deadly earnest. I'm terribly tired of this game.

I lay down on my chaise. A moth crossed the stream of light that broke through the lattice blinds. Well, how would it have been to live easy like the moth, predetermined? I felt like a wing-scorched insect dragging my body up a fogged mirror that exposed my naked underside. I wasn't a moth, I didn't want to fly around. I am, and have always been, a chicken. (As a matter of fact, my pelvic area was aching as if I *were* carrying eggs.) I'm a nester, not an adventurer. In what beds will I deposit my

474

immortal longings only to abandon them again. But I can take no other stand. If independent responsibility doesn't save us, nothing will.

To the very end life seems to force on women a morality of abnegation; a giving up of the personal, whether of sensuality, or ease or creative fulfillment. There are no sanctified cop-outs. A child's cry of need has the power to recall a woman from her deepest sleep, her most vivid dreams to her specific domestic responsibility. In taking responsibility for my anarchist grandson I was defending the order of the generations. I was acknowledging my link with nature, as well as with civilization.

But can I do it? Can I venture another beginning? Can I repeat the process: come out into foreign air crying at contact with the new element, then crawl, dragging my placental tatters after me, and heal another mammalian scar, another umbilicus? (With so many births I should sport a row of belly buttons, craters, veritable calderas, to outline my extinct volcanoes.)

Liberationists, remark this! Eve, naked Eve, not born of woman, she had no navel. "The man without a navel yet lives in me," wrote Sir Thomas Browne. Say I, "The woman with a novel yet lives in me."

*   *   *

In the press of Christmas tourists my chauffeur and I drove across the Canadian border. He wore a peaked cap and a conservative suit as rigid as a uniform. I too had dressed again for that man, that guard on the border. I wore a fur cape, a blue velvet hat — Washington crossing the Delaware; our cameras were visible, our luggage, what little there was of it, discreetly hidden. We were saluted through.

Muddle-headed life, how do you hit the target! Some drunken bully at a carnival, picking up the gun and shooting backward and over his head, one of fate's invulnerable idiots, could have come no nearer the mark. It was snowing.

Epilogue

"It is not the fashion to see the lady in the Epilogue."

— SHAKESPEARE

IT'S MY BIRTHDAY. Which one? That hardly matters. Every birthday arouses hopes of beginnings as well as intimations of letting go; as the idea of writing a novel evokes the idea of not writing a novel.

I wake to exile. I am in the vast solitude of a foreign environment, looking out on black hemlocks and white snow. Between the light-eating trees thin smoke is spreading and flattening from a hidden chimney. It is snowing the way it does only in tall tree country, straight down yet in every direction; falling through the gray light as it will fall forever here, on the black forest, on the white plain, on the winters of my childhood, on my parents' winters.

I stand by the window trying to distinguish features in the black and white landscape — a rail, a rise, a dip that seems to be a path leading to a collapsed enclosure. There are mounds. They are mounds in what seems to be an abandoned burial ground. It is small like those left on Western plains by pioneers. Where the wind has blown them free of

477

snow on one side, the stones and a few shrubs are edged in a black line.

With that random bravura achieved only by nature, a black mongrel bitch — low-slung, heavy-bellied — crosses the white surface leaving footprints like cast-off daisies. At the head of the tallest marker she squats.

I seem to hear the hot urine hissing, see it freezing yellow as it cuts into the smooth skin of snow. Why am I outraged? Why am I frightened? Why am I banging on the window like a horrified immigrant child? The dog had to urinate and snow is a natural phenomenon whose crystalline order invites the outrage of reality.

The air around me is buzzing. I hear a high electrical beep as of a faulty transistor. It is irregular, which makes it impossible to disregard. It seems to be every eighty seconds or is it one hundred seconds or is it pulsing down? No! There it goes accelerating again . . . a high ma . . . ma . . . ma . . . something like the unsure onset of labor. Is it now? Is it not now? Is it a twinge, or the final thing?

There it goes again. Count the contractions. I'd better pack and get myself to a maternity hospital. Oh Ariadne, who do you think you are, Sarah, the senile mother of her people? Jeremy, my old physician, I am comforting myself again with fictions, looking to literature again to verify my life.

To whom shall I write this letter?

Dearly Beloved,

All of you, indifferent as you must be — men, women, children, grandchildren — have you seen those admonitory signs in drugstore windows? *If you notice unusual bleeding . . .*

I have noticed. Every morning. Not on my handkerchief. No longer on my conscience. At the bottom of the toilet bowl. There lie droplets of blood. Where, but from the womb? I watch for them now. I watch them swirl apart the way the scarlet poppy tincture from Aunt Giselle's brush slowly became part of the surrounding fluids.

Father, I have the answer to your question, "What will we take with us when we cross the border?" Everything. Greedy everything. Costumes, photo albums, the heart of the enemy, sonnets, mandolins, original sin, unicorns, obsolete fables, old china, unmasked ideologies, fishing poles, garden tools, chess sets, the whole bundle — our past with all my present into their future. I want to carry it with me across the border, the whole incoherence of what was, is, and is to come.

And the truth.

Even the truth that resides in the essence of a cup.

I go back to my typewriter, my new portable. My hands are shaking but I write:

Dear Father,

Let me begin again.

Give me time. Not chicken time, I need sequoia time. My past has been a Prologue.

I'm not ready to be an Epilogue.